The Teacher

A Justin Barnes Novel

BY

ROBERT BANFELDER

BB

~~

BROADWATER BOOKS

Riverhead, New York

Broadwater Books
141 Riverside Drive
Riverhead, NY 11901

www.robertbanfelder.com

The Library of Congress Cataloging-in-Publication Data
is available on file.

ISBN: 978-09859486-3-4

Printed in the United States of America

10 9 8 7 6 5 4 3 2

BB
~~
BROADWATER BOOKS
New York

For Jacqueline
Inspiration is the be-all and end-all

BOOKS BY ROBERT BANFELDER

Fiction:

Trace Evidence

Knots
A Justin Barnes Novel

The Author
A Justin Barnes Novel
Award Winner: 'Best Suspense Thriller'~ NewBookReviews

No Stranger Than I

Nonfiction:

The Fishing Smart <u>Anywhere</u> Handbook for Salt Water & Fresh Water

The Buzz About *The Author*

"Robert Banfelder has turned up the suspense content in *The Author*, which speaks volumes for his newest work. Malcolm Columba is a mastermind turned serial killer who has placed his agents around the globe, both into terrorist groups and law enforcement agencies with equal success. It has long been thought that genius is next to madness, but could Columba's madness be a diabolical means to an end? *The Author* is filled with twists and unexpected turns that will keep readers on the edge of their seat until past where you think this one will end. But wait, this is just the beginning. Outstanding! Unspeakable crimes, a thrilling chase and a mesmerizing tangled plot. What more could you ask for? Banfelder has written another award winner!" - Mark Reid, NBR

"Banfelder's descriptions are detailed, the novel well plotted, and his imagination without bounds. The book is well researched and has much to offer those interested in fishing and its gear, boats or environmental pollution. It gives the reader a peek into the world of police investigation and Mafia manipulation and control. Like the wonderful meal prepared at the Bella Sera restaurant, the thrills and chills just keep appearing, course after course after course."
     - Donna Gestri, author, *Sweet Figs, Bitter Greens, For Jennie, Time Takes No Time*

"Bloody, long, and really good. Banfelder is a student of the criminal mind, specifically the serial killer. He has a knack for being inside the victim's and the killer's head simultaneously. Extremely original and a good tale. You should go out of your way to read *The Author.*"
     - Regan Batuello, *Suffolk Times*

"I recently picked up a copy of *The Author* and reached a point where the antagonist, Malcolm Columba, accosts young Becky Dawson while ice skating. I had a knot in my stomach in anticipation of the outcome. What an excellent level of suspense in such a compact chapter. Very well done! Great description and visualizations throughout! Banfelder is a very talented fiction writer who manages to weave his knowledge of the outdoors into his works. His novels are expertly crafted and positively compelling. Like *The Teacher*, *The Author* will have you sitting on the edge of your seat waiting for what comes next. - Angelo Peluso, author, *Fly Fishing the Surf, Saltwater Flies of the Southeast and Gulf Coasts, Fly Fishing Long Island, Saltwater Flies of the Northeast*

Acknowledgments

Rather than categorize, then expand upon the virtues of those special souls who contributed in their unique way to my success, be it through your friendship and support during trying times, or via your areas of expertise, I choose, instead, to lump the lot of you together upon these pages—realizing, of course, that where I truly hold each and every one of you accountable is a very special place . . . reserved within the confines of my heart.

Mark Ahrens, Sister Barbara, Cris Betancourt, Maryanne and Ken Birmingham. Brendan Byrne, Barbara and Thomas Cousins, Dr. Bruce H. David-former director of Kirby Forensic Psychiatric Center, Robert Dore, the folks at Eastern Flyrodders of Long Island, Detective Sergeant Robert Edwards-Deputy Commanding Office, Homicide Squad-Nassau County P.D. (retired), Geoffrey Freeman, Susan and Gene Frohnhoefer, David and Claudia Fulton, Detective Lieutenant John Gierasch-Commanding Officer, Homicide Squad-Suffolk County P.D. (retired), Edward Goodfield, Joseph Grattan-Chief of Police, Riverhead P.D. (retired), Pamela Hogrefe, Robert Johnsen, Dr. Geraldine Kammerman-owner/editior *Towers News* (retired), Kay Kidde, Kathy and Sergeant Paul LaGrasse-Suffolk County Sheriff's Department-Academy Bureau (retired), the LeRoy family, Marlene and John Mandrafina, Lt. John McGann-Suffolk County Sheriff's Office, Mary and Russ Moran, Julie and Kevin Nethercott, Monica and Diego Peña, Selma and Frank Perlman, Dr. Anthony Perillo, Mary Jo and Robert Perlow, Steve Randall, Wayne and Alice Robinson, Nancy and Richard Roberts-New York Court Clerk, Suffolk County, Sister Mary Ronald, Joseph Russo, Jean Schuler, Marjorie and William Smith, Meryl Spiegel, Gail and Joel M. Steinberg, Luce Skrabanek, Dr. Susan Snyder, the Tchilinguirian family, Elva Victoria, Peggy and Dennis Weinand-D.A.R.E. Officer, Riverhead P.D. (retired), Thomas Wernikowski, John and Renée Wolf.

Additionally, I wish to profusely thank my son, Jason Banfelder, and Donna Derasmo who, once again, truly know the meaning of the word *sacrifice*.

Finally, I offer my gratitude to an individual who wishes to remain anonymous . . . a person who helped pave the way for sensitive scene selections for *The Author* as well as *The Teacher*.

Robert Banfelder
July 2013

Chapter 1

With thin wrists firmly secured behind a scrawny back, her head and body locked solidly in place within a wooden makeshift vise, Grace Littleton lay face down on a sheet of Lucite, naked and shivering, although the building was sufficiently heated. The serial killer's caged and spiritless songbird hung silent upon her stationary swing—a scaffold suspended in a vaulted ceiling, seventy-seven feet from dome to doom. Between two planks spaced but a pinkie finger's width apart, San Francisco's opera star could certainly see but not cry out to the work crew cutting and laying a stone tile floor far below her. Wide strips of duct tape smacked across the singer's malleable mouth made her doubtlessly mute. The monotonous and interminable sound of several grating ceiling fans muffled any sob, moan or groan she might emit.

I'm up here, Grace wept with barely an inch of wiggle room. *Here. Here. Here,* she cried quietly, trying desperately to move her head and body. *Please. Just look up and see me. Why can't any of you see me?*

Because you are part of the framework, anyone in the know could have told her. Because your temporary coffin is camouflaged, built atop the platform upon which restoration artists will not set foot until mid-spring—that is, if things go according to schedule, which they rarely do, as any contractor could tell you.

Billy Baxter, Clarence Emery's accomplice, certainly could have told her, for the foreman surely knew.

The old courthouse had been slated for demolition several years ago, but the new town board put it out to bid and hit pay dirt when a developer saw its potential as storefront and office space. It was prime real estate that could readily be converted into plush shops and suites, housing affluent merchants and practitioners who wanted waterfront property and, for openers, were willing to pay one hundred and fifty dollars a square foot.

It took Grace little time to realize that no one could or would see her, even when the workers happened to look briefly toward the vast celestial ceiling with its paint-chipped angels holding golden harps and trumpets that hovered before her eyes.

On the third day of captivity, Grace believed she saw the worker in charge look up at her and wink. He was loud and animated on the floor below when directing his crew; quiet as a cat when he suddenly appeared just before dark, then once again in the early morning to remove her body waste and feed her through a tube.

With a rough cold cloth, Billy Baxter enjoyed sponge bathing the quivering form as he gruffly uttered the same few words on each occasion:

"Lift. Higher."

Grace could move but a fraction, achingly then painfully raising her pelvis from the diaper so that he could clean her. Next, with fetid filthy fingers, the man would rip the sticky duct tape from her face, find her lips and insert a clear flexible plastic straw into her mouth.

"Here, drink."

Through the tube, the anorexic greedily drank a soupy, spinach-like concoction. When she finished, Billy would dry her mouth before resealing it with fresh gray strips of the gummy adhesive, reminding his charge to remain quiet or he would have to kill her as instructed. After he left, Grace would stretch wide her mouth and attempt to force the tormenting tape away with the tip of her tongue, a tongue which Professor Clarence Emery had promised to have ripped from her head if she so much as made a single peep.

Before leaving for New York and putting Billy in charge, Emery had given Grace a modicum of hope, promising that her daddy would call by the end of the week if all went well; that is, if the director of Kirby Forensic Psychiatric Center could take direction. Otherwise, the imprisoned soprano would suffer a fall from grace, he swore, adding that, if she could only keep herself composed until then, the young woman could easily lose the additional five pounds she was hoping to shed before her next concert appearance—a *crash* diet if she could not.

"Hope springs eternal," Clarence Emery had concluded with a winning smile before raising her to the rafters.

Chapter 2

Without letup, a heavy afternoon March wind whipped the southwest wall of Kirby Forensic Psychiatric Center on Ward's Island, situated on the East River, two-thirds of a mile east of Manhattan. A sudden downpour pelted, then steadily pounded the tall brick building as a gale-force wind drove the gelid rain against barred or grated window panes, distorting the dismal view beyond. Within a corner office, two men sat across from one another. The hospital's director, Doctor Timothy Littleton, listened most attentively from behind his mahogany desk, staring fixedly at his straitjacketed patient.

"It's so good of you to see me, Timmy. I kept telling the other doctors that I had precious little to say to any of them; tons of tales to tell their director." Professor Clarence Emery grinned maniacally. "Among many things, they wanted to know why I mismatched one of the heads and bodies, where I put the other, as well as why I went berserk, although I view my actions as nothing more than letting off a little steam. They wanted me to start at the beginning. But there is no beginning, just as surely as there is no end to it all. It's all a vicious circle. A cycle if you will, with no definitive point of reference to mark the beginning of my so-called illness."

Doctor Littleton sat patiently.

"They say there were *signs*, Timmy," Clarence Emery continued. "Like when I drove up to the teller's window at EAB in Riverhead one winter. *PLEASE TURN VEHICLE ENGINE OFF*, the Scotch-taped instruction sheet read. The exhaust fumes were apparently reaching the tellers just as surely as fumes of impatience were getting to the customers waiting as long as twenty minutes to complete a simple transaction. Twenty minutes! If they had been clever about it, management I mean, they could have added an incentive to the sign, such as: *SAVE A GALLON OF GAS WHILE IDLING AWAY THE HOUR*. Of course, there were those who initially complied until sub-zero temperatures forced a few warm-blooded creatures to restart their engines and turn up the heat. I don't see how blowing my stack along with the horn until security arrived labels me a nut, do you?" Emery tarried a moment for a response, blowing a wisp of white hair away from his face. "I wonder if I were to wait as long for some sort of reply from you, Timmy, as I did my deposit slip, would you get the message."

"And what might that message be, Clarence?" the psychiatrist asked directly.

"That I'm running out of patience with you as I did the teller at that drive-up window."

"Why don't we focus for a moment?"

"Focus?"

"Yes. On why you're here."

Emery shook his head. "I want to focus on the nuns first."

"The nuns?"

"Yes. The nuns."

"What nuns?"

"The nuns who are getting abused and raped in Africa, as in other parts of the world. I don't do anything quite like that."

"I'd like to keep this dialogue close to home, Clarence. I'd like to—"

"Fine. First off, I don't see as how we're engaging in any sort of dialogue. More of a monologue, I'm sure you realize. I'm trying to avoid a tirade here, which is kind of difficult when you just sit there like a zombie in a trance. Close to home, you say? All right then. We'll talk about the nuns who, here on our soil, are getting abused and raped as well. But I want input, Timmy. To use your word, I, too, wish to establish a dialogue. You see, I want to learn as much about you as you wish to learn about me."

The psychiatrist smiled.

Clarence Emery shook his head. "No good, Timmy. Too difficult to read."

"What's that?"

"That smile of yours. That shit-eating grin. In this case, a picture is *not* worth a thousand words. A smile of complacency? A patient smile? Well, I'm not really into guessing games. I'm into fair play, rules that are established up front and unchanged. A level playing

5

field if you get my drift. Without a gully or a glitch. Go ahead, call me an idealist. Guilty as charged. But unless you contribute and make meaningful conversation here, Timmy, I'm afraid our session together is just going to be a total waste of time. *Verstehen?*"

Doctor Littleton picked up his pen. "Clarence . . . ."

"Yes, Timmy?"

"How was it that you came to take the lives of those two young women in a parking area at Pipes Cove in Greenport?"

Clarence shook his head sadly. "Sorry, Timmy. It's just not that cut-and-dried. It's a matter of degrees. You would first have to evaluate each and every facet like so many marks on the rim of a compass card if you're to fully and truly understand. For there are many ranges of reference you'd have to explore in order to chart the course of my actions. I'm trying to head you in a given direction if you'll let me. We can start or end with littering or loitering or lobbying. Anywhere you like. But we must come full circle. Then and only then will you understand madness in the making." Emery raised his eyes to the diplomas along the wall. "Those degrees, Timmy? Just forget about everything you ever learned in school. Not applicable, here. Understand?"

Doctor Littleton stared silently at his obstreperous patient.

"Not much better, Timmy. But I'll continue. The abusers and rapists of nuns were priests. I'm sure you'll agree that those brides of God were even easier *prey* for bishops and cardinals, too, if you'll pardon the pun as well as the accused."

"Clarence—"

"'*Safe targets in AIDS-ravaged Africa,*' was quoted in the *National Catholic Reporter,* Timmy, and from the Vatican as well. Sister Mary O'Donovan, from Point Pleasant, was anything but that when she was taken by a deacon, and then afterward to a Catholic health clinic for an abortion. She died during the procedure and was later given a Requiem Mass by the prelate who impregnated her at a cloisters."

"Clarence!"

"Yes, Timmy?"

"Please. I've asked that you call me Doctor Littleton."

Emery threw back his head and glowered at the ceiling. "All those tiny, tinier and teensiest holes in the acoustical tiles, Timmy? The

6

science of sound and still you don't hear me. Have I not asked you, nicely in fact, to call me Professor Emery if you insist on such formality here? So much for science, Doctor Do-little. There. I've met you halfway. Now. At least show me the courtesy of calling me *Teach*."

Chapter 3

The parking lot at the Bella Sera Restaurant in West Tiana could accommodate well over a hundred vehicles and was almost always filled to capacity for lunch and dinner—seven days a week—from Memorial Day to Labor Day. The three rooms held forty-five tables and seated more than two hundred and fifty customers now that the new extension was complete. However, January, February and most of March were bleak months in the restaurant business in general, and this past winter was no exception.

Jacqueline Rubino, the manager of the restaurant, and Justin Barnes, a source of her irritation at the moment, spoke quietly but animatedly in the back bar area of the expanded premises. It was near closing hour.

Jacqueline shook her dark head emphatically. "No, J. Absolutely and positively no. I don't even understand how you could ask me to do such a thing."

"We did it before," the handsome black man put forth plainly. "Did it for God and country," the six-footer added soberly.

"That's baloney and you know it. You did it for you. *I* did it because Don Ciccio and his people had a stranglehold on my family," the beautiful thin-framed woman affirmed. "I did it for survival, J. My father and uncle didn't work day and night for thirty years in this country so that some gangster could walk in here and take control. I did what I had to do, and that's that. Over and done with. Duty and obligation completed. I'm the manager of this restaurant. Not a murderess."

"I really need you on this one, Jackie. I—"

"No! You're nuts. We were lucky last time. Lucky we're both not sitting in prison for the rest of our lives. I was raised a strict Catholic, Justin. You know my upbringing. You know what I have to live with for the rest of my life. I can only hope that God will forgive me in the end. I ask for His forgiveness every day. I pray for you, too, J. I never told you that, but I do. But if you're hell-bent on taking out Clarence Emery, you find yourself someone else or go it alone."

"Jackie, listen to me. Please."

Jacqueline smacked the bottom of an empty carafe firmly upon the black granite countertop. "What do I have to say in order to get through to you? How can you walk in here and ask me to do this, Justin Barnes? Tell me! What right do you have to ask me this? But let me ask you something. Emery's locked up in a mental ward, correct?"

Justin nodded. "Kirby Forensic Psychiatric Center. Ward's Island."

Jacqueline laughed lightly. "Well, I think *you* belong there, fella. Let them handle him. Why do you want to get involved like this? He's finally off the streets."

"For how long?"

"What do you mean for how long? Forever and a day. He'll either receive the death penalty or life in prison without parole. He's not going anywhere."

"Then you really *don't* know him. I know that if I hadn't sent Emery's mentor to the bottom of the sea back then, he'd have somehow surfaced back into society—just like the professor will."

"You don't know that."

"What I know is, if Malcolm Columba were still alive, he'd have found his freedom by now."

"How?"

"The same way Professor Clarence Emery is going to find his."

"How, J?"

"Escape."

"Get real."

"I'm as real as they come, Jackie. And so are you. It's the reason why we're a team."

"Wrong. If you're looking for a team, try coaching Little League, or settle down and find a lasting teammate instead of just stringing that nice girl along. But just leave me the hell alone."

"You know how brilliant and bad this guy is, Jackie."

"I don't care. And you shouldn't care or get involved either.

You did enough in dealing with The Author and the others. Let it go and get on with your life."

"This *is* my life, Jackie. When they recruited me, I found real meaning in my life for the first time. A family. A purpose."

"Fine. Then you should know how *I* feel. My family is *my* life, Justin. My husband is the foundation of that life. My purpose is running this place. And you ask me to jeopardize all that?"

Justin ran a large hand atop his nappy pate. "I'm asking you to look beyond one family for a moment and think about many lives, about how many families Emery's already destroyed and about how many more he will destroy before somebody puts him down. That's what I'm asking of you."

"He's locked up, J. He's confined. What do you want me to do? Pay him a visit and put a bullet in his brain, then surrender myself? Huh?"

"What I want you to do is tell me that you'll work with us, and I'll lay it all out for you."

Jacqueline stared at Justin in disbelief. "Do you know why you're still standing there?"

The swarthy man smiled and shook his head.

"Because this is a public place," she said. "That's the only reason. If this were my home, which in a sense it is, I'd ask you to leave. So. There you have it. My answer is no. Now. Do you want something to eat or drink before I change my mind?"

"I thought the kitchen was closed."

"Do you want something to eat or drink?" she repeated.

"Will you just sit down with me and listen?"

"Not a chance."

Justin Barnes shrugged. "He goes absolutely wild over gorgeous Italian girls, Jackie—with the emphasis on wild."

"I'll remind you that I'm a Sicilian woman."

"He's suspected of murdering scores of young women, maybe hundreds, including a female homicide detective. Suddenly, he shows up in New York and gets himself arrested."

"Captured and arrested and now confined."

"All too easy, Jackie. It's nothing more than a little visit. But he'd surely let you pay him a call if we gave him half a reason."

"You're out of line and out of here. Understand?"

"I understand that most of them never saw their twenty-first birthday."

"Then I'll also remind you that I'm thirty-one."

"You don't look a day over nineteen, and you know it."

Jacqueline restrained a smile.

"Gorgeous Mediterranean types he just loves to clock and cut," Justin pushed.

"I just might clock *you* if you don't leave or change the subject."

"Not a one of them over a size six."

"Out!"

"That's where *he's* headed, Jackie. Out. I guarantee it."

"*Zu* Phil!"

"Crying uncle's not fair, Jackie," Justin scolded quietly behind a waning smile.

"*Zu* Phil," Jacqueline called again, firmly forming her full lips into an angry frown.

"What happened to that nice sweet girl I knew?"

"I grew up."

Phil Cancilla walked out of the kitchen, drying his hands on a clean white dishtowel before tucking the cloth at the small of his back.

"Hey, J. How are you?"

Justin fondly took the man's hand.

"Fine, Phil. I was just telling Jackie what a fine job she's doing with the place. Not an evening I drive by when the parking lot's not full."

"Well, I been booking a lot of parties lately, otherwise we'd be a little slow this time of year. You hungry? Kitchen's never closed to you, you know."

"Sweet of you, Phil. But I gotta go."

"Full parking lot or not, you stop by anytime and we'll find a table for you and Ursula. How's she doing?"

"Terrific. Only I wish you or Tomas would give her cooking lessons, and someday soon. I suggested she make fried calamari one evening, and she suggested reservations, here."

The owner laughed. "That's a good one."

"He thinks I'm kidding, Jackie. Tell him the face she made when I bought fresh squid from the market."

"Justin was just leaving," Jacqueline said evenly.

"Right. Gotta run. Get to yackin' and I don't know when to shut up."

"Got that right," she said with a smirk.

"Well, take care, Phil. Jackie. And say hello to Tomas and Frankie for me."

"Take care, J." Phil said and smiled warmly, taking the man's shoulders in for a hug. "And give Ursula our best."

"You bet." Justin turned to Jacqueline. "Size four if I had to guess," he practically whispered, appreciatively taking in the woman's tall, slim figure. "Ursula is an eight but tells me she's given up fried foods." Addressing them both, he asked, "Hear that joke about squid? Here on the South Shore they call it sushi. Know what they call it over on the North Shore?"

Phil Cancilla shook his head.

"Bait." The black man grinned.

Phil laughed heartily. "Now, that's a *real* good one."

Jacqueline stood fixedly with a stone-cold stare.

"*Bait*, Jackie. Get it?" Justin winked. "Think about it."

"*Ciao*, Justin," she managed, forcing a tight smile.

"Bye, kid."

Chapter 4

The weather turned sunny but remained raw as a persistent wind swept across Ward's Island, sending debris and ripples of water along the surface of flooded roads and parking fields, submerging the tops of tall grasses near the shoreline. Severe flooding over the past twenty-four hours had receded from knee to ankle-deep depressions throughout the muddy area.

"Another thing that drove me crazy, Timmy, was when I walked into a pub one summer and ordered a burger and an ice-cold beer. I told the waitress I want my burger rare. Not medium rare, but rare. Oh, 'and a thick slice of raw onion, please,' I specify. I even show her my requirement with a measurement between a thumb and forefinger. Do you know what comes out of the kitchen besides a host of excuses? A burger on a stale kaiser roll along with an inert stack of thinly sliced cellulose rings. 'I said I wanted a *thick* slice of raw onion, Miss,' I explain. 'Not a limp package of pulp. Just one nice, thick, crisp slice of pungent bulb,' thinking that by *now* she's got the idea. But she tells me that the onions are pre-sliced and that that's the way it comes, period. Some onions those folks have, I mean to tell you, Timmy. Some crust. Next, I cut into the burger. Medium-well. 'Well now,' I complain, 'does this look like a rare burger to you, Missy?' 'Want me to take it back?' she asks. 'Nooo,' I say. 'Just give me a tossed salad instead. What kind of dressing do you have?' I ask politely. 'All the dressings are listed on the menu,' she declares with a bit of an attitude. I remind her that she took the menu away when she took my order, asking if it would be too much trouble to list the dressings as I lifted the glass of piss-warm beer to my lips. She saunters over to her station by the register and returns with a menu and a frown. Yet she's *so* surprised and upset when I turn the tables on her, along with three or four chairs. The Public House on East Main Street in Riverhead, Timmy. Do not venture there unless you have the patience of Job and a tolerance for the absurd."

"Clarence."

"Yes, Timmy?"

"Can we stay focused, please?"

"Sure thing. Ever try ordering eggs over easy? I mean anywhere. Greasy spoon. Upscale diner. Brunch at the best restaurant in town or country. I guarantee you're going to be disappointed."

"Clarence, please."

"Yes, Timmy?"

"What did you do with the body of the first woman and head of the second woman at Pipes Cove?"

Emery shrugged his shoulders and shook his white head of hair. "If I were you, Timmy, I'd be more concerned about other matters."

"I have a job to do, Clarence. I'm sure you can appreciate that."

"It seems to me you're trying to do the job of the police. No? Isn't it up to them to find and fit together the missing pieces? I would think your job is to find out whether or not I'm fit to stand trial. And what even makes you think there were two women?"

"Come on, Clarence. The head of one? The body of another? Along with blood typing from the crime scene for openers."

Emery's bright blue eyes seemed to twinkle. "Openers? Pun intended, Timmy? Because I did open them up like a can of worms," he clarified. "Anyhow, trying to locate parts or, for that matter, establish whether I'm fit to stand before a jury of my peers is going to be a total waste of time I can assure you."

"Why is that, Clarence?"

"A: I'm not going to put the missing pieces of the puzzle together for you just yet, Timmy; and B: I'm not going to be here long enough for you to make a competency determination, although I think you've already made up your mind."

Doctor Littleton smiled. "You plan on going someplace?"

"As a matter of fact, I do. And soon."

"That so?"

"Quite."

"And where would you go?"

"Bonefishing in Belize."

Timothy Littleton couldn't help but laugh. "That a fact?"

Clarence laughed, too, darting his eyes about the room and resting them on the fish photo that hung crookedly on a wall by a corner window to the right of the director's desk. The prisoner raised a shoulder and rubbed an itch just below his left ear, noisily scraping his unshaven face across the rough material of the straitjacket.

"Yes, I'd do the tarpon flats with a fly rod in the lower Keys, but the place is crawling with retired cops this time of year. I even guided one a few seasons back. Homicide detective. Very pretty. Casting a streamer to one hundred and fifty pound giants. She wanted one badly for her trophy room. The irony being that she wound up as *my* prize. You should have seen her expression when I told her who I really was. She couldn't believe her pretty eyes or ears. I told her she was part of my retirement package. But the pressure homicide put on me forced me out of retirement, Timmy. They wanted to play. Well, here I am. Playtime personified. And now it's almost time for me to go again."

"Just going to walk out on us, Clarence?"

"Not without saying goodbye to you first, Timmy."

"Have a plan, do you?"

"It's been set in motion. Many months of preparation, I might add."

"I guess you won't tell me how you plan on getting out of here."

"Sure I will, Timmy. All you have to do is ask."

Littleton grinned. "Got a key, do you?"

"You're my key, Timmy."

"Me."

"Yep."

Doctor Timothy Littleton's curiosity piqued as Emery leaned forward in his restraints, focusing with a degree of satisfaction on the psychiatrist's furrowed brow.

"Mind if I bring in a colleague to hear what you have to say, Clarence?"

"Oh, I don't think you ought to do that, Timmy."

"Why is that?"

"Because you won't want anyone to know it's you who's going to release me—and make good my escape."

Littleton laughed, believing fully that his prisoner/patient truly was delusional.

"Clarence."

"Yes, Timmy?"

"I know you're not stupid."

"Certainly not."

"I know you know there are a few ways that this can go."

Clarence irritably brushed the other side of his face against his right shoulder. "Really only one, but go ahead . . . speaking hypothetically, of course."

"Thank you. I could declare you competent to stand trial."

"And my attorneys would, if I let them, seek out doctors who could argue that I'm not."

"Let me finish, please."

"Sure."

"I can declare you incompetent to stand trial—"

"Diminished capacity and—"

"Please, Clarence. Listen to me."

Clarence shook his head. "It's all moot is what I'm trying to tell you, Timmy. I could still be tried and given the death penalty or life in prison without the possibility of parole. Unacceptable, buddy. Even if God handed out a miracle and I was confined to a mental hospital instead of prison—which is not going to happen—cured and eventually released back into society, I'm telling you here and now that I wouldn't mind my p's and q's. Anyhow, do you really think I'd hang around for a minimum of ten to twenty years and hope? If that were the case, then you'd *have* to label me crazy, Timmy. See what a Catch-22 this whole business can be?" Emery laughed delightedly. "See what a farce this whole thing truly is?"

"Just to remind you, you're on suicide watch, Clarence. Twenty-four hours a day. So if that's what you have in mind, forget it."

"Now, how in this world am I going to go bonefishing in Belize if I pull a stunt like that?"

"What are you saying, Mr. Emery? That I'm going to just let you walk out of here?"

Emery nodded emphatically. "Yes, Doctor."

"Now, I suppose you expect me to put in writing that you *are* crazy. Is that it?" Littleton sighed his exasperation.

"I believe that you believe that, but still wouldn't give me the benefit of the doubt if I stood on my head in Times Square in my birthday suit. And that's precisely why I had to be prepared for you before we met."

The director's eyes narrowed. "What are you talking about?"

"Your daughter, Doc. You don't think I didn't know where I'd be headed when the authorities picked me up in Nassau County, near your second home? You don't think I didn't know who the director of Kirby Forensic Psychiatric Center was or that we'd eventually meet?"

"What *about* my daughter?"

"Haven't heard from her in over a week, have you? Really not unusual given your busy schedules and the distance between you, both in terms of miles as well as differences. But I know that you love her insanely, though I understand she's not too crazy over you of late. But just imagine how she'll feel when she learns the sacrifice you made. Nobody has to know but the four of us. My associate is holding her in *suspense*, shall we say." Emery stared up at the acoustical tiled ceiling. "The science of sound, Timmy. You're all ears, I see. Better to erase any recording if the wheels within your desk drawer are reeling like your brain, buddy. Of course, you'll want proof that she's still alive and kicking as they say. Alive and kicking. Believe me, Timmy; last I saw, she couldn't move a muscle. Still and all, I told her to conserve her energy, that she'd need every ounce of strength if her father didn't initially listen to reason. But I assured her that you'd eventually come around. In fact, I bet my life on it."

Chapter 5

A dreary dark night veiled the dim lighting along the corridor leading to Doctor Littleton's office. Behind the closed door, the psychiatrist's cozy little corner was minimally lit by one low-watt bulb cast from the desk lamp's incandescent three-way. The two men sat across from one another. One relaxed. The other tense and terrified.

"Couldn't reach her at home or through her friend's office, could you?" Clarence Emery grinned.

"You piece of utter garbage," the director put forth insanely.

"You don't want to upset me, Timmy. Believe me, you don't," the professor stated gravely. "Think about what's at stake here. Think about Grace. Think about her poor mother. Your daughter's life is in *your* hands at this very moment."

"How do I know you even have her?"

"Oh, I know you know I do."

"I know nothing of the kind," the director declared, fidgeting with a metal paperweight, wanting to smash his patient's skull precisely where he sat.

"Sure you do. Somewhere deep down. But I also know you need something more substantial. Something tangible. So. Here's what I'll give you on account. You'll find a set of earrings on the missing head of the woman the police are searching for at Pipes Cove in Greenport. Not just any earrings, Timmy, but the pair you sent to Grace on her last birthday. Little Dalmatian puppies. Not 'a hundred and one,' but rather two gold and silver doggies. Hey, brighten up, buddy. You look as though you've seen a ghost. It's not Grace, I can assure you. Not yet, Timmy. You need not worry at all if you're careful and do exactly as you're told. If you wish to get a jump on the police in order to identify the earrings, fine. But I would definitely advise against it simply because I think you'd puke if you saw her. In point of fact, she has no ears to hang them on. The police will find those trinkets firmly affixed to each nostril. You have no idea how unphotogenic she appeared at the close of our little session, so I doubt they'll want to show you any pictures. Therefore, do insist on seeing only the genuine articles." Emery sneezed. "Excuse me, Timmy. Please don't jump up and wipe my nose." The serial killer giggled with a satisfactory grin.

"Anyhow, the head you're to concern yourself with is frozen solid, so it won't offend in that sense unless you had a loss of power at your home in Great Neck. Nice digs, Timmy. She's downstairs in your freezer bin, buddy, tucked neatly away in the bottom right-hand corner of the chest. I can't understand why you didn't get an upright so you don't have to dig every time you want to find something. And no, it's not in clear wrap so that you or your wife could have a heart attack after realizing it isn't a roast. I'm not insensitive, Timmy."

The psychiatrist cringed. "Why did you do this, Clarence?"

"Simple. I want to show them all that no matter where they put me, I always have a trapdoor in the floor, the wall or ceiling through which to escape. That's all."

"Suppose the authorities come and take you out of here right now? Then what?"

"Then you'd be attending a funeral; that is, if I even bothered to tell you where the body pieces were. Grace's I'm referring to. My assistant is standing by."

"I can't just let you walk the hell out of here," Doctor Littleton proclaimed.

"Sure you can. And you will."

"How?" The man hedged, thinking he'd lose his mind at any moment.

"Oh, I'm sure you'll figure a way. I have faith in you, Timmy. Truly I do."

"You're insane."

"But you'd never ever put that in your report to help me out, now would you? You'd like to see me receive a lethal injection or rot away in some upstate prison rather than give me a shot at treatment and a cure. Am I right? Please don't lie to me, Timmy."

"If I determined that you could benefit—"

"Cut the crap, will you, Tim?" Clarence Emery smirked. "The politicians in this state wouldn't let that happen unless Hannibal the

Cannibal was elected to office. Oh, and just for the record, Timmy, I don't eat my victims' vitals. What I do is purely for fun, not fare. It's my weekly entertainment. I'll freely admit to you that I enjoy their shocked reactions when I tell them what I have in store. And I'll also confess that I'd be very sad to miss out on your daughter's fall from grace if daddy fails her in the end.

"By the way, that's a really fine diner near your Great Neck home, Timmy . . . where the police apprehended me while I was taking a leak in the parking lot. I would so enjoy another pastrami on rye and a Doctor Brown cream soda before heading back."

"You *let* yourself get caught—on purpose. Didn't you?"

"Slow on the uptake, but bingo, buddy."

"Just to have this moment."

Emery shook his head. "No, Timmy; for the moment when I walk out of here and into the night. For the moment I'm back to bonefishing in Belize, or God knows where."

Littleton seethed. "How do I know you'll release her unharmed?"

"Come on, Timmy. You know the answer to that. You *don't* know, but you have little choice. On the first day that you delay, starting today, you'll receive her pinky finger. By the fifth day, you'll have received all four fingers and her thumb. After that . . . ."

Littleton teared. "Please don't harm her." The man caved. "She's all I've got."

"No. You have a young wife. Now, if she was ten years younger and twenty pounds lighter, I'd have given her some thought," the madman declared half-jokingly.

"Please, Professor." The director wept and trembled, putting aside the paperweight.

"Good, Timmy. You see, we're finally having a dialogue. And to show you I'm not a monster, maybe just a bit perturbed, I'm going to arrange for you to speak to Grace. How does that sound? But first I have to be reassured that you won't do anything foolish, like clue the authorities."

"I won't, Professor Emery. I swear it." Littleton continued to cry and wiped his bloodshot brown eyes with several sheets of Kleenex taken from a box on his desk.

"I believe you, Doctor Littleton. And I want you to believe that when this is over and you have your precious daughter back safe and sound, with all ten fingers and toes, do you know what's going to happen as a result of her having been abducted? Do you? I know you know, so let me hear it. Come on now. All choked up and can't give me a straight answer, I can see. So I'll give you the appropriate response. You're all going to be one big happy family again. And I won't even send you a bill, Doc. Reason being is that I wouldn't dare give you my real address, or risk a money drop." Clarence Emery giggled happily.

Littleton went for broke. "I'll agree to a simultaneous exchange. Nothing less. Is that clear?"

Emery chuckled good-naturedly. "Unacceptable, Doc. You're in no position to deal. I hold the trump card. I'm going to be a day away from here before I release her. If I'm followed—and believe me I'll know—she'll die a horrible death. Understood? I said is that understood?"

Doctor Littleton surrendered an inflamed yet exasperated, "Yesss."

"Yes, what?"

"It's understood. But if you harm—"

"I know, I know . . . 'one hair on her head,' you'll hunt me down and so on and so forth. I've heard it all before, Timmy. You see, what we're establishing here is trust. So sit back and enjoy the game."

"I want to speak to her. I want to know that she's all right."

"Now, didn't I just say that a moment ago? Didn't I? Patience, Doc. Patience."

Chapter 6

Doctor Timothy Littleton's office was locked as was his mind when the call finally came through. The psychiatrist stood and grabbed the cell phone from his belt but almost dropped the instrument to the floor, recovering and practically shouting into the mouthpiece before collapsing into the chair behind his desk at hearing his daughter's frightened, trembling voice.

"Da-daddy? Daddy, please—"

"I'm right here, Grace. Hello! Baby, is that you?"

"I w-want to come home, Daddy."

"Tell me you're all right, sweetheart. Please tell me—"

"He's going t-to k-kill me if you don't do as th-they say." Grace began to cry.

"You know I would never let that happen, don't you? Say you know."

"I know. I love you, Daddy. I m-miss you so much. Please. Please don't let him hurt—"

Doctor Littleton lost the connection and thought he'd lose his mind. "Oh, God. Get her back on the phone, Professor. Please. I beg you, Professor Emery." Littleton helplessly held out the phone as if his straitjacketed patient could even place a call.

Emery beamed. "Now, look. My assistant and I are not asking for a dollar figure here, Doc. Not one thin dime. Long distance isn't cheap you know. And seeing as how we're operating on a shoestring, I think you should be satisfied that she's all right—for the time being. So. Do we have an agreement?"

The director stared blankly at the instrument in his trembling hand and nodded, putting the Nokia down upon his desk. "I'll have you out of here tomorrow night. You'll release her the following day. Yes?"

"On my honor, Doc."

"What if you're hit by a car or lightning or—"

"Then just make sure I have clean underwear when I leave here." The lunatic laughed. "Best insurance against calamity a man can have. Now. Have you got things worked out without involving another soul?"

"I swear it."

"Good. So lighten up. Everything is going to work out just fine."

The director's heart was pounding in his chest. "I pray to God for her safe delivery."

"I hope I'm included in your prayers, Timothy. You've got to put the horse before the cart. Yes?"

"Yes, Professor."

"Know what?"

"What?" Littleton's heart raced.

"I'd prefer it if you'd call me Teach. Really."

"Te-teach." The psychiatrist's voice quivered quietly.

"Great. If I weren't confined in this jacket, I'd give you a great big hug. Nothing tentative, mind you. Oh, and one more thing, Doctor."

"What?"

"Just a reminder that in case little ears were listening in, they can forget about trying to trace or track the call. I can assure you that my associate and Grace are now cell-less as we speak. By now, they're a good distance away from where the call was placed," he fibbed, "because my man knows that the authorities can home in on them to some degree. Even if the police narrowed down the area, they'd have to find the building and the bomb before it blew," he stated in half-truth, studying Littleton's fearful but telling eyes.

"I told no one. I told you before that I have no intention of doing anything to jeopardize my daughter's well-being," the man declared in sheer defeat.

"Good man, Doc. Well, if you would be good enough to have someone escort me back to my pad, I'll leave you in peace for now." Clarence Emery winked pleasantly. "Try and get some rest. You really look like crap, you know."

Doctor Littleton stood and stepped around from behind his desk. The two men stared at one another for a moment before the director buzzed for a turnkey.

Chapter 7

Detective Lieutenant Theodore Groche, Commanding Officer of Suffolk County Homicide, Yaphank, sat pensively behind his desk. Upon its massive mahogany surface were neatly organized piles of paper and folders: memorandums, file reports, magazines, several out-of-town as well as local newspapers.

Justin Barnes knocked, entered, then closed the door and crossed the room, planting a buttock upon a corner of the desk, his back to the floor-to-ceiling windowed wall that ran the length of the front office.

"Take a chair," the lieutenant invited, reaching for and opening a confidential file.

"Won't be staying long. Just wanted to report to you in person."

"She bite?"

"With her bare teeth. Snarled first with fair warning."

"Lay it out for her?"

"Never got the chance."

"I was afraid of that. How far did you get?"

"Through the door of the restaurant and over to the bar area. Told her what we needed."

"And?"

"And she practically threw me out."

"Think she'll come around?"

Justin shrugged. "Maybe when she learns who the two women were and it has time to sink in."

"You didn't tell her?"

"Wouldn't 'ave mattered much at that point. She'll need time to sort things out. Digest some of the gruesome details. The fact that they were very good customers ain't gonna do it for her. Let her read it in the paper for herself rather than hear it from my mouth. I'll tell her later who was missing exactly what."

"Missing four quarts of blood wouldn't do it?"

Justin shook his head. "Trust me. I know how her mind works."

"Maybe *you* should deal with Emery at Kirby. Then you could poison him yourself."

Justin smiled uneasily. "By the time I completed the application, he'd be gone."

"How?"

"He'll figure a way. Believe me."

Theo grinned and shook his head. "This is not the movies, J. Sure he could beat the death penalty if we don't stop him in his tracks, but he's not going anywhere."

"Really believe that?"

"I do."

"Then why are you sanctioning this business now?"

"Because of the nature of his violence. Because of the sheer number of young women whose lives he's taken. Main reason? Because he'd kill again *wherever* the state puts him."

"Not because he took the life of one of your own?" the maverick added to the mix.

Lieutenant Groche ignored the remark. "We've got some time. But if you're right, and I'm not saying that you are, J—"

"You just wanna hedge your bet," Justin jabbed.

Theo looked up from the file and smiled. "Tell you what."

"What?"

"If he evaporates from Kirby, or points between there and prison before we pull the plug on this freak, I'll let you call the shots in hunting him down. How's that?"

"I want that in writing; in stone—or even parchment paper will do."

Theo put aside the report and leaned forward, extending a bony hand. "This will have to do, J."

Justin stared at the lieutenant's spindly fingers. "I want you to take your finger and make a capital U in the center of my palm, boss."

"What for?"

"I told you. I want it in writing."

"Meaning?"

26

Justin just sat there grinning, exposing his pearly whites for all they were worth.

The commander laughed. "Meaning 'U da man'?"

"You got it. This way you won't forget so easily." Justin held out a sizable mitt.

The lieutenant took it and drew an invisible U upon Justin's palm, then balled the black man's fingers into a fist. "There. Signed and sealed. How's that? Happy, now?"

"Either way, we're gonna deliver this fucker from evil. But if he boogies on outa there, can I wheel an' deal from behind that desk of yo's, bossman?" Justin questioned with a drawl, slipping into the role of his sassy, streetwise savvy self.

"Don't push it, cowboy."

"Oh, no sa. I's never ever do dat."

"Press is going to release the names and some new details concerning the Greenport victims tomorrow. Besides being a good customer at the Bella Sera, one of them went to grammar school with Jackie. Maybe you can try her again in the afternoon."

"Try her patience for sure."

"So, you never got to tell her how The Professor himself would call her in."

"Told her he'd invite her there for a visit if we gave him half a reason."

"Tell her again tomorrow. Our local newspapers will print what I give them and hold back what they may learn on their own—for now."

"Will do."

"Now get your black ass off my desk and go to work."

"Comments like dat be one o' da reasons why mos' my brothers choose unemployment, boss." Justin grinned broadly.

"You could be next in line yourself if you don't watch your step."

"And jus' what kind o' step dat be, bossman? Dat be a shuffle, o' a lazy-ass attitudinal sashay?"

"Don't matter much to me because we white guys just take you boys in stride."

"Say what?"

"Out. Got work to do." Theo closed the file then pulled a stack of papers in front of him.

"You know, Lieutenant? I got to thinking. I've got the best job in the world and get paid pretty well; eliminating white folk with a serious sort of social problem, like our professor there." He pointed down at the file. "Ever take notice that few black folk get caught up in this serial killer shit? Sure, we cause a lot of the crime. But we ain't fuckin' sick like that. Ever stop to think about that, boss?"

"I thought you weren't staying long. Your words."

"Yeah, and I got your word right here." Justin held up a palm like a catcher's mitt.

"You sure do. But first he's got to fly the coop like you believe he's going to do before 'U da man,' J," the man in charge reminded him with an impatient look.

Justin slid his backside off the lieutenant's desk and stood quietly.

Theo sighed. "What now?"

Justin tested. "Doesn't it bother you that she could possibly do some serious time?"

"Who?"

"Who. Jackie. That's who. Even if she pulled it off, she'd be suspected and maybe even indicted."

"Who's going to indict her?"

"Them." From Yaphank, Justin gestured eastward toward the county seat in Riverhead. "D.A. and his entourage."

"*Them* is with us," the man put forth matter-of-factly.

"Maybe in another lifetime and some other jurisdiction."

"You're not around here long enough to know how things really work, J."

"Why don't you enlighten me so I can give her some reassurance?"

"Maybe in time."

"Doesn't worry you, does it?"

"Worries you, I see. Otherwise, you would have pressed her harder. Hey, didn't we take care of everything last time out?"

"Right, boss." Justin nodded with a degree of satisfaction before taking his leave. "That you did."

Chapter 8

The two men descended a staircase then headed along a dark, dank tunnel. Holding a long black Mag-Lite, Doctor Littleton walked several steps ahead of his patient. Professor Emery had to take faster steps in order to keep the pace.

"Another thing that gets my goat, Doc, is mismarked items in a store. After checking the action and all the snake guides, hook keeper ring and reel seat on an Ugly Stick, spelled S-t-i-k, fly rod during a Rod Riot Sale at Kmart, I brought the item to the counter and pointed out the special sale price to the woman at the register. She rang it up at sixty-nine dollars plus tax, nonetheless. 'No, no, no,' I said, showing her once again that it was clearly marked $9.99. Well, she called over a young fellow who ripped the red price tag off the rod. 'Mistake,' he claimed. 'Then you have several mistakes back there,' I said, pointing to the sporting goods department. 'It's a mistake,' he repeated. 'Fine,' I told him, 'but you've got to sell me the rod as marked for $9.99.' So he calls over a woman manager who proceeds to tell me—"

"Emery!" the psychiatrist snapped, stopping dead in his tracks.

The professor practically stumbled over the psychiatrist. "Yes, Timmy?"

"I don't give a good flying fuck about fishing poles—"

"Fly rods."

"—or any of that crap. All right?"

"Just trying to help you out, Timmy. When they come looking for me, and I'm not here, you've got to be able to tell them some of the doctor/patient things we talked about. Correct?"

"Let me worry about that. Okay?"

"Okay. But I was just—"

"Just be sure that nothing happens to my little girl, else I'll find you and kill you myself. Do you understand me, Emery?"

"Like I told you before, Doc, I'd prefer it if you'd call me Teach. And I'd also appreciate it if you'd take this confounded jacket off me now. I almost broke my neck."

"When we're there."

"How much further is it?"

"Right around the bend."

"Wait!" Emery looked ahead in alarm.

"What?"

The man shivered. "A rat!"

"There are no rats down here. Trust me."

Emery slowly lifted his gaze from the floor of the tunnel to Littleton's face. "That's what our relationship is based on, Doc. Trust."

"Just remember to keep your end of the bargain."

"I promised you that I'm going to release her the moment I arrive safely, and I'm going to keep that promise."

When the pair reached the end of the passageway, Doctor Littleton put down the flashlight, removed the straightjacket from his patient then stood back from the middle-aged, white-haired man.

"I never did anything in my life like this, Emery. I always considered myself a moral person. What I'm doing here is sinful in both the eyes of God and man. I'm a very selfish soul. I'm unleashing a madman back into society. I know this is wrong, but I'm begging you to do what is right and to let her go."

"I will, Timmy. I'll do exactly that."

"Allow some good to come out of my very selfish, evil act."

"You're boring me now, Doc. Gotta go. Is that the door?"

"Yes."

"Open it."

The director withdrew a key from his pocket, unlocked and pushed the heavy steel door ajar. Light from a distant lamppost lit a corner of a parking field.

"Here." Littleton handed Emery a set of car keys and a banded roll of hundred, fifty, and twenty dollar bills. "You take my car. It's got a full tank of gas. It's to your right in the next parking field." He pointed. "A blue Volvo. Probably the only vehicle there at this hour."

"Timmy."

"Yes?"

"Good night," the killer said abruptly. And in an instant, he was gone.

Doctor Littleton pulled the door shut tight then locked it. He picked up the flashlight and pointed the bright beam dead ahead of him, praying as he wept . . . wept and prayed, making his way unsteadily back through the narrow cobblestone labyrinth, feeling much like a sewer rat that his delusional patient had presumably seen.

Chapter 9

Grace Littleton held onto a glimmer of hope both in her mind and heart. The trouble being that her fine mind also told her that her captors, whoever they were, might never let her go free in the end. Especially the foreman. For she could easily pick him out in a sea of men as she had throughout the workdays: his light saddle-colored and badly scarred, well-worn work boots; particularly the toes. The way in which he wore his high-cuffed denim pants. The cotton canvas field coat. The scratchy timbre to his voice when he hollered orders to his men, or held the cell phone to her ear and whispered instructions as precisely what to say to her father as he had the night before.

Tell him you're scared for your life and to do what we say if you ever want to see your doctor daddy again, he had said with heated stale breath as he put himself on top of her and slowly dry-humped her buttocks through his clothing while she lay flat as a mat. Her legs were stretched to their max, fastened firmly with lengths of nylon rope tied to metal rings aft of the slotted wooden box.

His succinct but firm commands when he came to clean and feed her.

Lift. Higher. Here, drink.

Until that moment when Grace spoke to her father, she had never seen the foreman's features up close and personal—not until he lowered his frightfully disfigured face and gave her a hideous grin, exhibiting a severely scarred countenance.

Tell him you want to come home and that you're homesick and scared, he had slathered through a whisper.

He did not have to tell her anything. She was scared beyond belief, beyond words, beyond description. The best narrator in the nation could not put the fear she felt into proper context. The best musician in the country could not make the strings of her heart sing ever again, she swore. A mind for music she was losing by the minute.

Grace believed she was a sponge bath away from insanity when she heard a pair of voices within the ceiling: the foreman's and that of the man who had put her in the box.

The door within the dome opened in back of her.

"Hi, there."

Grace unquestionably recognized the voice but could not stretch her neck nor move her head a fraction to see the figure's feet let alone the form. But she knew the man called Clarence was back. God willing, he would let her go free.

"I said, Hi, there. Has Billy been a good boy to you while I was away visiting daddy dearest? Was he?"

Grace Littleton's entire body trembled.

"I guess that's a yes." Clarence Emery's voice grew closer and colder. "Have you been a good girl? Didn't try and tip off the workers, did you?"

Grace's temples swelled and pounded against the vise-like wooden frame that locked her head firmly in place. She could *feel* the sound of Emery's heavy footsteps upon the platform . . . *hear* the boards creaking throughout her entire bony body with the weight of the two of them. Emery was down on his hands and knees, crawling alongside her brittle bones.

"Wow! You did lose some weight, didn't you? Wouldn't want you as skinny as a toothpick, though. Now would we? Which reminds me. I brought you back a little present. Look." Emery unwrapped a tiny wooden tube and put it in front of her face before pulling off its cap. "It's a toothpick holder. Isn't that neat? Holds better than half a dozen toothpicks, but all we're going to need here tonight are two." Emery removed two toothpicks and snapped off the fancy thicker tooled end from each. "Billy, if you'll just hold onto this, I'll do the honors."

"Yes, Teach." The foreman put the holder in his pocket.

Grace fought furiously but futilely against the restraints that bound her body, along with the yoke-like block that firmly held her neck and head in place. Emery took his thumb and forefinger and roughly stretched the upper and lower lids of Grace's right eye. He held them wide open before inserting the sharp ends of the toothpick into the soft flesh in order to keep them peeled as the singer emitted a muffled endless scream. A drop of blood fell upon the plastic viewing

33

floor. Next, her tormentor repeated the operation on the young woman's other eye.

"There we go. Hand me that, Billy."

Baxter handed Emery a clean cloth with which the killer dabbed and blotted Grace's eyes. "Now you can see exactly where you're headed. As soon as that blood congeals and Billy wipes the floor of your coffin clean so that you have an unobstructed view, we'll send you on your way. You'll be home before you know it. Just like I promised the good doctor. In the meantime, Billy needs to readjust some ropes and pulleys. Shouldn't be too long."

Billy Baxter fussed with a line or two. When he finished, he cleaned the floor of Grace's cage.

"What your daddy was insistent on, Grace, to the point of being downright belligerent, was releasing you the moment I arrived. So, without any further ado, seeing as how you're not equipped with a pair of tiny wiper blades to clear away those tears, we'll send you, now, from heaven, here, to hell. Billy, will you *please* stop crowding me. There's hardly enough room up here for one without you breathing down my neck. Now move back a bit. And don't forget to pull the pins to the box after I back out of here. Otherwise, when you release the rope, nothing will happen. Then you'll have to come back out here and hook everything up again. Understand?"

"Yes, Teach."

"Good man. Good man."

Chapter 10

Once again, Justin sat at the rear bar of the Bella Sera Restaurant near closing hour. Jacqueline uncorked a bottle of Valpolicella, then slid a wineglass out from a wooden rack suspended from the ceiling, reluctantly pouring half a glass of claret before her only customer, decanting the rest of the contents into a large carafe. A waitress entered the room from the kitchen and said good night. Jacqueline looked up and gave the woman a pleasant smile and instructions in Sicilian before turning her attention back to the thorn in her side.

"If the wine's for me, Jackie," Justin said playfully, "you know I prefer the Montepulciano."

"We're out. Like I expect you're going to be shortly. We're closing in fifteen minutes."

"See the paper today?"

"Why didn't you tell me who they were?"

"Would it have mattered any? Would you have listened then?"

"No."

"So what would've been the point? Besides, Carmela Fontana wasn't positively ID'd until late last night."

"The point is I knew them both. The point is I went to school with Carmela. The point is they were both very good customers. The point is I would have been prepared," she snapped, removing and washing the filter from the cappuccino machine.

"Were you friends with Carmela? I mean socially."

"No, not really. We were never what you would call close. Neither of them, actually. I dated Carmela's stepbrother once or twice. High school. A hundred years ago."

"You're thirty."

"Thirty-one, I keep reminding you. I met you when I was twenty-nine. Recall? Sorriest day of my life."

"Yeah, and you could've been bussing tables for Don Ciccio today."

Jacqueline ignored the comment. "Jesus, J. She was decapitated, the paper said."

"Yep. Both of them."

"Why would he do such a thing?"

"Why don't you call and ask him yourself? Better yet, I can arrange an exclusive interview before his lawyers hit the scene. A bit surprising there hasn't been contact yet," Justin mused aloud. "Or, if you prefer to play Nurse Nightingale from Florence, I'm sure the professor would love for you to take his pulse while yours races as you slit his throat. We have several methods in mind to work you in," he half-teased and tested.

"I couldn't and wouldn't get near him, J."

"I told you before. It's all laid out. It's the *wouldn't* part that we have to work on."

"You don't give up, do you?"

Justin shook his head. "I wouldn't let anything bad happen to you. You know that."

"You already have."

"He cut Carmela's roommate up like cardboard before he beheaded them, Jackie. I'm afraid it's going to take a while for the authorities to come up with a matched set. Nassau police just found your good friend's head in some freezer."

The manager's face froze for an instant. "I just told you she wasn't my good friend. A childhood chum and customer. Ancient history. I know the families. And I'd say this whole business is not your business. You know I don't approve of what you do. You're not a cop, J. You're a hired gun. An assassin for the Suffolk County Police Department. If anything happened to you, they wouldn't know you from Adam."

"Sure they would." Justin smiled broadly, displaying pearly white and perfectly formed teeth. "You couldn't mix us up too easily."

"You joke, but they'd turn their backs on you quicker than you could blink."

"Look, Jackie. I didn't have much goin' for me before Kim and Brian took me under wing. And I'm grateful for the second chance I got. With Emery, we're talking pure evil here. God knows that. What I do is justified. All right?"

But Jacqueline flagged a finger of realization before the man's face, taking her thoughts to a higher plane. "Maybe that's it. Maybe you feel you've got to sanctify your actions instead of just walking away from the past. If that's the case, go do what you have to do, but like I told you before, leave me the hell alone."

"And I told you before; I can't do this without you. You're the key. We have the recipe less one ingredient. You. You're exactly what this madman ordered to a tee."

"What ever happened to the law, Justin?"

"It's broken, kid. We've got to fix it first."

"And this is your answer to the problem? This is how you're going to fix things?"

"It's a temporary solution."

"Of which I'll have no part."

"All right."

"All right, what?"

"I'll have something to eat."

"I didn't ask you."

"You asked me the last time I was here."

"That was then, and this is now. We're closed."

"I see."

"I don't think you really do. J, look at me. You're a good man. There are a dozen things you could be doing with your life. Why put it on the line like this?"

"Dozen things, huh? Washroom attendant. Car wash attendant. Garbage collector. Gas pump jockey!" he extolled facetiously, extending the fourth finger of his right hand in her face before folding all of them angrily into a firm fist. "I got a good shot fo' dat las' po·si·tion, seein' how folks in dis country's tired o' pullin' up to da pump and dealin' with a dot head who can't speak mo' dan two one-syllable sentences. Dey be happy to see a nigger who can count change and tell 'em what da weather fo'cast be fo' da next few days."

Jacqueline sighed irritably. "Just drink your wine and go. It's late."

Justin smiled with bittersweet disappointment. "Jackie, we have to stop saying goodbye this way."

"Night, J."

"Say! If I just pack it all in like you say, you think Phil might give me a shot in the kitchen, or maybe waiting tables with Warren and the gals? Better still, I could sweep and mop up after closing. How 'bout dat? I could start right now if ya like. Whattaya say, woman?"

"Maybe I'll just give you a shot myself right now. End your misery. How about that?' she said, raising a gun finger to his head.

"Oooo-eeee, girl! I jus' knew you still had it in you. All someone has to do is get under your silky skin. Well, let's see where we go from here," he needled.

"From here, you're going to the door," the manager snarled. "There are three of them to choose from. So finish up and take your pick."

"You used to be the sweetest girl in the whole world. Remember?"

"I used to be innocent before I met you. Recall?"

Justin Barnes swung his legs off the barstool and placed a ten dollar bill upon the counter before exiting the nearest door.

Jacqueline's husband, Tomas, came out from the kitchen. "What did he want?"

"Oh, you know. Wanted us over to Ursula's for dinner," she fibbed.

"What did you tell him?"

"Told him we were busy with parties; catering and such," she outright lied.

"Wasn't he just here the other day?"

"Yes."

"Persistent."

Jacqueline nodded and smiled anxiously. "He has trouble taking no for an answer."

Tomas shrugged. "We got fresh cod, flounder, salmon and striped bass for tomorrow night."

Jacqueline jotted down the items, considering tomorrow evening's special before closing out one of the registers.

Chapter 11

The last thing Grace Littleton saw before her cage crashed against the stone tile floor of the old courthouse was the illusory race between clouds and angels with musical instruments, seemingly ascending into the heavens. Whites and pinks and blues flew by her at a rate of speed and direction that appeared to defy gravity, lifting Grace's soul from the box as her body shattered and splattered while ropes and pulleys swung aimlessly through space.

As the blades of the large ceiling fans within the dome completed their last revolution and ceased, not a whisper of air moved a speck of dust until the doors were opened to the building on Monday morning. Construction workers moved helter-skelter across the terra cotta quarry-tiled floor.

"What the f—!" one man exclaimed as he entered from the bay side of the building, staring at the busted bloody skeletal frame of a woman with long dark hair, thrown clear of the splintered cage that had held her like a helpless songbird. A simile that wasn't far off the mark when the construction worker later learned who she was. But for that moment, all he could do was gaze between the broken catwalk-like bridge hanging high above him, then down at the naked body of the dead woman. "Oh, dear God," he whispered. "IN HERE!" he screamed to the others.

The police had identified the woman as Grace P. Littleton, daughter of Doctors Timothy and Victoria Littleton of New York. Grace was a promising young opera singer, musician and composer who had been scheduled to give her first overseas performance in Milan next month. Throughout San Francisco, she was more noted than the mayor; certainly more talented in all respects, it had been bantered about from one end of the city to the other. It was reported that Grace suffered from anorexia. The disorder had been the bane of her parents' existence. The least of their problems at the moment. The tabloids played the story up big. Fans along the busy seaport, where they lived and breathed her music, wept bitterly.

Eve Sterling, Grace's dearest friend and mentor, immediately boarded a plane from Rome when she received the shocking news.

Chapter 12

With his lawyer present, Doctor Timothy Littleton, quite agitated, sat at police headquarters in Great Neck. Two detectives stared in silence as the psychiatrist wiped his bloodshot eyes, blew his nose, then brought both fists forcefully down upon each knee.

"We've told you everything," Littleton's lawyer said solemnly.

"Maybe *you've* told us everything, Ed," one of the detectives said derisively. "He's told us virtually nothing."

"Look. We—"

"Look, nothing. I asked him when Emery first told him about the head in the freezer."

"Don't answer that, Tim," Ed Willis warned.

"Come on, Ed," Detective Prescott pressed. "I'm not the prosecutor here. We're just trying to establish a time frame. Not build a case."

Littleton raised his hand in anguish. "I—"

"I'm telling you as your lawyer, Tim, not to answer that or any question until you run it by me. All right?" he added resoundingly.

"No, it's not all right," the younger of the two detectives squawked.

"Well, I'm afraid it's going to have to be," the attorney balked. "This meeting is over. And unless you're going to charge and arrest my client—"

"Ed," the detective in charge interrupted.

"What?"

"Consider him arrested, all right?"

"No, it's not all right."

"Look. You don't like me telling you how to do your job, just like I don't like you telling us how to do ours. You don't tell us when this interview is over, Ed. We tell you."

"Interview? You've had him in here for four hours. You know

what's going on in California. The man has a plane to catch."

"And I'm going to hold him here overnight unless *he* starts answering our questions. Now."

"Give the guy a break, Fred."

"We're the ones who need a break, Ed. We got Looney Tunes out there running back and forth between the coasts killing young women. For all I know, Emery's sitting in some diner or luncheonette around the corner laughing up his sleeve at all of us. We've got to know each and every detail. Every second of every minute and every word that nut case told your client, as well as anyone else in that facility."

"This is not going to be your investigation, Fred," the attorney brayed heatedly. "You know that. The body of one woman turned up in Greenport—"

"And the head from another wound up in your client's freezer, or don't you get the connection?" Detective Frederick Prescott jousted angrily.

The younger detective laughed.

Detective Fred Prescott swung around in his seat. "Find that funny, Lee?" he asked of his subordinate.

"Sorry."

The senior detective faced back around. "Suffolk. Nassau. We're both involved. Surely, I don't have to tell you that, counselor."

Edward Willis opened up his briefcase and threw his legal pad and pen inside. "Let him go to California and take care of his daughter's arrangements. He'll surrender to you upon his immediate return. I remind you that this man came in voluntarily."

"And I remind you that we have a serial killer loose out there who has claimed some two dozen lives last we looked and will undoubtedly kill again, Ed. God only knows how many more we're talking here. So. Do I have you and your client's full cooperation, or do I book him now and hold him for the D.A.? Believe me, we'll do a better job than the doctor, here, did with Emery."

Willis stood and stuck his hands deep into his pants pocket. "Let me have a few minutes with my client—alone."

"Sure thing. Lee. Give these gentlemen some space."

Detective Lee Henris got up and, together with Prescott, left the two men to themselves.

Chapter 13

As there were no nonstop flights out of LaGuardia to San Francisco, Doctor Timothy Littleton caught a Boeing 767 from JFK International Airport. In the first-class section, most everyone was fed and content, watching a movie, reading, or relaxed in polite conversation. Everyone, that is, except Doctor Littleton. Three hours and twenty minutes into the flight, and with special permission, the psychiatrist received an expected, important call on his cell phone. Without hesitation, believing it was the psychiatric center, he removed the instrument from his briefcase and answered.

"Hello."

"And another thing that irks me, Timmy, is when people threaten me. You didn't think I'd let that go, did you?" Clarence Emery put forth peevishly. "You really pissed me off, you know. It took everything I had inside to control myself so that you wouldn't think I'd somehow lose it in the end. Maybe change your mind about releasing me. Nevertheless, I did keep my word, Timmy. I released her. Just as soon as I arrived. I even told Grace how *you* screwed things up just before I let her go. She was most disappointed in you, Tim. You could see it on her face. Most upset. I'm sure it was her very last thought as she dropped to her death. No up-and-coming concert in Milan, Doc. Not for Grace Littleton. She already did her solo yesterday evening, as you well know. From seventy-seven feet, shrink. What's *your* altitude now, Doctor? You do want me to call you doctor, don't you? Some thirty-five thousand feet, I do believe, Doctor Do-Little."

"You're fucking dead!" Littleton shouted. "Do you hear me, Emery?" the psychiatrist droned, dropping his voice to a whisper as he wept.

"No, you are. Oh, and by the way—the only rat I saw in that maze before I left Kirby was you. Now, I want you to summon stewardess Desirée Milo. She's a tall drink of water. Five-foot ten in stocking feet. One hundred and twenty-three pounds, last I looked. With long blonde hair that she usually wears in a ponytail. Today, I hear it's up in a bun. Like my associate, she was born in the Midwest, but raised in the extreme northern part of Italy. Lecco. Just above Milano, not far from where Grace was to make her overseas debut. I want you to tell Desirée that she'll be heading south soon, along with two hundred and twenty-one bodies including yours and the crew. Think you can do that for me, buddy? Think you can pass along the word? B-o-m-b," Emery spelled out slowly and deliberately. "Bomb. As in ba-boom! Sort of like your daughter's fall from grace, Doc. Only you're going to experience a more sudden kind of crash. Are you hearing me, Timmy?"

Doctor Littleton was seated on the aisle, listening to the madman's threats. Listening like he had listened to thousands of patients over the course of years. The psychiatrist had immediately signaled to a male flight attendant to listen in on the conversation, too.

"Tell Desirée that you brought the bomb aboard yourself, which indeed you did, Tim," Clarence Emery ranted. "Right under the nose of airport security and bomb-sniffing Labrador retrievers donated by the Australian government for the purpose of breeding. That ought to get the crew's attention, since they're all familiar with a terrorist plot that's been brewing and how badly those dogs are needed.

"Tell the suits everything they needed to know, Timmy? You see, I knew the police would allow you to say goodbye to Grace one last time. Knew too, that her body wasn't going to be air-shipped to New York. Dead set against your daughter's wishes, Doc. She wanted to live, die, and be buried in San Francisco. Your wife's a wreck, so Grace's friend will be taking care of all the necessary arrangements, I hear. In that ci-ty by the bay," Clarence Emery crooned. "Not 'the city that never sleeps,'" he recited, "because that one's good old New York. Oh, by the way; did you take out flight insurance, Timmy? I always had a problem with that. Damned if you do, damned if you don't kind of situation—don't you think? But I'm sure the wifey's well provided for. Not that she isn't well-off in her own right."

At the mere mention of the word *bomb*, the male purser had grabbed a dark-haired stewardess, and the two disappeared into the cockpit. Doctor Littleton took his carry-on bag out from under his seat and set it upon his lap. His hands trembled as he unzipped the canvas Lands' End case.

"Where?"

"Where what, Timmy?"

"The bomb," his voice quavered.

Other passengers seated around the man, including an elderly woman seated beside the window next to him, began to stir uncomfortably.

"What did you say?" she insisted nervously.

Littleton ignored her, searching deliberately through his bag.

"Bomb," the boy behind them repeated. "He said, bomb."

"Timmy, are you there?" Clarence Emery questioned calmly.

Littleton had the phone wedged between a shoulder and an ear.

"Timmy! Are you still with me?"

"What?"

"Are you busy looking through your carry-on? Did you do like I asked, Tim? It's not in your bag. Do you want to know where the bomb is?"

"Tell me."

"You're the bomb. You listening? You failed your daughter. You bombed as a father. As a husband, you're hanging by a thread. What's all that commotion around you, Doc? You got those people worked up into a frenzy, do you? Well, I'll tell you what. You can put their minds at ease. Know why? It's April First. April Fools' Day, Timmy. You can tell them it's all a big joke. Tell them your cousin or someone called and played a practical joke. Go ahead. Tell them. Do it now. You don't want a panic on your hands, do you?"

The purser and stewardess came back down the aisle with another uniformed woman hurrying behind them. Tall. Very attractive. She wore her blonde hair pinned up in a bun. She spoke fluent Italian with a concerned look on her face, addressing the purser. The trio hurried past Littleton and headed into coach. Heads bobbed and bodies leaned into the aisle; worried faces and looks of wonder followed the threesome. Several men and a young lady got out of their seats. In a loud voice, a woman passenger demanded to know what was going on.

"It's just a joke," Doctor Timothy Littleton told everyone. "My cousin's sick idea of a joke. April Fools."

"Then where are they headed in such an all-fired hurry?" the loudmouthed woman demanded, pointing toward the crew members as they vanished into the rear compartment.

"Something's up," one of the men insisted.

"Damn right there is," another declared.

"I think you're the sick one," someone said of the doctor. "What the hell are you hiding in that bag?"

"I'm not hiding anything," Littleton barked.

Professor Emery was busy buzzing in the doctor's ear.

A moment later, the purser and two stewardesses returned, escorting a heavyset man with a disfigured face up the aisle toward the cockpit. The blonde stopped in her tracks as the three continued briskly forward.

"Sit down," the head stewardess told a husband and wife who were still standing. "Everyone buckle your seat belt—now," she instructed with an accent. "Everything is fine, but we're just taking a precautionary measure. Sir, I asked that you sit," she insisted in a calm but firm tone.

One of the passengers questioned her in Italian, and she answered the man directly.

"Excuse me," Littleton interrupted the woman in charge. "Is your name Desirée Milo?"

Desirée turned around abruptly with some surprise.

Doctor Littleton handed her the cell phone.

The stewardess took the instrument without taking her eyes off Littleton. "Yes?" she spoke into the mouthpiece with consternation written across her pretty face.

"Remember me?" Professor Clarence Emery asked.

"Who is this?" she insisted, an edge to her voice.

"Physics, Chemistry, and Biology. Cal. Tech. Remember how you refused to open up that friendly little frog?" Emery chuckled. "I insisted that you call him Croaky."

Littleton watched the woman's face grow cold with fear.

"Emery?" She still had her bright blue eyes set on Littleton.

"What a memory, dear. You were one of my rising stars, and now you fly beneath them. But in exactly two minutes and thirty seconds, you shall be well above them. Part of an expanding universe. Miss me? Miss the university, Mrs. Notaro? Yes, I heard that you got

46

married and have a lovely two-year-old bouncing baby boy. Bet he'll miss you madly, but only for a while, and then he'll soon forget. Sad. Oh, the man next to you is a doctor." Desirée was already heading up the aisle and over to a panel with Littleton's phone to her ear. "A psychiatrist. He was mine for several days at Kirby Forensic Psychiatric Center. I told him a moment ago that I'm just fooling around, being it's April One. But you of all people know me better than that." A flashing red sign told everyone to buckle up. "Don't even bother looking for the bomb, Dee. You'll never find it in the minute and fifty-five seconds you have left to live. And even if you did, what would you do with it? Maybe if you had stayed after class and paid more attention to me, you'd have some idea. At least you'd have a fighting chance. All you have now is Billy Baxter. I called your captain earlier and reported him. Remember Billy from class? You probably don't even recognize him. He bombed out. Face like the inside of a furnace, but loyal as they come. Always called me Teach, while you insisted I was mad. Do you know why I didn't bother pursuing you a second time up until now? I wanted you to have something to live for. Husband. Kid. But you were always on my list of things to do, Dee."

"My husband will track you down and kill you, Clarence Emery," the woman whispered, disappearing into the cockpit, shouting orders to her assistant to go back out and calm the passengers, passing along information to the pilot and co-pilot, pressing a reticent Billy Baxter for a clue, turning her attention back to Emery. "Slowly. He'll kill you slowly, Emery," she swore.

"One minute, twenty seconds. Want to spend them threatening me? Mr. Anthony Notaro is going to have to get in a long line, dear."

"He'll find you, Emery."

"You'd do better if you thought about finding the bomb. Know what? I'm going to give you a big hint. No. Even better. I'm going to tell you where it is. Or should I say, who it is? It's Billy, Desirée. Yes. Billy's the bomb. You always said he had an explosive personality." Emery laughed. "Very busy was Billy today, Dee; booking a flight from coast-to-coast and back again, reassuring me it was really Desirée Milo in the flesh, scheduled for the return trip, too. Well, you have fifty-five seconds to dismantle him, Mrs. Notaro. He's sitting in tourist class. He was always a second class citizen, I'm sure you would agree, my dear." Emery chortled maniacally.

"He's standing right beside me," Desirée snapped. She turned to Billy Baxter before putting down the phone. "Your pal says you're a human bomb, Billy. Want to die with us up here?"

Billy quickly shook his head.

Desirée ran her hands all over Billy's body.

The pilot received permission to land. ETA for an emergency landing was a hopeless seven minutes away. They were somewhere over Kansas.

Desirée and the male purser stripped Baxter down to his shorts and socks. She grabbed and searched the accomplice's crotch and buttocks, firmly pressing in and around his privates with her schooled fingers.

"Where is it, Billy? Where did Clarence put the bomb? Tell us," she insisted.

Billy Baxter was crying and pointed to his mouth before running a finger slowly down the front of his shirt and stopping at his stomach.

"Oh, my God!" Desirée swallowed hard and, in an instant, made her way to the serving station and back again with a thick-bladed carving knife that had been used to slice skirt steak earlier. A dampened scream followed by a gush of blood sluiced from Baxter's throat as the senior flight attendant firmly planted the point of the blade above Billy's collarbone. The man crumpled before her.

"Are you mad?" the captain shouted.

The purser stepped back, saying nothing, but simply cringed.

"Have you lost your mind?" the co-pilot blasted.

"Had a good teacher," Desirée said evenly as she ran the sharp knife along Baxter's gut while the three men looked on in horror.

The head stewardess opened up Baxter's stomach as the man's body twitched involuntarily. She grimaced, searched, then removed a good-sized coated white capsule filled with glycerin, she believed. *Nitroglycerin*, Desirée envisioned. The capsule was partly dissolved. But then how could Emery precisely *time* its disintegration, she wondered, realizing that he could not. Frantically, she traced and raced through the contents of Baxter's small intestine when suddenly a thunderous roar erupted within the belly of the aircraft—which a nanosecond before had been the baggage compartment.

The explosion tore violently through the fuselage, separating the plane into three sections as a million pieces of debris filled the bright sky high above the cloud cover . . . forming a fiery mass somewhere over the central United States . . . a ball of orange, ringed in red and yellow . . . a pall-like cloak of blackness blanketing the clear blue space.

Clarence Emery dropped his cell phone into the Sound of silence with a splash, then thought aloud. "Now, where ever am I going to find a replacement assistant on such short notice? I imagine I'll just have to go to some nearby campus to recruit a new student with a flair for the dramatic. Yes, indeed, I might. Then again, the theater hosts some indubitable talent every now and again. Hmmmm."

Chapter 14

Justin Barnes was awakened by the phone. It rang quietly but interminably before he finally fumbled for and found the receiver, focusing on the dim red numbers of the clock radio. He said nothing, holding the mouthpiece upside down against his ear.

"Justin?"

Justin inverted the receiver and listened.

"Justin! It's me."

"It's me, too. And it's two a.m." He looked over at Ursula, who did not move so much as a muscle.

"I know what time it is, J. Did you see the news?"

"Yeah, over four hours ago. Why are you calling me now?" Justin listened to her silence for a moment, then hung up. The phone rang again seconds later. He grabbed for it on the first ring. "You have me on speed dial or something?"

"I want to talk."

"That's what phones are for, Jackie."

"I need to talk to you in person."

"Last couple of times, you didn't even treat me like a person."

"I'm sorry."

"Sorry don't cut it. You comin' in or what?"

"I said we need to talk."

"And I say, good night." Justin hung up the phone again, reached down and unsnapped the tiny plastic plug from the receptacle along the baseboard.

Ursula stirred. "You hung up on her?" she questioned, her sleepy voice muffled by the feather pillow.

"Go back to sleep."

"Not very nice hanging up like that."

"She needs to stew a bit."

"She coming in?"

"You're not supposed to know or ask about things like that."

"Right."

"Go back to sleep."

"Who is this Desirée Notaro—the former Ms. Milo—who I heard about on the news? And how is she connected to Emery?"

"Was."

"Who was she, J?"

"Paramilitary."

"Para-who?"

"Special unit trained by Special Forces before she wound up in airport security."

"Special Forces?"

"We'll talk about it in the morning."

"No, I want to know now." Ursula rolled over and sat up straight. "What's Special Forces exactly?"

"Army elite."

"Rangers?"

"Green Berets."

"I thought Rangers were the elite."

"That was World War II."

"My grandfather was a ranger."

"Army?"

"Forest."

Justin turned on his side and sank his elbow into the foam pillow. "Funny girl."

Ursula gave a sleepy crescent smile. "Were you ever trained in warfare?"

"Yeah, informally on the streets of Harlem and New Haven."

"I'm serious."

"So am I."

"You never had any formal training?"

"Nope."

"You were never in the service?"

"Nope."

"How come?"

Justin put the pillow over his head.

"How come you were never in the service?"

"Can't hear you."

"Punctured eardrum? Flat feet? What?"

"Criminal record."

"Anything I should be concerned about?"

"Yeah, murder if I don't get my proper rest."

"How'd she wind up a stewardess?"

"Operation some years ago went sour or something."

"Like how?"

"Like, whattaya writin', a fuckin' book?"

"They were very vague about her on the news. I figured you could fill me in."

"At two in the mornin' I'm gonna fill you in?"

"Well, I hardly ever get to see you since the Emery business broke. You're either at the restaurant tryin' to re-recruit Jackie, or out looking for this phantom."

"That a word?"

"What?"

"Re-recruit."

"I don't know. All I know is when we were at the restaurant last time, the two of you *didn't* talk about him. And when she and Tomas are here for dinner, we definitely *can't* talk about him. Then when you and I are alone, you *won't* talk about him. So, I figured I'd try you when you're vulnerable, sleepyhead."

"Talk about something else."

"Frank Sinatra had a punctured eardrum."

"Frank Sinatra was home fucking groupies while their boyfriends were away fighting the war."

"Couldn't be," Ursula affirmed.

"How's that?"

"Because I saw him in *From Here To Eternity*." She smiled and stretched her arms toward the high ceiling.

"You're a riot, Ursula. A regular riot," he said in his best Ralph Kramden impersonation.

"I want to know about Desirée Notaro. How did she wind up a stewardess, considering her *elite* background and higher education? News said she had a degree in biophysics and chemistry and was once a student of Professor Emery's. I find that just a bit too coincidental."

"You're not going to let me get any sleep till I tell you, are you?"

52

"Nope."

Justin rolled over onto his back. "No further inquiries into Jackie's role?"

"Promise. Desirée Notaro has my full attention."

"Her professor tried to take her out."

"On a date?"

"Not on a date, Ursula, for Christ's sake. He stalked her and tried to kill her."

"What happened?"

"He failed."

"Not tonight he didn't. Tonight he scored big. Desirée Notaro *and* Doctor Littleton. Not to mention two hundred plus passengers and crew."

"Certainly hit a home run this time, didn't he?"

"How'd she get away from Emery the first time out?"

"It's a long story."

"Then give me the abridged version."

"Can't."

"How about a little background?"

Justin surrendered a weary sigh. "Emery would sponsor select students for work-study programs in countries like Turkey, Central and South America. Only the work part involved smuggling drugs into this country. One way was by his couriers ingesting specially lined bags of cocaine. Nothing really new there. Drug enforcement agencies had been on to tactics like that for years. Then came people and their pets. What was unique about Emery's approach was that, if things ran afoul for his crew, they were instructed to swallow specially designed capsules conveniently hidden on their person but very accessible. Like under a shirt collar or lapel, or in hairdos and such, explaining to his charges that the compounds were calcium channel blockers that would neutralize stomach acids and prevent the bags from breaking open—if those runners were detained for any length of time. But investigators soon learned that the capsules contained compounds that, when consumed, would react and cause the body to convulse. Death would soon follow."

"So how did Desirée Notaro fit into the scheme of things?"

"She was part of airport security when one of Emery's couriers was taken into custody. Less than an hour later, the guy took out two guards, the detaining area, a lounge and a lunchroom."

"How?"

"Explosion."

"He had a bomb?"

"He *was* the bomb."

"What?"

"That's what she claimed. She was lucky and suffered superficial cuts and bruises. According to her, the young man had been thoroughly searched when put under arrest. No weapons. No contraband. But she said she'd seen him take something from under his collar just before they made the arrest, pop whatever it was into his mouth, then swallow and smile at her. Less than an hour later, an explosion followed that took out part of the building."

"J."

"What?"

"I minored in chemistry."

"And?"

"And what you're suggesting is . . . wild."

"Why?"

"Let me see if I understand this correctly. This courier—this student—supposedly swallowed a capsule just before he was arrested, turning himself into a human bomb."

"That was her take."

"Let me tell you something. Okay? You'd need three things to make something like that happen. A pre-mix, oxygen, and a spark. Ain't gonna happen the way that went down."

"How about the plane that went down?"

Ursula Pratt sighed. "It just couldn't happen like that, J. But let's say somehow it did. A body exploding is not going to take out an airliner, much less sections of a building as you described. Do you have any idea of the amount of explosive you'd need to ingest? Certainly not a capsule or horse pill or anything that size."

"That was the consensus some of the investigators came away with back then."

"Oh, now we're getting somewhere. What do they *think* actually happened?"

"That there was a device planted in the detaining area beforehand, and somehow the student triggered it."

"Now, that I'd buy into."

Justin nodded dubiously toward the ceiling.

"You don't seem convinced."

"Second time around the block with one of these couriers, another guy admits to Notaro when she arrested him that he took two capsules just before deplaning. Know what she does? Drags this guy from Arrivals to a Dumpster outside and throws him in it—handcuffed —then runs to get a dump truck filled with sand parked across the Tarmac, drives back across the runway and dumps the entire load into the bin. Practically buries the guy alive. Personnel thought she was going bonkers." Justin yawned and scratched his hairy chest.

"Well, what happened?"

"Nothing. No explosion or anything. But no one was in a hurry to pull the asshole out."

"Why? Did they believe the bin was going to blow sky-high, sending this sandbox and courier into oblivion?"

Justin didn't answer.

"What happened next?"

"Stone cold dead by the time they got to him."

"Drugs? Suffocation? Heart attack? What?"

"An undetermined substance found in his system."

"Undetermined?"

"Unknown. Undetermined. Unclear. See, that's what's so weird. Had there been drugs or shit in this guy's system that ate through his stomach lining and killed him, it'd be an open-and-shut case. There'd be a full report to that effect. But there's nothing but speculation. No one's talking."

"Who's no one?"

"Toxicologists—of the government kind."

"What did they put down on the death certificate?"

"Initially, they tried to sign off on congestive heart failure, then backtracked when some military forensic team stepped in and listed the cause of death as unknown. The file is sealed."

"Well, I'd have heart failure, too, if someone dumped a truckload of sand on my head. So they take Desirée off the ground, where she can't cause any more trouble, and put her in the air." Ursula shook her head in disbelief. "You wonder how a woman with that kind of military training, a B.S. in biophysics and an M.E. in chemical engineering, winds up as a flight attendant after being bounced from ground security," Ursula stated in exasperation. "She'd have been better off finding a teaching position somewhere."

"Interestingly, she wanted to teach. But rumor has it that Emery had her blackballed. She wanted a position at Cal. Tech., where Emery taught. Then *any* university or college, there came a point. But word was out. Emery made sure of that, the story goes. He had her labeled a nut, a thief who stole lab equipment, a temptress who seduced her professors—married or single, male or female—trading sexual favors for favorable grades."

Ursula's mind was reeling. "What do you think went on up there this afternoon, J?"

"I don't think we'll really ever know. What we do know is that William Baxter was on that plane; a former student of Emery's, too. We know that someone called the airport and reported that Billy-Boy was smuggling drugs. And we also know that Doctor Littleton received a call from sunny California."

"From who?"

"Clarence Emery, if I had to guess."

"What's the likelihood of actually finding him, J?"

Justin shook his head. "A snowball's chance in hell if you really want to know the truth."

"Why?"

"Because he's absolutely brilliant, a master of deception and disguise, rich with resources from drug trafficking, while enjoying sanctions within a wide criminal network throughout the world."

"How?"

"Because he's not greedy. Because he shares and shares alike. Because he's more interested in the game of cat and mouse than he is in profit or power or anything else. He's made his multimillions."

Ursula was silent for a moment, thoughtful. "What would you say might be your single hope in apprehending him?"

"I'm not interested in apprehending him, Ursula. All I'm interested in is finding him. That's it."

"Uh-huh. I sometimes forget, or try to, what it is you really do."

"Forget about it for good and you'll sleep nights," Justin suggested.

"I'll ask you again. What would be your one hope?"

"A good night's sleep," Justin Barnes said, closing his eyes and shutting down his mind for the time being as the hour was 2:15 a.m. In less than a minute, the man was fast asleep.

Ursula slid quietly out of bed, stooped down and plugged the phone wire back into the plastic receptacle. Stepping into an oversized pair of slippers, she made her way to the bathroom, combed her hair, got dressed and headed home.

Chapter 15

Justin Barnes ignored the ringing and beeping. Jacqueline Rubino kept her black Lexus several yards behind Justin's back bumper. Both vehicles were traveling east on the Long Island Expressway, well over seventy miles an hour. Justin got off at Exit 72 and slowed down to forty. Jacqueline held her phone up before the windshield, waving it back and forth like a wiper blade, signaling for Justin to pick up his cell phone. He unzipped and ripped the phone from its pouch.

"Yeah?"

"I said I want to talk to you."

"I'll repeat my words from last night. That's what phones are for. Start talkin'."

"You better not hang up on me this time."

"I said, start talkin'."

"Pull over. I don't want to do this on the phone."

"You know where the Riverboat Diner is at the circle in Riverhead?"

"No."

"Then follow me." Justin terminated the call.

Chapter 16

Anthony Notaro held his sleepy two-year-old son close to him before putting the boy to bed. Closing the door to the child's room, he walked down the hallway and into the kitchen, punching three significant size dents into the upper door of the refrigerator-freezer. Dissatisfied, he drove his elbow sharply against one of the new floor-to-ceiling custom cabinets, splitting the face of the solid white oak door in two. The man slowly sank to his knees before the oven door and punched through one of the double square panels of tempered glass. Finally, he stumbled to his feet and wept, supporting one bloody hand within the other, heading over to the double sink.

A moment later, the doorbell rang—and rang—and rang. Three minutes had passed while the late-night caller, standing in a light rain on the stoop, intermittently pressed the lighted bell button.

Anthony angrily pulled open the front door. "Who the fuck are you?"

Justin turned his head and looked high and low behind him. "Me?"

"Yeah, you asshole. You another fuckin' cop?"

"Cop? Do I look like a cop to you?"

"What are you doing here? What do you want?"

Justin fixed his eyes on the man's bloody hand wrapped in a white towel the size and shape of a boxing glove. "What'd you do to that hand?"

"Foreplay. I'm not gonna ask you again," he threatened, looking the tall black figure up and down like an opponent in a boxing ring.

"What if I told you I came here to burglarize your home? Wanted to make sure no one was around."

The man looked past Justin to the woman sitting in the car. "Interracial burglars on the prowl, fella?" Notaro questioned sarcastically, studying the woman's striking features from sixty feet away.

"Nah, I just bring'er along for good directions."

Anthony set his eyes impatiently back on Justin. "What do you want?"

"Professor Clarence Emery."

"Figured you for a cop."

"I'm not."

"Then what?"

"Can we come inside and talk?"

"She a cop?"

"Manager of a restaurant."

"You the busboy?"

"Knew I liked you right off. Maybe she could look at that."

Blood was dripping from Anthony's hand through the thick terry towel. He set his dark eyes back on the stately figure stepping from the car before he turned around and disappeared inside the house.

"Wipe your feet," he called from a hallway.

Justin was putting up water for tea and instant coffee while Jacqueline attended to the man's hand over the adjacent sink. The hydrogen peroxide fizzed and bubbled and burned the fist of the stocky six-foot-three commercial pilot as she poured liberal amounts of the solution upon the open cuts.

"I think this one could use a few stitches," the woman strongly suggested as she steadied the man's hand, gently dabbing at the deep slices between the first and second knuckle. "Hold still."

Anthony tensed his body. "I'll be all right."

"Thick, like the oven door and cabinet," she scolded, pouring on more of the antiseptic for good measure.

"Damn it!" he whined and winced.

The colorless liquid hissed and formed a white foam as Anthony writhed and fought to withstand the stinging pain.

"Stay still," she insisted.

"Easy for you to say."

"You put those dents in there, too?" she asked, gesturing toward the refrigerator while leading him over to a table. "Sit."

Jacqueline held a large, white gauze pad in place, pressing it firmly against the face of the big man's fist. "Put your other hand here," she ordered. "Hold this tight." Jacqueline dexterously wrapped a strip of first aid tape around Anthony's right hand, cut across the sticky band, then wrapped another strip along the outer edge of the bandage. "There. We want this to breathe. Now let's have a look at that elbow."

Justin stepped back from the stove, running his eyes along the wall of cabinets.

"Cups are in that one above you," Anthony said. "Coffee, tea and sugar's over there in the pantry."

Justin gathered up the items and removed a quart of milk from the refrigerator, bringing them to the table. "Spoons?"

"By the sink; top draw on the left."

Returning to the table with the silverware and pot of boiling water, Justin splashed a little on the tablecloth near Anthony as he poured her tea.

"We want to clean him up, J. Not scald him," she said with a smile. When Jacqueline smiled, she could brighten a pitch-black room. "You guys have your coffee. I'll take care of this mess first."

Justin looked down at the bandages and dressing and grinned with approval. "I told you we could have passed you off as Nurse Florence Nightingale at Kirby."

Jacqueline said nothing but went on about her business, picking up shards of glass from the floor in front of the oven, wiping the area clean of blood.

When the three of them were more or less settled at the kitchen table, Anthony Notaro was the first to speak. "I'm going to find that bastard, and I'm going to blow a hole in his skull. He's going to pay with his life for what he did to Dee."

Justin nodded his understanding, for he knew what the man was going through, having lost someone he truly cared about, too. Someone very near and dear to him, he reflected. A distant kissing cousin but close enough to be labeled mistress, friend, mentor, and so much more. Monisha Washington. Found suspended from the Mackinac Bridge in Michigan, near where she attended college. Murdered at the hands of Professor Clarence Emery's cohort two years earlier. Malcolm Columba: The Author. A serial killer who had known and worked closely with Emery. A homicidal maniac who mentored and molded the professor. A monster that Justin had finally found and murdered in cold blood, having warmed to the idea of deep-sixing others of that ilk. Secretly sanctioned and sanctified by Suffolk County's hierarchy.

"We'd like to help you accomplish that end," the maverick stated matter-of-factly, returning to the moment.

"Help, how?"

Justin took a sip of coffee. "May I call you Tony?" he asked politely.

"No, you may not. No one calls me Tony. No one ever has."

Pompous ass, Justin thought. "We're really getting off to a swell start here, Anthony. You don't mind if I call you Anthony. Or is it Mister or Captain Notaro, pilot extraordinaire?"

"Anthony would be fine."

"Would it now?"

"Want some lemon?" Anthony asked the woman as she quietly sipped her tea.

Jacqueline shook her head. "I'm fine."

"Tell me what you want," Anthony asked Justin directly.

"Already told you. We want Emery."

"Not any more than I do," Anthony snapped, wanting to put his good hand through the top of the table. "I lost my wife. And that boy in there lost his mother." Anthony Notaro almost lost it again, fighting the urge to bawl before the both of them.

"We want him just as badly as you do, Anthony. Believe me when I tell you that. I know what you're going through. Believe that, too."

"Did he take away your wife and make an orphan of your kid? Did he?" he challenged, glaring across the table, sorry he had let the two of them into his home. "He might just as well be an orphan." Anthony looked over Jacqueline's shoulder in the direction of his son's room. "Might as well be an orphan," he repeated, "because I'm as dead inside as his mother." He bit his bottom lip to keep from crying.

Justin felt the man needed a little information in order to place them all on the same page. He glanced over at his partner, then looked back at the wreck of a man before him. "Hear about those two women at Pipes Cove in Greenport?"

Anthony nodded. "Read about them in the paper," he whimpered.

"One of them was Jackie's old school chum and good friend," he exaggerated for effect. "Her head wound up in the freezer in Doctor Littleton's home in Great Neck. The director of Kirby, where Emery was being held. She had on the psychiatrist's daughter's earrings. Fixed to each nostril. Couple years back, I lost someone, too. Murdered by another madman. Malcolm Columba. Remember him? Emery's associate. I also lost some other people I truly cared about. So, we *do* know what you're going through."

Justin had Anthony's full attention.

"You're that guy . . . ." The pilot's mind flew back in time. Many unanswered questions followed the death of that serial-killer. "I recognize you now from the papers and the news."

"Not as a cat burglar or a busboy?" Justin grinned like the Cheshire cat.

Anthony held a straight face and the look of respect. He looked across at the beautiful woman. "What did you say your name was?"

"Her name is Jackie, Anthony. But you may call her Jacqueline," Justin answered for her with a put-on arrogant air.

Anthony Notaro almost cracked a smile. "You got a plan, Justin and Jacqueline?"

"Oh, do we have a plan," Justin assured the man. "Do we ever."

Jacqueline looked over at her partner, giving nothing away—certainly not the fact that she had no clue as to what or where Justin was going with *his* plan.

Chapter 17

The new chef *extraordinaire* had finished scaling, gutting and cleaning up the ten-pound silvery salmon before placing the whole fish—head, body, fins and tail—upon a stainless steel poaching rack. His assistant, a portly young man in his teens, looked on with curiosity.

"We've never done a salmon here before," the lad said.

"Wait. When Al sees the finished product and the customers taste it, they're going to flip."

"How long you let it cook for?"

"Forty minutes."

"How do you know?"

"Hand me that ruler, and I'll teach you a little trick."

Howard Urban handed the chef the wooden ruler from an overhead shelf.

The man wiped one end on a clean damp rag and held the straightedge upright against the middle of the fish. "How thick is it at its center, Howie?"

The lad leaned over the table and looked. "Four inches?"

"You asking me or telling me?" the chef questioned congenially.

"Telling you," the boy answered placidly.

"Then, at ten minutes an inch, how long are you going to simmer, not boil, but simmer this fish?"

"Forty minutes? I mean forty minutes," the boy said with certainty.

The recently hired chef nodded approvingly, lifting then carefully placing the glistening fish and shiny new rack into its pan of simmering water, covering it with the lid. "There. Step number one."

"What's next?"

"Next, we make fresh mayonnaise."

"Make?" Howard remarked with genuine surprise. "We don't make mayonnaise here. We have it in gallon containers over there."

"That's one of the reasons why this place had the reputation of a second-rate restaurant, and why I've been hired to turn the place around. And turn it around is what we're going to do, Howard. You and I. So pay strict attention. Someday you'll be training others. If they don't fall in line, we'll dump out that processed junk and pickle them in those containers. How does that sound?" the man in charge declared.

"You're the boss," the boy said delightedly.

"Boss of the kitchen, yes. But when I'm finished here and move on one day, Howard, you could be in charge. Learn well what I teach you, save your money instead of running around with those losers I see you hanging with, and maybe you'll open up your own restaurant when the time is right. What do you think of *them* apples?"

"Apples?"

"It's an expression."

"Yes, sir."

"Forget this sir and boss stuff. All right?"

"All right, but what should I call you?"

"How about anything but late for dinner?" the chef chaffed.

The heavyset youngster laughed heartily. "But seriously, o' chef whose last name I can't even pronounce," Howard bantered back good-naturedly, "what do I call you?"

"Let me think on that for a while," the man considered. "But for the time being, how about calling me by my first name."

"Really?"

"Sure."

Howard nodded happily. "All right, Mike. How do we make fresh mayonnaise?"

Clarence Emery smiled. "Empty that shopping bag of fresh herbs over there behind you. I'll get the eggs and olive oil, and we'll get started."

"Sure thing, Mike," Howard replied enthusiastically.

Forty minutes later, Howard removed the pan's lid and inserted a wooden spoon through the looped handles at each end of the draining rack as his tutor had instructed, carefully lifting out the perfectly cooked salmon.

The recently hired chef transferred the fish onto a large oval tray. "Now, while the skin is still hot, we can gently scrape it off with a knife, like so; from in back of the gill, here, to a couple of inches before the end of the tail, right there. On both sides. Being very careful not to damage the fish when we turn it. I'll do this side, and then you can do the other."

"Then why did you scale it if we're taking the skin off anyway?"

"Because we'd have a real mess on our hands if I hadn't."

Howard watched his mentor meticulously remove the rest of the silvery skin from the flesh, revealing its beautiful light pink color. Painstakingly, Howard did the other side of the salmon, from its gill to within two inches of the tail.

"Beautiful," the master chef declared. "Perfecto."

Howard was very pleased with himself.

"When the fish cools, we'll spread the mayonnaise along its surface. Not before, otherwise the mayo will melt and make a real mess. In the meantime, let me show you how to prepare veal that will melt in your mouth. You like veal?"

"I love food, period. Can't you tell?" Howard gleamed, slapping his gut affectionately. "I tip the Toledo at two ten, Mike."

Emery smiled. "Well, we're definitely going to have to do something about that."

Howard's face went from one of happiness to sheer horror in a hot second at the mere thought of having to lose weight.

"Not to worry, Howard. I'm going to teach you how to eat properly. Eat practically anything you want, but eat healthy; you'll learn to eat in moderation. You won't even know you're on a diet, except for the fact that I'm going to instruct you on exactly what to do. Where we'll use olive oil and clarified butter for our customers, *you'll* substitute with canola or peanut oil when whipping up a little something to eat—with the emphasis on little. Things like that. You overeat because you're bored. You learn what I teach you, apply it, and you'll never be bored again. What do you say?"

In his entire life, Howard never had a person take an immediate liking or interest in him, and he quickly seized the opportunity. "Yes, sir. I mean, Mike."

"Good man. Good man. How are you with the ladies, Howie?"

Howard looked down shyly and said nothing.

"Well, we've got to do something about that, too."

"Really?"

"Howard, when I get done with you, the women are going to be eating out of your hand."

Howard looked baffled.

"That's also an expression, Howie," the chef stated with a warm smile.

"I know," Mike's assistant acknowledged. "That one I heard for sure. But I'm lucky if they even ask me the time of day," he said so sorrowfully.

"Well, that's all going to change," Clarence Emery assured him.

After the salmon had cooled, Emery spread the creamy dill mayonnaise sauce over the pink portion of flesh.

"Looks pretty," Howard said.

"You haven't seen anything yet. This is just a savory paste, which we're going to decorate with scales."

"Scales?"

"Yes. Now, what I want you to do is slice up some cucumber, very thin, like I'm doing with this daikon radish."

"Want me to peel mine?"

"No, the skin will give it some added color."

"How's this?"

"Thinner, please. Translucent."

"Trans-who?"

Emery smiled patiently. "I want those slices so thin that you can practically see through them."

The boy sliced a tenuous ring, closed one eye, then held the thin flat piece up before the master. "How's this, Mike?"

Emery nodded his approval. "Excellent. Do the rest. Next time, we'll be sure to have a mandoline."

"Mandoline?"

"Not the kind you play, Howie. But the kind with which you cut vegetables. Makes the job a breeze, along with perfect slices."

The two worked together as a team. Howard carefully sliced

the cucumber; Emery did likewise with the radish.

"Next, I want you to arrange yours in rows of two. Overlapping them like this. Starting from the tail. See how they stick to the paste? Go ahead."

Howard gingerly laid one slice over the next, constructing and simulating the scales of the fish. When the lad completed two rows, Emery laid the radish slices in a similar pattern.

"See how we work from the tail toward the head of the fish in order to replicate the Creator's design? Note how the scales are streamlined from front to rear, as the fish itself would move forward through the water. What would happen, Howard, if God reversed the order and started the scales at the other end of the fish?"

"There'd be . . . uh . . . resistance?"

"Exactly. So, we not only want to create a beautiful presentation here, we want to be accurate in detail, too. Yes?"

Howard nodded his head in agreement. The two worked conscientiously. Just before Emery reached the gill, he stopped.

"Hand me that knife," the chef directed.

Howard handed his teacher the blade by its handle.

In a flash, Emery removed and discarded the fish's gill, sliced through part of a peeled red onion, then rearranged the purplish rings into the cheek cavity, brightening and giving new life to the captured creature of the sea, completing one half of the presentation. Ripping a sheet of clear wrap from a roll, he laid it atop the salmon, then deftly turned the decorated fish over and onto a bed of simulated sea grass.

"I want you to do this half by yourself," Emery directed, washing and wiping his hands before removing the chef's hat from his head and passing his fingers through a crop of recently dyed black hair.

"Moving right along." The teenager beamed proudly.

Emery was through bonding for the moment.

"Where you going?" the chef's assistant asked.

"Do some shopping."

"Where'd you ever learn to cook and cut like that?" Howard asked as his newfound friend headed out the rear of the kitchen.

"CIA," Professor Clarence Emery called back with a grin, putting on a pair of thick horn-rimmed glasses—although his eyesight was twenty-twenty.

"The CIA? Really?"

"Culinary Institute of America."

"Oh," Howard said with just a hint of disappointment scrawled across his flaccid countenance.

Chapter 18

The police commissioner finished proofing the *Newsday* article for Sunday's edition with some degree of satisfaction, lifting his bloodshot eyes and setting them on Detective Lieutenant Theodore Groche.

"Well?" the homicide commander asked.

"It's on your head if there's fallout from this, Theo."

"I understand."

"I don't know if you really do. I realize you're putting in your papers in January, so we're not talking career here. But it could mean your pension. It could even mean prison."

"We've been through this before, Kevin."

"We've been through this when I was in the catbird seat and could protect you, when my position was secure, Theo. Come June, you're on your own. Come June—"

Theo put up his hands and smiled benignly. "Everything's going to be all right. We're going to be all right with this."

Commissioner McGruder smiled, too. "Always the optimist, Theo. Always looking on the bright side, seeing the silver lining in every dark cloud that passes by. And the good Lord knows we've certainly seen our fair share of those."

"It'll be all right," the lieutenant repeated. "So tell me what you think."

"It's good, Theo. Damn good. I just hope it works. And if it does, I pray that all goes well from that point on. For your sake. We're not dealing here with *one* of the best, but, by far, the *very* best. This guy sees shit through a brown roofing shingle; he'll smell a trap a mile off."

"But there's truth in every word she says, and *Newsday* will print it."

"That's your edge, Theo. Hopefully, it'll draw him out. But

then watch out. Emery will have every base covered."

"Won't matter much if we hit a home run."

"That's where you're wrong, Theo."

"How do you mean?"

"Your player still has to run those bases. And that's where you're going to have to be very careful. Even when heading into home plate, you're not going to be home free."

Theo nodded with understanding. "We'll be careful."

"I know you will. But will you be as cagey is my utmost concern. The guy is absolutely brilliant."

"But positively nuts."

"And in that lies your *added* edge." The commissioner smiled benignly.

"Then it's a go, thank God," Theo said with some relief.

"Your funeral if you fail. No ticker-tape parade if you finish first," the stout man reaffirmed with a frown.

"Never was, Kevin."

Kevin McGruder put aside the article and picked up the black and white photograph, staring down at the stunning woman. He raised his bushy eyebrows. "A suggestion, Lieutenant?"

A suggestion from the commissioner was like a warning from the Almighty.

"I'm listening."

"I wouldn't run the photo."

Theo waited for the explanation.

"It spells *trap*. Let him look her up and over himself. Another thing. I'd put the story on page five or six. The words are powerful enough to get his motor running. Make it a feature story, and you might just as well put her picture on the front page with a headline that reads: "Find Me, 'Cause We're Gonna Fuck You Up Real Bad When You Get Here, Chump."

Theo nodded. "I've been tossing the idea of the photo around a lot."

"Toss it out would be my advice, Theo," McGruder set forth solemnly.

"Yes, sir."

"He'll see her for himself soon enough. Couple more things. I'd wait awhile before I run it. Let the word circulate. And forget

Sundays. Let it appear midweek. Emery misses nothing."
    Theo nodded in agreement.

Chapter 19

After flying a shipment of medical supplies from the Midwest into Islip Airport, Anthony Notaro headed home. He was tired and irritable. The eastbound traffic on the Long Island Expressway was moderate, Anthony thanked the stars. Westbound travel was a nightmare. Bumper to bumper.

Had he been headed toward the city, he'd have given new meaning to the term road rage, he swore. Anthony turned north, crossing Route 25 toward Wading River. As he pulled into his driveway, the comely woman, holding his toddler in her arms dotingly, came outside to greet him. She waved both her and the child's hand before the Buick came to a stop.

"Daddy's home," Jacqueline said succinctly in the boy's right ear. "And I think he's brought you a present," she whispered sweetly in his other, giving the infant an affectionate peck on the cheek.

The child lifted his head toward the heavens, ignoring his father and the handsome woman who held and hugged him dearly.

"You're back early." Jacqueline smiled, giving Anthony a kiss on the cheek, too, as he stooped forward to take the squirming bundle from her arms, putting a small plastic plane in his son's tiny hands. The baby immediately put the tip of one wing into his mouth and gurgled. "I think he said Gabreski or Grumman," Jacqueline swore and giggled, alluding to the airport in Westhampton as well as the one-time manufacturer of aircraft in nearby Manorville.

From his jacket pocket, the pilot took a small black velvet box and handed it to his purported lady-in-waiting . . . waiting for the madman to come to her; waiting for Clarence Emery to make his move, if he dared.

"I didn't have time to wrap it," Anthony said apologetically. "Hope that's all right."

Jacqueline smiled awkwardly.

"Well, open it."

She opened the little box and stared.

"It's a friendship ring. Nothing more. So don't look like you're going to have a kitten. Okay? Justin insisted. He believes each of Emery's victims was supposed to have a checkered past, as he put it. It's a good thing he called instead of telling me this in person because I would have decked him right there. Desirée did nothing to warrant —"

"Shh," she interrupted, gently pressing a finger to the pilot's lips. "Justin called me, too. It's what Emery *believes* in his sick and twisted mind is all. It's important that he sees us as an item so soon after Desirée's—" Jacqueline searched for and swallowed the word, "—demise. It's vital that he sees me, a married woman, spending a good deal of time with you and Nicholas. We're going to cover all the bases, Anthony. All right?"

Anthony took a deep breath and nodded calmly. "I know. It's just that—well, Desirée never, ever—forget it. So. You're supposed to be something more to me than just my assistant, helping me find this nut."

"J and I spoke at length. I'm supposed to be your live-in as of this minute, helping you take care of your kid and home and supposedly your needs. Your mistress of the moment," she said uncomfortably. "This is a bit awkward for me, too. Believe me."

"How are you going to manage things—the restaurant—and your own family?"

"Officer Ruth O'Connor is going to help me play a part, too," Jacqueline explained.

Anthony slowly shook his head. "I don't know if Emery's going to buy into this."

"Why not?"

"Because I never had the reputation of being a lady's man. Because I never gave another woman a second look. Never had to. Desirée was all the woman I ever wanted in the world."

"And that's how I feel about Tomas, too. Look at me, Anthony. You and I were thrown together as a matter of circumstance, both hell-bent on revenge for certain. We want Emery to see us together. If he sees the article, we have a shot at him because everything in it, with the exception of an insinuated intimate relationship," Jacqueline parenthesized, "is true. If we're good actors—you and I and Ruth—and we keep to the script, we're going to nail this son of a you-know-what. We'll let things leak out slowly and naturally. Starting with your nosy neighbors down the road." The gorgeous woman smiled and gestured.

Anthony turned and faced the nearest property, peering through the sparse wood lot. "Giving you the evil eye, are they?" he said and nodded with a knowing grin.

"Like radar when I drive by those homes."

"I guess that's good," he added disconcertingly.

"Good so long as you don't let it bother you. Good that they see you taking up with another woman."

"So soon after Desirée's—death."

Jacqueline nodded. "Sorry, but it makes us appear . . . well, checkered," she said unabashedly.

"You know something? I really don't give a good god—give a darn about what people think," he declared, staring down into his son's big, bright blue eyes. "Right, sport?"

"Then that's good, Anthony, because Justin wants us to go out and be seen in public. Just you and me," she elaborated. "One of your local haunts. Up to it?"

Anthony nodded. "Ruth inside?"

"Out of sight, of course, but never out of mind," she put forth plainly.

"You know, you two *do* look remarkably alike from a distance."

"I thought you never gave women a second look," she said teasingly as she pulled him by the arm toward the stylish Cape.

"Looked a little," he said so shyly, "but I never—never mind."

Jacqueline stopped him at the front stoop. "I want you to look at me and listen very carefully, Anthony. I want you to believe what I'm about to say."

"What?"

"There is absolutely no doubt in my mind that we're going to succeed."

Anthony looked into the serious woman's alluring green eyes. "Then put that ring on your finger, give me another kiss on the cheek for the world to see, and make me a cup of coffee, mistress," he kidded, hiking Nicholas in his arms.

Jacqueline smiled and extended a hand to the heavens, sliding the silver band on the ring finger of her right hand, skipping the kiss and gently guiding both father and son up the front steps and through the entrance to the home—turning and double-locking the door behind them.

The policewoman stood off in a corner of the room in the exact outfit Jacqueline was wearing as the couple entered the home.

"Ask you something?" Anthony asked.

Jacqueline looked up.

"May I call you Jackie?"

The woman smiled invitingly. "You may and you better," she insisted cheerfully. "In spite of what Justin Barnes said when we first met," she underscored in a tone that immediately cemented their working relationship.

Chapter 20

Clarence Emery and his young assistant, Howard Urban, were busy in the kitchen preparing shrimp and grits with tasso ham. The line-crew was stirring pots, scouring and washing out sauce and sauté pans, whipping heavy cream, slicing and dicing red and green onions, while talking about the serial killer who had escaped from a mental facility up in New York a month ago.

"Motherfucker cut their heads clean off with a butcher knife and stuck them in a freezer," the Cuban dishwasher declared loudly while running steaming water into a large cauldron before scrubbing its interior with a fist-sized stainless steel scouring pad.

"Stuck *one* of their heads in a freezer," an elderly South American cook corrected, filling several dozen littleneck clams on the half shell from a pastry bag packed with creamed spinach. Using a pair of scissors, he then began topping off each moist morsel with a thin slice of center-cut bacon, picking up a rhythm as he snipped away.

"Blew his psychiatrist up in a plane while the man was flying out to California to bury his daughter," the Cuban continued. "Luckily, his wife was on an earlier flight."

"Yeah, real lucky. So she could bury the both of them," a young Mexican busboy said, setting down a bin full of dirty dishes.

"She didn't have to bury nobody," the old man said, shaking his head sadly. "The daughter's been cremated and the father's in a million pieces," he explained rather graphically, clipping the raw strips of bacon noisily for emphasis as he worked.

"Hey, how come you know so much about the murders, Octávio?" another man wanted to know. "Maybe *he's* the serial killer," he announced to everyone, pointing a long-handled oven spatula at the Brazilian. "Maybe we should check the freezers *here*," he kidded.

"If you read the papers, Yankee, you'd know he's a forty-five-year-old American professor of physics. Do I look American or forty-five to you, gringo?"

"I *do* read the papers," the pastry chef said defensively.

"Yeah, the funny papers," Octávio Fernandez joked.

"Which just goes to show how fucking old you really are. They're called comic strips today, you donkey. Gonna retire your ass soon to the funny farm."

Clarence Emery smiled. "Maybe you should do less talking and concentrate on that garlic bread before you burn it, Smitty."

"Shit!" The man scurried over to one of the ovens.

"Yeah, last week he burned four loaves," Howard ratted.

"Yeah? Before Mike came here, you didn't even know how to make garlic bread," Smitty snapped, taking out the fresh loaf in the nick of time.

"Before Mike came here, I didn't *have* to know how to make garlic bread," Howard retorted good-naturedly.

"That's right because you bought it—like everything else—in the supermarket. But I always make *all* the desserts from scratch."

"Before Mike got here, not a one of you knew how to cook a damn thing right," the young Mexican man decried. "Locals called this place the Road Kill Café," he reminded them as well, cradling a stack of clean plates piled from crotch to chin before disappearing from the kitchen.

"Listen, let me tell you all something," Smitty put forth. "My desserts are what kept this place goin' before Mike ever got here . . . no, it's true, and I'm gonna tell ya why. The entrée can be fair to middling because the entrée generally heads the list. Right? But my desserts are the *last* thing the customers remember when they leave here. It's that lasting impression that draws them back. That's psychology," Smitty affirmed, slamming the oven door closed with a thrust of his hip.

"Road Kill Café, my ass," the Brazilian brayed beneath his breath.

"Well, Mike here is sure as hell gonna kill me off before I ever make it to retirement," the Cuban snipped. "I've never seen so many dishes, except maybe in a restaurant supply house. I liked it better when Howard virtually piled everything on one plate and sent it out. No offense, Mike."

"None taken," Clarence Emery said evenly.

A pretty waitress rounded the kitchen while lining up several plates of salad along a slender arm. "And *I* liked it better when I didn't have to run back and forth so much," Laura Ingrilli agreed. "But I'll tell you guys another thing; I sure as shootin' appreciate the tips I'm getting these past four weeks," she avowed quite happily, exiting as the Mexican reentered through the adjacent door.

"Yeah, well don't forget the dishwashers, busboys, and other slaves to kitchen's hell," Ignacio Vázquez implored, calling after her as he stooped to store a pot below the shelf in front of him.

"From what I understand, Laura and the other girls give you guys about ten percent more than what you were getting before," Emery commented. "Am I right?"

"That's true, Mike. Every word and penny of it," Ignacio agreed. "Ten percent more money in our pockets; thirty percent more dishes." The Cuban frowned.

Emery smiled. "Maybe I'll suggest to Alfredo that the help back here deserves, and should therefore receive, a decent raise. How's that? I think the boss can well afford it now."

The Cuban man, the Mexican boy, the elderly South American fellow, as well as everyone else in the bustling kitchen, slowly widened their eyes along with astonished smiles.

"O*rr* right!" a young Chinese cook standing in the corner exclaimed.

"That's only if you stop with the sticky rice," Howard warned. "This is not some cheap Chink take-out joint like next-door."

"No make sticky *l*ice no more, Howie," the lad swore. "Nice and f*r*uffy *r*ike Mikey *r*ikes it. That's an expression," he needled his coworker, then turned, smiled and winked at Mike affectionately. "O*rr* right, eve*l*y one?"

"O*rr* right," Howard and everyone bantered good-naturedly, including the head chef of the up-and-coming establishment.

"Hai*r* to the chief!" the Asian teenager exclaimed, saluting their hero smartly.

"Here, here," two of the crew rejoined, one of them removing a headband in tribute.

Clarence Emery, alias Mike Chardavoyne, took a modest bow before grabbing a chicken from a counter and cutting the plump bird into a dozen pieces before the Oriental could fill a two-quart pot with cold water.

Chapter 21

Only after having called downstairs to the desk clerk, the San Francisco Police Department, Suffolk County Police in New York, then finally hotel security, did the distraught woman unlock and open her door the length of the chain that secured it. The hotel manager had supposedly scrutinized Justin Barnes' letter of introduction, along with credentials of the man whose swarthy complexion first appeared on the other side of Doctor Victoria Littleton's peephole that morning. Barnes was back upstairs.

"It doesn't look like you," the stately woman hedged, holding the door ajar.

"Well, it's me, Doctor Littleton," Justin snapped indignantly. "Usually, I carry around a negative for funky white folk who just can't tolerate living color," he jawed. "But I figured all I needed was a letter of introduction, which I know the sunshine boys faxed over to you earlier as did Suffolk County homicide. So. Do I just stand out here all morning like I don't belong in these swanky digs while you place, yet, another call, or do I come back wearing a bellhop's uniform?"

With a degree of ambivalence, Victoria Littleton closed the door and removed the chain. She reopened the door, glancing anxiously down the hallway. "I guess if hotel security says it's all right," she surrendered quietly, offering up a nervous smile, standing before the tall, well-dressed, broad-shouldered figure at the threshold.

Justin smirked. "What hotel security? I walked right past the doorman and the desk clerk, who thought I was Denzel Washington coming up here to read a script."

"But they told me—"

"They told you what you wanted to hear, is all. If you called the feds, they'd have told you the same thing. To put your mind at ease with a false sense of security, they probably have this hallway covered with video and sound. If I were Emery or an accomplice set on foul play, you'd be dead and I'd be in custody by now. So relax. You want security? You want to feel safe? Go out and get yourself a Doberman and a double-barreled shotgun, lady. These are the times we live in. Now, you want to invite me in so that they can go back to playing gin rummy or whatever it is feds do with downtime?"

"You don't sound like a cop to me," Doctor Littleton said, stepping back into the room.

"Told you on the phone; I'm not a cop."

"What are you exactly, Mr. Barnes?"

"Consultant."

"Consultant?"

"Yes."

"Well, Mister Consultant. Come in and have a seat."

"Well, thank you very much, Vickie dear," he spewed with an air of arrogance and annoyance, following the attractive woman into a spacious parlor.

She turned and apologized. "Look. I'm really sorry I had you wait so long."

"And I'm really sorry you lost your daughter and husband. I'm sorry you're running scared. I'm sorry that son of a bitch is still out there. Apologies aside, I want you to tell me everything your husband told you about Professor Clarence Emery." Justin was directed to and settled into a comfortable overstuffed club chair. "Then I want you to tell me everything you can and can't about your daughter's life. Everything. Her musical career. Her love life. Her anorexia. Places she visited both here and abroad."

Victoria sighed wearily. "I'm afraid there isn't very much left to tell that I haven't already told the authorities. My husband never brought his work home from the office, meaning that he never ever discussed his patients."

"Tell me about his mood during the last days with that maniac. I'm sure you can tell me something in his not having told you anything at all. His demeanor. His tone at the dinner table. His behavior before and after he went to bed."

Victoria nodded. "I knew something was wrong."

"You'd have to be an idiot not to," Justin put forth bluntly, leaning forward in his seat as Doctor Littleton took hers.

"I don't think I've ever met anyone quite like you, Justin

Barnes," she said uncomfortably.

"I don't think I'll ever meet anyone quite like Clarence Emery —when I finally do get to say hello. So, you gonna try and help me find him?"

"I'll try," she affirmed.

"Atta girl," Justin said warmly, loosening the Windsor knot at his throat.

"May I ask you something before we get started?"

"You may ask."

"You're the man who . . . who found Malcolm Columba two years ago, aren't you?"

Justin nodded a response.

"I remember your picture on the news and in the papers."

"Yet, you didn't recognize my puss through the peephole, nor match it against the photo the authorities faxed over with the letter," Justin jabbed.

Victoria Littleton dropped her eyes to the carpet. "I recognized and remembered you, Justin Barnes."

"So what was the problem?"

She ran the tip of a finger along the upholstered armchair. "The problem was that I read between the lines."

"Meaning?"

The woman raised her eyes and met the man's stare. "Meaning that I think you found and murdered that man . . . Malcolm Columba. Clarence Emery's associate. And I ran a little scared."

"Would it bother you if that were the case?"

Victoria held Justin's gaze for several seconds before she slowly shook her head. "It would bother me greatly if you didn't say hello to Emery for me and Timothy and Grace. It would bother me terribly, Justin Barnes, if you didn't say goodbye to him for all of us, too." Without a change of expression, a series of tears rolled down the pretty woman's face.

"Well, I hate goodbyes, Doctor Littleton," he said, carefully weighing his words. "Worst of all, I hate seeing garbage like Emery and his kind littering the planet with bodies. So, I'll just say hello to Mr. Emery for you and yours when I see him. All right?"

Victoria nodded soberly and began her story from the first night her husband returned from Kirby after receiving Professor

Clarence Emery as a prisoner/patient. There was very little to tell, apart from the fact that her husband had mentioned that the Nassau police arrested the notorious serial killer. Next, the bereaved mother launched into Grace's history, explaining at the end of her monologue that she was remaining in San Francisco to be close to her daughter's music and memory.

Chapter 22

The petite and pretty dark-haired waitress from Alfredo's Restaurant in downtown Baltimore was putting a key in the door to her apartment just as a figure came around the stairwell, startling Laura Ingrilli.

"Jesus, Mike. You scared me for a second. What are you doing here?"

"It's about Howard," Emery said quietly.

"Howie? What about him? Is he all right?"

"He's fine." Clarence Emery looked up at the ceiling as if there were no place else to look. "Can we go inside for a minute? I won't take but a moment of your time. Promise."

"Well, sure Mike. I just put a load of laundry in the dryer downstairs. But I want to warn you ahead of time that I'm not the world's best housekeeper," she explained. "And I know how fussy you are and all."

"This is not the kitchen, and I'm not here for a white-glove inspection," he assured her along with a wink and a bright smile.

"Come on," she said, pushing open wide her door and eyeing the package at his side. "What have you got there?"

"Oh, just some things I picked up for the restaurant."

"I thought maybe it was a big box of candy," Laura trifled, closing the door behind them. "Thought for a second you were calling on me."

"Well, you sure are pretty enough to come calling on, but I think I'm a little too old for you, Laura."

"Be surprised," she said with a flirtatious grin. "Guess how old my boyfriend is."

"You mean the one who drops you off at work in the afternoon?"

"Uh-huh."

"I don't know. Maybe thirty-three, thirty-five."

"Try forty-two."

"Really?"

"Yep. Acts like he's sixteen sometimes, but I love him just the same. Treats me like I'm somebody special."

"Howie says that fella sometimes treats you very mean. Sorry. I guess it's none of my business. But he did tell me he saw that guy of yours slap you once and push you out of his car, right outside the restaurant."

Laura shrugged. "Once in a while he gets like that. Not often, or I'd dump him in a heartbeat. I mean, what relationship doesn't have its ups and downs? My parents . . . never mind, Mike. Don't get me started on that. Anyway, let me offer you something to drink, then tell me what's up with Howie. Scotch all right?"

"Nothing really, Laura. Maybe you could point me in the direction of the bathroom."

Laura laughed. "Tell you what, Mike. If you can't find it for yourself in ten seconds flat, I'll give you my share of tomorrow's tips. How about a beer?"

"How about a glass of water?"

"Tap or bottled? Pellegrino from the restaurant. I'm becoming a lady of fine taste since you arrived, Mike. Never ate so well, either. I think I gained seven pounds the first week. That hadda stop or I'd turn into a blimp. You're a genius in the kitchen. Dangerous, though."

"Regular water's fine. Be right back." Emery headed down the hallway to the bathroom.

"Only door on your left, Mike," she called after him. "Can't get lost."

A moment later, Emery returned and took a seat in the corner of the studio as Laura stepped from the kitchen alcove, holding two tall glasses of ice water with a lemon wedge set along the rim of each.

"Not there, silly," she scolded with a feigned sour puss. "Come on over here and sit by me."

Emery got up from the wooden rocker and went over to an upholstered chair next to her.

"There. That's better. Here," she said, handing him his drink. "I even took the pits out of the slice like you taught us, Mike."

Emery nodded approvingly. "Thanks."

"Well, this is a surprise. My one night off a week, and I have the pleasure of your company. So tell me. What's up with Howie that I can help you with? Let me guess. He ate up all the profits and you want to talk to him," she said decidedly. "No? I know. It's not about Howie at all. You're here because Alfredo sent you over to lay me off 'cause he couldn't muster the courage to do it himself. He wants to replace me with that bimbo with the big boobs who's always hitting on him at the bar. That Yolanda dame. No? Thank God. Because I'd kill him along with you for doing his dirty work."

Emery laughed and shook his head. "You're the best waitress this side of town, and you know it. This *is* about Howard, Laura."

"Christ, you sound so serious. You said he's all right."

"He's all right. Problem is he adores you, Laura."

"And I adore him."

Emery shook his head again. "I mean, a lot."

"You mean . . . like an infatuation kinda thing?"

"I mean, like he's crazy-nuts about you."

Laura put down her drink. "He tell you that?"

Emery nodded.

"He's just a kid, Mike."

"A big overgrown kid of eighteen who's wild about you. Head over heels. He's lost ten pounds in four weeks and vows to lose forty more before he proposes to you."

"Proposes?"

"I put him on a special diet, and I think he's going to stick to it."

The pretty woman shook her head in disbelief. "I've got better than a decade on him, Mike. I'm like a big sister to that kid. I never thought he thought of me that way."

"Thought of you that way since the day Alfredo's opened."

"He told you that, Mike?"

Emery sipped his drink, then nodded again. "Indeed he did, Laura."

"Seems both you guys had quite a talk."

"He did most of the talking; I did the listening."

"And?"

"And I'm going to ask you to do me a favor."

"What kind of favor," she asked suspiciously.

87

"A dinner date."

"I have a boyfriend, Mike. He'd kill me. I just can't."

"Can't kill you if he doesn't know, and I happen to know he's out of town for the week, which you casually mentioned to Howard. So what about tonight?"

"Tonight? You want me to have dinner with Howard tonight?" Emery smiled warmly.

"Mike. That's only going to make matters worse. You know as well as I—"

The chef raised a finger to his lips for silence. "I have a plan."

"A plan?" she questioned, shielding and squeezing the wedge of lemon before depositing it into her glass.

"Yes. A dinner plan."

"Mike. You're asking—"

"For a favor. I wouldn't leave you alone in this situation," he assured her. "I'll be right here. I'm going to be chef and chaperon. He'll assist me."

"Chaperon? And what do you expect me to be?" she asked incredulously.

"You? I'd expect you to be yourself, Laura, while Howie and I prepare a feast right before your eyes this evening."

"Where, here?"

"Why not? Just the three of us. A little dinner party. And no one will be the wiser."

"And what do you think that's going to accomplish? Huh? Then he'll expect a date same time next week, if not tomorrow night. Without a chaperon. Or maybe he'll want to take me out dancing. Why would I want to encourage that, Mike?"

"Because I want you to help me build a bit of confidence in that young man. I want him to see that it's not impossible to get a date with the prettiest girl in all of Baltimore, if not the whole state."

"My, but you are a flatterer, Mr. Chardavoyne. Are you sure it's not *you* who's making a play for me?" She batted her eyes playfully.

"Miss Ingrilli, I have enough things to worry about with running a kitchen. I honestly have no time for play," he stated quite formally. "Howard's at a crossroads in his young life, and I want him to have lots of dates and choices and happiness."

"What if your plan backfires and he finds that I'm the only one in the world for him?"

"He won't."

"How come so sure?"

"Because next week I'm fixing him up with Yolanda Quinones," he joked.

Laura giggled deliriously. "Well, then I guess next week is when you're gonna get him laid," she said mischievously, gradually turning down the corners of her mouth into a promiscuous jealous pout. "That being the case," she needled deceptively, "I just might invite him to stay over after dinner and send you home alone. How's that? Give him lessons in foreplay, which that devourer, Yolanda, probably forgot a century ago. What would you do then?" she asked, leaning forward seductively in her seat.

"Tell your boyfriend on you," Emery answered straightaway.

"Bet you would," Laura scolded coltishly. "Well, what are you guys going to make tonight?"

Emery grinned from ear to ear. "It's going to come as quite a surprise, Laura. I won't give anything away. Here." He handed her a slip of paper.

"What's this?"

"Howard's phone number. The mother will probably answer. When she puts him on, invite him over and tell him to bring the items I asked for earlier."

"Pretty sure that I'd say yes," she remarked. "Yes?"

"Pretty sure that I could count on a pretty remarkable pretty young woman."

"You're sweet, Mike. Howie's very lucky to have a friend like you. Thank you."

"For what?"

"For being you. Oh!"

"What?"

"What time do I tell him?"

"How much time do you need?"

"Couple of hours. I have laundry to fold, straighten up around here a bit, bathe and put on a happy face. How's that?"

"Then call and invite him for seven o'clock sharp. All right?"

"Seven it is, Mike."

Emery stood and headed for the door.

"You forgot your package." Laura pointed to the floor beside the rocker.

"I think I'll leave that here, if you don't mind. Howie and I can use some of the items I bought in preparation for tonight's feast."

"Sure. But don't go overboard. Is there anything I should have on hand?"

Emery thought. "Candles?"

"Got 'em. Yankee Candles, and candles for all occasions. Ya know, I think this is going to be fun."

"See you at seven."

"And I've even got a bottle of very nice dry red wine."

"Not from Alfredo's cellar, I trust."

Laura put a forefinger to her full lips. "Shh. Took it before I started making decent money there, thanks to you, Mike. I won't do it again," she promised, lowering the same finger to her chest. "Cross my heart and hope to die."

Chapter 23

Howard Urban caught his breath and briskly wiped his feet upon the welcome mat, firmly lifting one knee and then the other in order to balance the pair of heavy bundles wrapped in both arms. Glancing at his watch, he rang Laura Ingrilli's doorbell at precisely a quarter to seven, stepped back and waited patiently, repositioning the shopping bags.

A moment later, Laura opened the door. "Hi, Howie," she announced excitedly with a beautiful, big smile.

Howard sheepishly dropped his eyes to the carpeting before bravely running them up the hostess's trim figure, continuing his gaze toward the ceiling. "Hope I'm not too early," the teenager said awkwardly, chancing a glance at her cleavage. "You look terrific, Laura."

"Well, it's not every day you get to see me in a dress, now is it, Howie?" she asked gaily, turning around completely and showing off her sexy low-cut sea foam green chiffon. "And Mike did say it was a dinner party. Will you stop standing out there and come in please?"

Howard stepped beyond the welcome mat and craned his head around the room. "I know I'm a little early, but the bus driver called out your stop and I had nowhere else to go with these."

"You're fine. Why don't you put those bags inside on the counter by the sink?"

"Oh, and I wiped my feet real good before I rang the bell, Laura," Howard offered, traipsing into the kitchen alcove and setting down the groceries.

Laura put the tips of her fingers to her lips and smiled. "That's very thoughtful, Howie. Now, please come and relax while I make you a drink."

"Mom has me take my shoes off when it's wet outside, and I'd have done that if it was raining."

"Well, I'm not your mom, Howie. And it's beautiful out there tonight. So, go make yourself comfortable and relax. How about a beer? I'm saving wine for dinner."

"Oh, no, Laura. Mike wouldn't like that one bit. He has me on a very strict diet. I've already lost ten pounds. My goal is fifty. And then do you know what I'm going to do?"

"No," Laura answered uncomfortably, fidgeting with her charm bracelet. "How about a Pellegrino with a twist?"

"Sounds great."

Laura disappeared into the kitchenette. "Lemon or lime?"

"Whatever's handy, Laura."

Choices, she thought. *Mike wants him to have choices. Fine.* "Lemon or lime, Howie? Make up your mind," she prompted, giggling under her breath.

"Lime would be nice, Laura. But I don't want you to go to any trouble. Mike and I are going to do everything this evening. He says you wait on everybody, so tonight we're going to wait on you hand and foot. Another one of his expressions," Howard felt he had to explain.

"You look very nice tonight, Howie," Laura complimented the boy, handing him a glass.

"And you look smashing."

"Smashing?"

"Uh-huh. Know what I'm gonna do when I lose fifty pounds, Laura?" he repeated.

Laura said nothing, but shook her head.

"I'm going to buy myself a brand new car."

"Really?"

"Yep. No more buses and trains for this fella."

"What kind of car are you thinking of buying?"

"Well, I thought about a Camry. But Mike says it's an old man's car—that it definitely ain't cool. He says I should get a Camaro, or something more sporty like that. But to tell you the truth, Laura, in case you haven't noticed, I'm really not that cool a guy."

Laura stepped up to her guest and ran her slender fingers through his silky blond hair. "Howie. I think you're the coolest guy of the lot we've got working back there in Mike's kitchen. And if I wasn't so head over heels in love with a jealous boyfriend, I'd ask you to take me for a ride in your car when you get it. Camry or Camaro. New or old. Wouldn't matter nohow."

Howard almost spilled his drink. "You would?"

"Yep. I definitely would. And I'll tell you something else. Whatever kinda car you get, you're gonna look real cool behind the wheel, whether you lose twenty pounds or fifty pounds or gain back five. Know why?"

Howard shook his head.

"Because it's your personality that shines through, Howard Urban. Women notice that more than a shiny set of wheels. Intelligent women, that is. Not the kind of women who hang out at the bar and fall all over Alfredo."

"You mean like Yolanda whatever her name is?"

"Exactly that sort of woman," Laura agreed emphatically.

"She's a real tramp," Howard said with disgust.

"But you have to admit she's got *some* body," Laura teased and tested. "A figure to die for."

"Yeah, some body, but not a brain between the two of them."

"Her ears?"

"I meant Yolanda and Alfredo," Howard clarified. "Um, this is good. Very refreshing. Mike got me away from soda and crap like that."

"You like him a lot, don't you?"

Howard nodded. "He's my best friend. I don't know if I'm *his* best friend, but he's certainly *my* best friend. Male friend, that is. You're my best female friend, Laura," he added, setting down his drink.

Laura studied Howard for a moment before she spoke. "Tell me something, Howie."

"What?"

"When you lose this weight and buy yourself a car, what do you plan to do?"

"Do?"

"Yeah, you know. Like take a trip. A little vacation maybe?"

Howard looked down at the carpet, then back into Laura's shining big brown eyes. "Keep a secret?"

"Sure thing."

"You know that woman who comes in with her daughter on

Friday nights and takes a table in the back off the kitchen?"

"Know the woman? Worst tipper in the world." Laura caught Howard's heavy-hearted expression. "But that girl is sweet as honey," she recouped.

"Oh, shit."

"What's wrong?"

"I forgot the honey. Mike'll kill me."

"You mean for tonight?"

Howard nodded nervously, getting to his feet.

"I have honey here in the apartment."

"How much?"

"Quart, quart and a half. I'm a tea drinker. I always have honey and lemon on hand."

"Got a quart unopened?"

"Pretty sure. I'm almost positive. Let me take a look inside."

Howard followed her like a puppy into the alcove.

"Yep. Here we go." Laura took the sealed container from a cabinet. "Let's see. And I also have a little less than half a quart in the refrigerator."

"Do you mind if we stick the unopened one in here so Mike doesn't think I forgot anything? I'll replace it tomorrow, I swear."

Laura rearranged several items, then set the full container of honey in the bottom of the shopping bag. "Done. Now, are you going to go back out there and relax?"

"You're a lifesaver, Laura. You know that?"

"Go."

Howard took his seat and another sip of sparkling water, glancing at his watch. "Made it right under the wire. That's an expression, Laura," he said with a titter.

"What does Mike need a quart of honey for? What are you guys making tonight?"

"I honestly have no idea. He says it's a secret."

"Talking about secrets, you left off with the girl and her mother," Laura coaxed. "Gonna tell me more?"

Howard looked around the room as though someone could be eavesdropping.

"Come on, Howie," she urged animatedly, as if she were shaking excess water from her fingers. "He's going to be here any minute. You know how punctual he is. I want to hear this. I swear I won't tell a soul. Mike, or anyone else for that matter."

"Oh, Mike knows."

"But I don't," she insisted.

"I think she likes me."

"The girl?"

"No, the mother," Howard said with a straight face, then laughed heartily. "Of course, the girl!" he exclaimed. "What did you think?"

"I was thinking the mother can't be a day older than me," Laura sounded, sighed and shook her head with questionable relief. "Now, shut up and tell me everything."

"Well, whenever I come out of the kitchen—and I always make it my business to come out—finding any sort of excuse," he confessed, "well, she smiles at me."

"And?"

"And I smile back."

"That's it?"

"It's the *way* she smiles at me, Laura," Howard said proudly. "A guy can tell, you know."

"No shit?"

"Stop," he said with an embarrassed smile. "I know you're teasing me."

"How long has this smiling thing been going on, Howie?"

"Well, I saw her the first week I started there. But you mean from the time she first noticed me?"

Laura nodded.

"Past six months."

"You like this girl a lot, don't you?"

Howard put his head back down and nodded. His face and neck were turning ruby red.

"And you say you told Mike all about this, like you're telling me now?"

"Mike and you and no one else."

"So, what's all this business with a car and losing weight? What are you waiting for? You going to ask her out or what?"

"Well, I just can't go up to her and say, 'Would you like to go to a movie next week, Zena?' That's her name. Zena. And then what would I do? Walk or more like waddle to the station and explain to her that we have to take a bus?"

"Why not?"

"Come on, Laura. That definitely ain't cool. I'm supposed to be eighteen years old and, if you want to know the truth, I'm really seventeen and lied to get that job. All right? Mike doesn't even know that part. I told him when I lose the weight and get a car, I'm going to ask her out. Not before."

Laura stepped toward Howard, leaned forward, and planted a kiss upon the boy's forehead. "You're my best friend, too, Howard. Know that?" she said, brushing away a joyful tear from the corner of one eye.

Suddenly, the doorbell rang.

"You get that," she said, quickly heading for the bathroom. "I have to fix my makeup for that storyteller friend of yours."

Chapter 24

Clarence Emery began removing the grocery items from the brown paper bags.

"So, let's see what we have here. Parsley, carrots, root celery—excellent, excellent. Sometimes hard to find, but much better than regular celery branches. Nice big bag of onions, gallon of cider vinegar and a quart of honey. And here's a good white wine I bought that we'll need for the marinade. Never use cooking wine that you buy in a supermarket. Remember what I said, Howie? If you can't enjoy drinking it, why in the world would you use it in your cooking?"

Howard nodded and Laura looked on curiously as Emery emptied the contents of the other bag.

"Box of kosher salt. Curing salt. Five pound bag of sugar. Good. And I take it this is the smoked back fat I asked for. Yes?"

"Yes, Mike. I had a little trouble getting it, but I managed," the boy affirmed happily.

The chef unwrapped the contents from the butcher paper, then removed several squares of fat, setting them down on Laura's cutting board and giving Howard a thumbs-up. "Bay leaves, thyme, whole black pepper, allspice, coriander. Howard, my boy, you did very well."

"Did you say marinade?" Laura questioned. "We plan on eating sometime tonight?"

"Not to worry, folks. Some meats might take a week to marinate, while others take no time at all," Emery clarified.

"So we're having meat," she said, smiling her approval.

Emery smiled back.

"You know, I already have about half the ingredients in this apartment that you had Howard go out and buy."

"Well, this way we know that we have everything we need and need not empty your pantry. Correct?"

"I guess," she agreed.

"Howie, do me a favor and get the package next to the rocker."

"Sure, Mike."

When Howard walked out of the alcove and into the main room, Laura was tempted to inquire as to why in the world the man standing right beside her had told such an outlandish story—a tall tale about Howard having a crush on her, when, in fact, the chef was supposedly aware of his assistant's designs concerning a customer's young daughter, Zena. Laura felt certain that no mention of a proposal was ever made by the young man of seventeen. *Why would Mike say such a thing?* she wondered. *Strange.*

"Here you go," Howard said, setting the case upon the counter. "Whattaya have in here, bricks?"

"Just a few things I picked up at a restaurant supply shop earlier. Go ahead, open it up."

Howard unpacked, then opened the box. "Wow!"

"What's all that stuff?" Laura asked.

"Knives and a carving fork," Emery answered.

"I know that, silly. Not those. That thing there," she bade with a tentative gesture.

"The steel?"

"The what?"

"A rod for sharpening knives. It's called a steel."

"All right, smarty-pants. I'm not talking about the steel. I'm asking about *that*," she emphasized, touching the tip of the narrow silver implement attached to the stainless steel tube.

"That? That's a needle," the chef remarked casually.

"Com'on, Mike. I can see it's some kind of needle. But for what? Tell me."

"It's called a larding needle."

"What's it used for?"

"Larding meat."

Exasperated, Laura turned to Howard. "Does he *always* behave like this with that crew back there in the kitchen? I think they'd throw a fit."

Howard shrugged. "In the kitchen, you can't shut him up," he said, somewhat at a loss for Mike's laconic behavior. "He explains *everything*. At least to me," he added in a pompous, privileged tone, then caught himself. "Sometimes, more information than a person needs to know," he recouped jocularly.

"Certain meats cook dry because they're lean," Emery made clear. "Like venison. Fat moistens the meat and, at the same time, gives it a nice flavor. So, you lard the meat by threading the needle with a strip of back fat, inserting it into, say, the shoulder portion or the upper leg," he elaborated, gently brushing the tip of his finger along the top of Laura's left thigh.

Laura instinctively took a step back. "So glad I asked. Oh, my God! We're not having venison tonight, I hope," she said, cringing and screwing up her face.

"No, but I'm thinking about putting it on the menu come fall; that is, if I stick around that long."

Laura grimaced. "Do me a favor, Mike. Cook it on an evening I have off, all right? I'll remind you again as we approach the season."

Emery looked at Laura with mild amusement, then with outright disappointment.

"Oh, I know, Mike. I've heard all the stories. 'If it's prepared right . . . if it's a young deer . . . if it's eviscerated immediately—not having spent the night wounded,' et cetera, et cetera."

"Eviscer—who?" Howard asked.

"Ah, you didn't know I knew such a fancy five-dollar vocabulary word. Hey, fellas?" Laura laughed lightly. "Well, my dad was a big deer hunter. Both with gun and bow and arrow. I heard every story you could imagine. My parents had venison seven ways to Sunday. That's an expression, guys," she teased the two of them. "Sorry. I just couldn't resist. Me? I never touched the stuff." Laura looked back down into the polished mahogany felt-lined box. "And what's that big gismo you got there?"

"A brining pump," Emery answered straightaway.

"And what do you do with a brining pump? And don't tell me brine," Laura forewarned with a sportive fist.

"Inflate the meat with the marinade that I'm going to prepare," the chef announced rather quietly.

"That's terrific, Mike," Laura lauded. "But now for the sixty-four thousand dollar question. I see vegetables, and I see herbs and spices. But I don't see, nor do I have, any *meat* in this apartment. Where's the beef, buddy?" she absolutely bellowed.

"That's the surprise," Professor Clarence Emery proclaimed.

"Maybe it's you," Laura went on hysterically, playfully kneading the fold at Howard's chubby cheek.

"Maybe it's you," Howard said in kind, gently poking a stubby forefinger at the pretty woman's nose.

"Well, it can't be Mike," Laura challenged friskily, grabbing for Howard's hand.

"And why not?" Howard questioned, reaching for one of Laura's wrists, and then the other.

"Because he's the chef," she cackled.

"Maybe the plan is to have you both on a silver platter," Emery concluded with a great big grin.

Chapter 25

Police Officer Ruth O'Connor placed the newspaper down upon the kitchen table next to her empty coffee cup, flipped through several pages, then turned Wednesday's *Newsday* article around so that the headline and picture laid directly under Anthony Notaro's nose.

"What's this?" Anthony asked through an interminable yawn from a virtually sleepless night.

"You," the policewoman stated flatly.

The pilot focused on the four-by-six inch picture of himself holding up a recent photograph of his wife. The half-inch high headline read:

HUSBAND SAYS: "I'LL FIND MY WIFE'S KILLER."
Fed claims serial killer is going to be hard to nail

"Well, it's about time," Anthony mumbled with a bite of a muffin in his mouth, then began reading.

By Kate Brand
STAFF WRITER

Anthony P. Notaro, a commercial pilot and Wading River resident, whose wife was a flight attendant aboard the doomed passenger airliner last month, has vowed a "life-long commitment if necessary" in seeking the alleged killer, Mr. Clarence Emery, formally a biophysics professor at the California Institute of Technology in Pasadena.

Mr. Emery was apprehended in Nassau County in connection with the murders of two women at Pipes Cove in Greenport, Long Island in March of this year. Emery was then transferred to the Kirby Forensic Psychiatric Center on Ward's Island, from which he escaped after seventy-two hours.

Sources close to the investigation believe that its director, Dr. Timothy Littleton, was coerced into arranging Emery's escape. Littleton was on the ill-fated flight en route to his daughter's funeral in San Francisco when the plane exploded.

Authorities in San Francisco reported that the psychiatrist's daughter, Grace Littleton, a promising opera singer, musician and composer, was being held hostage within the dome of a former federal building undergoing reconstruction when the scaffolding supporting a cage in which the woman was confined collapsed, killing the twenty-eight-year-old. Police suspect that Emery, working with a male accomplice who was on the flight, is responsible for the airline explosion, killing all two hundred twenty-one passengers and crew.

Young women of Italian extraction are said to be Emery's primary targets. Unconfirmed reports list as many as several hundred victims, which, if accurate, could make Emery the most prolific serial killer in U.S. criminal history.

Joining Anthony Notaro in his quest for Emery is Jacqueline Rubino, a former schoolmate of one of the Greenport women, Carmela Fontana, whose decapitated body was found near the remains of Theresa Pelicano. Both women were longtime residents of the East End. Mrs. Rubino spends a good part of her busy day caring for Notaro's two-year-old son whenever the pilot is on assignment flying medical supplies throughout the United States.

When Notaro was asked if he was making progress in his search for information, the man replied, "My job affords me the opportunity to research leads that take me from New York to California; from North Dakota to Texas. Headway, like a headwind, is always a difficult course. But when I pick up a tailwind, the media will be the last to know about it," Notaro affirmed. When pressed to answer why he agreed to be interviewed, Notaro said, "To let Emery know that I'm coming after him full-bore."

Rubino was asked in a separate interview how she found the time to manage a South Fork restaurant, while devoting countless hours to helping Notaro, as well as her reasons for assisting the pilot.

Rubino replied: "As an Italian-American of Sicilian descent, I feel a responsibility to my people and my community. Carmela Fontana was a schoolmate. Both women were very good customers, and I know the families well; good and decent families. I find the time by making time; sleeping less. I am simply helping a man who, like myself, is committed to finding Clarence Emery."

Rubino says she is researching countless articles and documents concerning the murders Mr. Emery is purported to have committed over the course of several years, in the hope of providing Notaro and the police with relevant leads.

Asked if she and Notaro believe they can do more than federal, state and local governments could achieve with unlimited resources at their disposal, Rubino smiled and said, "We can only try. But try we will."

Emery is believed to have returned to California, having used the alias Clifford Giordano, said a law enforcement source from Pasadena who would not disclose further details of the probe.

FBI investigators, however, believe that the 45-year-old fugitive may have fled the country. A special agent, who spoke on condition of anonymity, said, "A physical description of Emery would prove moot, misleading, and meaningless, as the man changes the color of his hair, eyes and even his skin like a chameleon. He can and has appeared tall, short, heavyset, thin, bald, and lionesque. He could play the part of a cripple or pole-vault a ten-foot fence, as in one daring escape from Dallas police several years ago. He could appear young, old, male or female and has made precisely those types of appearances as an aficionado of the performing arts."

Emery is said to be considered extremely dangerous, viciously attacking and killing his victims with carving knives.

According to the U.S. Government's International Broadcasting

---

See SERIAL KILLER on A62

Anthony stopped reading and turned his attention back to the unflattering photograph of himself. "I thought Jackie was supposed to be the bait," the pilot said with some surprise. "From what I read and see here, I'm the hook, line and sinker. Not that I don't relish the idea, because I absolutely do."

"Emery's profiled as a predator of young Italian women. So, unless we put you in a dress and shave a decade off your age . . . ." the policewoman razzed her charge.

"Thank you very much, Ruth. But I really don't get this."

"We make things too obvious, Emery's going to smell a rat. Put Jackie's name in there, but don't beat him over the head with it, we may draw him out."

"You really think this will draw him out?"

"Profilers do."

"Feds think he's out of the country."

"Probably part of the cover story, like in a fairy tale."

Anthony stared back down at his picture. "They make me look ninety here."

Officer O'Connor stepped away from a window and came back around the table, peering over his shoulder. "Angry. Not ninety. Maybe seventy," she wisecracked mischievously.

"Thanks again, sport."

"Don't mention it, champ."

"What if he's in a place where they don't get *Newsday*?"

"I think you're going to see that picture and hear the story on several news channels shortly. The AP will pick it up and run with it, if they haven't already. If Emery's interested, he'll follow-up—fill in the gaps for himself."

"How? What if he really is out of the area? Where would he look for information?"

"Libraries. The Web. Believe me, he'll learn what he needs to know, if he has a mind to. Meaning, he'll find you and Jackie."

"What makes everybody so damn sure he'll bite?"

"Narcissism—his love of self, as well as the game of cat and mouse."

Anthony looked up from the picture and into the policewoman's patently pretty face. "Can I ask you something personal?"

"Thirty-four C, but I have them toned down with Kevlar."

Anthony smiled for the first time in over a month. "Seriously, how—"

"I'm serious. It would have been easier for me to pad Jackie up than it is to hide these boobs. But before Emery comes a-callin', he'll know whether she wears tampons or sanitary napkins. He'll know how many teeth she has in her pretty mouth and how many hairs on her head. Think I'm kidding, huh?"

"What I was going to ask you was how does her husband react to all this . . . . "

"Business?"

"Yeah, you know what I mean. How does he handle it? Her coming here and staying overnight several times a week. You pick her up in her own vehicle. You take her home. You must see and hear what's going on there. Clearly, he knows the risks. The potential dangers. Surely, he must get upset."

"No, I told you before that he pretty much takes it all in stride," she lied. "Tomas is a very strong and self-assured individual. Very confident. Very trustful. If he even thought you were having unclean thoughts about his wife, he'd come here and cut your ball off."

"Ball?"

"I had to tell him you were something of a eunuch," she said with a straight face.

Anthony Notaro actually laughed. She had never seen him laugh and took it as a positive sign that the man might one day heal. Maybe.

"I told him, too, that you didn't quite have the usual high-pitched voice accompanying harem guards, but that you still sounded rather faggy. Better hope he never sees and hears you on the network news. But if the papers run the picture of that old geezer there," she stated casually, striking a comic arthritic pose above the photo, "I'd say you're in the clear."

Anthony laughed heartily before his mirth suddenly melted into a murmur as he focused on the picture within the picture—the portrait picture he was holding up of his murdered wife. A flood of tears fell uncontrollably down his face as if someone had unexpectedly opened up the gates of a dam.

Ruth stepped away from the table and went over to the coffee maker just as it stopped percolating, pouring yet another cup that morning. So much for all her courses in psychology, the policewoman fretted . . . for better or for worse, she seethed.

Chapter 26

Before the lieutenant could even respond to the man's sharp double-knuckled knock at the door, the maverick had entered Theo's office. The commanding officer gestured for Justin to take a seat, but the undercover civilian remained standing.

"What's up, J?"

"I want you to authorize additional overtime for Officer O'Connor."

The head of homicide could not help but smile. "If I give Ruth anymore overtime, fella, she'll be collecting more than yours truly. Now, how would that look? Huh?"

"Three or four hours tops, Theo."

"Weekly?" the lieutenant tested with a grin.

"Daily. Starting today."

"What's the problem?"

"Jackie."

"What about Jackie?"

Justin looked up in frustration at the ceiling.

"Well?"

"I need to keep her alert and in the picture. I feel she's having second thoughts."

"Spell it out."

"She's just not herself lately."

"I'm not following."

"She's tired, Theo. Growing weary. Waiting it out through the cold war. Jackie's a very special person. Very giving of herself."

"Get to the point."

"She's been juggling her life around 24/7. I think she realizes she's been spending too much time away from her family and the restaurant."

"You feel. You think. Look. You brought her in. You find out exactly what's bothering her and deal with it. If it's a case of Ruth having to put in a few more hours, we'll work it out. How's she doing by the way?"

"Great. Real good at holding Notaro together. I can tell you that. And as far as filling Jackie's shoes, from twenty yards away you'd swear she *was* Jackie. She's picked up her mannerisms quite nicely. Flawlessly, in fact. Got her smile and laugh down pat, if you can believe that. Even captures the way she seems to glide across a room. Ever notice Jackie work a room at the restaurant?" Justin jawed.

"No, I'm just dead from the neck up," the head of homicide deadpanned. "Let me ask you something, J."

"Ask away."

"Could Jackie actually go toe-to-toe with Emery if—"

"Toe-to-toe. Face-to-face. Asshole to elbow," Justin interrupted.

"Let me finish, please."

Justin placed the tips of ten fingers together to form a pyramid of patience.

"Let's just say, for argument's sake, that Ruth is indisposed."

"Oh, you mean like taking a crap or something," he snickered. The lieutenant ignored the crass comment. "This time around, it's not going to be the same as putting a gun to someone's head and pulling the trigger at her choosing. Emery will come at her when he sees fit. How he decides. Where he chooses. That's the big difference here, J."

"Jackie, Ruth and I are a team, Theo."

"You're not listening to me. You and Ruth may not be around when that moment comes. But if you are, *Team* is exactly what I want you to keep in mind," Detective Lieutenant Theodore Groche stated firmly, turning quite serious. "Team is how we think and how we win."

"Yes, sir."

"Now, once again. If Ruth were out of the picture, for whatever reason, could Jackie still handle Emery if push ever came to shove?"

"No contest, Lieutenant. I wouldn't put her or the operation in jeopardy if she couldn't handle the job. You know that. That's why I'm bringing this matter to your attention now. Unless you can deliver an eight-day week, Jackie just needs a few more hours for herself and family. Other than that, the girl's loaded for bear. I shit you not. She's packin' a PPK around-the-clock and ridin' roughshod over security at the restaurant with a ready 9-mm sub—a magazine of thirty, set for three-round bursts. If Emery came collectin' as the paperboy, he'd collect a head full of lead for his trouble. You know she's deadly when it comes to weaponry. In hand-to-hand, she'd seal his fate in a heartbeat. Knife or not. Not nearly as neat as our boy, but she'd slit his throat and have his kidneys out in seconds flat. A fourteen-year veteran from the elite Emergency Services Unit told me he never saw anyone quite like her for her size and weight. She's lightning fast on her feet. She put him and one of his top instructors down for the count before they knew what hit them. Of course, you know who trained her," he said immodestly, grinning from ear to ear.

"She's also personally involved. Not good."

But Justin shook his head emphatically. "Look, Theo. This is not anything akin to her first assignment concerning Don Ciccio and company. This is not about her immediate family now, nor about a childhood acquaintance that she went to school with, or those victims' families. This is not about Desirée Notaro, the crew or passengers aboard that downed airliner. There's nothing personal here to get in the way of Jackie performing her job."

"Nothing short of her being of Sicilian descent, you mean."

"Come on, Theo. That's like saying I should never pursue the likes of a Wayne Williams because I'm black."

"Wayne Williams." Theo recalled the name.

"Black man. Alleged serial killer of many young black boys."

"Atlanta area."

"Early eighties."

"Convicted."

Justin nodded. "Serving two life sentences for the murders of two black boys."

"Valdosta State Prison, last I recall."

"That's right."

"Then why do you say alleged?"

"He never confessed to any crimes."

"Neither has my mother-in-law."

Groche's hired gun smiled banally. "Told you once before,

boss. Very few black folks ever get caught up in this serial killer shit."

"So, you think Wayne Williams is innocent?"

"Don't know. All I know is that Georgia jurisprudence is slow as molasses with the results of DNA tests that could answer that question today. Back then, although testing was available, it was seldom applied. Such was the situation in Williams' case.

"But getting back to Jackie," Justin continued, "this is purely police business on her part. A good Samaritan with a capital S. Period."

"Then fine, if that's truly the deal. But if you have any other concerns about her, the slightest whatsoever, then I have concerns."

"My concern is not about any personal involvement, or her tangling with Emery one-on-one, if she had to. My concern is keeping her in a holding pattern until the target lands. At that point, his fucking ass is grass because she'd craft and draft him a brand-new asshole with his own fucking carving knife."

The lieutenant reclined and laced his hands squarely behind his head. "Do you know you have a warped but wonderful and colorful way with words, J? Ever thought about putting them into poetic form?"

"Nah, but I could hum a few bars if you like."

Theo laughed and shook his head. "It takes a nut to catch a nut, I guess," he said, knowingly.

"Not nice, boss," Justin bantered back playfully, displaying his pearly whites.

"Go to work."

Justin remained standing before the commanding officer's desk.

"What is it, J?"

"I want to know the overtime's a done deal, bossman. I want a written guarantee. Not just something you say you're gonna work on." Justin extended his hand, palm up.

"So, we make Ruth rich with overtime and cut Jackie a little slack in the bargain," the lieutenant agreed, reaching across his desk and, with a forefinger, drawing an invisible letter U upon Justin Barnes' mitt-like hand. "*You* still da man," Theo assured him. "Happy now?"

Justin stepped back and saluted smartly—simultaneously

clicking together the worn, black leather heels of his size twelve Oxfords—did an about-face, then exited the office.

Chapter 27

In a corner of the bathroom, Laura Ingrilli's pate sat surreally atop a small vanity, like a stylist's poll exhibiting a wig.

"You see, Howie. There is absolutely no reason to leave the head on like we did the salmon. Absolutely no reason whatsoever. I mean, it would be like serving up, say, the backstraps of Bambi with its noodle still intact," Clarence Emery put forth graphically. "Rather gross, wouldn't you think? Now, let's recap. You marinate a one hundred twenty-five pound creature, such as Laura, for about five days to a week. Carrots, root parsley and root celery, if you can find them; otherwise, parsley leaves and celery branches will do nicely. No need to peel the vegetables, Howie. Just scrub them and trim the ends."

Laura's headless, skinless carcass lay in a bloody bath, covered with slices of roots and spices.

"A glass, ceramic, plastic or stainless steel container is fine. But always avoid aluminum, as the acids in some ingredients tend to react with the alloy, and you could be left with a bad taste. In this situation, the porcelain bathtub is just perfect. So. We've added the vegetables, cider vinegar, white wine, bay leaf, thyme, crushed whole black pepper, allspice berries and coriander. Mixed the marinade together, lavishing it over the *meat*. There's no need to cover the entire flesh because we've turned her over several times. Of course, if the weather were warmer outside, we'd have no choice but to refrigerate. But with the window open a crack, I think we're all right.

"Next, we'll want to cure her for smoking. That's where the honey comes in because the flesh is somewhat acrid. What we need to do is balance out the bitterness to give it a nice flavor. Now, it's absolutely necessary to know the weight of the honey, Howie. Not that honey lying in the tub," Emery tormented, "but the container of honey. If you think that one quart equals thirty-two ounces, well, you're sadly mistaken because it actually weighs forty ounces; that is, two and a half pounds. Watch." Emery set the plastic container on Laura's food scale taken from the kitchen. "See? If you read the label, it will tell you. I've worked out a formula for curing Italian women. Zero point thirty-two ounces of honey per pound, times Laura's weight of one hundred twenty-five pounds, give or take away her noggin," he lectured with a wink, "is approximately a quart. What we'll do now is run some water from the sink until it's nice and warm, in order to dissolve the honey."

When the water was tepid, Emery closed the faucet and inserted the stopper before pouring in a quart of clover honey, mixing the solution by hand.

"Paying attention, Howie? Four to five cups of warm water; next, seven to eight cups of cold." He opened the other faucet. "It's important to get the cure to forty degrees. I've been doing this awhile, so I know when the solution is just about right," he said with satisfaction.

The madman added measured amounts of both kosher and pink curing salt, mixing the brine thoroughly.

"If you weren't incapacitated, Howie, I'd ask you to assist me with the brining pump. But you just sit there and watch."

Emery drew the liquid up from the basin and into the stainless steel tube.

Howard closed his eyes tightly and turned his head away as his instructor injected the fluid into Laura's skinless shoulders and thighs.

"I said, watch!" Emery demanded. "Don't make me tell you again."

Howard opened his eyes and witnessed the purplish flesh swell.

"Brining shortens the curing time, Howie."

The boy's naked, flabby chest and shoulders rose and fell with convulsive heaves.

"Christ, Howie. I think you're going to suck all the air out of this tiny space with all that heavy breathing." Emery chuckled, putting down the pump. "I can't imagine she'll need a vanity in here after this, can you?" he questioned, glancing at Laura's contorted countenance. "What a sourpuss. Though it would be a mistake to mask that mug for special delivery," the chef declared, leaning over the bathtub and tearing off several lengths of clear wrap from a roll, first carefully laying the transparent sheets along Laura's limbs and torso before tucking in the edges to form a sort of seal. "I told you I was going to fix you up with a woman. Didn't I, Howie?"

Emery got to his feet. Using the box of wrap as a makeshift handle, he pulled out a short section and stepped over to the vanity, then heedfully encircled Laura's head as though he were winding a turban of bandage around a patient's skull.

The crinkling sound sent a series of shivers through Howard's entire body.

"I think I'm going to send this package off to Jacqueline Rubino, in care of the Bella Sera Restaurant on Long Island, Howie. After that, I could head on up to Wading River and hand-deliver Jackie's head to Tony Notaro. The nerve of those two! Or I could send Tony's head—oh, how he hates being called Tony—to Jackie's husband, Tomas. I wish I had the time to take up pickling. Well, Howie? Are you ready for some more larding, fat boy? Maybe I'll have you learn the process firsthand. We're all out of back fat as you can plainly see, Tubby. Now, where do you suppose we can get some more without leaving this little room? Oh, I know," Emery said in mock surprise, tilting his head to one side and looking Howard Urban squarely in the eye.

Gagged and taped and tied, Howard squirmed about the toilet seat.

Emery looked back down at what was left of Laura's body . . . the strips of marbled back fat that he had injected throughout her lean frame with the larding needle . . . lacing and crisscrossing the lithesome muscles of the arms . . . breasts . . . stomach . . . her long and once lovely legs.

Howard's eyes pled for mercy.

"You should have let me hook you up with Yolanda Quinones, Howie. We could have had some fun. But no. You had your eyes set on that pip-squeak. Zena Nobody. Not even an ounce of Italian blood coursing through her veins. And speaking of blood, buddy, I wonder who's going to clean up this awful mess," the fugitive questioned, looking about the tiny bath. "Certainly not I."

Chapter 28

The kitchen crew at Alfredo's Restaurant was going berserk. Smitty Dawson appeared useless without the benefit of careful supervision. Ignacio Vázquez's area was jammed with dirty dishes. Octávio Fernandez was cursing in Spanish and English as he prepared his clams casino/Rockefeller. Sweating buckets, the Mexican busboy carried in a plastic bin brimming with piles of dishes, glasses and utensils. Ignacio mumbled something under his breath. The Asian cook shouted orders in Chinese at the Brazilian stand-in chef who gave the Oriental the finger, who, in turn, gesticulated, throwing up his hands in frustration then stormed past a waitress picking up an order at her station.

"Orr right, I quit!" Tang Lee shouted, pushing past the pair of swinging doors leading to and from the kitchen.

The proprietor got up quickly from a barstool and approached the young man.

"I quit," the cook repeated.

"You can't quit," Alfredo said calmly.

"Why?" Lee demanded to know.

"No one quits unless I fire them," Alfredo explained. "It's un-American. That's why. You want me to tell your father you're a quitter? He'd have your hide."

"I'm not afl/aid of my father," Lee said insolently. "I'm not afl/aid of anybody."

"You afraid of the Mafia?" Alfredo challenged, not knowing what else to say.

"You afl/aid of the Chinese Mafia?" Lee shot back.

The elderly South American charged out of the kitchen. "Tell him a cook doesn't order a chef around," Octávio insisted. "Tell him it's the other way around."

"You hear that?" Alfredo said sternly.

"He's too s*r*ow," the cook complained. "He takes fo*level* to cut and *r*ay the bacon on the c*r*ams. And he's no chef. He's jus' a *r*ine cook—jus' *r*ike me."

But Octávio was emphatically shaking his head. "He shouts orders at everybody in Chinese, when you can't even understand his English," the old man barked. "With Mike and Howard out—only God knows where—*I'm* the boss in the kitchen. I'm the chef. You tell him that."

"You too o*r*d."

"What?" Alfredo asked.

"He says I'm too old," the Brazilian translated. "We're really backed up in there, Al. Set this snotnose straight."

"You talk like that to your grandfather, Tang? You call your father's father an old man to his face?"

Tang Lee immediately put his head down in shame. "No."

"Then I want you to show the same respect to your elders here. All right?"

Lee turned around on his heels and marched briskly back into the kitchen. Octávio Fernandez followed after him.

Alfredo went back to his girlfriend at the bar. "Fuckin' Chink tried to threaten me with the Chinese mob!" he fumed, sitting back down on his corner stool.

"So why don't you fire him?" Yolanda instigated with a '*don't cry on my shoulder*' look as she sipped and stared fixedly at her meal ticket over the glass of Scotch in her hand.

"Ah, I know his family," Alfredo offered lamely. "His father and grandfather are friends."

"That's no reason for the boy to disrespect you," she said flatly.

"You're right. I'll have him shot on sight during the Chinese New Year. How's that?" Alfredo said decidedly with a smirk.

"When's that?" the buxom woman asked rather seriously.

"Finish your drink, honey. I gotta go in there and pinch-hit in a minute. We're shorthanded tonight."

"Where's Laura?"

"She didn't bother to come in or call, either. When it rains it pours."

"I could put on an apron if you let me keep the tips," she

suggested seductively.

"No, you're liable to smother the customers when you lean over to serve the soup. Then I'd be held liable." The owner caught and laughed anxiously at his own unintentional pun.

"Hey, that's pretty funny," Yolanda said decidedly then tittered, too. "Liable, liable. I get it. I get it."

Chapter 29

A large package was delivered by Airborne Express to the Bella Sera Restaurant in West Tiana, and signed for by one of Phil Cancilla's nephew-in-laws, Frankie Sunseri. Frankie placed the white Styrofoam container on the counter behind him, then went to work, first washing and drying his hands thoroughly before sprinkling a cloud of flour upon a large, circular wood-handled board.

Tomas Rubino arrived at the restaurant an hour early and started prepping for a formal luncheon, working beside his cousin.

"That package came for Jackie," Frankie said.

"What?" the cook asked absentmindedly, looking for his cleaver. "I wish people would put things back where they find them," he complained.

"You got steaks delivered this morning."

"What are you talking about?"

"Steaks addressed to Jackie."

"From who?"

"Omaha Steaks."

"We didn't order any steaks."

"No, but someone sent them to her."

"Who?"

"I don't know. I don't touch things that don't belong to me." Reaching into a refrigerated compartment, Frankie grabbed a cylindrical tin. Inverting the aluminum container, he removed and placed the moist mound of dough upon the floury white board, then kneaded the leavened ball.

"You see my cleaver?"

"Phil was using it, last I looked. Check back there by the double sink."

Tomas headed through the swinging doors and over to one of the sinks, then sighed. "I wish he'd put things back where they belong," he said upon returning to his station. "I tell him all the time."

"Package is there on the counter behind me," Frankie directed, shooting a thumb over his right shoulder.

"What package?"

"Package of steaks or whatever."

"Maybe Phil ordered them."

"Addressed to Jackie?"

"Well, she is the manager."

"But not the meat manager," Frankie said through a yawnful grin. "Know the prices we'd have to charge if we started serving Omaha Steaks?"

"They're expensive?"

Frankie exhaled a heavy breath. "Out of sight, oh cousin of mine. Corn fed. Frozen, but still expensive. Packed and shipped in dry ice."

"Wonder who sent them."

"An admirer, no doubt," he said mischievously.

"She has too many admirers," Tomas whined.

"Beautiful woman like that? Of course, she has admirers. Remember last year when she got a case of fine wine as a gift?"

"Yeah, and who drank most of it?"

"Well, you put it out."

"I didn't put it out. Jackie put it out."

"And when you two come over to our place, what do you think you get?"

"Grape juice," Tomas teased.

"The very same wines we serve here. That's what."

"Yeah, but I always serve you and Salina the best of the lot. Sometimes even *better* than we carry here. So what are you bellyachin' about?"

"Sure, but I still have to pay cost for mine. You got that fancy case free. Twelve bottles. Just like those steaks," Frankie reminded him with a persistent grin, gesturing back toward the carton while he worked and widened the circle of dough above two balled fists.

"You want steaks? You come over next week. I'm gonna serve you frozen steaks. How's that?"

"Seriously, I hear they're pretty good."

"We'll see."

"Salina and I will bring Antinori, red."

"Which Antinori? Solaia?"

"Whattaya crazy? Maybe a Chianti Classico Riserva, or a 'Peppoli'."

Tomas grinned. "Let's compromise. Tignanello; a '96."

"Just how much do you think those steaks are worth anyhow?"

"I don't know. You're the one who said they're expensive."

"Maybe they're not even steaks. Maybe they're hamburgers."

"Somebody's gonna send my gorgeous wife hamburgers?" Tomas shot back playfully, cutting up a series of cutlets with the cleaver, letting his cousin know that all the teasing in the world wouldn't get to him—which, indeed, it always did.

Frankie shook his head. "I got to admit that Jackie's definitely good for business. Maybe that Notaro guy sent them to her as a gift," he goaded, spinning the disk of dough high into the air.

Tomas shot Frankie a troublesome look. "Don't get me started on that again."

"Why don't you open the box? I'm sure there's a card inside."

"Because, like you, I don't snoop around and open up other people's things."

"I see."

"And if that carton was addressed to Salina?" Tomas questioned soberly.

"It'd be opened, inspected, and wrapped back up like it was never touched," Frankie confessed.

Tomas shook his head, pounding the cutlets thin with the edge of the thick blade. "You're bad, my friend. Know that?"

"Yeah, well I wouldn't even bring a bottle of Valpolicella Masi to your home for dinner until I knew exactly what was in that package," the counterman persisted, spiraling a thick, rich tomato sauce from a ladle before showering a series of condiments, followed by a fistful of cheese upon Bella Sera's famous thin-crust pizza. "But for filet mignon, which Omaha Steaks is famous for, I'd select a decent wine. If they're burgers, I'll bring the beer," Frankie finished, folding his lips firmly between his teeth to keep from laughing, grinning down devilishly at the floor.

Chapter 30

Howard Urban's death was imminent. The end was a paradoxical footrace between slow bleeding and a rapid pulse rate overtaking respiration, brought about by pure unadulterated fright. The obese boy's body temperature was as low as his bulky frame that lay motionless on the cold white tiled floor.

"Another thing that bothers me, Howie, is when people say one thing and do another. Like you picking away at everything as we prepared the marinade. Nibbling away at the carrots and celery like a big fat rabbit is one thing. Sticking your finger in the container of honey is quite another. I don't know if you were even aware of what you were doing. You were on a diet to *lose* weight, not gain it back in a single evening. With me, it's a bit different. I've been on a steady diet of starch and high protein in order to bulk up. You wouldn't even recognize me in another month from now, given the opportunity. And I sure as hell wouldn't recognize you," Emery remarked in earnest.

"You really didn't think I was going to lard you, like I did Laura, did you? With all those holes in you from the brining needle, you'll probably die from infection first, than from loss of blood.

"You know, Howie, maybe when I get to New York, I'll take a day job as a delivery driver, or perhaps find work in the evenings as a short-order cook at Vincente's. That's a café across the street from the Bella Sera on Long Island," he expanded. "After sending Laura's head off to Jackie last night—who, by the way, was a waitress herself not so long ago—I'm sure she and the family have their tongues wagging away by now. It's only a matter of time before the Suffolk County boys and the Baltimore police will be comparing notes. Laura's body, I'll leave here with yours. Maybe Alfredo could feed the homeless. Go back to being known as The Road Kill Café," he chattered. "You know, I'm going to miss those fellas at the restaurant, though. Ignacio and Octávio; Smitty and Tang; that new busboy, Xavier; even good ol'

Al. I'm even going to miss the girls. You know what's funny, Howie? All those employees working at Alfredo's Restaurant, and not a one of them an Italian, except for Laura here. I'll bet Al puts Yolanda Quinones to work in less than a week. Care to take the wager? Fifty bucks. I'll send the money to your mother if I lose. No?

"Tell you what. If I don't read or hear anything about the discovery of both your bodies—oh, let's say after several days—I'll phone in an anonymous tip. Promise. I wouldn't want your mother too hysterical. I'm sure she'd want an open casket instead of a portrait sitting atop a closed coffin. Then again, there is just so much an embalmer can do with all those puncture marks, Howie. With all the money she'll save, she can hire a professional mourner, and the two can do a duet.

"Look at it this way, Howie, my boy. No more worrying about weight loss, or Zena, or wheels to pick her up. You won't even have to worry now about the color of the car. Bet I know the color of the vehicle in which you'll be riding face-up shortly," Clarence Emery stated solemnly, along with a smirk and a wink, closing one eye and then the other, stepping back blindly toward the bathroom door.

Emery's eyes flew open wide at the sudden sound. "There's that blasted phone again, Howie. Laura's boss or boyfriend, no doubt. One last chance to make a wager, kid. No? Guess gambling, unlike gluttony, isn't your other vice, fat boy. Well, toodle-oo, ol' chum. Always think of me as Teach. At least in spirit, anyway," the professor lamented sadistically, picking up his case of knives and needles and accoutrements before taking a final look at the teenage boy: tied and taped, gagged and stretched out on the tile floor like a buckshot mini whale, beached between the commode and the broken basin.

"God, I take pity on the crew who has to clean this mess up," Emery said in all seriousness, stepping from the room and out into the hallway, taking one last look around the bloody studio apartment.

The phone stopped on the sixth ring.

"Thank you, God."

Chapter 31

A bridal luncheon for fifty at the Bella Sera had gone off without a hitch, Phil Cancilla was pleased to note. Several ladies from the party were still saying their goodbyes along the arched and Roman Doric column walkway when the manager of the restaurant pulled up at 4:30 p.m. sharp. Ten minutes later, Jacqueline stood before a table in the front kitchen, cutting the straps off the sizeable Styrofoam carton addressed to her, wondering who could have sent such a gift. Having worked the family restaurant as a waitress for six years, she recalled receiving many presents from customers: flowers, candy, perfume, even a case of fine wine. Never had the young woman gotten a gift from Omaha Steaks. Separating the squeaky-snug Styrofoam lid from the weighty white container, she suddenly gasped as the enveloping gelid vapor from the refrigerant rose above the dissembled stone-cold stare.

"Oh, my God!" Jacqueline whispered. "Tomas! Frankie! *Zu* Phil!" she shouted.

From the back kitchen, Tomas bolted forward with cleaver in hand and was the first to reach his wife. From behind the front counter, Frankie flew through the pair of swinging doors, rushing to her aid wielding an eighteen-inch stainless steel pizza knife. Phil Cancilla came running from a restroom, stopping dead in his tracks before clenching a knuckle of his right hand between a set of vise-like teeth.

The four figures stood gazing down at the distorted, frosty frozen face framed with jet black hair.

"Do we know her?" Phil beseeched them.

Jacqueline threw up her hands in uncertainty, then wept quietly.

Both Frankie and Tomas led her away from the table. Several waitresses and a waiter standing near an entrance off the kitchen were immediately ushered away by Phil.

A regular customer poked his head in a distant doorway, asking what was wrong.

"It's all right," Phil said, forcing a crooked smile, hurrying along the passageway to intercept him. "Jackie burnt the garlic bread, is all."

"I don't smell nothin'," the patron replied.

"Please, Gino. Go sit down. We have everything under control here."

"You say so, Phil," the big man said skeptically.

"Everyone—" Frankie said to the other employees gathered at the threshold between the two dining rooms while shielding the Styrofoam box with his body "—please. Please go back to work."

Jacqueline dried her eyes. "Who signed for that?" she demanded after the others had returned to their stations.

"I did," Frankie answered.

"What time?"

"Ten o'clock this morning."

"You have an invoice or anything?"

"I just sign on that electronic thing they carry around. Airborne Express. Overnight delivery. Driver's been here a dozen times before." Frankie turned to Tomas. "I think I saw a slip of paper in the corner," he gestured toward the carton.

"Don't touch anything," Phil Cancilla ordered. "Wait till the police come."

Tomas went back to the table and pulled on a pair of latex gloves, then removed a Ziploc bag with a folded sheet of paper inside. It was a note addressed to Jacqueline. He looked at them tentatively before reading it slowly to himself. He struggled with the English, but certainly caught the gist.

"That's it. *Basta!*" Tomas shouted at his wife as if there were no one else present. "*E Finito!* You call Justin Barnes, and you tell him that it's finished." He handed her his cell phone, then snapped his wrist when she hesitated. "You want me to do it?"

Jacqueline snatched the phone from her husband's hand while Frankie took and hid the carton from view.

"Don't throw out those packing straps, or touch anything else," Phil barked at Frankie. The owner turned obliquely. "You gonna tell us what it says?" he practically demanded of Tomas.

Tomas ignored him. Seething. Staring deliberately at his wife.

Jacqueline spoke quietly into the miniature mouthpiece. "Hello, J. It's me. I just opened a present from Clarence Emery, sent to the restaurant, ten a.m. this morning. Airborne Express. A women's head packed in dry ice. Twenty-two to twenty-five years old. Long black hair. I think she was very pretty. Definitely Italian. That little chat we had the other day concerning hours? No problem. We're gonna nail this son of a bitch."

Tomas sent his foot against a steel cabinet.

"No, Tomas is holding a note or a letter as we speak. He won't show it to anyone. Doesn't want me spooked. ... That's correct. You two can discuss it. ... No, I'm fine." She scrunched the phone between her neck and shoulder, withdrawing a pistol concealed beneath a frilly feminine lace apron at the small of her back, sliding the receiver back fractionally, double-checking to be certain that a round was secured in its chamber. "Loaded for bear, Justin Barnes. We're going to take that monster down."

Jacqueline returned the weapon to its holster and handed the cell phone back to her husband. When he faltered, she snapped her arm sharply and angrily, smacking the instrument back into his hand.

Tomas took the phone and smashed it to smithereens against the face of a stainless steel refrigerator.

"That's out of *your* salary, buster. Not mine," she said calmly, brushing past him and heading toward the main dining area.

"You're not going to listen to me, are you?" he called after her.

"It's too late for that," she answered firmly.

"Well, I'm calling your father," Tomas insisted. "I'm calling Dominic right now."

Phil went over to Tomas. "Leave your father-in-law out of this. Hear me? My brother doesn't need this trouble. I just called the police. Let them handle this," he said, passing a trembling hand through his thinning, dark receding hair.

"He's right," Frankie agreed. "Let the police and Justin handle this. I'll talk to Jackie. She'll listen to reason."

"She'll listen to Justin," Tomas blew. "Not to you, or me, or anyone."

"No, she'll listen to the police," Frankie swore. "I'll make them talk some sense into her."

"Justin *is* the police," Phil added awkwardly, lowering his voice.

"That's bullshit and you know it," Tomas snarled. "He's an exterminator working undercover for them, and my wife's his bait. How I *ever* let her get talked into this, I'll never know," he whined, pacing the area before the pair.

"Hey! You know exactly how," Phil insisted. "And keep your voice down. You, you think I'm stupid—that I don't know what went on with Jackie two years ago? No, we don't ever talk about that. Like it never happened."

"Look, I didn't know about that other business until it was over and done with," Tomas swore. "*Capisci?*"

"Well, I sure as hell didn't know either," Phil assured him. "She just took it upon herself—"

"All right, let's stop it," Tomas warned, waving a latex-gloved hand along with Emery's note through the air. "This is what it's come down to. She took nothing upon herself. It was that *melanzana* that planted the seed in her head," he fumed.

"Yeah, well it was that *melanzana* and Jackie who took care of family business when I let that mafioso put a gun to my head," Phil declared. "We could have lost this place. Thirty-two years now, Tomas. I came over here and worked that front counter out there when I was still a kid; just like Frankie's doing now. Just remember that. You let Justin see that paper first. You hear me? We owe him that much."

Tomas threw up his hands in disgust and stormed out of the kitchen with the note.

Phil turned to Frankie. "You keep that box out of sight until J arrives. And you keep your mouth shut. *Capisci?*"

Frankie nodded obediently.

Chapter 32

Justin was returning from the Bella Sera, traveling north on Route 24. It was after midnight. He held the cell phone to his ear.

"I was just about to call you, J."

"Did you hear me, Theo? He's contacted Jackie with a note," Justin told the lieutenant, who was sitting barefoot alongside his bed.

"I heard you. I heard you." The man stood, holding the phone in one hand while putting on his robe with the other.

"I want you to listen to this and tell me what you think."

"Where are you?"

"In the car," he answered ambiguously.

"Forensics finished with that package yet?"

"They're already out of there. You listening?"

"When and where did she get the note?"

"It was in the carton with the head."

"Hidden?"

"Not hidden, Theo. Off to the side of the carton. You wanna hear this or not?"

"Why am I only hearing about the note now?"

"Because Tomas didn't give it to me until now. He waited till the police cleared out. Got it?"

"Who's Tomas?"

"Jackie's husband, for cryin' out loud. The head cook at Bella Sera. You've only met him maybe a million times."

"Seen him, maybe. Never really met him," Theo stretched. "Well?"

"Well, what?"

"You want to read me the note, or what?" he yawned indifferently, slipping his feet into a pair of funny-looking fish slippers with plastic eyes.

"Can't. I just entered a tunnel," Justin fibbed. "You're gonna have to wait now." He figured he would teach the man a lesson.

"Turn on the overhead—your map light or something."

"Bulbs are burnt out," he outright lied.

"Don't you keep a twelve-inch Mag-Lite handy in a compartment on the driver's door?"

"Can't hold a light and steering wheel and read at the same time, Theo," Justin stalled, surprised that the lieutenant even remembered that he had a flashlight, let alone its length, or where he stored it, having had the man in his car but once—well over two years ago. *Strange what the head of homicide recalled and didn't; selective memory,* the maverick mused.

"Try holding it in your mouth," Theo suggested facetiously, lowering his reading glasses to the bridge of his nose.

"How about I stick it . . . never mind."

"Just pull the fuck over."

"Told you. I'm in a tunnel. I could lose the signal any second."

"Tunnel or approaching the 105 Bridge in Riverhead?" the lieutenant simpered.

Justin stared into his rearview mirror. "Now, how'd you know dat? You havin' me tailed, copper?" he questioned with some concern.

"Emery just called me at my home, J. I repeat. At my fucking home. Told me you just left the restaurant. Told me that you were traveling north and that you'd probably be calling soon to compare notes. But in case you didn't have it handy, he read me a copy. So let's stop playing games. Okay?"

Justin turned serious and immediately pulled over. "Okay."

"I'll read; you follow along." Theo began reading the note that he had transcribed from a recording.

Justin held the original beneath the map light.

Hi, Jackie,

Did you miss me? I know you did. Know why? You walked right by me when you headed across the street to borrow two bottles of seltzer water from Vincente's. I was

128

emptying the garbage. I got a
real good look at you, girl.
Wow! Heads-up, kid.

The Teacher

"Then he hung up on me. Your note read like that?"

"Exactly that."

"I just sent a couple of our boys back down there to speak to the manager at Vincente's. Poor guy was heading home to bed. A crew coming in behind them is going to collect and go through the garbage. They'll be using a Waste Management vehicle so that nothing looks out of the ordinary."

"Waste of time, Theo."

"Probably."

"You want me to swing back?"

"No. Go home and get some rest. Who else knows about the note?"

"Just you and me and four family members: Phil, Jackie, Tomas and Frankie."

"Frankie?"

"Phil's other nephew-in-law by marriage, or is that redundant?"

"Think this Frankie can keep a lid on it?"

Justin smiled. "That's exactly what he did until he turned the carton over to forensics."

"Anybody else know anything?"

"Some of the other employees know that *something's* going on. But as to what, they haven't got a clue."

"Nor do we," Theo bantered.

"We'll get him, Theo."

"Jackie all right?"

"Right as rain. She wants to reciprocate the gift-giving by handing Emery his own head. Trouble is that Tomas did an about-face when he read the note. He wasn't too keen on the idea to begin with, as you know. But Phil knows how to handle him."

"Is the husband going to pull the plug on this?"

"He's doing his damnedest."

"Emery finally bit, J."

"Yeah, while Tomas is biting her head off. Oops! Bad choice of words."

"What the hell did he expect? None of us knew how or when or where Emery was going to come at her. Or even if he would. And now that reality has hit them squarely between the eyes . . . ."

"It's definitely the *how* and *where* part, boss," Justin set forth rather reverently. "How Emery managed to get the head shipped via Omaha Steaks, as well as where it wound up, without one of us the wiser, is what spooked Tomas. Can't say I blame him. He can't help thinking that might have been his wife's head in that box. I think Tomas wanted to put mine in there to keep the other one company."

"Well, Emery was supposed to get the idea that Jackie was playing house in Wading River with Notaro, and attempt to hit them there. Not send her a present to the restaurant."

"I know, Theo. Believe me, I know. But we both know Emery ain't gonna do what he's *supposed* to do. Anyhow, Ruth's on her way to the restaurant to pick Tomas up. She'll spend the night at his house as Jackie. Believe that one? Thanks to Phil, Tomas is listening. Reluctantly. But he's listening nonetheless."

"Where's Jackie now?"

Justin smiled brightly. "Got her safely tucked away."

"So you're telling me Tomas is going to go along with the program."

"For the time being."

"I guess he still doesn't know just how involved Jackie and Notaro are supposed to be."

"No, and thank God for small favors, Theo. She's been able to keep him somewhat in the dark on that account. Ruth's been covering nicely for her, too. We can count our blessings he reads the Italian newspaper and not *Newsday* or the weeklies."

"Good, because we've got a *News-Review* reporter lined up who's going to happen by that Sports Bar off 25A that Notaro and Jackie have been frequenting lately. He'll do an on-the-spot interview concerning their progress on the case. Turn up the heat a bit. Timing may be just about right on that account. They'll run a photo of Jackie, which is probably moot at this point as far as Emery is concerned."

"Then I'm glad Tomas and Anthony are on distant shores. And

I wish you'd tell me these things ahead of time so that I could run interference if anything popped up."

"I just did. *Suffolk Life* and *The Traveler Watchman* even got one of Notaro's nosy neighbors to add her two cents worth today," Theo elaborated. "But if Jackie leaves the loop for whatever reason, Ruth will just have to stand in 24/7. Won't be a walk in the park, but we'll have no choice."

"Just make sure those papers don't run any pictures of our two rising stars holding hands or making kissy-face, 'cause we don't need another murder on our hands. I'm hoping that maybe between Ruth and Phil, Tomas'll chill out some."

"Well, you could always tell him it wasn't really his wife but Ruth," Theo half-kidded.

"Nah, you can fool the customer but never the cook."

"Hey, that's pretty good."

Justin liked it, too. "Think maybe we'll be able to identify that woman anytime soon?"

"If she's a missing person and not a runaway, which I tend to doubt."

"Maybe we could clean'er up and run *her* picture?"

"Not a bad idea if we were working with *The National Enquirer*. But I was thinking more along the *lines* of a sketch," Theo quipped.

"Lines of a sketch. Is that supposed to be cute?"

"Hey, I can be clever at this hour, too," Theo said through yet another yawn. "Listen, I tend to doubt that we're going to find her prints or anything revealing on that note or package."

"Or the bag either, I'd wager."

"What bag?"

"Emery had the note in a Ziploc. And you're right; zip is what we'll probably get. He likes to make things difficult, sport that he is."

"Hold on a sec, J. Got another call."

Justin held.

"Listen, gotta go," Theo said rather anxiously.

"Emery forget to say good night to you?"

"It's my mother."

"After midnight?"

"Chest pains. Gotta run. And watch your back."

Justin heard a click, then secured his phone, heading the Cadillac carefully off the shoulder and back onto the county road.

"Why didn't you tell him I was with you?" his passenger questioned from the backseat.

"My dear," Justin answered in his best W. C. Fields impression, "the less the police know about your business, the better off you are."

"You don't trust him?"

"I don't trust phones, German shepherds, pit bulls or Dobermans."

Jacqueline smiled. "Can I sit up now?"

"No."

"Tell me who and what else you mistrust or dislike," she asked sleepily, planting an elbow on the edge of the supple leather seat, resting her head in the palm of a hand.

"Babies, kids, and mixed drinks," he continued with a classic Fieldsesque timbre.

Jacqueline lay there amused. "Can you tell me what Theo said?"

"Not-now, my-dear," he persisted, stretching out his syllables as well as the performance, looking into the rearview, then both side mirrors before stepping down smoothly and steadily on the accelerator.

"Where are you taking me?"

"Where you'll be safe for the evening."

"And where's that, I'm afraid to ask?"

"My place."

"Yeah, right."

"But first I have a quick stop to make in Riverhead."

"I'm not going to your place. Period."

"Well, let's see now. If you add it up, you've spent, what, seven or eight nights off and on at Anthony's house? In his bedroom no less—"

"In his *guest* bedroom, at the other end of the house, mister," Jacqueline punctuated by punching the back of his seat with a fist to make her point felt. "And with Ruth as watchdog and ward, buster."

"In his bed for all intents and purposes. I mean, if we have to paint you as a woman of questionable character, let's get it right,

132

sweetheart. All right?"

"So, now you want to take me home with you. You want to show me off to your nosy neighbors, too? Want to give them something to *really* talk about? Is that it?"

"No, I want to show you off to Clarence Emery. I want him absolutely *wild* about you."

"I think he's wild enough already. Don't you?"

"Yeah, but shackin' up wif a black dude from Mastic/Shirley, that ought to drive him positively nuts. It's jus' fo dis evenin', sweetcakes."

"You told Tomas you were taking me to Ursula's."

"Told him what he wanted to hear."

"You keep in mind what you just told Theo about Tomas having your head wind up in that box."

"That sweet little guy of yours?"

"Sweet as honey until he loses his temper. You think Anthony's got a short fuse?"

"Well, you just rest assured I ain't gonna put the moves on some skinny-ass white broad from the other side of the tracks," he assured her, adjusting the rearview mirror to catch her glare.

"Skinny? Ursula runs right about the same dress size I do," she stated evenly yet defensively.

"What? In her dreams. Maybe her hat size. She's put on a good twenty pounds since I met her. You and your family's fault. She never knew Italian food till she discovered Bella Sera."

"What would she say if she found me in your apartment?"

"She'd say, and I'll quote, 'Get that skinny-ass white ho da hell outa here,'" Justin answered, readjusting his rearview mirror and picking up a pair of high beams closing in on them.

Jacqueline's eyes darkened mightily before they closed sleepily.

Justin enjoyed the quiet and the fragrance of her perfume as he drove without having to say another word—first stop, Riverhead. He had to awaken her when they arrived in Mastic/Shirley.

Chapter 33

Clarence Emery lay stretched out on an old but comfortable mock leather sofa, his head supported by a thin, folded polyester pillow. He was reading the local paper when the tenant unlocked the front door and entered the fifth floor walk-up apartment.

Emery looked up and smiled. "How was school today, Xavier?" he asked the young Mexican busboy.

"Fine, Mike."

"Good, good. Glad to hear it. Did you get your English essay back yet?"

Xavier Sanchez removed his backpack in a single motion. He unzipped its top, reached into the bag, and produced the paper. "B minus," he announced proudly, smiling in elation.

Clarence sat up straight, planting both feet solidly upon the bare wood floor. "Well, this calls for a celebration. Don't you think?"

Xavier nodded excitedly.

"What I think you should do is call Tang Lee and ask him if he'd go next-door to that Chinese takeout joint where he used to work and order us up some grub," Emery kidded. "Think he'd de*r*iver here when he got off work?"

The handsome young man laughed with mild amusement, laying his essay upon the coffee table in front of his newfound friend and mentor.

The professor reached for and took the composition, perusing the piece while continuing the conversation. "An authentic Chinese establishment adjacent to Alfredo's, and Al had me teaching the Oriental how to make a Bolognese escalope of veal. Go figure. Well, with Howard gone, maybe you'll have a shot at helping Tang and Octávia whip up some of those sauces and specialty dishes instead of collecting and carrying heaps of dirty plates and pots and pans back to Ignacio at the sink. Keep in mind that the old Brazilian is not going to be around forever. Have you been practicing like I taught you?"

"Yes, Mike."

"Good man."

"You think Howard will ever come back?"

"Oh, I don't know."

"What about Laura?"

"I think she may have taken a waitressing job elsewhere. Might have even taken Howie with her. I told you; I overheard those two talking on the q.t. Or maybe she ran off with her boyfriend."

"How about you? Why do you wanna leave?"

"Oh, it's not that I want to leave. It's just that it's time for me to go."

"Go where?"

"Wherever destiny leads me," Clarence Emery stated reservedly.

"I'm gonna miss you, Mike," the lad said sadly and sincerely, taking off his jacket before plopping himself down in a tattered club chair.

"What you're going to miss is having someone stand over your shoulder and show you how to do everything. That's what you're going to miss. But I taught you how to study and how to further your culinary skills. Correct?"

Xavier nodded indifferently.

"Then what's the matter?" he questioned, reading Xavier's instructor's notes in the margin.

"Alfredo's will never be the same without you."

"Oh, the place will do just fine. Octávia, Tang, and Smitty will hold down the fort, and you'll make your bones in time."

"Bones?"

"It's an expression. Like make your mark."

Xavier nodded.

"Hold down the fort you understood perfectly, you mixed-up Mexican," the teacher teased. "You understood it because your descendants once overran a fortress one hundred and thirty-six years ago. Remember?" Clarence Emery coaxed.

"The Alamo," Xavier acknowledged.

"But then six weeks later, the Texans rallied and kicked your ancestors' butts but good."

"Maybe *you'd* be a busboy today, and I'd be the head chef at Alfredo's if the war had turned out differently," Xavier retorted.

Emery smiled complacently. "And maybe we'd all be eating rice and beans and farting our way through one big state of chaos as the result of constipated thinking. What do you think about that?"

"I think you're making fun of me, Mike."

"Just funnin' with you. There's a difference."

"I know a lotta things you say go right over my head," Xavier confessed. "Most everything, I guess."

Emery shook his head. "If that were so, you wouldn't have gotten my drift at all. Right?"

"I guess. But . . . ."

"But what?"

"Well, like you was sayin'—"

"*Were* saying."

"Like you were saying 'bout rice and beans, and all. I got the fartin' part, but lost the rest," Xavier said with a bit of a blush, passing a palm high above his head.

"All right then. Let's go through the banter step by step. Okay?"

"Okay."

"But first you have to learn to relax your mind and reason out the words without clouding your brain, because then you won't be able to think at all. Understand?"

"I think so."

"Farting our way through one *big state*," the professor repeated, raising his bushy black brows in question.

"Texas!" Xavier exclaimed, smacking a knee in realization.

"Good. Now if beans are a flatulent, meaning that they make you fart, rice on the other hand binds or restricts the bowels. Too much starch will do that," the instructor reinforced.

"Constipates you! Right?" Xavier caught on.

Clarence Emery nodded. "Constipated thinking, Xavier. Ever sit upon the porcelain throne and try to defecate until you thought your head would explode?"

Xavier laughed and grasped the metaphor.

"Net result?" Emery pressed.

"Chaos!" Xavier stated emphatically.

"Then you wind up with shit for brains," the educator swore.

Xavier roared, smacking the palm of each hand squarely upon both knees. "How do you . . . . "

"How do I what?"

"Put all those . . . things together in your head so fast, the way you do?"

"*Things*, Xavier?" Emery chided. "Think, man. Say what you mean."

"Thoughts," Xavier said crisply.

"Good."

"How the heck do you do it? Think real fast on your feet like that. So . . . cleverly."

"Well, like I said. First you have to empty your brain of the kind of crap that clouds reason. Unclutter that airy attic, Xavier. The skull is not a kind of cup-like closet, but rather a housing for a hard drive; a human computer that needs re-programming and updating from time to time. Think and be yourself, Xavier, no matter how silly or serious you feel you might sound to others. If your mind is lazy or set on satisfying other folks instead of what is truly in your head and heart, your reasoning is going to be constipated. Got it?"

"I think so."

"Let pure unadulterated reasoning flow forward from you naturally. Not that foul-smelling effluvium, which contaminates the minds, bodies and souls of lesser men."

"Effluv-a-what?"

Clarence Emery raised and crooked a forefinger like a tiny periscope, slowly rotating his wrist and pointing to a position directly behind them, digesting the rest of Xavier's essay.

Xavier popped up from his seat and went over to the unabridged dictionary on the table. "a-f-l?"

"e-f-f-l."

"u-v-i-u-m. Got it." Xavier studied the meaning of the word. "Mike?"

"What?"

"Where are you going when you leave here?"

"I have business waiting for me in another state."

"Another restaurant?"

Emery nodded. "Yes, Xavier. Another restaurant."

"Well-known?"

"Will be after I put it on the map."

"Are you gonna be the head chef there, too?"

"The head chef," the man mused, putting aside the essay and staring up deliberately. "You might say that. Yes."

"Why are you smiling?" Xavier asked, returning to the chair.

"Because I just might deliver someone's gourd on a silver platter, after I sever it. Personally."

"Come on, Mike. Really."

"Really and truly, I might."

"Someone mess with you?"

Emery ignored the question.

"How come you don't want nobody—I mean anybody—to know you're staying here, Mike?"

Emery just smiled. "How many credits are you carrying this semester?"

"Nine."

"That's nothing."

"I work full-time. Remember?"

"When you apply what I taught you, you'll find that school and work's a breeze. Next semester, I'd like to see you handle twelve credits, work part-time in the kitchen as a cook, while making twice as much money than you're making now."

"I wish you'd be around to see that."

"You're going to wish your life away, Xavier."

"When do you think you'll be leaving?"

"In a while."

"Like when?"

"I might be out of here by tomorrow."

"You kidding?"

Emery shook his head.

"When were you gonna tell me this?"

"You'll be glad I'm out of your hair and have the place back to yourself."

"That's not true. You could stay here forever, and I mean that, Mike."

"That's very kind of you, Xavier. I appreciate that."

"So, you won't be here when I get home?"

"I don't think so."

The two said nothing for the next few minutes. Emery leaned back and closed his eyes while Xavier contemplated a crack in the ceiling.

"Well?"

"Well, what, my friend?"

"My essay. What did you think?"

"I think I'd have given you a C minus and told you to write something about the Alamo."

Xavier dropped his eyes to the floor, smiled and shook his head. "Want me to order in for us?"

"Sure, why not?"

Chapter 34

At Smitty Dawson's insistence, Alfredo Termotto reluctantly drove both his pastry chef and part-time waitress over to Laura Ingrilli's apartment. Alfredo parked the car and shook his head in disgust.

"I've got Yolanda closing out the registers and locking up the place, just so I can drive the two of you out here. I hope you remember this when I ask you to do *me* a favor," Alfredo yammered.

"We will, Al," Smitty promised. "Right, Brenda?"

"Sure thing," the redhead said.

"And I'll tell you what you're gonna find up there," Al went on. "You're gonna find that her boyfriend talked her into going on a little vacation with him. That's all this is. That's why she won't answer the phone; that's even if she's back. Either that, or, like Xavier said, she and Howie found employment elsewhere."

Smitty shook his head. "She would have called by now."

Alfredo laughed. "Do you know how long I've been in this business? How many employees I've had and the excuses I've heard? Too damn many. 'I couldn't find a working phone.' 'My mother was so sick that I couldn't think straight.' 'I got drunk and couldn't call, and the next day I was too embarrassed—then it just got harder and harder to make the call at all.' And my favorite. 'I was in a car accident and banged my head; when I came to, I didn't even know who I was.'" Alfredo laughed sarcastically. "But they all wake up and remember payday, all right."

"Laura's not like that, and you know it," Brenda brayed.

"None of them are like that, until one day, they're like that."

"Never thought of it quite like that," Smitty said behind a stifled smile.

"You sit where I sit, and you'd see."

"I'm on my feet all day in the kitchen. When do I ever get a chance to sit?" Smitty joshed.

"You're sitting now, aren't you? When we could all be home in bed. Well, go on up there and satisfy yourself. I've still got to drive the two of you back, and it's getting late. So move it."

Smitty stepped out, then helped Brenda from the backseat. He turned back to Al. "You don't think it's strange that Mike and Howie didn't call in either? Well, maybe Mike. Who knows what his story is? But Howard's never missed a day since he started. It's not at *all* like him."

"Not like you either, I suppose," Alfredo barked.

"And what the hell is that supposed to mean? Whether I'm sick or slick, I still call you, Al," Smitty declared matter-of-factly. "And Laura would do the same."

"Slick is more like it," the employer jeered caustically. "So. Got your slick-ass story ready for the superintendent in case Laura doesn't answer the door?"

"We got it," Smitty rasped.

"Good. You guys ain't back in fifteen minutes flat, you can grab yourselves public transportation."

"Sweet guy, Al," Brenda said before giving her boss the Bronx cheer.

After ringing and knocking and trying Laura's door, Smitty and Brenda rode the elevator down to the superintendent's basement apartment and pressed the buzzer.

"Yeah?" the man answered, opening the door a crack.

"Hi, I'm Laura Ingrilli's sister, Brenda," Brenda Harrison flat-out lied. "And this is my brother-in-law, Smitty," she prevaricated, too. "Sorry to bother you so late."

The tall blond Nordic superintendent nodded good-naturedly.

"My sister was mugged and badly beaten," Brenda began. "She was visiting me in New York when—"

The Scandinavian immediately brought a cupped hand to his mouth. "Oh, dear God!"

"She wanted to speak to you personally, but her jaw is broken and . . . ." Brenda let her words trail off as she accepted a handkerchief from Smitty, along with a comforting hug.

"Is she going to be all right?" the man inquired in a heavy

Norwegian accent.

Brenda gave a brave smile. "She'll feel a lot better when she has some of her own clothes and the checkbook that she asked me to —"

But the superintendent was shaking his head. "I can't do that," he stated firmly.

Brenda began to sob. "They stole e-everything from her. Money. ID. Her keys."

"The police strongly suggest you have the locks changed as soon as possible," Smitty chimed in.

"And because she's out of state, the hospital insists she pay part of her bill up-front, since the insurance doesn't cover everything. Laura wants to write a check to pay her rent as well. What she owes now, plus one month in advance because the doctors want to keep her there awhile to run some more tests," she informed the man who she knew, from past conversations with Laura, to be the landlord's nephew.

The super stopped shaking his head and began scratching it. "I don't know," he said. "I don't think I—"

"No problem," Smitty spoke up abruptly, taking his fictitious sister-in-law's hand firmly into his. "We'll just buy Laura what she needs and find her another place while we're here." He set his eyes back coolly on the squarehead. "Her boss is waiting out there in his car," he added, pointing upward toward the street. "He said, 'anything she needs.' I think Alfredo will also agree that she needs to look for another place." Smitty reached inside his jacket pocket and produced a sealed envelope marked PERSONAL. "Laura said if there was any problem to hand you this letter to give to your uncle to get her two months security back. She has other bills she has to pay and needs her checkbook, along with a few articles of clothing."

"Look. I can't just let anybody in there, Smithy," the man said defensively.

"It's Smitty. And you're not just letting anyone in. You're letting her sister and brother-in-law in for five minutes, while you stand there as we collect a few of the personal belongings that she asked for."

"Her boss is Alfredo of Alfredo's Restaurant. *Ya?*" the superintendent asked anxiously.

"That's right," Smitty answered straightaway.

"My wife and I were at the restaurant last month after Laura told her they had a new chef. It was really a wonderful meal."

"I'll tell Al you said that. Or better still, you can tell him yourself. He's right outside," Smitty reminded him.

The Norwegian was staring at the envelope. "What is it you want to take out of there?"

"Just some toiletries, undergarments, couple of outfits and her checkbook," Brenda chimed in.

"I don't think there should be a problem with that. Wait here a second, please." The man disappeared for a moment, returning with a set of keys. "No furniture or small appliances or anything like that?"

Smitty looked at the superintendent with some surprise. "Whattaya think, we're here to rob the place?"

The Norwegian shrugged. "I had a nice old man come to me last year and tell me he was here to pick up his son's laptop computer to take to the repair shop. When the tenant returned home in the evening and reported it missing, I told him what had happened. He told me his father had been dead for twenty years."

Smitty and Brenda shook their heads understandingly.

Olaf Hanson unlocked then opened the front door to Laura's apartment, flicking on a wall switch that lit the overhead as well as a beige ceramic pedestal lamp next to a wooden rocker. He summoned the two impostors inside.

Brenda surveyed the small studio and immediately crossed the cherry-red carpet toward the narrow hallway leading to the bathroom. "I'll get her toiletries and some outfits. You look for her checkbook in that desk, Smitty." She opened up one of the closets along the way, and then another.

Smitty went over to the mahogany secretary standing in a corner beside the lamp, pretending to search for Laura's checkbook.

The superintendent walked across the room to the dimly lit alcove kitchen. He looked around in confusion, staring wide-eyed at the mess along the countertop: the stained walls, the sticky bowls and utensils sitting in the sink, the pile of garbage lying on the linoleum floor in the corner. Olaf turned the dimmer knob clockwise for more light, when Brenda suddenly let out a horrifying scream from the bathroom. Smitty dropped a pack of monthly bank statements and went to Brenda's aid as the superintendent ran from the studio, banging on doors and yelling for the tenants to call the police.

From inside the safety of their apartments, two of Laura's neighbors slid open the disks that shielded their peephole, as no one dared to open their door. An elderly woman across the hallway immediately dialed 911.

Chapter 35

Spring was drawing to a close, and there were no new leads on Professor Clarence Emery. Xavier Sanchez had been questioned by both Maryland and New York homicide detectives several times. The young man had apparently been quite shaken by the experience of having a serial killer staying in his apartment. Needless to say, Xavier's landlady and neighbors were distraught, too. There were many nights that the young Mexican boy could not fall asleep until it was practically time to get up and go to school or work.

Laura and Howard's brutal murders were still on the tip of everyone's tongue throughout the city. Xavier could not concentrate on schoolwork, and his test scores and grades reflected as much. At Alfredo's restaurant, the boss himself had threatened to demote him to a position lower than that of a busboy, if only Alfredo could think of one. As it was, the young Mexican performed virtually all of the menial tasks, including sweeping and mopping the floors after closing hour.

"You can't even do that right," Alfredo complained one evening, grabbing the broom from Xavier. "I want the dust and crap in the dustpan. Like this. See? Not swept under the counter and—"

"I didn't sweep anything under no fucking counter."

"—then left there to be mopped and spread around."

"Mr. Termotto," Xavier snapped.

"What is it?"

"I'm not responsible for Howard and Laura's death. But you and some of the others here make me feel like I am. All I did was give him a place to stay. I didn't know who or what he was. None of us did. But somehow you're all blaming me. Well, I can't work here any longer. You can mop up after you sweep up to your own satisfaction. You can find someone else to clear and cart your dirty dishes. I quit!"

Alfredo Termotto watched Xavier turn and head out the

swinging doors.

"Listen," Alfredo called after him, "you can't quit. Only Tang Lee can quit. You hear me? And then we make the peace. Xavier! Get your wetback, spic-ass back in here now, man. We'll talk, goddamn it."

But Xavier was already heading out the front door of the restaurant.

"Shit!" Al sounded. "It's all your fault, Ignacio," he barked at the Cuban dishwasher.

Ignacio Vázquez smiled glumly. "Yes, boss. It's my fault if you say so."

"I say so, fuckface."

Tang Lee and Octávio Fernandez looked at Alfredo as though he had lost his mind.

"What are you two gawkin' at?" the boss barked.

The two cooks said nothing.

"Well?"

"A rear jerk," Tang Lee managed.

"What did you say?"

"You heard me, Arfled. You a rear jerk."

"And you're fucking fired, jerk-off," Al shouted. "You can't quit on me, but I can sure as shit fire your sorry ass. So consider yourself fired."

"Oh, rearry?"

"Yeah, rearry, you—you tongue-tied chicken-shit Chink. Go. Go find work next-door. And don't let either of those double doors hit your ass on the way out."

Tang Lee took off his apron.

Octávio did the same. "If he goes, I go."

Ignacio Vázquez looked over and shook his head. "I never thought this day would come," he said, untying his apron, too, and tossing it on a counter.

"And what day is that?" Alfredo asked with an angry look.

"The day we all wake up—and up and leave your sorry ass," Smitty Dawson said, washing then wiping his hands clean upon a dishtowel snapped from Ignacio's shoulder.

Alfredo Termotto stood wide-eyed with his mouth agape; no further wisecracks nor a single word was uttered. He turned around and watched as the crew marched out, one by one.

A moment later, Yolanda Quinones walked into the kitchen. "Is something wrong, Al?"

Al looked absently around the entire kitchen before he spoke. "We're closing for a spell."

"How come?"

"How come? I'll show you how come." And with that pronouncement, Alfredo lifted a cooling pot of marinara sauce from the stove and hurled it against the nearest wall while Yolanda stood by in horror. "RENOVATIONS AND REDECORATING!" he shouted at the top of his lungs, heaving a thick, solid oak cutting board through a back window.

Xavier was at home in his apartment reading the newspapers when the phone rang. He let it ring, looking down at the picture of Timothy McVeigh who was executed one year earlier for the Oklahoma bombing, killing one hundred and sixty-eight people. He turned the page and saw the unfamiliar face of Clarence Emery; the headlines: **Wanted**...*Still at large*...**Extremely Dangerous**. The young man wondered how many men and women 'Mike' had actually murdered. Xavier considered the question carefully, staring fixedly at the couch where his so-called friend had slept.

The phone kept ringing and ringing. Someone knew he was there. Probably someone from the restaurant, Xavier figured. Probably Alfredo.

Clarence Emery hung up the phone in disgust.

Chapter 36

It was a mild summer's day along both shores of Long Island, with temperatures in the low to mid-seventies. But about mid-island, within the confines of the homicide commander's office in Yaphank, tempers were rising rapidly.

"So you're just going to abort," Justin Barnes questioned Theo incredulously.

"He's out of the country," the lieutenant stated flatly.

"And what if he's not? What if he's just waiting for us to let our guard down?"

"Interpol assures us that—"

"Yeah, assure this," Justin steamed, obscenely grabbing his crotch.

"Do you know what this is costing the county, J?"

"Do you know what this will cost us if he strikes like the snake he is?"

"We can't draw this thing out forever," the lieutenant tried to reason.

"Three months is not forever, Theo. So what if it's another three months? Or a year? He's going to go after Jackie, I'm telling you. He'll try and kill her. He'll go after Notaro, too."

"We'll have someone shadowing them for a while. We just can't afford to run this operation the way we have."

Justin shook his head in disbelief. "I didn't know we were operating under a timetable or on a shoestring, Lieutenant."

"If it means anything to you, I didn't think they'd pull the plug on this either, J. That's the God's honest truth. McGruder retired, and it's a whole new ball game."

"I can't believe this shit."

"Look. They figured Emery would strike by now."

"No, you look. We have too much time and energy invested,

Theo. And furthermore—"

Theo was shaking his head.

"You're not even listening to me, Lieutenant."

"I've been listening. You're the one who's not listening. There's nothing we can do unless he makes another move. I've explained all this to you."

"All right, all right." Justin's mouth was racing miles ahead of his mind. "They're pulling Ruth off. Get me someone else, Theo. Pull some strings. Call in a favor. Take someone out of retirement. Just get me the help I need. I'm asking you as a friend."

Again, Theo was shaking his head. "You don't understand."

"That's right. I don't. I don't understand how you people can allow me to put the lives of two civilians and their families on the line and then pull the plug on this. I don't fucking understand that at all."

"I've been trying to explain it to you, J. But you refuse to listen."

"Wrong. I refuse to understand, but I've been listening to a bunch of bullshit, which is all that I've been hearin' all fucking morning." The man threw up his hands. "All right. I know this is getting us nowhere."

"Got that right," the commanding officer stated heatedly.

"So, here's what you're gonna do to meet me partway."

"J."

Justin put a palm out like a stop sign. "Just hear me out. I didn't say halfway, or even a quarter of the way. I said partway."

Theo tossed a pen on his desk, pushed his chair back and reclined.

Justin sat on the corner of the lieutenant's desk and leaned in on the man.

"Get your ass off my desk and your face out of mine."

"Sit up straight and pay attention."

Neither man moved an inch.

"You gonna listen to me, Lieutenant?"

Theo locked his eyes icily on Justin's.

"You go ahead and pull the plug like you were ordered. Only you don't pull the plug. You buy me time. Let the word leak out that the operation's over, and I swear to you, Theo, he's gonna strike. You leave me Ruth for a week after you pull whoever you have to pull off

Notaro's digs, as well as Jackie's home and place of business, and I'll find my own security force. That's all I'm asking, Theo. A week with Ruth and my own people on this. It's not like I'm asking for the moon," Justin begged. "One fucking week, man." Justin's expression turned to a dark cold fix. "It's too late to train anyone to fill Ruth's shoes."

"I don't know, J," Theo pondered.

"One fucking week."

"How are you going to pay for the kind of security force you're looking to replace?"

"I've got a few bucks tucked away from more lucrative days, boss. If you ever need a loan, Theo—"

"Don't make this sound anything like a bribe, J."

"Who, me? Why I wouldn't think or dare *influence* da Man. No, siree. Dat be a pretty dumb thang for a ne'er-do-well nigger to do, now wouldn't it, bossman?"

Theo slowly nodded his head in surrender. "One week from the time I pull the stopper, J. No more. Then Ruth's out of a sundress and back into uniform. Understand?"

"Problem is, boss, I understand things too damn well. Anyhow, Ruth O'Connor and I thank you from the bottom of our hearts. And when we nail this motherfucker shut in his coffin, you can thank Anthony, Ruth, Jackie and me personally."

"We'll see, J."

"Goddamn right we will," Justin said, removing himself from the corner of the lieutenant's desk.

"Anything else?" Theo smirked.

"Yeah. How many warm bodies will you have protecting Jackie and Notaro once you abort?"

"One and one."

"Well, golly gee, fella. 'Bout as safe as a couple of kittens in a logjam. I'll add one to Jackie's home, one to the restaurant, and two more to watch Anthony's home and property."

"Your show. They better be good or they'll all be tripping over one another's feet and tongues."

"Thanks, Theo—for small favors."

"Ingrate."

Chapter 37

The only person who truly concerned himself with David Klein's whereabouts and well-being upon his release from FCI Camp up in Otisville, New York, was his program counselor. It was not that relatives and friends were callous, or at least a wee bit curious. It was more a matter of self-preservation, for whenever David involved a member of his clan in any of his questionable dealings, it usually spelled trouble with a capital T. The latest tax debacle that had landed the con man six months in federal prison, along with stiff fines and home detention, was an illuminating example of the afflictions the seventy-two-year-old caused himself and others. With magnificent homes in California, Manhattan, as well as several apartments scattered abroad, David's travels were strictly limited to the confines of his East End residence in East Quogue, mandated by district court.

The phone company had installed a separate line in the man's upstairs master bedroom; another was placed downstairs in the office behind the kitchen, along with a FMD: an electronic Field Monitoring Device. The new line and number were not and could not be tied into any other. No call waiting or call forwarding, nor any of the other bells and whistles were permitted. The line was installed for the express purpose of Klein's counselor being able to check and see if the man was where he was supposed to be for the next six months; that is, warehoused 24/7.

Although house detention was a far cry from his quarters in Otisville, it still did not spell freedom. Not the kind of freedom most people take for granted. Not the kind of freedom he had known and enjoyed every day of his life before being sentenced. Initially, David was able to escape boredom vicariously. Books were his vehicle. Fiction. Nonfiction. Cookbooks in particular. There, in the commodious kitchen off his cozy office, David could be found cooking up a storm, utilizing every culinary gadget imaginable to man. The inordinate amount of pleasure he would derive from concocting meals for himself was in no way equal to the joy he received when he cooked for, and relaxed with, his guests. But after being home for a week by his lonesome, he thought he would go stark-raving mad. Another week went by before he languished and figured out a way to beat *the system*—the phone system—now and again enjoying a good neighborhood restaurant, keeping his escapades to a minimum.

Late Monday afternoon, David's preparation of borscht was interrupted by the doorbell. Furtively, he peered out the window at the vehicle sitting in the driveway, simply shaking his head in frustration, ignoring the persistent ringing. Finally, he marched barefoot toward the door in a long, white silk robe that concealed the altered ankle transmitter.

"Yes, who is it?" he answered—like he didn't know.

"Phone company."

David unlocked and opened the door. "I didn't call the phone company," he grumbled, staring past the man and back toward the white Verizon van. "I called Petro to service and fix this fucking air conditioner for the final time. First it was the fucking furnace when I was away. I almost lost the house with the winter we had. Then I call the stone mason to correct a crooked cobblestone he laid. I called the blinds and shutters guy to straighten a rod over the bathroom sink he broke. I called the roof guy to find a persistent leak. Next, I called the screen man to learn it was the saleswoman who ordered the wrong sized screens; and, in addition to a nice breeze I occasionally get off the ocean, I wind up with mosquitoes the size of adult carpenter ants, which, by the way, are attacking these wooden pillars as we speak," the owner harangued. "But I didn't call the exterminator yet because I'm building up a list of those who are bugging the hell out of me. Now, what is it that *you* want?"

The man smiled pleasantly. "I need to check the new line."

"Nothing wrong with it. I was just on it before," he lied.

The man looked down at his report sheet. "This is marked, URGENT. Reported dead on the other end early this afternoon," he explained.

David sighed. "Dead on the other end is how I'd like to see the guy who reported it," he ranted, wondering just how much the man standing before him knew about his *special situation*. "Wipe your feet good, and come in. I just had all the floors and carpets redone. If it was wet outside, I'd make you take your shoes off, or put on those little booties," he added, pointing down to a box of workmen's paper footwear beside the door.

"Ukrainian or Russian?"

"What?"

"Your borscht. Smells delicious."

David smiled proudly. "You like borscht?"

"Love it. What's your broth?"

"Anything but a fish stock. Usually beef. Sometimes chicken."

"You put in pork?"

"I'm a Jew! I make a beef or chicken broth and vegetables. Russian recipe. My mother's. But I've made it with pork and frankfurters for my gentile friends. Most of whom are dead. Think there's any correlation?" David questioned with a gamesome grin.

"Nope, been eating Ukrainian style all my life, and I'm as fit as a fiddle," the phone man assured him.

"You look fit. Listen, I'll send you home with a container. Should be cooled by then. Think you'll be here long?"

"Long enough to take you up on your offer."

"You got it. Well, I got a line coming into the office over there. Beige phone. Another upstairs in the master bedroom to your right. Need anything, just holler."

"Thanks. Mind if I start upstairs?"

"Just don't steal anything or I'll report you to my cleaning lady. She's a cross between Attila the Hun and Göring."

"I'm bonded," the man announced defensively.

"Don't mean shit. I was bonded in the building trades and stole everything that wasn't nailed down, then went back with a claw hammer and finished the job. A Jew who doesn't know how to use tools can't call himself a real man. Problem being that we're not *supposed* to handle tools. So if Christ was really who He said He was, He'd have given Noah a hand with that fucking ark instead of handing down a set of measurements. Cubits, my ass. Now, if they'd have told me Jesus Christ was a custom tailor, maybe I'd have bought into that shtik. But a cocksucking carpenter? Who the hell did He think He was kidding anyways? I know, I know. Only half the world. Or if they had told me He was into chattel or securities, I'd have known for certain He was the biggest fraud that ever walked the face of the earth and would have at least shown Him some respect."

Shaking his head in mild amusement, the phone man disappeared around the top of the stairs, and David went back to his borscht.

Fifteen minutes later, the technician returned and was talking on a cordless phone while fussing with the instrument in the office. When he finished, he came back into the kitchen.

"Everything okey-dokey?" David asked, wiping the counter clean with a damp cloth.

"Workin' order," the man clipped his words, standing with his hands behind his back.

"So, what was the problem?"

"Oh, they were going to call off the whole operation and leave a few folks I took an interest in hanging in the wind."

David stared at the stranger queerly. "I'm afraid I don't know what the hell you're talking about."

"It's a long story," the man declared.

"Your borscht is over there on the counter."

The man remained exactly where he stood.

"What do you want?" the homeowner griped. "A tip?"

The man laughed quietly and shook his head.

"Get the fuck out of my house." David walked over to the counter and grabbed one of the plastic containers filled with soup. "Here." He stepped up to the fellow and handed him the quart. "Now leave."

Clarence Emery nodded nonchalantly before plunging a kitchen knife into the base of Klein's throat. The homeowner instantly shot a hand to his bloody neck and seemingly fought for a word or phrase.

"'Jesus Christ!' is what I wager you'd have said, David," the professor figured, relieving the cook of the calid container before the body hit the floor.

Klein writhed in his own blood for a good twenty seconds while Emery watched him die. Stepping back from the corpse, the impostor went over to the Corian countertop and dipped the tip of a finger into the caldron of tepid borscht cooling on the stove, tasting the crimson liquid.

"Umm. Heavenly . . . absolutely heavenly."

Next, he inserted the tips of all ten digits into the pot, removing and carefully placing his fingerprints upon a freshly painted white wall. "There. That should do quite nicely. That should put us all back in the game. You see. We just made Justin Barnes' deadline in the nick of time, David my man."

Chapter 38

Justin's girlfriend, Ursula, was running scared. The two had just finished showering and were getting dressed.

"He only targets white women, you once said. Young, pretty women in their early twenties. Women of Italian descent. Well, he's added a seventeen-year-old boy in Maryland to his list, and just murdered a man in East Quogue. Not to mention Doctor Timothy Littleton, as well as over two hundred passengers and crew of every age, color, race and creed. And not with a carving knife either, but with a goddamn bomb. You think I want him coming after me? Look. Ruth O'Connor and Jackie are trained professionals. I'm just a secretary between jobs. Why me?"

"Because I need you. Because you're available. That's why," Justin pressed.

"I can't believe you'd want to put me at risk like that," Ursula ranted, snatching up her comb off the bureau.

"Put you at risk how? By picking up Anthony Notaro at the airport while his car is in the shop?"

"What if Emery puts a bullet through my windshield?" she questioned, pulling the comb angrily through her curly, shoulder-length jet-black hair. "Huh?"

"You know he doesn't operate like that," he argued, pulling on a brown leather calf-high boot. "He stabs them in the heart or throat, then cuts them up like cardboard." Justin planted his foot solidly upon the hardwood floor and worked a trouser leg over the top of the boot. "No guns and bullets for that boy, Ursula. Promise. Up close and personal is how he behaves. White women with a past."

"Oh, so now you're some sort of punk-ass profiler. Well, I'm a black woman with a future, and it's going to stay that way. Did Laura Ingrilli have a past?"

"She was perceived that way. Yes."

"Give me fucking break. She was twenty-eight and had two serious boyfriends in her life, you yourself said. The first one dumped her after a decade."

"She was running around with an older, married man. In Emery's eyes, she was a tramp."

"Then I guess that puts a cross section of the black female population at risk, too. Doesn't it, grandpa? The only gal I ever thought of as lily-white was that honky broad on the Ivory Soap box, and she wound up in porn. Why didn't, or doesn't, he go after her? No, sir. He goes after svelte chicks with a good head on their shoulders, until he decides to cut it off for them," she said through a shiver.

"Well, there you go. A solid argument that I can hang my hat on. Just goes to prove my point."

"What are you talking about?"

"Emery would never-ever in a million years go after any wide-beamed, smart-ass nigger broad with a checkered past, present and future," Justin reviled roguishly, diving for cover as Ursula started after him.

"Who the hell are you callin' a nigger, nigger? Huh?" she shouted, thrusting the pointed end of a rattail comb before his face and fending arms. "Sta–stab yo' black ass—chauvinistic, macho motherfucker. Come 'ere, cocksucker."

Turning sideways, Justin shielded himself with the flimsy covering he ripped from the bed, but then faltered. "Hey! That hurt."

"Good." Ursula had driven the handle against his backside with enough force to cause him pain without injury.

"Enough," he warned, wrestling her to the floor like a broken broom.

"Ow! L-let go of me. You son of a bitch."

"Well, you asked for it."

"When I get up, I'm gonna kick yo' black ass."

"Gimme that comb, and I'll let you go."

"Oh, I'm gonna give it to you, all right. I'm gonna give it to you where you'll re-mem-ber. STOP IT! Goddamn you."

"Gonna be good?"

"No–y-es—you're hurting me."

"I can't hear you."

"YES, you—motherfucker," she shouted, struggling violently.

"Doesn't sound to me like you're gonna be a good girl."

"I'm gonna kill you when I get up. You hear me?"

"Nope." And on that note, Justin muffled her mouth with a ball of blanket.

Ursula writhed and wiggled and kicked and wailed before he finally let her go.

Without a word, she got up and stormed over to the full-length mirror, standing there with her mouth agape. Fiercely, she spun around to face him. "Look at my hair. Will you just look at my hair!" she shrieked.

Justin went over to the mirror and dropped his pants, staring at his buttocks to see if she had broken skin. "Oh, you're so lucky, lady."

"Oh, now I'm a lady." She studied herself in the mirror. "Give back my goddamn comb."

"You gonna pick up Notaro like I asked you to?"

"Not on your life. You get Ruth or Jackie or someone else to pick him up. And if I ever hear that you squirreled her away overnight for *safekeeping* again, you're fucking history."

"So, that's what this is all about."

"You heard me."

"That was weeks ago. She was here for one fucking night."

"One fucking night too many."

"Well, I asked you to move in, didn't I?"

"Oh, so I don't move in, and you bring her here."

"The one fucking night when Emery sent her a present. Laura Ingrilli's head. I slept on the couch, and Jackie slept—"

"In your fucking bed. But you weren't going to tell me, were you? I had to find her hair between the sheets, on your hairbrush, and in the shower drain."

"What did you do? Take apart the pipes?"

"I'm gonna take you apart if you ever pull a stunt like that again. Understand?"

"We were in a bind. You know what she went through that evening."

"And I'm sure you were *very* comforting."

"What's that supposed to mean?"

"It means, J, that you could have dropped her off at my place instead of taking her home to yours. But no. You come by after midnight, without even calling, and stick a gun in my hand for protection while she's sleeping in your backseat—telling me you're taking her to a safe house. Yeah. Some safe house. Yours."

"I couldn't risk leaving her with you. All right? Emery could have been following—"

"But you could risk leaving me all alone with a handgun, that I don't know if I could even use if I had to."

"Well, you had your fucking comb, if all else failed," he said cruelly.

Ursula stared at him in silence, then slowly and sadly shook her head. "I don't know how much more of this I can take. I try and understand you, J. I truly do. I see how this business is tearing you up inside. I realize what you're going through right now. I know it takes beaucoup bucks to put together a crew to watch Anthony, Ruth and Jackie—day and night—while you run off to God-knows-where to play detective. And now you want to pull me into this mess along with you. Do you know I have nightmares imagining that it could have been my head or yours in that Styrofoam box?"

"Black and white, or in living color? Your dream, I mean."

"Joke around all you like. But you want to know how all this is going to end? With one or more of us dead. That's how. Anthony, Ruth, Jackie, you or me. Mark my words."

Justin stepped clumsily over to Ursula and slipped an arm around her bare shoulders. "That's just not going to happen. You hear me? That's just not going to happen. Emery's out of the woodwork now. And he's fucking nuts. He's going to make a mistake. And that's when and how we're going to nail him."

"He waited till the last moment, J. Then he murdered that Jewish fellow in East Quogue. He *knew* Theo was going to pull the plug on Ruth. Emery *knew*. How did he know that? Tell me. He wants all of you back in the game. That's all this is to him. One big fucking game. He left his calling card just as plain as day so there'd be no mistake it was him. His fucking fingerprints on the man's wall. Emery would kill a man or woman, boy or girl, prostitute or priest. He'd use a knife, gun, bomb, or drop a body from the heavens, like he did Grace Littleton's. He'd just as soon kill a young black boy, me, or an ornery ol' nigger like yourself. Trust me, J. Don't try and figure him.

He's ten steps ahead of all of you. He'd do the most unlikely thing to gain the upper hand."

"Sounds like you got this guy all figured out, girlfriend. Sure you don't want to be on my **A** team?"

"**A** team!" she blurted. "A team of ten ain't shit, nigger."

"That was then, and this is now. We got hundreds out there hunting for his hide."

"Oh, yeah?"

"Yeah."

"Then how about you hunting up a chauffeur?"

"Tomorrow I could. Today I can't. Tomorrow things are going to be different."

"Sure, until Theo leaves you in the lurch again, because I'll bet you dollars to doughnuts Emery ain't anywhere to be found—until he's ready to be found. He's probably laughing up his sleeve at all of you right now."

Justin handed her back the comb, then skittered over to the bed, pulling on his other boot.

"He'll wait until you guys and gals are good and tired, like he did before. He'll wait till you go through another five grand."

Justin looked up at Ursula oddly. "Now, how'd you know how much money I put out there? You snoopin' through my records and personal *thangs*, woman? Huh? Like you was snoopin' 'round for strands of Jackie's hair?"

Ursula smirked, then sorrowfully and sadly shook her head again, staring atop the chest of drawers. "You're an open book, J." She walked over to the nose-high bureau and removed an open bankbook with a pink withdrawal slip stuck between its pages, putting the items into his hand.

"How did these wind up there?" he asked as calmly as he could.

"Wound up right where you left them."

"Right," he said, knowing that something was very wrong.

"What's the matter?"

"Nothing. Just getting careless, is all."

"That, my man, is something you can't afford to be. Hey. You hearin' me, nigger?"

Justin lifted his eyes and set them on Ursula. "Got that right, girl."

Except when traveling, Justin never had so much as a charge slip sit for more than a day in his wallet, let alone a deposit or withdrawal receipt lying around in plain sight. Not in the clandestine business he was engaged in. Records such as those were filed away immediately. The large withdrawal transaction he recently made, in order to cover the cost of his crew, had been duly recorded and filed away in a locked cabinet, along with the bankbook. He distinctly remembered securing those items. He was methodical when it came to money matters; orderly—to the point of arranging his presidents faceup before tucking them in his billfold.

Justin turned his attention back to the bureau.

Loose change would always go into a large cup sitting in a cupboard above the broom closet as soon as he came through the door. Yet, there, too, along the top of the bureau, sat a slew of coins. Mostly quarters and pennies. A heap of silver off to one side. A line of pennies to the other. *No!* Not in a line, he observed. But arranged in the shape of a hook.

"So, J. Are we going out tonight, or not?" Ursula demanded. "Well? Hellooo. I said, are-we-going-out-tonight?"

Justin looked at her curiously. "That your change on the bureau?"

"Say what?"

"I asked, is that your change up there?"

"Change, sport?" Ursula mocked, setting her dark eyes level with the polished piece of ebony furniture. She marched up to the chest. "That's chump change, champ. What are you tryin' to pull now? Gonna tell me next that's all you got on hand after what you dropped on your bad boys? I don't give or leave change on men's bureaus, mister. What I do is have my admirers take me out on the town: dinin', dancin' and romancin'. And if they're especially nice to me, it may—and I do emphasize, *may*—develop into a re·la·tion·ship."

Justin was hardly listening. Standing and staring at the pennies. *Yes. Like a hook—or the shape of a letter,* he pondered.

"J. Are you even listening to me?"

Justin glanced back at her. "You bet, baby. Hung on each and every syllable."

Chapter 39

Justin sat across from the commanding officer and waited anxiously for the man to hang up the phone. As the lieutenant spoke quietly and reassuringly to his mother, he shuffled interminably through the photographs that forensics had taken and the lab developed several hours earlier. Finally, Theo placed the receiver in its cradle and instructed his secretary to hold all calls.

"Sorry about that," he said, holding on to the pix and returning the items recovered from Justin's bureau.

"I'm telling you, as sure as I'm sitting here, that Emery or someone else was in my apartment."

"You're sure Ursula isn't messing with your head."

Justin shook his head deliberately. "I'm sure."

"Then you know what I'm thinking regarding the silver, don't you?"

Justin nodded. "Thirty pieces."

"Judas betraying Jesus."

"And the pennies lay out in the shape of a J, for yours truly."

Theo was in agreement. "Did you count the amount?"

"Sure." Justin took and consulted a spiral pocket memo book from his shirt. "Twenty-four quarters, five dimes and a nickel. Six dollars and fifty-five cents."

The lieutenant smiled and shook his head. "The *total* amount, J. Counting the pennies, too."

"What are you saying?"

"Eleven pennies," Theo added.

"Six dollars and sixty-six cents. Jesus Christ, Theo. 666."

"You're a whiz, kid," Theo funned.

"I can't believe I missed that."

"It's understandable. You were fixated on the initial **J**. So don't go beating up on yourself. You had the presence of mind to call me and not scoop up those coins."

"How the fuck did he or anyone other than Ursula get in, Theo?"

"I think the more important question is why he didn't snuff you when he had the chance. If he got *in*, why didn't he take you *out*?"

"The game, Theo. He loves the fucking game."

Theo contemplated the ceiling. "I can't believe he surfaced back here on the Island. But you were right again. I honestly thought he'd turn out to be somebody else's headache. I really believed he was out of the country, as Interpol did."

"I'll be honest with you, Theo. For the first time, I wish I was wrong. For the first time, I'm running scared."

"You'd be less than human if you weren't, J."

Justin smiled uncomfortably and shook his head. "I don't mean to pull this macho-man crap," he explained. "I'm not afraid for me. I'm afraid for Jackie, Ruth, and Anthony. I'm afraid for Ursula. I'm afraid because I don't know where he'll strike next."

"Where you least expect, J. You can almost count on it. No pun intended."

"That's just about what Ursula said."

The two looked at one another uneasily.

"Where's Ursula now?" the lieutenant asked with legitimate concern.

"Back at her place for the moment. I just had an alarm system installed in mine. She already has one. Also, I had all our locks changed and installed one of those security bars from door to floor for good measure. Plus I have someone watching her 24/7. She's either at her home or my apartment."

Theo nodded satisfactorily. "I can give you a warm body now, to watch her back."

"Appreciated, but I'll keep the guy I got for a while. Owes me. Only way I'll ever collect," he swore through a carefree smile.

"You mean the guy from Wyoming?" Theo stated flatly.

Justin smiled. "You got a tail on my tail?"

"Plate stands out like a sore thumb. Ran it through DMV. Nice company you keep, J. Guy did a nickel for car theft. He has a bogus license that we decided to let him hold on to because we figure you know what you're doing. You do know what you're doing, right?"

"He can be a mean-ass motherfucker when the chips are down. One of the best wheelmen in the business, to boot."

"May be a bit rusty after doing several years."

Justin shook his head. "Like a bicycle, boss. You get on it, and you go the distance."

"If you say so."

"Wanna laugh?"

"Could use one."

"Know what my pal, Milky, was doing as an inmate?"

"Time."

Justin chuckled. "Seriously. Tying flies."

"Every prison has its industry, J, as I know you know."

"Yeah, but tying flies?"

"Wanna know something?"

"What?"

"Know why they cut your boy loose early?" the commander asked in all seriousness.

Justin sat up straight with mild surprise. "Looks like you really did your homework, my man."

"The administration moved all its inmates into a new facility, deciding to curtail production down to sixty hand-tied flies per week per prisoner, from only God knows how many they tied before. Warden wouldn't say. Thirty tiers had to find a new pastime. So the outfit they tied for in Colorado had to move its production overseas. Your boy, Milky, being master of all he surveyed, so to speak, promised to supply several distressed officials, whose names shall go unmentioned, with the best of the best for the streams and rivers they fished out there—in exchange for early release. As the art of fly-tying was suddenly brought to a standstill, a couple of frantic hotshots who couldn't live without the goods, including the warden who tried unsuccessfully to keep the operation running, yielded to your friend's demands. The governor of the state cut nine months off his time."

"Jesus, Theo. When you dig, you really turn up dirt, don't you?" he remarked with some surprise.

"I've got friends, too, J. Only most of mine are on this side of the fence," he chaffed. "Let me ask you something. Can you really count on this guy in a pinch?"

164

Justin nodded. "My man Milky's cool. New York born and bred."

"Cool, if you say so. White as milk, I hear," Theo subsumed, staring down at an unopened file folder in front of him.

"Albinos usually are. You see, like black folk, they tend to overcompensate," he added wryly. "More to the point, Theo, in a pinch he'd stand by me."

"All right. But if you have to cut him loose for any reason, you let me know. Manpower is not the problem it was before Emery turned up in Klein's kitchen."

"Like a bad penny," Justin quipped.

"Like eleven of them," Lieutenant Groche concluded.

Chapter 40

The two men sat huddled opposite one another at a table toward the back of a delicatessen in Cutchogue, talking quietly. The incessant drone of an old air-conditioning unit drowned out most of their conversation, which they kept painstakingly private whenever the waitress came by with a pot of coffee. The blond gentleman sporting a crew cut and day-old growth of beard leaned way forward, dropping his voice to a whisper as a young woman exited the rest room and walked to the front of the store.

"You know what really got to me last night?"

"What?"

"I went out to a place to eat called Bell Sarah's."

The albino abruptly looked up from his sandwich.

"No, not the Bella Sera in West Tiana," Clarence Emery qualified. "Bell Sarah's Seafood and Steaks, in Quiogue. Not to be confused with Quogue, or East Quogue. It's actually a neat little bar/restaurant on the water. Rather quaint. Nautical setting."

"Thought you lost your mind there for a second," the man remarked, putting his face down close to the plate as he took another bite of the oily, vinegary wet hero.

"Anyhow, I take a corner table and order a draft from the menu. A Coors Light. No prices listed for the beverages, mind you. Just a list of half a dozen beers. Draft and bottle. Next, I decide on salad and a skirt steak. *Rare*. Marinated, of course." Emery winked. "Came with waffle fries and creamed spinach. Fourteen ninety-five. Fine. Food arrives. Nice presentation. Steak's perfect. Tender. Moist. Great. Scoffed that meal down, one, two, three. Check comes. I'm getting a bit ahead of myself, but guess how much for the draft beer? Twelve-ounce glass."

"I don't know. Three bucks a pop?"

"Try five bucks. For Coors Light! Draft, mind you. A glass of wine there is five dollars. Fine. Fair enough. But you charge the same price for a small draft as you do a glass of wine? Come on. Anyhow, I call the waitress over and question the bill. She says that's what it is. Okay. So I ask her how much they charge for a *bottle* of Coors Light. Know what she tells me?"

Emery's associate dropped two slices of oily onion from the corner of his mouth as he shook his head.

"'Three-fifty a bottle,' she says."

"No fucking way."

"I figure she's got her beers mixed up. Should be three-fifty for the draft and five for a bottle, I tell her. But then another waitress pipes up and informs this one that it's three-fifty for a bottle at the bar. I just shake my head and smile. What am I going to do? Create a scene? Bring more attention to myself when I got half the county out here looking for me?"

Again, the man shook his head and, with a forefinger, held back several oily rings of onion along with a slice of salami and provolone that was about to topple onto his plate.

"Finally, I learn that she charged me for some fancy-dan draft beer instead of the Coors. I wonder how many people they do that to in the course of an evening?"

"Fucking rip-off artists."

"Then get this. I'm reading a brief history of the family off the menu cover. They claim to have been there for four decades. Now, I know the Bella Sera in West Tiana recently celebrated their thirty-second anniversary. So, naturally I'm pretty impressed to learn that Bell Sarah's in Quiogue has been around for some forty years—or so I'm led to believe. As I was washing down that delicious meal with another beer, I walked across the room and over to a wall dedicated to a hero cop. The entire wall was filled with memorabilia: Pictures. Letters. Awards. Some pretty impressive stuff: Brummer Award for valor, heroism and outstanding performance. You should know all about that stuff. Plaque for community service. Medals. Ribbons.

"Anyhow, I soon discover that it's the owner himself who, twenty-three years ago, opened the doors to the establishment. Twenty-three, not forty. I figure maybe the guy's family owned it since the early sixties then turned it over to him. Not the case. Do the math. He had the place since '79. I then ask how it is that the family comes to boast four decades. Well, as it turns out, what the family actually means, the manager tells me, is that the end of 1979 concludes—yet still counts as—a decade, enumerating on her sticky fingers the seventies, eighties, nineties and into the year 2000. Can you believe the nerve? I told her with that kind of creative math, she could jump ahead to the year 2010, today, and charge folks ten bucks for a bottle of beer or glass of wine, claiming that they're way ahead of their time if anyone questions the inflated price."

Emery's associate laughed and licked the tips of his oily, vinegary fingers. "Funny. What did she say when you said that?"

"The manager said nothing. The waitress told me she'd appreciate it if I left the tip in cash rather than on the credit card."

"You used a credit card?" the albino asked incredulously.

"Klein's," Emery said evenly.

"You used his credit card? The guy you iced in East Quogue?"

"One of several he carried around in his wallet. The guy had more aliases than those coins I collected from his office."

"Kind of risky. No?"

"Not really. Actually, it was his brother-in-law's card. Besides, I got a contact who can tell me the activity on any VISA, MasterCard or American Express account so I don't go raising any red flags. Of course, I wouldn't use it out of state to charter a party boat, pay for a cruise, or an airline ticket to South America," he made clear. "In and out of a few nice out-of-the-way restaurants or a mall is perfectly safe. After a few days, I throw them out and use somebody else's card."

"But why even take a chance with *any* credit card? And only a few miles from where you wasted the guy. Quiogue. Quogue. East Quogue. What the hell's the difference?"

"Because those broads there really pissed me off. That's why. When the card's reported stolen, which I'll make sure happens shortly, the police will be all over those cunts with a hundred heavy-duty questions. It'll serve them right. Wish I could be there to see their faces."

"You said Klein would sneak out while under home confinement. How? I'm curious. I know he was monitored with an ankle transmitter. Leave the premises for any length of time, and authorities know."

"Never got the chance to ask him. But I can tell you this. Klein was really quite ingenious when it came to tools and tinkering. He put the system down a couple times a week and went out for several hours. He even screwed around with the phones so he could still take care of personal business. But I had another contact with the phone company fuck with the lines and cause him some concern. That's how come I gained access so easily. Klein knew the dedicated line was out before I ever showed up at his doorstep. He pretended like he didn't know anything."

"Why'd you pick him? Seems like a lot of trouble to go through just to ice some guy in East Quogue."

"It had to be someone close enough to the Bella Sera in West Tiana, but not too close because they're watching that place and the area like a hawk. I wanted it to be a Jew living on the water. So why not a prominent sort of chap who the police were monitoring day and night? Got to have a challenge, my man," Clarence Emery vaunted with a wink.

"I still don't fully understand."

"The handful of silver and pennies I had you leave on Justin Barnes' bureau?"

"Yeah, I got all that. Thirty pieces of silver, referring to Judas selling Jesus out. The pennies in the shape of the letter J. Bunch of coins totaling six dollars and sixty-six cents. 666. Sign of Satan. Where's all this leading?"

Emery simply smiled. "I told you, the coins were taken from Klein's office."

"So?"

"They were rare coins. Very old."

Frustrated, the albino shook his head. "Okay, aside from Jesus being a Jew, why a guy living on the water?"

"I killed him while the sun and moon were still visible in the late afternoon sky. When they discovered the body that evening, it was a clear and starry night."

Emery's accomplice thought hard. "What does all that mean?" he asked, bringing the sandwich back to his face.

"Means absolutely nothing," Emery declared delightedly.

The man stopped chomping in mid-mouthful. "Nothing?" he mumbled.

"Not a goddamn thing."

The albino smiled and swallowed. "You put a bunch of clues out there so that the police remain clueless, scratching their collective heads. Probably have them studying the Bible in relationship to astrological charts," he said through an appreciative grin.

"You got it."

The white-haired, pale-skinned, pink-eyed figure laughed and grabbed his coffee. "I love it. Fucking downright brilliant. Satan. Judas. Christ as a Jew. Sun and Moon together. Stars. Water. Rare coins. It'll keep them guessing till the cows come home."

"Guess I should have celebrated with a three-pound lobster and a fine wine that evening instead of a steak and beer."

"One more thing."

"What's that?"

"The letter J."

"What about it?"

"Well, it could stand for Justin, or Jackie, or Jesus. Who, exactly, was in your head?"

"Why not all three in a single Godhead?" Emery teased and tested.

The man nodded respectfully as he finished his sandwich. "A sort of Trinity."

"Bingo, buddy."

"Ask you something?"

"You can ask."

"All those women. You kill them because they were Italian?"

Emery shook his head.

"Because they were somewhat less than righteous?" the albino probed.

"Had nothing to do with it," Emery disclosed. "They could have all been patron saints."

"Then this is simply how you play the game."

"Again, you got it."

The man sat in admiration and awe.

"Just don't ask me too many more questions, partner."

"How come?" But Emery's accomplice already knew the answer.

"Because, then, I'd have to nail you to the cross," the man's mentor stated maniacally. "Cross my heart and hope to die," Clarence

Emery swore and signed.

Chapter 41

Ten minutes after Anthony Notaro was seated at a corner table in the dimly lit establishment, Officer Ruth O'Connor arrived at Phil's Sports Bar & Restaurant in Jacqueline's Lexus. The undercover cop parked in back next to Anthony's old but well-maintained Buick, entering the building from the rear. It was the 'couple's' favorite hangout. The same haunt in which Jacqueline had given her last interview to *The News-Review* months earlier. The same table in fact.

The July heat and humidity drove many of the locals to the pleasantly air-conditioned dining room/bar-lounge area for libations and luscious steaks, ice-cold beer and clams on the half shell, closed-circuit TV and conversations covering basketball, baseball, golf, tennis, boxing, fishing, hunting, trap, skeet and sporting clays. The talk and telecasting ran day and night.

"Where's Jackie?" the pilot asked, standing and pulling out a chair for Ruth.

"She and Tomas just had one hell of an argument. He's decided, once again, not to let her out of his sight. I'm lucky I got to borrow her wheels."

Anthony nodded understandingly. "I really can't blame him. If she were my wife, I'd feel exactly the same."

The policewoman nodded, too, moving her chair in closer to the table.

"Think he'll ever make a move?" he asked in earnest.

"Emery?"

"No, the boogeyman."

Ruth smiled prettily. "They're probably one in the same."

"Actually, I wish that were the case so—"

"So that we could all wake up from a bad dream and go home and get some rest," she stated, stretched and yawned, finishing her charge's thought.

"You know something?"

"What?"

"You even look like her when you cover your mouth like that."

"Practice makes perfect," she agreed, scrunching her face and crossing her eyes wildly.

"Now, that's certainly more you," he teased.

Ruth giggled like a school girl.

"Hungry?"

"Overtired but starving. Let's order," she suggested.

Anthony leaned back and took in his surroundings. "You know he'd never dare show his face here," he stated almost invitingly.

"You know that's not the idea. We're simply to continue to be seen all lovey-dovey. Then maybe, one day soon, he'll make his move."

"It's the maybe part that bothers me."

"Me, too," she admitted.

"Maybe he'll never come."

"Came back to the South Fork," she said encouragingly.

"And killed a man he didn't even know."

"Didn't know those women either. Not really."

"Certainly knew my wife, though."

Ruth said nothing.

"Ruth?"

Ruth forced a little smile.

"Is there something you're not telling me about Desirée. Something I should know about my wife and Emery? Before we were ever married, I mean. She never even once mentioned him. I find that rather strange. Dee was usually very open with me."

Ruth raised her eyes to the rafters. "Like what?"

"Like I don't know. But something."

Ruth shrugged.

"Like were they ever an item?" he pressed. "Like did Desirée do something to set him off?"

"Nothing that you don't already know. He wanted her to work with him on some project when she was his student, but she wanted nothing to do with him. End of story."

"I don't know. Something tells me it's not that cut-and-dried, Ruth. I sometimes think there's more to it than that."

Ruth reached for and took a sip of Anthony's seltzer. "That's all I really know," she said truthfully. But she, too, sensed that there was more to the story . . . more than they might ever know.

Anthony took back his drink and changed the subject. "You know what the worst part of sitting around here is? Not being able to have a *real* drink. I mean, like a double Dewar's on the rocks."

"Well, you could have just one. A single shot. I'll escort you back home after lunch. Keep a sober eye on you," she promised. "How does that sound?"

Anthony declined. "No, one'll lead to two, and then three, and then I won't be able to function, which might not be a bad idea."

Ruth nodded knowingly. "Tell you what. When this is all over, the two of us will come back here and get drunk. Give these folks something to *really* talk about instead of sports. How's that?" She placed a hand upon his as another couple entered the room. "Know them?" she whispered.

Anthony leaned forward and sent nothing but a warm breath into her ear.

Ruth pulled back deliberately and smiled. "Was that a yes, or a no, or a pass or what?" she asked coyly.

"That was . . . ."

"Well, tell me," Ruth insisted.

Anthony shook his head and began to sob quietly, his broad shoulders trembling like a leaf.

Ruth pushed her chair back and stood. "Come on. I'll follow you home and make us both something to eat there. Up and at 'em, flyboy."

Anthony waved her off and put a napkin to his eyes. "Sorry. I'm all right. Really."

"No, you're not."

"I'm all right," he repeated. "Honestly. Or I will be after I have that drink. Just one."

"You sure?"

Anthony nodded in embarrassment. "What are you drinking?"

"Trade you." Ruth took back his seltzer and sat. "One drink, and then we go," she insisted. "I don't mind cooking, if you'll do the dishes." Leaning forward, she gave him an affectionate peck upon the lips.

Anthony flushed, staring off into space. Never before had she done that. Neither in public nor in private.

"Hey. I got a good joke. Wanna hear?" she offered, raising her eyebrows and fluttering her eyelids for his full attention. "It's clean," she added with a Jacquelinesque pose, hands placed high above her hips, head tilted off to the side.

Anthony took a deep breath and forced a little smile. "Sure."

"Actually, I don't have any obscene ones in my repertoire because I forget them all five minutes after I hear them. Gotta learn to write them down," she jabbered. "Ready?"

"Go for it."

"This Jewish man's old dog passes away, so the distraught fellow goes to his synagogue right around the corner from his home and asks Rabbi Schatz to say Kaddish for his beloved pet. Well, the rabbi looks at the man with some surprise and says, 'Abe, for a dog you want me to say Kaddish?' But Abe goes on to explain that Pimm was a very special companion and feels that this is only right and proper. The rabbi smiles understandingly but suggests that Abe go down the block to the *reform* synagogue, further explaining that perhaps the rabbi there could be of some assistance. 'Oh,' says Abe. 'So, let me see if I understand you correctly. You want me to go down the block to Rabbi Perlman's synagogue to see if they'll say Kaddish for my beloved friend that I nurtured and cherished from a puppy?' The rabbi nods with some impatience. 'I see,' says Abe. 'And do you think, also, that Rabbi Perlman might accept the fifty thousand dollar memorial endowment I had planned on giving to *this* house of worship?' 'Abe!' declares the rabbi, 'you didn't tell me Pimm was Jewish.'"

Anthony leaned forward with his face buried in his hands, his head and shoulders shaking from an ambivalent mix of levity and depression. Frivolity seemed to Ruth to be taking the lead, although she really wasn't sure.

"Come," she insisted, popping back out of her seat again and pulling him to his feet. "Forget the drink. I've got a captive audience, and I think I'm on a roll. We're gonna hit a joint just down the road from here for the best Margaritas on the north shore. I'll drive; you'll listen." She dipped into her purse. "Seltzer's on me," she insisted.

Ruth laid a few singles on the table, then led him away along the windowed aisle. "So. There was this gay priest who every Sunday before services asked God's help and forgiveness for his many sins. Early one Sunday morning, a bishop enters his congregation and asks the priest, flat out, if indeed the rumors he heard were true. 'And what rumors might that be?' the priest asked the prelate, forestalling the inevitable. 'Well, I heard from a very reliable source that you engaged two altar boys—'"

Anthony suddenly grabbed Ruth's arm in a death grip, then quickly moved her away from a window.

"Jesus Christ!" Ruth hissed, tearing her weapon from its holster, ripping her cell phone from its holder, rapidly tapping in a number. "Come on, come on," she snapped, moving swiftly toward the back of the building. "No, not you, Anthony!" the undercover cop commanded. "Stay put!"

But Anthony moved briskly past her and out the rear doorway.

"Shit," she uttered angrily and quickly followed.

A light blue sports car immediately shot out from the crowded parking area, speeding along a gravel driveway, throwing up a shower of stone before spinning halfway around as the driver worked the accelerator and brakes, suddenly sending the vehicle rearward in a violent arc, creating a vast diaphanous cloud. The figure behind the wheel winked and waved before the car lurched forward again, gripping the asphalt pavement with authority. The passenger in the front seat put down his window and gave Ruth and Anthony the finger from behind a party of six elderly couples, frozen in fear. In a flash, the driver and his accomplice peeled off the macadam, leaving behind the acrid smell and taste of burning rubber as the pair disappeared around the corner, evaporating into a vaporous ribbonlike distance.

Ruth and Anthony ran toward the borrowed Lexus.

"Taborsky. O'Connor here. We're in pursuit of Emery, no disguise, and a male albino driver, heading west on 25A from Phil's Sports Bar, Wading River. Light metallic blue, late model Camaro; Maryland plate, Kilroy 6-7-6 Tango Edward. Do you copy?"

"Affirmative. What's your...ation? I...peat. I ne...crossro.... O'Connor, do ...opy?

"You're breaking up, Sergeant," Ruth fumed, staring down at two deflated tires: one on Jacqueline's left front Lexus, the other on Anthony's right rear Buick, parked alongside.

"Come ba...wi...your pre...ent position, O'Connor? Over."

"Betwixt and between," Officer O'Connor blew, angrily kicking one of the flattened wheels.

"Your situation! Damn it, O'Connor. Are you all right?"

"Upright and downright pissed at the moment, Taborsky. We're outside Phil's Sports Bar. We got two flat tires and—what are you doing? ... No, not you, Taborsky. Jesus, Anthony! What the hell— Christ.... What? ... Notaro's hot-wiring a customer's car."

"L...n...me. I...."

"Fuck! I'm losing you, Taborsky."

"LET'S GO!" Anthony screamed at her, slamming the floor shift rearward, shooting the vehicle into reverse and sending up a plume of dust and stone.

"Stand by, Taborsky."

"What on earth...going...there? ...think he's doing?" the duty sergeant hollered.

"Blind flying," Ruth bellowed, ripping the cardboard sunscreen from the windshield and tossing it to the ground. Without opening the door, she jumped into the front seat of the commandeered convertible just as Anthony smacked the gearshift into first, blowing the high performance sports car out of the parking lot, shifting the five-speed through all five gears, putting the vintage Porsche's accelerator to the floor in hot pursuit.

A detective grabbed the phone from the sergeant. "What is happ...?" Detective Kerrigan demanded, followed by the sound of steady static. "I repeat.........................

Ruth flipped the useless unit onto the backseat.

Chapter 42

The door to the lieutenant's office was wide open. Detectives along the entire hallway were moving busily back and forth like pedestrian traffic at a busy intersection during the height of rush hour.

"Fucking guy's got balls as big as water balloons," Justin blew. "Showing up at Phil's Sports Bar like that. No disguise or nothing. He's positively nuts."

"And what guy is that?" Theo asked calmly from his chair. "The guy we're really after, or that fly-by-night fly-tying friend of yours from Wyoming?"

"Maryland plates, Lieutenant. Ruth and Anthony reported Maryland plates. Not Wyoming," Justin insisted. "Milky has Wyoming plates on an old blue Mustang. Not a new blue Camaro. All right?"

"How many albinos does it take to make you distinguish black from white?" the commander fired back sarcastically. "Get real."

Justin said nothing for a moment. "I still can't believe it," he finally quailed in quiet disbelief, not quite sure what to make of the report.

"Well, believe it."

"Anybody bother to take tire impressions out there? Because the tread design ain't gonna match Milky's Mustang, nohow, I'm telling you."

"That don't mean squat. Besides, neither of those vehicles has been located. Nor has your so-called friend. What does that tell you? Huh? Now you know who entered your apartment and put the bankbook, withdrawal slip, and Klein's coins on your bureau. I'm surprised he or Emery didn't put a bullet in your brain and close the account," Theo snapped.

"Milky could have killed me or Ursula anytime he wanted to —but he didn't," Justin put forth lamely.

"As you yourself said, Emery loves the game."

Justin shook his head in sheer disgust. "Milky would never betray me, Theo."

"Who else could have gotten a key to your place, aside from Ursula? He probably went into her pocketbook, had one made up, and then returned it."

Justin paced back and forth in front of Theo's desk. "I still don't buy it."

"Then you're a damn fool. Where's Milky now? Tell me. He's supposed to be on Ursula's heels. Following her like a shadow. Protecting her. Just be thankful he didn't eclipse her."

"Maybe Emery found himself an albino look-alike. A double. Like Ruth assuming the role of Jackie."

But Theo was shaking his head. "You're fucking thick."

"Why not? Tit for tat. Anything's possible, Mister Know-It-All."

"Who handles a car like that, huh? You yourself said he's the best wheelman in the business. Ruth and Anthony never saw anything like it in their lives. The guy was playing with them, J. He led them on, and then ran circles around them. Literally. She couldn't even get a shot off without risking lives. The guy was cool, calm and collected. The guy fit the description of your so-called friend. When are you going to wake up?"

"Yeah, some description. Milky white and sitting behind a steering wheel. Sounds like reverse discrimination. Sounds like another form of racial profiling, if you ask me," he said sillily.

"No one's really asking you, J. I'm telling you. Want to hear more?"

Justin looked at his boss incredulously. "More? Just decided to tell me now?"

"Want to hear?" Theo asked patiently.

"Go ahead. I'm listening."

"The two were seen together the day before yesterday sitting in a deli out East. The waitress on duty had no trouble remembering your friend. She didn't forget what the man sitting across the table called him either. She thought it was the funniest thing in the whole world. Milky, she recalled."

"And you weren't going to tell me this, Theo? Like it wasn't important or anything?"

"I didn't think you needed more convincing."

"Where's this deli?"

"I want you to take a little time off, J. Rest. I want you to look after Ursula for a while."

"Where's this deli, Theo?" he repeated.

The detective lieutenant lowered his eyes to a pile of paperwork before him. "We got it covered, J. Now, go do like I ask."

Justin Barnes stood firmly planted.

Theo looked up, then back down at his paperwork. "Don't make me—"

"Make you what? Huh? I already went through five grand out of my personal savings to foot this race myself. And if need be—"

"That was your doing, Barnes. No one asked you to do that. You did that on your own."

"But I got results, Lieutenant. I got Clarence Emery out of—"

"You got Clarence Emery right where he wants you to have him. And that's nowhere, no time soon. Got it now? That's why I'm telling you to take a vacation from this. Take Ursula on a trip. I'll call you."

Justin did an about-face along with a slow burn and quietly left the man's office, slamming the door closed for the full effect.

Chapter 43

In bed before 10 p.m., hot and exhausted, Ursula and Justin argued with one another there in the darkness.

"Jackass motherfucker," Justin complained bitterly as she bore the brunt of his wrath, regardless of the fact that his anger was directed solely toward the commanding officer of Suffolk County's homicide squad. "Knows jack-shit 'bout Milky and the man he really is."

Ursula listened attentively, then tried to talk some sense, but Justin had a closed mind and narrow vision when it came to his friend.

"Fucking gall of him to put me on the sidelines."

"Theo's got a lot of people on this," Ursula reasoned patiently.

"He wants my ass outa there. But I'm the nigger who drew that sick fuck out for them. Me! Me and Jackie. Emery doesn't want Ruth or Anthony. He wants my big black ass and Jackie's little behind for trying to set 'im up. He wants to show me who's king of the hill, top of the heap."

"Sounds like Sinatra and those vagabond blues," Ursula jabbed in jest. "Sounds like you're feelin' mighty sorry for yourself, fella," she projected, inwardly joyous that, maybe, just maybe, the two of them could now have something of a normal life.

"Sounds like you've already taken sides and decided Theo's right, and that I'm wrong."

"Ruth and Anthony both identified Milky and Emery. All right?"

"Ruth and Anthony saw someone sitting behind the wheel of a car in a crowded parking lot with shit going down all around them."

"Hey! Even a waitress from some deli identified your pal."

"Yeah, but Theo won't even tell me what deli—will he? Won't let me interview her."

"Do you think you're going to learn something that the police don't already know? Do you, J?"

"The police who interviewed her didn't spend a year with Milky in the slammer. I did."

"That was a long time ago, J. People change."

"A leopard doesn't change its spots, Ursula. We were friends then, and we're friends now."

"Animals don't do to one another what people do," Ursula retorted.

"What are you saying?"

"That your friend Milky sold you out. That he went to work for the highest bidder. The man was sitting in prison tying friggin' flies, for cryin' out loud, J. How much do you think he came away with? Several hundred bucks? Money's a powerful motivator. And that's another thing. Those coins left on your bureau in the shape of a hook. A fishing hook, Sherlock. A not-so-subtle sign in that it had *his* signature all over it, if you ask me."

"Let me point out a couple things to you, all right?"

"So point," she said in exasperation, throwing back the sheets and turning her pillow over to its cooler side—the air-conditioning unit having quit moments after the couple got into bed for the evening.

"According to Theo, the waitress couldn't identify Emery's photo. True?"

"That's what you told me, my dear."

"Because we know that Emery changes his appearance like a chameleon changes color. Yes?"

"Go on."

"But supposedly she could identify Milky. Right?"

"So."

"So, couple days later at the Sports Bar, both Anthony and Ruth recognize Clarence Emery and give a description of another man who they never saw before."

"Yep, and who they later identified from a recent prison photograph as your butt-buddy, Milky."

"But isn't it just possible that Emery found himself someone who looks like Milky, then purposely put him on display in a public place to draw attention to this guy? Both at the deli and the Sports Bar."

"A double? A look-alike?"

"Why not? We got Jackie's double waiting in the wings for Emery to show his face."

"Why would he do that?"

"Why? To create confusion. To create distrust. It would be like Emery to do exactly that. It's his game, Ursula."

"Then where is your friend Milky, now? Why hasn't he called? Why wasn't he watching my back like he was supposed to? And above all, how did this look-alike, this double, this impostor, learn to drive so professionally like your good friend? Isn't it all just a little too coincidental, J?"

Justin conveniently avoided what he couldn't answer, covering the same ground anew. "Doesn't it seem just a bit strange to you that two men, who should want to keep a low profile, suddenly bring such attention to themselves in a public place, like a busy deli and a popular sports bar?"

"Doesn't it seem just a tad strange to *you* that these two men, who should *definitely* want to keep a low profile in order to avoid death or capture, show themselves at a public place where they *know* a woman and a victim's husband are just champing at the bit to put a bullet in at least one of their brains? The answer to that question is rather simple, J. You've made the argument yourself a dozen times before. Emery, and whoever else knowingly runs with him, has got to be absolutely nuts. Period. And you still haven't answered my other questions because you can't. Now let's get some goddamn rest," she snapped, flipping and fluffing up her down pillow. "And I want that air conditioner fixed before I spend another night here."

"It's not broken, Miss Smarty-Pants."

"What do you mean, it's not broken?"

"Just what I said."

"It went on the fritz soon after we got into bed."

"Turn on the light."

"What for?"

"Do it and you'll see."

Ursula leaned over and turned on the lamp. Nothing happened. She tried it again and again. Exasperated, she reached across Justin's sweaty naked body and tried turning on his lamp. "They're both broken," she said in a childlike manner.

"They're not broken, Miss Know-It-All. We lost the power after we turned the lights out and climbed into bed. Electric hasn't come back on yet. You see, sometimes things aren't always as they appear," he said evenly. "But your point is well-taken because it would certainly *seem* a bit too coincidental if both lamps blew independently of one another, along with the a.c.," he added sarcastically and somewhat satisfactorily as he rolled over onto his stomach.

"It's not the same thing and you know it."

"Is too."

"Isn't."

"Is."

Ursula turned her pillow back over, punched its center fiercely, planted her head into it, then tried to empty her mind of the horrors and dangers surrounding the two of them.

Justin fell sound asleep almost immediately.

It was a good hour before Ursula finally dozed off for a fitful fifteen minute nap.

Chapter 44

The structure in which the underwear-clad figure stood captive was no wider than a stand used for storing a set of foldable end tables, although erected exceedingly higher. It was a cage that Clarence Emery had constructed in a makeshift workshop, located off to the side of the cellar stairs. The top of the contraption consisted of a large wooden vise that held the albino's bloody head, clamped solidly in place. The man's bare, bruised arms were extended fully forward, his wrists clasped firmly through the framework, supported by a single post. Much like a pillory of sorts. The tips of the prisoner's toes barely touched the platform.

"Comfy?" Emery asked. "It won't be long before we squeeze the living truth out of you, Milky."

Milky wept bitterly.

"It shouldn't much matter to you anyhow, as your whole life has been nothing more than a living hell."

"Pl-please," Milky pleaded. "Please . . .dear Jesus."

"You sort of look a little like Him, on the cross, you know."

"I tol-told you . . . told you everything . . . everything there is to tell."

"No, you didn't, Milky. You spent a *year* with your friend, Justin Barnes. Locked up together in the joint. What you told me took less than five minutes. I want history, Mr. Melvyn Milken. I want details. I want to hear it all."

". . . t-told you."

"You told me nothing that I can use."

"Oh, dear God! I just got out. I di-didn't hurt you. All I did was wa-watch his girlfriend. Th-that's all I did. Please, Mr. Emery. I don't want to die."

"But you *did* hurt me, Milky. You went to work for Justin, against me. That's very, very bad. But you don't have to die. Just give me something good that I can use against him, and I'll let you go."

"You-you'll never let me go. Please. I just got out of prison. Please. Please, Mr. Emery. I'll work for you against him. I swear it. Just let me go. Then I'll come back and tell you what you want to know."

"Really, Milky? You mean kind of like a double agent?" The lunatic laughed.

Milky tried to move his head up and down but couldn't manage. "YES," he screamed. "I SWEAR IT!"

Emery craned his head and shoulders, addressing the figure standing in the background. "Well, what do you think?"

The man responded in the negative.

Emery nodded in agreement, turning back to face his captive. "So, what do *you* think of my main man—Milky number two? They say everyone has a double. Of course, he's a good deal shorter than you. Therefore, we had to prop him up a bit when we took that little drive out to Wading River to say hello to Anthony and Ruth. But my friend, here, still handled the wheel like a trooper. Actually, an ex-trooper. Trooper Vito Vitalo, Monroe Barracks, Monroe, New York. New York State Police. Medal of Valor, presented by the governor himself. Certificate of Exceptional Valor for Meritorious Acts. Law and Order Awards. Marksmanship and more. Man's been decorated up the kazoo. But we need not go into all of that. Talk about being light-skinned—even for a northern Italian. Don't you think?" Emery grinned ghoulishly. "Come on over here, Vito, you impostor you," he ordered laughingly, "and say hello to the real Milky."

Vito came from behind a sawhorse and stepped up to the platform, raising his beady eyes to meet Milky's.

"Vito, Milky; Milky, Vito. Not at all how we picture a state trooper; hey, Milky my boy? Imagine having this guy pull you over and ask for your license and registration. I guess that's why they tried to keep him confined to the barracks as much as possible. Except for height, hair and weight, you two guys pretty much look alike, you know. About the same age, too. Still, Milky, you have the unfair and added advantage of more than a few inches when you take into consideration the base of the platform and the fact that you're standing on your tippytoes. Actually, you appear to *tower* over Vito," Emery babbled. "Anyhow, all that stature stuff concerning law enforcement is a thing of the past. I mean, you can't be a midget, mind you. But nowadays you can be of average height, female, and maybe even follically impaired—campaign hat or not." The lunatic cupped his fingers and scratched the top of his head. "Imagine meeting up with some dikey-looking dish like that," he blathered. "I figure no amount of courtesy cards in the world would help a poor male motorist cruising along those highways and byways. Right, Vito?"

Beneath the ceiling of the cellar stairs, Vito held Milky's pleading pinkish eyes in the pale light of the single bare bulb burning high above them.

"P-please don't hurt me, mister. I beg you," Milky implored the man, as if their mutual features and inflictions formed an irrevocable bond between them.

"Can I put the screws to him now, Clarence? You promised me I could if I got us out of there in one piece when that Porsche came barrelin' up our asses."

"And a promise is a promise, Vito. Go ahead. But do *not* crack his skull open immediately, or you'll take all the fun out of it," he cautioned slyly.

Milky fought for but couldn't find the words he wanted, yet the fingers of each hand opened and closed in determination, forming a fist followed by an unintelligible plea for the sadist to back away. Milky tried to pull his wrists free of the wooden plank that held them fast. He tried to shake himself loose of the cage, but couldn't. When he caught and finally brought a breath back into the core of his being, a single seamless, ceaseless scream covered any and all sound emanating from the sizable squeaky screw-handles fixed to solid oak blocks—blocks that designedly began to crush his skull.

Chapter 45

Seated at a table toward the rear of a deli in Cutchogue, Justin Barnes had finished several cups of black coffee while poring through the sports section of three newspapers, having waited well over an hour for the waitress to finish her shift.

Finally, the young woman walked up to his table, set her hands upon her wide hips, and shook her head. "Why didn't you just kill some time shopping or walking around or something? Why did you insist on waiting for me in here?"

"Wanna know the truth? Because I didn't wanna lose you. That's why."

"I said I'd be here. Didn't you believe me?" she asked with a crooked smile that matched her yellow teeth.

"Oh, I believe that you believe that," Justin agreed. "But chances are your boyfriend might've come in and taken you out of here early. Or your boss could've told you to go home because things are slow near closing time. Then what? You gonna go runnin' 'round lookin' for me with or without your boss or boyfriend?" he asked frankly, his head cocked at a forty degree angle to add emphasis to his point. "A bad black dude like me?" the maverick added, smiling handsomely.

Inez Diaz dropped her head shyly and swept it back and forth. "I ain't got no *real* boyfriend," she said awkwardly.

"Oh, I see. You got yo'self one o' dem bogus boyfriends," he teased, sliding into the role of his streetwise sassy self. "The artificial, pliant type, I'll bet."

"Say what?"

"You know. The counterfeit kind. One o' dem blow-up dolls," he went on.

"I do *not*," she aired in an affected manner. "Besides, I ain't never heard of one of them male kind. I know they got blow-up *girl* dolls—but not boy dolls," the twenty-year-old affirmed.

"Sure they do. I had me one once growin' up."

"You did not," the waitress brayed.

"What'samatta? You never heard of Joe Palooka?" he questioned patently, sitting back in his chair before shooting three quick jabs toward the ceiling.

Two men in their mid-twenties, hanging out at the front counter, looked up with annoyance and an attitude.

Oblivious to the pair, Inez laughed and shook her head.

"No, it's true. He stood 'bout waist high," Justin insisted. "Made o' yellow plastic. Had a bunch o' beans or beads or somethin' in the bottom of 'im. You'd hit 'im, he'd rock back then straighten right up. Punch 'im good 'n hard, he'd hit the deck. But he'd pop right back up at'cha, each and every time. Joe Palooka." Justin had a faraway look in his eyes. "Anyhow, that was my blow-up doll."

"You look like that movie star, what's his name?"

"Ah, Sammy Davis!" Justin said decisively, closing one eye.

"No, silly. Not Sammy Davis. The tall handsome one. You know."

"Let me guess. Jessie Jackson."

"The actor!" she persisted, mad at herself for not being able to recall the name.

"Actor. Actor. Actor," Justin jived. "Got it! Colin Powell."

Inez was getting more frustrated by the second. "He was paralyzed in that movie . . . ."

"Denzel Washington," Justin delivered, showing off his pearly whites.

"Yesss," she said excitedly. "Him."

"Listen. Can we get out of here and go someplace where we can talk?"

"Sure. Where would you like to go?"

"To dinner."

Inez looked at him suspiciously. "You want to take me out to dinner?"

"Yep."

"Why?"

"So that we can talk and not be interrupted."

"Talk about that al . . . uh—"

"Albino."

"And that guy who was with him."

"Yep."

"We can talk here, if you like. I can put something together for us to eat. I'll tell Susan not to bother us. Or better yet, I can have her wait on us. And you won't have to pay for my meal because I'm entitled to it."

Justin shook his head. "I want to take you out to a nice place, Inez."

"Look at me. I'm not even dressed. I've been working like a dog since one o'clock this afternoon. I look a mess."

"You look just fine."

Inez thought it over quickly. "I've got to be home no later than ten though, to walk and feed my dog."

"Then ten it is."

"I just want you to understand that I told you guys everything I know. I hope I won't be a disappointment to you."

"It'll be like I'm hearing it for the very first time, Inez. Believe me. Besides, I'd really enjoy a fine dinner and the company of a very nice girl like you."

Inez blushed. "I never had no detective take me out to dinner before. But I did have a cop tell me once that he'd make sure I got bread and water if I didn't clean up after my dog," she griped. "I got away with a warning."

"Swine."

"That's exactly what I called him! Well, not exactly that—or to his face. But I think you get the idea. Oink, oink," she vocalized rather loudly.

A coworker and two customers at the front counter glanced back smugly.

"Oh, I do indeed, Inez," Justin assured her. "Believe-you-me, I do."

"I'll go get my bag, and we're out of here. Excuse me for just a moment." The waitress disappeared into the kitchen area, beaming excitedly.

The two men at the counter gave the stranger a rather disdainful look.

Justin got up from the table, ducked, bobbed, weaved,

crouched, then shot a menacing glare in addition to two quick jabs their way. *Punk-ass motherfuckers,* he thought, stepping forward and throwing a formidable left hook, followed by a short, quick blow that sounded through the aisle. *Go ahead, say somethin', fools. Don't wanna put me in no mean-ass fucking mood that you'll be sorry fo', flunkies.*

Inez returned after a few minutes, suggesting a new Italian restaurant near her home and right around the corner from the deli.

"They just opened up a week ago. It's fantastic. I have a friend who works there. I just called, and she's on tonight; she'll take care of us. This way, we can enjoy a meal without being rushed, and I can be home early enough to walk Buster."

Inez and Justin entered the refurbished building that ostentatiously displayed a gaudy gold banner announcing its Grand Opening. The place was crowded. Off the vestibule, Justin could not help but notice a huge, gaudy etched glass-faced refrigerator, containing a plethora of wine bottles standing upright alongside a sea of empty chilled carafes. A middle-aged hostess immediately walked up to the couple and escorted them to a table. As soon as the two were seated, Justin started questioning Inez as to the albino's general description.

"White, like I told the other two detectives."

Justin leaned forward. "Inez," he practically scolded.

"What? Did I say something wrong?"

Justin smiled. "Look around you, darlin'. Everyone in this place is white but me," he put out for openers.

Inez looked embarrassed. "I'm not prejudiced, you know."

"I know that. That's why you're sitting here with me now. Right?"

"That's right!" she said decidedly.

"Good. So tell me what you remember—"

"*The Bone Collector!*" she offered up ecstatically. "The movie with Denzel Washington. He was this para . . . I can't say it. Para something."

"Paraplegic."

"That's it. Anyhow, you look just like him," she said most emphatically.

"I look bedridden?"

Inez guffawed then groaned, holding her sides to keep from splitting. "Oh, you're too much," she declared when she finally caught her breath.

"So. Aside from being white, what can you tell me about this fellow? What did he look like? Hair. Height. Build. Anything you can think of."

"Well, aside from him being really, *really* white," Inez joked, "he had this really thick blond hair."

Justin couldn't help but smile as she fluffed her hair like Ursula would her down pillow. "Messy, you mean?"

"Very."

"High, bushy hair? Kind of like that guy sitting directly behind me in the checkered green shirt?" he questioned without turning around.

"Yesss. Definitely more like that," she said, admiring the man's power of observation.

"Color?"

"Actually, kinda in between blond and white. But I'd have to say more white. Definitely, more white."

"Go on."

"Well, what was really creepy were his eyes. Pink. Dead pink eyes."

"Dead?"

Inez nodded. "You couldn't help noticing them. You couldn't help but stare when you thought he wasn't looking."

"What about his height and build?"

"Stocky. Not like you."

"How not like me?"

"Not nearly as tall."

"How tall?"

"Short for a guy, I guess. About five-foot-six or seven. He was sitting down, but I got a good look when they headed out the door. Shorter than the other fellow he was with, for sure."

"Around her height?" he asked, as the waitress, apparently Inez's friend, approached their table. "The albino, I'm talking about," Justin made clear as he raised an arm toward the woman's head as a means of measurement.

The young waitress immediately took two steps backward.

"Yes," Inez assured him. "It's all right, Helen. He's okay," she explained, dismissing Justin's behavior as ordinary, everyday conduct for a cop. "He's a detective," she whispered quite proudly. "Detective Justin Barnes."

Helen took one step forward. "Still, I think I'll take your drink order from here," she said, unsure of the situation.

"No, he's cool. Really, Helen. I wouldn't introduce you to a molester or a rapist," she teased.

"No? What about that guy you fixed me up with last Monday? Arms and legs like an octopus."

Inez giggled deliciously. "A nice sea monster, once you get to know him, Helen."

"No, thank you. I'll make my own dates in the future. So, I thought these guys were finished with you."

"Just follow-up," Justin interrupted, extending his hand then gently pulling the young woman in like a rope. "Appreciate it if you'd keep this business under wraps. All right, Inez? Helen?"

Helen slid her hand from his and drew an imaginary zipper across her lavender lips. "Appetizers and specials are on the board over there. I'll bring you menus in a minute. Meanwhile, what can I get you guys to drink?"

"Inez?" Justin asked politely.

"I'll have a diet Coke, lemon, no ice."

"Nothing for me at the moment. But you can bring half a carafe of red with the meal. Two glasses."

"Burgundy, Chianti or Merlot?"

Justin looked across at his dinner guest. "Name your poison, darlin'," Justin offered genteelly, watching Inez's enthusiasm bloom.

The young woman glowed. "Merlot, please."

Helen leaned over the table and lowered her voice. "He ain't no cop, Inez," she said, staring directly into Justin's dark brown eyes. "But he is a gentleman. Still, I'd watch my step if I were you."

"No, I saw his badge and have his card, Helen," Inez said defensively. "He's a dick, all right."

Helen looked from Justin to her friend. "Guess you'd know that better than I," she said, waving the fingers of her right hand held at shoulder level before turning and taking her leave.

Inez lowered her eyes and bit her bottom lip. "Sorry about that. She can be a gas."

"Just as long as she doesn't pass it here."

Inez burst out laughing again. "You're a trip, you know that?"

Justin forgot about her crooked yellow teeth and skewed smile. "How about we pick some appetizers before Helen comes back?"

"Going all out, sport?"

"I got a hunch you're gonna help me nail these guys, Inez."

"What did they do?"

"Told you before. It's police business."

"You sound just like those other cops who came around."

"You give them a height and hair description same way you gave me?"

Inez nodded. "Told them just like I'm tellin' you. They tried to put words in my mouth, but I told them what I saw. The pink-eyed creep sat with his back to the door. The other guy sat facing front."

"Tell me about this other prick."

"Oh, no, Detective Barnes. He was really and truly quite nice."

"Really?"

"Oh, yes. Most definitely."

"Leave you a nice tip, did he?"

Inez anxiously set her eyes on the appetizer board.

Helen returned with Inez's drink. "One diet Coke, lemon, no ice and some menus. Be back in a moment to take your order."

"Hold on a second, Helen. You like shellfish, Inez?"

"Sure."

Justin quickly studied the board. "Half-a-dozen clams Casino; half-a-dozen oreganata."

Helen jotted down the order and poised her pen. "Do you still want the Merlot with your meal, or should I bring it with the appetizers?"

"What an efficient waitress you are," Justin responded sincerely. "Bring the wine with the appetizers."

Helen took her leave.

"So, did this nice fella leave you a good tip?" Justin pressed.

"I was hoping you wouldn't come back to that."

Justin remained silent.

"What I did wasn't so nice, but I can explain."

Justin didn't say a word.

Inez lowered her voice to a whisper. "He left me twenty dollars, which I immediately questioned. But he insisted there was no mistake. So I stuck it in my apron and put a ten in the tip jar we all share. No one ever leaves a twenty-dollar tip in a deli. And how would that bitch, Susan, I work with ever know? That's why I did it, Detective. Because the woman's a bitch from the word go. God, I can't believe I'm telling you all this." Inez went into her handbag and brought out a packet of tissues, bringing a single sheet to her eyes. "Sorry."

Justin reached into his back pocket and withdrew his wallet. He removed a ten-dollar bill and pushed it across the tablecloth toward her.

"What are you doing?"

"Paying for information, Inez."

"I can't take—"

"Shut up and listen to me very carefully. All right?"

Inez nodded her head vigorously, took another tissue and dabbed her eyes and nose. "Sorry," she repeated.

"There are two kinds of sorry people in this sorry-ass world we live in, Inez. People who are sorry they get caught, and those who are truly sorry for what they do sometimes. You fall into the latter category. Understand? Now, you'll take this money and put it back in that tip jar tomorrow, hear?"

Inez's shoulders were trembling. "I'll put it back," she promised. "But I won't take your money, Detective."

"Look at me."

Inez raised her head and met his eyes.

"The information you just gave me regarding this albino's height and hair, Inez? Very important, like I said. Now, I've got to know if what you're telling me is absolutely accurate or not. If I can find these guys, I might be able to save some lives. I don't want to see you sorry like this tomorrow for having told me less than the truth today."

Inez looked Justin squarely in the eyes. "I told you everything, Detective. I told you before about those piggy pink peepers of his. Running his eyes over me while I poured their coffees—" she elaborated through a sniffle "—spilling his cream. The cream in the container, I mean," she giggled nervously. "Later, he spilled some sugar because he was laughing so hard, which I cleaned up right away."

"Whoa! Who spilled sugar and cream? The albino or the other fellow?"

"The albino. He kept pouring tons of each in his coffee. Light and sweet was how he took it."

"And you're sure it was the albino."

"Absolutely. The other guy took his black. I had to come back four times with full containers of cream for the creep. Everything I'm telling you is absolutely so."

"I believe you, Inez. I truly do. Now, please take this ten and put it back tomorrow. And don't ever do anything like that again that you'll be sorry for later. It's simply not worth it."

Inez shook her head. "This dinner is payment enough. You're treating me like a princess, Detective."

"Please call me Justin."

Inez smiled and nodded. "Justin. I like that name a lot."

"Well, I'm stuck with it whether I like it or not."

"Justin's a fine name, and you're a fine man, and I mean that."

"Thank you."

"You're welcome."

"Now, before I burst your bubble and tell you we're goin' Dutch treat next time out, I want you to take and put that sawbuck in your bag, girl. Hear me?"

Inez scrunched her shoulders as her eyes lit up like a pair of halogens. "Next time out?"

"Why not? We only have till ten o'clock, and I believe you've got more information stored in that pretty head of yours than you could possibly imagine."

"I do?"

"Yep. Besides, I want you to sleep on some questions that you might not be able to answer here tonight. Okay?"

"Sure."

"Now, put that bill away before I make you leave the tip. And believe me, I'm a pretty big tipper myself."

"You're just pretty," Inez replied warmly, then blushed. "I know my shortcomings, though. But once I get to the dentist, I'm going to straighten out my life," she avowed, finally taking the bill and depositing it into her handbag.

"Ah, there's Helen with our wine and appetizers," Justin said happily, spying the server across the room, just off the kitchen.

"And not a minute too soon."

"You that hungry, too?"

Inez giggled and waved away the question. "With that ten on the table, she'd have thought the worst."

"Oh, I'd have told her it was change you gave me from a hundred," he teased.

"And why ten bucks, Justin Barnes? Thinking that I'd even give you change," she gave back in spades.

"Carfare back to Shirley. Oops."

"That your girlfriend?"

"That's where I live. Mastic/Shirley. Dividing line; between the two towns."

"Then why the oops?"

"Cop never tells a paid informant where he lives."

"I'm no informant."

"Sure you are."

"Am not."

"Did you just give me information?"

"Sure, but—"

Helen set the dishes down and kept her tongue.

"Did you not accept money?" Justin needled.

"Shut up."

"You's a paid informant, woman."

Helen was shaking her head in an *I told you so* fashion. "Did I, or did I not tell you to watch yourself with this guy, Inez?" she mouthed-off as she poured the wine.

"Shut up, Helen," Inez snapped.

"Can't."

"Why not?"

"Because I want to get your order in."

"We haven't even had our appetizers or looked at the menus yet."

"Trying to do you a favor, friend. Kitchen's backed up and—"

"Whatta you running out of back there?"

"Patience."

"Justin loves flounder; he told me on the way over."

"Well, we've got plenty of that. Nice and fresh. Not frozen."

"Then we'll give you a holler when we're ready."

"I'm off in ten minutes."

"Then why do you even care?"

"Habit."

"Break it."

"I break them every day."

"Your *bad* habits? I rather doubt that," Inez mocked.

"Glasses and dishes."

"That's what I figured."

"If you decide on the veal, and I don't mean sometime toward the end of this century, you're going to have to speak up now. Two orders left."

"You know I love the veal."

"Rollatini with prosciutto. Yes?"

"Great."

"Pasta?"

"Penne."

"Justin? Flounder, plain or crab-stuffed?" Helen asked politely.

Justin had followed the playful back-and-forth bantering like a ping-pong match, deciding the competition to be a draw.

"Crab-stuffed, please."

"Mashed or baked?"

"Mashed."

"Gravy?"

"You bet."

"Vegetables are mixed."

"Fine."

"Be back shortly." Helen left the two of them to their appetizers.

"Inez."

"What?"

"Did this fellow sitting across from the albino ever call him Milky, by name?"

"Why, yes he did. When the container of sugar slipped from the other fella's oily fingers, 'cause he ordered his Italian Hero nice and wet, and he made a mess on the table like I told you before, he first called him butterfingers. Then, 'cause the man's lips were covered with this milky, oily mess, his friend said, 'Hey, you know. I think I'm going to call you Milky, too, from now on.' Those two shared a great big laugh over that one."

Justin nodded discerningly. "Can you tell me how much you think this Milky guy would weigh in at, Inez?"

"Oh, I'd put him somewhere between one eighty-five and one ninety . . . give or take two submarine sandwiches he devoured all by himself," she answered with a grin, removing a clam from its shell with the wrong fork before placing the colorful morsel into her mouth.

Justin raised his glass to her health.

"Got another confession," she offered, picking up her glass and touching his.

"Tell Father Barnes."

"I always thought this wine was pronounced Mer*lot*, like in p*lot*," she said, taking a single sip.

"Want to hear *my* confession?"

"Sure."

"Two years ago, I couldn't even read or write."

"Get out of here."

"It's true."

"Then how did you become a detective?"

"I'm not."

"Then what are you?"

"I'm a paid assassin for Suffolk County P.D."

Inez put down her drink and absolutely roared.

Justin took a sip and laughed, too.

"You have got to be the funniest man in the whole world, Detective Justin Barnes. A regular rip."

"That's me."

"Do you think you'll find these guys you're after, Justin?"

"Oh, indeed I do."

Chapter 46

Theo stood just outside the doorway to his office on the second floor. Directly across the hallway, two detectives in shirt sleeves sat in apparent apprehension behind their cluttered desks as Justin railed before the commanding officer about the incompetence of certain members of a certain team. The seated pair suddenly rose from their chairs as the maverick physically moved the lieutenant toward the threshold. Theo stiffened his body to block the entrance.

"Fine," Justin blew. "You don't wanna do this behind closed doors? You want to do it out here in the open? Fine by me."

"I want you the hell out of here, is what I want," Theo stated angrily.

"You don't wanna hear what I have to say? You want me the hell out of here?"

"I want you in another county. I want you out of the state, in fact."

Several detectives came hurrying along the hallway toward the ruckus and joined the two men standing on either side of Justin's heels.

"For openers, the albino at that deli in Cutchogue stood five-foot-six or seven—tops, Theo," Justin bellowed. "Milky is six-foot-one in stocking feet," he managed to get out of his mouth as one of the detectives tried to grab hold of him.

"—fuckin' hands off-a me, asshole," Justin parried—and a detective sergeant flew back against the wall.

Another detective of gargantuan proportion grabbed Justin in a headlock.

In a single sweeping motion, Justin broke the hold and easily sent the burly figure head over heels, landing him solidly against the tile floor to the sound of a sickening CRACK. The cop screamed bloody murder as a number of detectives pulled Justin aside, pinning the civilian firmly against a wall.

"Let him go!" Theo ordered.

Six men held him fast.

"I said, let him go."

The band of men backed off. Justin straightened out the collar of his shirt, mumbling to himself, massaging the side of his neck. The cop on the floor was holding his elbow, shrilling and writhing in pain. Four of his buddies went to his aid, lifting the big man back to his feet before escorting him away.

"Get in my fucking office before I have you shot," Theo commanded.

"What the fuck-a you gawking at?" Justin barked, taking a giant step toward the pair who stood like stone pillars in his path. "Huh?"

The two parted like the proverbial Red Sea.

"Get-in-here," Theo repeated, taking Justin firmly by a sleeve.

"Ah, yessa." Justin shuffled through the open doorway, allowing himself to be led like a misbehaving child. Once inside, Justin shook off Theo's grip. "You could have avoided all that crap out there, Lieutenant. But you just couldn't—"

"Don't you dare stand there and lecture me on what I could and couldn't have done. Now, you sit down there and shut your mouth."

Justin strode heatedly over to a corner of Theo's desk and immediately took a seat.

"I should really lock your ass up and throw away the key," the head of homicide burned.

"No. I think you should swallow it along with some of that fucking Irish pride and thickheadedness."

The detective lieutenant sighed heavily, sinking into his chair. "How did you find her, J? I gotta worry about a snitch now?"

Justin had to laugh. "How did I find her, he asks. 'A deli out East,' you said. How many albinos you think we got parading around out there?"

Theo was boiling mad but also seemed impressed. "Took ten of my men two days just to pick up a lead. Awful lot of delis on those two Forks," he tested.

"Tell me about it. But I got lucky. I figured I'd find the deli and your waitress on the North Fork."

"How?" the lieutenant demanded.

Justin knew that he had the man's interest now. "The place Milky's staying at is on the North Fork."

"Yeah, so tell me something I don't know."

"I believe Emery and his accomplice snatched him from his flat. I didn't think they'd travel very far. Emery never does. Does his victims close to where he holes up."

"So, we're back to this phantom albino of yours?" Theo smirked.

"No phantom, Theo. Emery's man is shorter than Milky by at least a half a foot, and with thicker, longer hair. A good twenty pounds heavier, too."

"Not too much of a coincidence for you that this guy can run circles around Ruth and Notaro, and did? Literally. Your wheelman. A guy they clearly saw sitting well up in the driver's seat?"

"Problem being, you're all shortsighted, near as I can see," Justin jabbed.

Theo's face reddened. "You're getting to be a regular wise guy. Know that?"

"What I know is that Milky would never do anything to harm me. I know that it wasn't Milky at the Sports Bar in Wading River with Emery. I also know that he would never run off without a word."

"No, just his clothes and his car. And I'll remind you that there were no signs of a struggle at his apartment, J." Theo got up and went over to a window. "What do you think happened to him? Huh?"

"Told you. I think Emery's got 'im."

"Well, so do I," Theo blasted. "In the palm of his hand."

"Not funny, Theo. I think Emery's holding him captive, or worse."

Theo turned around and shook his head, still unconvinced. "My detectives interviewed this waitress, Inez Diaz. Twice."

"Your detectives went in with preconceived notions after that incident in Wading River. It's you and your detectives who are falling right into Clarence Emery's trap."

"My boys came home with a different description than what you're handing me now with regard to weight, hair and height," the man declared. "You think that just might be because you persuaded

Miss Diaz to see what *you* wanted her to see? Huh?"

Justin shook his head emphatically. "I spent hours with her, Theo."

"And maybe when you got finished with her, she'd have said Milky was a Martian, if you'd wanted her to."

Justin wanted to drop the little man precisely where he stood. Only the clear glass partition separating them from the hallway filled with suits and sensibilities prevented him from doing so.

"You're a piece of work, Theo. I swear to God."

"J. I've got a lot of work to do. I want you to go home and forget about this business. Let us handle it. If you don't, if you cause any kind of trouble like you caused out there, I'm going to have you locked up. And I'm not fooling. And put that bogus badge, which I'm not supposed to know about, on my desk—right now. I don't want you contacting Inez Diaz, or anyone else for that matter. You have no authorization. Am I clear on that?"

"Clear as Clarence."

"What's that supposed to mean?"

Justin held the badge in abeyance and his tongue in check.

"J. If you had something good, I mean something absolutely solid, I'd take a second look. But I'm afraid you're just spinning your wheels. You thought you had a friend, and he betrayed you. You refuse to see that. I feel for you. You may not believe that, but I do."

"Finished?"

Theo looked at Justin with sheer contempt. "*You* certainly are. Badge and ID. Now. Push the envelope, and I'll pull your pistol permit."

Justin shook his head. "Sir, I save my best for last."

Theo stared at Justin queerly.

"Milky is lactose intolerant and diabetic. This impostor kept adding cream and sugar to his coffee. Milky wouldn't do that in a million years."

"Inez Diaz told you this?"

Justin nodded in the affirmative. "She kept refilling his empty cup. And this guy kept pouring heaps of sugar and cream to the top. My man, Milky, takes his black, like me. Like Emery, too."

Theo walked over to his desk and picked up the phone. "Get me Bobby Lee, now!" A moment later, a stern look crossed the lieutenant's face. "I don't give a flying good fuck if his elbow or *asshole* is broken! Quite frankly, I don't think he'd even know the difference. No, I'll wait."

"God, is that who you sent out there to question her?"

Theo put a hand over the mouthpiece. "He was available, J."

"So's his wife from what I hear. Had I known it was him, I would have dropped him on his head instead of his back out there. Who'd you send with him?"

"Hendricks. Why?"

"Why? Because I once watched Hendricks question his golden retriever for twenty minutes as to why Gretchen wouldn't fetch the fucking newspaper that he was beating her with. That's why."

"What do you want from me, J?"

"Two discreet detectives of the right complexion to canvass a twelve-block area surrounding Milky's flat. Darkies, in case you have trouble in translation. Shouldn't be too difficult to find someone who might have seen one or two albinos in a black neighborhood, now would it?"

"Why did you ever stick him in The Greens, J? Just tell me that."

"Cheap rent, which I'm payin' for, and proximity to Ursula's."

"Ursula's home isn't in The Greens."

"Close enough. Right along the outskirts."

"I hear she's staying at your place now."

"Off and on. She's safer there."

"Well, if it's any comfort, I got Mosely and Richardson watching her back."

"Good men, Mosely and Richardson." Justin nodded his thanks.

"Glad you approve of some folks around here." Theo took his hand off the mouthpiece. "What do you mean he can't come to the phone right now?" The commander listened to someone's bellyaching for a few seconds before slamming down the receiver in disgust.

Chapter 47

Clarence Emery descended the cellar stairs with his accomplice, Vito Vitalo.

"Well, well, Vito. Looks like Milky here has a splitting headache,"

Milky drifted in and out of consciousness like the steady rhythm of a tide. Several times a day, in fact. His most lucid moments were when he was being fed soup or other liquids.

"So far, you haven't told me very much at all about Justin Barnes, Milky."

"He hates white folks," the bloody figure mumbled and wept.

"You must have told me that half a dozen times, Milky. How come he likes *you* so much?" Emery put forth scornfully. "Tell me. He a queer?"

"No."

"Why are you two friends?"

"I don't know."

"Oh, but I think you do."

"Just are."

"Were you his asshole buddy in the literal sense? Did you bend over backwards and forwards to please him, Milky?"

"No!" Milky cried. "He was and is and always will be my friend. He protected me in the can."

Emery laughed. "Sure he didn't put it up in there? What do you think, Vito? You know these types as well as any man. Do you think Milky, here, took or takes it up the ass?"

"I don't know. Maybe we could find out with that broomstick over there."

"Pl-please don't hurt me anymore . . . please," he pleaded. "I've done everything you asked me to do. I've told you everything I know. I'll say an-anything you want me to say . . . do anything you want. Just please don't hur-hurt me anymore."

"I haven't hurt you, Milky. Vito here hasn't even begun to turn the screws to you," Emery said calmly.

"You have! I h-heard . . . . heard my head crack." Milky raised his eyes as if he were trying to see inside his own skull. "The pain is unbearable," he murmured, drooling a stream of blood. "If you're going . . . . going to kill me, kill me fast. Please. Just shoot me. Don't kill me slowly like this. I nev-never did anything to hurt you."

"And I told you that you did. So there."

"I can't b-bear this any longer," Milky wept. "Kill me now. Get it over with. Please."

"You will be amazed at just how much more pain you can and will endure. Trust me, Milky. Trust me. Vito, would you please crank that handle up a notch?"

"NOOOO!" Milky howled. "No more. No more. Please, no more." Milky lost consciousness once again.

"Handy having a stove, sink and refrigerator in the basement, Vito. No?"

"Handy," Vito said sullenly.

"Well, you don't sound too happy about it."

"I'll be happy when we're out of here."

"Soon, Vito. Soon." Emery studied Milky for a moment. "Are you back with us, Milky my boy? No? Vito, do me a favor and fill that mop bucket over there with cold water. We'll do like they do in the movies and douse him. See if that brings him around or drowns him."

Vito walked over to the double sink, filled the plastic bucket to the top, then wheeled and raised the heavy pail over to the platform.

"Right in his face, Vito. That should clean him up a bit, too. Good man. Good man. We don't want to give the lady of the house too much of a fright when she discovers him." Clarence Emery began to giggle. "Justin Barnes is another story. I want him stark-raving mad," the serial killer proclaimed and positively pealed.

Chapter 48

Justin took Ursula's house keys and handed her the mail. The two entered the modest dwelling. He switched on the light, turned off the alarm, closed and double-locked the front door, finally anchoring the steel security bar firmly into the floor plate. She followed closely as he crossed the living room and headed toward the kitchen, flipping on two more lights along the way.

"Feel better now, Miss Nervous Wreck?" he needled, more than a bit relieved himself, although he didn't want to admit it. "I told you, you got good people watching this place 24/7. I just wish you would have waited awhile."

"Three days is awhile. Besides, I couldn't stay away forever. It's good to be back home," she smiled happily, starting to relax. "Coffee?"

"Fine." Justin stepped into the hallway and ran his eyes along a bookcase, taking a volume off a shelf. "Ever read this *Moby Dick*?"

"Can't hear you."

Justin walked back into the kitchen with the book. "Ever read this?"

Ursula looked over a shoulder and nodded. "Only a dozen times."

"Then it's good, I guess."

"You guessed right. You can borrow it if you'd like. But I want it back."

"Guess that's what borrowing is all about," he chaffed.

"Not when *you* borrow. When *you* borrow something, I never get it back."

"So what you're saying is that I'm a thief."

"Not unless you stole my half-and-half along with half a quart of milk," she complained, stooping and staring interminably into the refrigerator before navigating a hand past jars of relish and olives and plastic containers—sliding bottles of juice and cans of diet soda aside. "Shit. I could swear . . . ."

"You just did. But I've heard worse. Still, never-ever from your lips," he needled, beginning to unwind, too.

"Well, *you* can have coffee 'cause you take it black anyhow. I guess I'll have to settle for tea." Ursula removed a lemon from a bin, then went over to the sink and filled a two-quart pot with cold water.

Justin was flipping through the pages of the book. "How long did it take you to read this?"

"Oh, I don't know. Maybe a few days the first time around." Ursula measured out two tablespoons of French Roast, poured half the water into the coffee maker, set the pot upon the stove, then lit the burner. "Be a few minutes."

Several minutes later, the two of them sat down at the kitchen table to tea and coffee and butter cookies. Justin was still absorbed in the tome.

"I can't believe someone can sit down and write a book this big. It must have taken years. Guy probably wrote it in prison," he joked.

"Put the book down and drink your coffee while it's hot." Ursula reached for the sugar bowl and removed the lid. "Well, I'll be damned." She picked herself up and went over to the pantry, reaching for and withdrawing an open five-pound bag of sugar. "Here. Take this." Justin got up, and she handed him the bag. "Over by the sink, please. You pour; I'll hold the bowl. Otherwise, we'll have a mess."

"Yes, ma'am," he said, setting the classic aside.

"Weird."

"What's weird?"

"I could have sworn I had half-and-half and milk in the house before I left. And now this sugar."

"What's the matter with it?" Justin tipped the bag and carefully poured a steady stream of crystals into the ceramic bowl.

"I would never rip open and leave the bag like that. Was this you?"

The flow of sugar fell past the bowl and into the sink as he abruptly set the bag down upon the countertop.

"What's wrong with you?" she chided.

Justin gestured for her to remain still as he withdrew his

handgun and moved cautiously from the kitchen to the adjoining room, cradling his weapon close to his chest before rounding the corner and springing forward like a cat. Crossing the space, he opened wide the bathroom door, stepping in and sliding aside the shower curtain, scanning and fanning the stall with the pistol extended the length of his arm. Next, he thoroughly checked Ursula's bedroom and all her closets, satisfied that they were secure. Under the bed. Then the guest room. Finally, he moved toward the cellar stairs, yanking open its door. The single bulb was burning dimly. Justin started down the steps. The smell of fresh cut lumber, combined with a rancid odor, was overpowered by a putrid stench that filled his nostrils as he cautiously made his way around the staircase. There on a small Formica table were the missing containers of milk and cream, along with cups and bowls and silverware. Suddenly, his head went light and his heart grew heavy at the figure standing upright off to the side of an old table saw. Milky. The man's skull was crushed within the monstrous jaws of a makeshift wooden vise.

"No," he whispered. Then louder. "Oh God, no!" Justin's heart was pounding fiercely as he approached a puddle below the platform upon which his friend stood fast. "What did they do to you, Milky?" Milky's head, face and body were streaked with blood. "Why in the world would they do this to you, good friend?" But of course, Justin knew the answer.

"Who are you talking to down there?" Ursula demanded with a pitch to her voice that sent an additional chill along his spine.

"Don't come down here," he insisted in a tone that told her she had better listen. "Stay up there."

"I'm calling the police," she yelled from the top of the stairs, gnawing the nails of two fingers between gnashing teeth.

"You do that, Ursula," Justin said in such a way that sent her scurrying for the phone. "You do that little thing," he repeated quietly, the emotion of hatred—fraught with guilt—welling up within his brain, then spreading through his entire being.

He stepped up to the body and examined the red, white and blue 3½ x 2-inch P.B.A. card held fast behind the elastic waistband of Milky's bloody briefs. The emblem depicted in the center of the card loomed in front of Justin. Its purple band and silver buckle above the brim and below the crown came slowly into focus as Justin brushed away his tears. Stars and stripes encompassed the symbolic gray felt campaign hat. NEW YORK STATE TROOPERS underscored the cover. HONORARY 2000, printed in yellow, ran the margins. *Serving Our Members For 56 Years* was inscribed along the bottom of Vito Vitalo's two-year-old calling card.

Two phone calls to and from the New York State Police revealed that a state trooper—an albino—from the upstate Monroe Barracks on Dunderberg Road in Monroe, had retired the year before. The five-foot-six, one hundred and eighty-seven pound decorated officer enjoyed a spotless record spanning eighteen years of exemplary service until an incident occurred—an incident no one wanted to elaborate on at the moment; an incident that apparently forced the thirty-eight-year old veteran's early departure from law enforcement and ruined an otherwise resplendent career. A messy divorce, a year of reclusion, the sale of the couple's home, then Vito's sudden disappearance—that was all the authorities could or would speak about.

How Vitalo hooked up with Emery was anybody's guess. Detective Lieutenant Theodore Groche learned that a deal had been cut, whereby the trooper would resign rather than face serious criminal charges. The record was sealed. The state boys were stonewalling. Groche reminded them all that he was investigating a homicide directly connected to the ex-state trooper. Theo's boss, the new police commissioner, found it necessary to threaten a defiant judge with a leak to the press if certain information was not forthcoming.

In the end, it was revealed that there was serious suspicion and speculation that Vitalo may have murdered a female motorist on his watch. No proof. Only supposition and conjecture. For one reason or another, the Orange County district attorney's office, seated in upstate Goshen, did not feel comfortable going to trial with purely circumstantial evidence. The prosecutor probably believed that Vitalo's flawless record would prejudice the jury in the defendant's favor. At least that's what Theo surmised from the set of sketchy circumstances.

Chapter 49

Tomas and Jacqueline Rubino passed through the rear of the restaurant shortly before it opened for lunch. As manager, she usually arrived for work at 4:30 in the afternoon to prepare for the busy dinner crowd, but Tomas had insisted she stagger her hours for no other reason than to break her set routine. The two took a seat and found a moment alone at a table off the kitchen.

The exhausted woman threw up her hands in frustration. "I'm falling behind in everything," she complained. "I've got a million things to do around the house. I've got—"

"You've got things to do right here," her husband stated firmly. "If Emery knows you're at the restaurant, instead of playing musical seats with that policewoman, he'll get tired and leave," he reasoned reassuringly. "What's so funny?"

Jacqueline's smile evaporated as quickly as it had materialized. "Sorry."

"No, I want to know what's so damn funny," he insisted.

The hint of a smile reappeared upon his wife's angelic face. "It's musical *chairs*."

"What?"

"Musical chairs," Jacqueline repeated. "Not musical seats," she began to explain, unable to contain a giggle and a grin.

"Chairs. Seats. What's the goddamn difference?"

"Nothing really."

"You better smarten up and listen to me. This is no game."

Jacqueline wanted to tell her husband that is exactly what it was. Emery's game. Not hers . . . that she was a player who had little choice, now, but to see things through to the end.

"Tomas—" she looked deeply into her husband's dark brown eyes "—I love you, and I know you mean to protect me." She struggled for the right words and an easy way to tell him to back off.

There wasn't one. "I know you don't want to hear this, but my changing hours and spending most of my time here with you isn't going to change whatever sick plan Emery has in his equally sick mind. But they'll get him," she said with utmost conviction, glad that she hadn't used the contraction, *we'll.*

Tomas was shaking his head. "Leave well enough alone and he'll go elsewhere, especially if he sees you're here with family. Look at the time and energy all of you wasted. You have a double: your policewoman friend, Ruth. So Emery went out and found himself a double. A state trooper, no less."

"Shh," she whispered, placing a finger gently to his lips. "Uncle Phil and Frankie are not to know about this."

"Emery showed all of you that two can play the same game," he continued, lowering his voice. "So let it be over. He'll get tired and he'll go away."

Jacqueline wished his words were true, but she knew in her heart and mind that it was far from over. The game would not be over until Emery was dead. Then and only then would her family and friends find any peace. She held her husband's stare before finally nodding in agreement, forcing a counterfeit smile that belied her good looks and character.

"That's my girl," he said with some relief, putting on a false face, too, that assumed an air of great confidence and calm. "We have the state and local police and others helping us. We have our own security force. Emery will get tired, and he'll go far away. Okay?"

"Okay," she acquiesced with fingers crossed and hidden within her lap. "Just don't complain that things aren't getting done around the house."

"Me? When do I ever complain?"

The two of them shared a light but genuine laugh, despite their unsettling situation.

Phil and Frankie entered through the front dining room and went over to the couple.

"Glad to see you two smiling for a change," Phil interrupted politely, addressing his niece directly, "and that you're here nice and early, Jackie."

Frankie nodded in agreement.

"What's up?" she questioned, anticipating a problem with

perhaps a waitress who called in sick at the last moment, or a last-minute item that needed to be picked up at market.

Phil shrugged his shoulders. "Nothing. Just glad you're here," he repeated.

Again, Frankie nodded in accord.

Jacqueline looked from Frankie to Phil, then back to her husband. "Ah, a conspiracy," she acknowledged, smiling warmly at her caring and loving family.

Phil leaned forward and put an arm around Tomas' shoulder. "Everything all right?"

"Never better," Tomas answered, getting up from his seat.

"That's good. Very good," Phil added with satisfaction.

Frankie's gaze strayed to one of the chairs. He stooped forward and picked something from its seat. "What's this?"

The four of them looked at the feathered item curiously.

"Must have fallen off a customer's hat or something," Frankie suggested, turning the streamer fly over in his palm.

The exhausted woman stood and hunched her slender shoulders. "Probably some woman's pin," she said and yawned politely, covering her pretty mouth.

"Nothing to hold it," Frankie noted, running a finger along its colorful shank. "Probably broke off."

"Let me see that," Phil said, taking the decorative article from the young man's hand and examining the fly carefully. "It's not broke. See? No clasp. Not a pin. The point's been filed so nobody hurts themselves. A decoration, is all."

"That's what I said," Frankie chimed in. "Probably fell off some guy's fishing hat. You know, with all those flashy flies," he illustrated, circling an index finger above the top of his dirty-blond hair as if he were drawing himself a halo.

"Jesus, Joseph and Mary!" Jacqueline blurted out, grabbing the streamer from her uncle's hand.

"What?" Phil asked, taken aback.

Jacqueline scrutinized the lengths of pale-white hackle and hair and the pair of pinkish eyes with bright red pupils that seemed to stare directly back at her as she turned the artificial fly over in her hand.

With furrowed brows, the three men stared down at the

streamer.

"Mother of God," she intoned, dropping the fly to the table. "It's him."

"Him, who?" Phil asked apprehensively, fearing he knew the answer.

"Emery. He was here."

"Impossible," Tomas insisted. "Absolutely impossible."

Jacqueline firmly shook her pretty head. "He was here," she repeated quietly. "It was either Emery or that trooper."

"What trooper?" Phil and Frankie asked in unison.

Jacqueline stood silent.

"What trooper?" Phil repeated his question.

"A *state* trooper?" Frankie queried.

Jacqueline remained silent.

"You tell us what's going on, Jackie," Phil put to his niece insistently. "We have a right to know."

"I can't discuss it," she said firmly. "It's classified."

"Classified!?" Phil excoriated in total disbelief. "You're my niece, for God's sake. We have no secrets. You're not the police."

"We had a state trooper in here for dinner the other night," Frankie set forth matter-of-factly, pointing to a corner table next to the fireplace. "Sat right at that table over there, facing the wall. Hat and dark glasses. Never took them off. I thought maybe he was a member of Justin and Jackie's team that I'm not supposed to know about."

"That's right!" Phil recalled aloud.

"What night?" Jacqueline demanded.

"Thursday night," Frankie replied.

"Of course it was Thursday night!" she said with sudden and utter understanding. She looked at her husband. "He *knew* both you and I were off that evening."

"Who is this guy?" Phil demanded.

Jacqueline ignored the question and began shooting a barrage of questions at her uncle and cousin as she thrust a chair aside and strode over to a phone behind the bar.

Chapter 50

Addressing Detective Lieutenant Theodore Groche and his people, the forensic scientist held up a clear plastic evidence envelope containing the four-inch saltwater fly found at the Bella Sera Restaurant in West Tiana. "This streamer, gentlemen, imitates a menhaden," Lester Townsend explained.

Justin stood at the rear of the room filled with mostly homicide detectives.

"A what?" one of the suits questioned.

"Bunker bait for bluefish," Justin chimed in.

"Actually, any of the Clupeidae of the genus Brevoortia," hair and fiber expert Townsend pontificated. "A classification of teleostean fishes comprising sardines, shads, herrings and menhaden; the latter of which is commonly referred to as, yes, bunker or mossbunker. Very good, sir," the specialist said condescendingly. "You're Mr. Barnes, I believe?"

Justin nodded.

"So, troops, bunker bait for bluefish is certainly on the mark; not to mention striped bass that enjoy those oily creatures equally as well. A good friend of mine ties this streamer in a chartreuse pattern— only with black and golden eyes. However, it's more the overall configuration than its color or the eyes that attracts Pomatomus saltatrix; that is, bluefish, gentlemen," the scientist continued, wrinkling his nose and sticking out his tongue in sheer disgust. "Yucky, yucky stuff."

"What are you talking about?" one of the seasoned detectives protested. "Bluefish are delicious."

"Delicious when they're small," another man argued, facing the palms of his hands less than a foot apart.

"Cocktail blues, they're called," Ruth O'Connor rejoined. "I catch them all the time. Two to three pound class."

"They're the best eating size," a fellow officer agreed. "Dynamite on the grill."

"Well, I wouldn't take one if you gave it to me," Townsend reinforced the point. "Couldn't care less if it were two or twenty pounds. I wouldn't feed it to my cat."

"The really little ones are fun to catch and eat," a rookie detective piped up enthusiastically. "I'm talking only a few inches bigger than that streamer you're holding. My son and I catch them by the bucketful."

"Right," another veteran detective reflected. "Used to be you could keep them all, too. But now the DEC sets a limit. Ten, I think."

"Ten per person," Theo cut in rather impatiently, catching the eye of his fledgling. "So, your son and you can still come home with a pailful, Noel. Now, if we can all get back to the business at hand."

"Snappers," someone said, paying no heed to the commander.

"What was that?" Theo snapped.

"The little guys. They're called snappers. Baby bluefish," another clarified.

"I still wouldn't give a one of them to my cat." Townsend insisted.

"You and your cat don't know what you're missing," the father-fisherman proclaimed.

Lowering his voice, Theo shook his head and leaned in toward Justin. "You started all this, you know."

"Just wanted that horse's ass up there to speak plain English, boss," Justin offered in explanation. "Menhaden to some of these suburban and city geeks is just a piece of expensive real estate south of the Harlem River. To Kilpatrick, over there, it's a cocktail with a dash of bitters and a maraschino cherry."

Theo could not help but smile. "You're a rip."

Justin could not help but frown, thinking of Milky lying in his grave: RIP.

"All right, all right," Doctor Townsend spoke up pompously, dimming the lights. He turned on the projector, then stepped up to the screen and tapped his pointer at the enlargement. "This is a blowup of the artificial that I'm sure you've all had a chance to examine by now. It was constructed by a professional flytier. Of this, there is no doubt. The hackle, that is the pale-white saddle feathers, here," he indicated, running the pointer along the length of the lure, "are from a common chicken." The mad scientist lowered his stick just long enough to cock his arms against his sides and cackle like a hen. Everyone laughed or smiled politely. "The hair, however, is human." The scientist encircled several strands of the thin white hair that swept rearward from the top of the streamer. "I'm sure you'll be interested to learn that these hairs belonged to one Melvyn Andrew Milken, a.k.a. Milky, who was Mr. Barnes' friend, I understand."

All heads turned to take Justin into their sights.

Justin flashed his eyes to the ceiling, then just as suddenly lowered them to the floor.

Those who refrained from taking notes, now had their noses in their notepads—scribbling as fast as the hair and fiber expert spoke.

"Now, the eyes, gentlemen. The eyes are of significant importance. The eyes are the window to your serial killer's soul . . . assuming, of course, that he even has one." The forensic scientist rested the tip of his pointer on the reddish-violet hue at the center of the streamer's pupil. "The eyes are an extremely accurate representation of Mr. Milken's orbs." Townsend hit the remote and a blowup of the menhaden's left eye matched the victim's in a striking juxtaposition that jolted one man in his seat.

"Jesus!" another homicide detective remarked.

Lester Townsend drew a concentric ring around the artificial eye. "Note the iris. Most folks believe that albinos have to have pinkish-reddish eyes, when, in fact, the color of the iris may vary from a muted gray to shades of blue and even brown—the latter of which is common in ethnic groups whose skin is of a darker pigmentation." Townsend was staring directly at Barnes. "The pinkish-reddish area we see here is reflected off the retina; that is, the membrane within the eye. It's very much like when the light from a flashbulb reflects the red-eye you see in photographs." The man paused as if being blinded by the flash of a camera, covering his eyes and staggering two steps backward for the full effect.

No one cracked a smile or batted an eye.

"Of course, lighting conditions vary. But let's not focus solely on color gradation. Let's look at this white blemish called Bitot's spots on the conjunctiva; that is, the mucous membrane that lines a good portion of the visible eye. Note how the two images correspond precisely. Next, let's compare their right eyes. Again, artificial and human." Townsend pressed the remote, then adjusted the focusing knob. "There we go. Note the same locations of the pinkish triangular-shaped mass called pterygium on the eyes' cornea."

"Wow!" Officer Ruth O'Connor replied in full appreciation for the detail she was witnessing on the screen. "I can't even apply mascara or eye shadow without making myself a mess."

"Take a look at this," Townsend declared, projecting all four images on the screen at one time. "Left eyes. Right eyes. Fly and fellow."

The slides showed up sharply, but the presentment was compact. Those toward the back of the room came forward for a better look. Those in front leaned well forward in their seats.

A moment later, Townsend raised the lights and turned off the projector.

Ruth's hand shot up together with her question. "What kind of material was used for the artificial eyes?"

"Good question, Officer O'Connor."

Ruth was surprised that Townsend knew her name, let alone the fact she was a bluecoat sitting in civilian clothes before him.

"A very good question, indeed. Any takers?"

"Glass."

"Plastic."

"Ceramic."

"Porcelain."

It was as if Lester Townsend delighted in shaking his head in the negative while announcing an implacable, "No."

"Mylar?" Justin questioned.

With wonder, the scientist fixed his eyes on Justin. "Once again, very good, sir. Hats off to you. You're absolutely correct."

Theo looked at Justin oddly, while the rest of the troops eyed the maverick with some suspicion—including Officer Ruth O'Connor.

"What's Mylar? And how did you happen to come up with that, J?" Ruth asked.

"Yeah, I gotta hear this one for myself," an undercover cop in tattered, dirty street clothes questioned as well.

Justin looked down in embarrassment. "To tell you the truth, I don't really know what Mylar is, actually. All I know is that my friend, Milky, made some of the eyes for his artificial flies from it. It's kind of like tinsel you use to decorate a Christmas tree. But the stuff he worked with usually came in sheets. He once told me how he spent hours crafting the eyes. Selecting just the right colors. Matching them to 'match the hatch,' he'd say. He was a perfectionist. I can tell you that." Justin left out the prison part of the story, which he figured most of them knew about anyway.

Lester Townsend could hardly wait to expound on the properties of the material but had restrained himself from interrupting until Justin finished speaking.

"Lady and gentlemen," the forensic expert continued with a grin, facetiously acknowledging the fact that he had a woman in the midst of more than a dozen men. "The chemical composition constituting—"

"Why, thank you," Ruth broke in politely. "You left me out of the mix when we first got started, Irwin Corey; but I'm glad you caught and corrected your faux pas. Now, just tell us what the fuck Mylar is and how it relates to this bug so that we can all get the hell out of here 'cause we got work to do, mister."

Two detectives sitting on either side of Ruth glanced over at one another. One came apart at the seams, while the other could barely keep a belly laugh from building.

Theo chuckled, shook and scratched his head.

Townsend appeared flustered but went on with his colloquy, ignoring the policewoman's rude remark. "Mylar is a trademark for a synthetic fiber; a thin, reflective, relatively strong polyester film used in photography, recording tapes and insulation products. Its reflective property particularly lends itself to the construction of both fresh and saltwater flies. It's a sought-after material by flytiers around the globe, sold in sheets and strands and tubes and even thread. It comes in a wide assortment of colors and shades thereof. Its strands and threads are generally used to wrap the body of a fly, glistening as it travels through the water column. The sky's the limit when it comes to utilizing this material, leaving construction to the imagination of the artisan.

"All sorts of artificials have been created to fool fishes," the man drawled on monotonously. "Minnows. Crabs. Shrimp. Et cetera." Townsend paused to pick up the envelope containing the streamer anew and held the item high above his head. "Mass-produced eyes are readily available by the millions; however, one cannot simply go out and purchase what you see here. These eyes have been meticulously sculpted from Mylar, then carefully layered to create not only the desired hue, but contour as well. They were not, as you can plainly see, just simply glued or tied in place as you would sew a button on a shirt. The workmanship is truly remarkable. Whoever tied this is a master flytier, as I said. An artist in the true sense of the word. Tiny pieces of pink, white, brown, red, blue and gray Mylar were used to construct the eyes, right down to those blemishes you saw magnified on the screen a moment ago; executed with precision."

Executed was the word that caught in Justin's craw. Milky was the flytier who produced the streamer that Townsend was holding in the air, Justin firmly believed. He remembered the day his friend had shown him a miniature crab he replicated from a color photograph, a crustacean the warden had wanted copied. Its mottled body was not made of Mylar, but rather a tiny nutshell . . . painted in acrylic . . . its little legs and larger claws finely formed from feathers and foam . . . wee eyes resting on short stalks made from molten monofilament. It was, indeed, a work of art. The warden had wanted two dozen, for openers, after seeing the finished product.

"This is simply a preliminary examination," Townsend went on to explain. "We're still processing information before we start dissecting this little fella. But we wanted to give you what we have at this particular juncture so that every swingin' dick can get their asses back to work," he remarked and grinned broadly, scanning the room before coming to rest his eyes fixedly on Officer Ruth O'Connor.

Chapter 51

It was late evening when the cell phone sounded atop the night table. Justin stirred and finally answered on the fifth ring.

"Yeah?"

"Hiya there, buddy."

Justin's gut wrenched. "Who's this?" he mumbled, though he believed he knew. There was no reply. Pushing back the top sheet and swinging his legs out of bed in a single motion, he leaned over and turned on a table lamp, then grabbed a notepad and pen from the pocket of his shirt that was draped across the back of a chair. "I asked who the fuck this is."

"It's Milky's executioner, Justin Barnes. Actually, I acted more in the capacity of the governor and decided not to commute his sentence," Clarence Emery answered through a chuckle.

The words cut through Justin like a steel blade, sending a chill across his shoulders and down the spine.

"You fucking bastard."

"Veritably, it was Vito who pulled the switch. Or should I say, really put the screws to Milky."

Justin held the phone in one hand; with the other he scribbled notes.

"Getting it all down, pal?"

Milky's mourner looked up toward two windows. The shades and curtains were drawn. Yet, he felt certain Emery was watching him —not in the physical sense, but in a sense that made no sense at all.

"Where are you, fuck-face?" Justin cursed the killer and the night.

"Not far from your thoughts, now am I, J? Did you like the little touches with the loose change on your bureau and the barbless hook they found in Bella Sera? I didn't want anyone there to prick themselves." The maniac giggled like a girl. "Theo and the team scratching their heads, are they? Come on, tell me. You know I'm dying to know."

"Oh, you're going to die, all right."

"Of course I'm going to die. But not tonight. Tonight, the trooper is going to die. He knows too much, you see. Vito's become a liability. You'll find his body in green pastures surrounded by still waters. You can't say that I don't give you guys and gals all kinds of clues. Bye for now, J." Emery terminated the conversation.

"Motherfuckin' , cocksuckin' son of a bitch," Justin blared into the mouthpiece of the cell phone in his trembling hand. A second later, the telephone on the other night table rang. Justin picked up where he left off, repeating the last line of profanity that had fallen on deaf ears.

"J."

"Gonna take you down. Gonna cut your fuckin' heart out. Hear me?"

"Guess he called you, too," Theo said calmly.

Justin slowly let the air out of his lungs before taking a deep breath, then expounded on Emery's conversation, leading up to and concluding with the madman's threat to kill the state trooper.

"Think there's anything to it?" Theo asked through a yawn.

"I really couldn't care less," the livid soul answered through his teeth. "Don't really give a fuck at all. It'll save me the trouble of puttin' down two scumbags if it's true."

"I hear you, J. Normally, I wouldn't lose any more sleep than I have already over something like this. But if we can find Vitalo, sooner than later, it's just that much closer we'll be to finding and nailing Emery. Early discovery may give us an important lead."

"I know, Theo. I know. Just let me have a second to wind down."

"I'll give you two . . . there. How's that? Now, let's start brainstorming these so-called clues of his and see what we can come up with. All right?"

"Yeah, sure. You wanna do this here and now? Or you wanna meet somewhere?"

"Here and now, partner."

"Oh, so now I'm your fucking partner."

"Don't start, J."

"No, I won't start. Meaning you can go first. 'Green pastures surrounded by still waters,' Theo. Just jump right in anytime, partner."

"Funny man."

"I'm waitin' on ya, boss."

"Twenty-third Psalm."

"Never heard of it."

"I can see this is going to be a long night."

"I put my Bible back where it really belongs."

"Okay. I'll play straight man. Where?"

"In some motel room drawer. Long time ago."

"That's what I figured."

Chapter 52

Ex-State Trooper Vito Vitalo's bones lay scattered throughout a rich green pasture on Shelter Island. The cows that grazed along the bank were raised strictly for milk rather than beef. Paradoxically, an outbuilding near the water's edge, where the murder actually occurred, appeared to be nothing short of a slaughterhouse.

The cruelty with which Emery had administered pain and punishment upon the man's body was noteworthy to say the least, as witnessed by teams of detectives and technicians teeming across the land and along the docks and shoreline—combing the entire property before returning to the butcher's block: a large rectangular table set in the center of an abandoned building where Vitalo's flesh had been carved clean of its skeletal frame. There at the dairy farm, in the steadily rising temperature of midmorning, authorities drew diagrams, took still and video pictures, ran tape measures, collected samples, compared notes, then simply shook and scratched their collective heads; not over any question concerning the crime scene in general, for things were pretty much cut-and-dried. Only in terms of trying to ascertain the reason *why* anyone would want to do what Emery obviously relished, did the police even bother to speculate.

Why on earth would a man cleave and carve another to the bone? The answer was basically elementary. The man in question, Clarence Emery, was, is and always would be, truly insane. Madness personified. Still and all, it was a concept that was difficult to grasp, even for the assembled group of seasoned homicide cops. And although it was not law enforcement's ultimate responsibility to reason *why*, for the shrinks would have to deal with that aspect in the end—should it come to full fruition—the squad of detectives, nevertheless, couldn't help but ponder the question beyond that fundamental factor.

It was Justin's job to make certain that the latter phase of police procedure and operation—one of the final cogs in the complex machinery of a civilized society and system, with its courts of law and convoluted brands of justice—would never come full circle, would never ever see the light of day; that is, the culprit's capture and categorical confinement. It was Theo's and Team Three's task to see that Justin succeeded—though in each detective's heart of hearts there stood a mountain of jealousy heaped with envy, as most would have sold their soul to the devil for the opportunity to pull the plug on Clarence Emery themselves. Teams One and Two had more than an inkling as to Justin's true role as a civilian affiliated with homicide. All other law enforcement personnel involved in the case remained in the dark on that bleak account, having been told that the maverick served somewhere along the lines of a consultant. Whether they believed it or not was irrelevant.

Though unofficially an official player on the team, Justin could view but was not permitted to handle evidence, such as the carving knives and splitting tools used to murder and butcher Vito Vitalo; that is, not until the detectives and forensics team had finished their preliminary examination. Not until their tool marks maven had signed off on a particular item would Justin Barnes be allowed to touch anything.

Justin peered curiously at the cleaver and knives arranged neatly along the butcher block table set off to one corner of the room. The list of cutlery Emery had used on his victims over the months was growing steadily. Each crime scene paraded a new set all its own: chef's knives, paring knives, offset serrated and flexible boning knives. Some of Solingen steel. Others of high-carbon vanadium. Cheap to very expensive. All displayed by different manufacturers: Wusthof. Henckels. Global. Chicago Cutlery. F. Dick. A few were from Germany; others from Austria, Japan and America—and now another brand.

Without the aid of the requisite magnifying glass others had borrowed from the tool marks man, so as to decipher the illegible engraving on the fillet blade, Justin copied down the manufacturer's name and origin by literally drawing the inscription in his notebook. He had some difficulty interpreting one of the letters, along with the odd markings just above it. Albeit incorrect, it was the best that he could manage for the moment:

T. Martlüni Finland
Hand ground stainless

"And Theo complains about my handwriting," he mumbled to himself.

Having noted Justin's frustration, the tool marks man came over and put the magnifier in the black man's hand.

"Guy's good and getting better," Detective Kilpatrick bantered with another cop standing off in a corner, referring to the serial killer's handiwork.

"I think he's ready for a side of beef," a junior grade detective suggested playfully.

"Nope. He had his chance. That field is full of moo cows."

"I *dink* he had *udder* ideas," the coroner clowned, casually walking up to the bloody table.

"Cause of death here, Matty?" Kilpatrick questioned with a facetious glare.

"Kind of hard to tell right now," the examiner joshed. "Organs are everywhere but where they should be."

"Still, I'd list it as a heart attack."

"Nah, I'd say loss of blood along with appetite," a senior man figured through a ridiculous frown. "Emery never would've gone to the trouble if the guy was already dead from fright."

"He's got a point, you know."

The coroner turned his attention back to the butcher block. "Yeah, and I think Emery made *his* quite clear. Over fifty of them," he recounted, staring down at the length of punctured bloody skin, laid out like a pelt.

"You know, along with a body bag for the bones, I think we'll still need the Wet/Dry-Vac."

"Yeah, then we can just pour him in a collection jar when we're finished."

"Hey, J," Kilpatrick called over. "You look like a real sleuth now, my man," he mocked. "Making any headway?"

Justin looked up from the magnifying glass. "Having a little trouble with the name on the fillet blade," he admitted.

"Let's have a look-see." The cop came over and looked down

at Justin's notes. "That's a capital *J*. Not a *T*. And it's *M-a-r-t-t-i-i-n-i*. Two t's; three i's. Not, *t-l-ü*, like you have there. Whatja think the dots were? Umlauts? Gotta learn to cross your t's and dot your i's, J," he teased. Kilpatrick withdrew his pen. "You mind?"

Justin shook his head, handing over his pad to the man.

The cop crossed out, then rewrote the name rather than correct it:

J. Marttiini

"There you go. Granted, it looks like a capital *T* and an *l-ü-i*. But it's not."

Justin scratched his head. "Mind if I ask you how you know this?" he questioned, believing the man was positively brilliant.

Kilpatrick grinned broadly. "Follow me." He walked over to a large black suitcase and withdrew a clear plastic evidence bag. "Here. Take a peek."

Inside the bag was a leather sheath with the first initial and surname clearly printed in capital letters across its top; the name of the country beneath it.

J. MARTTIINI
Finland

It was the sheath that had obviously contained the fillet knife.

It was the capital **J** that bothered Justin, on more than one account.

It was the knife maker's surname, too, suggestive of the lead detective's favorite cocktail—a martini—that raised the hair on Justin's nape. For it was the case detective, Detective Brian Archer, who, together with his partner, had been busy combing parts of Europe, following up on a supposedly promising lead. A bogus tip as it turned out. Probably set in motion by Emery himself. The two detectives were en route home.

"I know what you're thinking," Kilpatrick said. "Probably just a coincidence. Don't read too much into this."

"No, of course not," Justin replied uncomfortably, handing back the evidence bag.

Chapter 53

In the commanding officer's corner office, Justin sat beside the lieutenant, each of them staring blankly out separate rain-pelted windows that overlooked a dusky skyline. Faint flashes of light followed by claps of thunder resounding in the distance broke the prolonged silence between the two contemplative souls.

"Know what I think, J?" Theo said after serious consideration. "I think you know something you're not telling me."

Justin turned his attention back to Theo and laughed mockingly. "Me? You don't tell me a goddamn thing unless it's on a need-to-know basis. Know that?"

"I'm being serious."

"So am I. Treat you like you treat me," he trifled. "See how you like it."

Theo shot a short column of air through his nostrils. "I need to know what it is you're not telling me," he pressed.

"What ain't I tellin' you? You tell me."

"Like what that fly your friend, Milky, painstakingly tied, all means. Why he tied it, certainly realizing that Emery and Vitalo were going to kill him in the end. Why they put his head in a kind of vise like that. And where is all that fly-tying equipment, J.? The vise for tying flies? The materials used? None of it makes any sense."

"Why does it have to make sense? Emery's a sick bastard who loves to toy and torment. Maybe to Emery, Milky was just some kind of giant bug he was studying. Just like that vise-like contraption he constructed for Grace Littleton—sticking her in a cage like a songbird, high in the heavens, so to speak. Maybe Milky, in Emery's sick mind, was a lowly bug he killed in Ursula's basement simply for giggles. Who the hell knows? I doubt if Emery knows himself."

"A fly with eyes like Milky's, J. Remarkably distinguishable so that there'd be no mistaking it," the lieutenant pressed.

"I don't even know if Milky brought any of those tools and materials back with him from Wyoming. I tend to doubt it."

"But why have Milky go to all that trouble?" Theo reiterated. "Lester Townsend's people tell us that with all the steps involved in constructing the streamer, it must have taken days. What's Emery trying to tell us?"

Justin went back to gazing out the window. He sat there for a considerable moment before he spoke. "Know what pinkeye is?"

"You mean conjunctivitis?"

"I had it in prison. Couldn't see out of one eye; could barely see out of the other."

"And?"

"Had a good case of it, too."

"And?" Theo repeated.

"And Milky took care of it for me. Homey hailing from the same state is the only thing we had in common. That and a criminal record."

"How did he take care of you?"

"Got his hands on some antibiotics and eyewash; ointments, salves."

"Infirmary couldn't handle it?"

Justin snorted a laugh. "Get real, Theo. Doctors there couldn't and didn't care."

"That's pretty contagious stuff. You could infect an entire—"

"Group of niggers? That's right, bossman. They practiced segregation on our tier. We slept, ate and shat in separate quarters. Sick call was for those malingerin' white boys. Dispensary for a black man was when they dispensed with your sorry black ass in a box."

"How did he manage, if you were all cut off from one another?"

"Man, you don't know shit for the *po·si·tion* yo' in. Know dat?"

"Different place, different time, I guess," Theo reasoned defensively.

"Ain't no different there or here or then or now, T." Justin called the lieutenant T whenever he thought The Man was getting thick between the ears. "Here, like in any joint in the country, things get taken care of in the yard. The yard can be busier than a midday marketplace in a Third World country. 'Course the screws were mostly blind to the business goin' down 'round them; but not the inmates, dude," he drawled. "Screws be da guards, 'case yo' didn't know dat, boss."

"That much I know," Theo said with displeasure, hating it when Justin acted out, like he was doing now.

"Anyhow, Milky took his lumps for gettin' and givin' me da med."

"The med?"

Justin slowly shook his head. "My *med·i·cine*."

"Oh. Then what happened?"

"Whattaya think happens to a nigger-lover in prison, T? Especially when you're an outcast for openers. An albino wif a pink-eyed Panther fo' a pal. Huh?"

"Tell me."

"You're a trip," he remarked, raising his eyebrows to the ceiling in an expression of disbelief.

"So, then what did you do?"

"Had to set a few o' those white boys straight, is all."

"Cost you?"

"Two weeks in the hole, but it was worth it."

"How do you mean?"

"I'm surprised at you, man. I don't think you *really* know or understand the value of a friendship. Milky got his ass beat bad for helping me. It's not like he didn't know what could happen. Lucky they didn't cut his throat in his sleep."

Theo was beginning to understand why Justin believed that Milky would never betray him. The commander nodded respectfully.

"J."

"Yeah?"

"Once again. Why would Emery grab Milky and force him to tie a fly like that?"

"You don't give up, do you?"

Theo studied Justin closely. "Aren't you curious? Don't you want to know?"

"To tell you the truth, Theo, I'm more concerned with what Milky was trying to tell me through his art than I am about what Emery has in his sick fucking head. All right?"

"You think Milky was trying to communicate something?"

"I honestly don't know."

"The lab unraveled every feather, thread and hair for a clue. You know that, don't you? You saw the report."

"Yeah, and they were looking for anything that would tell us something about Emery, not necessarily something that would tell me what Milky was trying to say, if anything."

"That's why you and I are having this little chat."

"You think I'm hiding something."

"I didn't say that. What I said was that you're not telling me everything."

"You mean like my case of pinkeye."

"Case in point."

"I don't know what else there is to tell."

"I think Emery grabbed Milky, not only because he was your friend, but because he wanted certain information from him."

"What kind of information?"

"Information that Emery could use against you."

"Like how?"

"To discredit you. To hurt you psychologically. Maybe make it easier and even fun to kill you."

"Now, why in the world would he do dat?" Justin kidded.

"Come on, J. You know Emery knows you're coming after him."

"You tell him dat?" he toyed.

"You did, on the phone the other night. He knows that you're relentless. He knows that you found and murdered his associate, Malcolm Columba, along with several other players connected to that pack two years back."

"Then what you're really asking me is whether or not anyone outside the department, other than Jackie and associates, knows what I *really* do for you? In other words, did I tell Milky? Not that it matters much now."

"He was your friend, J."

"Friends don't have to tell friends everything in order for them to remain friends."

"Did you?"

"He knew I was working undercover. That's it."

"Good."

"You wouldn't be sitting here asking me that question if you'd given me the manpower I needed earlier. I had to go out and recruit warm bodies myself. Milky might still be alive today." Justin raised his eyes to the ceiling again, nodding with agitation, framing the allegation solidly in his mind.

Theo shook his head. "I kind of doubt it. He came to you, remember? Needing a fresh start. You'd still have given him an assignment. Am I right? And Emery would still have gotten to him because Milky was your friend. Simple as that."

Justin did not argue because he knew that Theo was probably right.

"So. Are *you* gonna tell me more about this Vitalo business, bossman? Or you gonna keep me in the dark?"

The lieutenant laced his hands behind his head and leaned back in the chair. "What do you want to know?"

"How a piece of shit like that ever became a Mounty."

"Trooper, you mean."

"Same difference. Same hat. Both horses' asses."

"Love to bait me, don't you?"

Justin cracked a smile.

"The guy excelled in everything he tackled. College all-star quarterback. President of his class. Marine lieutenant. Awarded the Bronze Star in Vietnam. All Vitalo ever wanted after his discharge was to be a cop."

"Albinos have low vision problems. How'd he make it into the marines and the state police?"

"Daddy. Retired Colonel, U.S.M.C. More money in his pants pockets than in all of Monroe, it's bantered about. Connections up the kazoo. The Vitalo name is golden up there. Vito got whatever he wanted. Then came the divorce."

"What really happened? Why'd he flip out? Plenty of people cut the knot and get on with their lives."

"Vito married his childhood sweetheart and homecoming queen, who suddenly upped and left him for an old flame. Her own childhood sweetheart: a cheerleader with a three-year-old child. Seems both women came out of the closet about the same time and were living happily ever after somewhere in Middletown."

Justin was beginning to get the picture. "Wouldn't just happen to be the same woman motorist who state police found brutally murdered along 17A near Goshen?"

"Emery certainly does find them, doesn't he? Both victims and accomplices."

"Still doesn't explain how or why Vitalo got himself hooked up with Emery. Especially after he beat a murder rap."

"Not until you stop and realize that being a cop meant everything to him. He found himself out on his ear, and daddy couldn't fix it. Vito wasn't needed anymore. However, Clarence Emery could use a cop. A good one. One who could penetrate surveillance. One who could run riot over Ruth and Anthony, like he did in Wading River. One who could pull Milky out from under your nose. You recruited an ex-prisoner. Emery recruited an ex-cop. Good guy, bad guy. Perfect match. Wouldn't you say? And in almost every way. Want to take this a step further? Emery always uses a knife, insofar as we know."

"In·so·far?" Justin rejoined with a frown.

Theo paused, his brow wrinkled in thought. "Poor word choice. So far as we know," he rephrased. "Up close and very personal. It was probably Billy Baxter who sent Grace Littleton to her death, then planted the bomb aboard the plane that killed Notaro's wife and the entire crew. The point I'm trying to make is that it was undoubtedly Vitalo who put the screws to Milky. Perhaps Vito Vitalo was looking in the mirror, figuratively putting the screws to himself. Or so says the shrink up in Albany, who evaluated him after he was brought in for questioning a year ago."

"Shrinks say a lot of neat things after the fact, Theo. The fact is, if doctors released half the patients who they say truly belong in their hospitals, and admitted the other half who they honestly believe could function well on the outside, know what would happen?"

Theo shook his head.

"Absolutely nothing. Not a goddamn thing would change. Everything would somehow even out. Psychiatrists are like TV weathermen, Theo. If one predicted fair weather, and the other forecasted a storm, there'd be a fifty percent chance you'd find the failure on another channel. Point being is that they'd *all* still be working, and we'd still have these conditions called madness and weather."

Theo smiled broadly and unlaced his fingers from behind his head. "You have an interesting way of putting things, J. Always told you that. Maybe you should consider becoming a preacher one day."

"Nah, my people'd see right through me in a minute. Then again, it's you white folk who could really use my help and support," Justin declared quite brazenly with a serious grin.

Theo surrendered. "What are you going to do now?" he asked, moving himself forward in his seat and picking up a report.

"Find out where Emery acquired those fly-tying materials and equipment, 'cause they sure as hell didn't come from Ursula's basement, or anywhere in that house."

"Nope. The lab's been all through that place with their vacuums and fine-tooth combs. Only feathers they found were upstairs in the bedroom from her down pillow, or was that one yours?" he asked with a silly grin.

"I hate feathers. Mine has to be either foam or polyester."

"Well, I wish you luck, J. But I have a feeling it's going to be like looking for that proverbial needle in a haystack. Or should I say a particular feather in a down coat or pillow factory," Theo concluded, burying his face in the report, indicating that their meeting was over.

"And since down coats and pillows are comprised of geese and duck plumage, if I found just one chicken feather amongst the pile, I'd probably have discovered Emery's safe house, sure as shootin'," he jived, pointing a gun-finger at the lieutenant's head. "But we're not looking for a particular feather, Theo. We're looking for the *eye* of the storm."

"Think you'll find it, hot shot?" Theo challenged, glancing up.

"Found that waitress, didn't I?"

"Not without ruffling a few feathers, you didn't."

"You trying to be funny now?"

"Trying," Theo admitted as his smile went on the wane. "I just want to let you know that the teams have been through every fly-tying shop from the tip of this Island to Timbuktu."

"Well, we'll soon see about that. Won't we?"

"Out of here, now. I've got work to do."

"I love and appreciate you, too, boss."

Chapter 54

Eastern Flyrodders of Long Island held their meetings on the second Tuesday of each month at the Indian Island Golf Course off County Road 105 in Riverhead. Justin tracked down the club's president, who gave him the name and address of an individual who could possibly provide answers to some questions concerning the menhaden streamer fly with its unusual eyes. Eyes that matched his friend's, Milky, to a tee. Justin carried around a color photograph of the unique streamer.

Tom Cousins was unique in his own right. A man of seventy who still suffered severely from a horrendous automobile accident that happened a week after he and his wife retired to North Carolina several years earlier. A car crash that almost claimed both Tom and Barbara's lives. Tom had remained in a deep coma for a fortnight as the result of severe brain trauma. When the man regained consciousness, he could not remember anything—neither his name nor the fact that he had been an educator, as well as a grant writer for close to fifty years. Nor could he recollect a single night at the opera, of which there had been many. Furthermore, Tom could not remotely recall that he had been an avid golfer. In truth, the man could not even bring to mind the fundamentals of how to properly hold a club. But a fragment of recollection that eventually did resurface, after a nurse at the hospital had encouraged Tom to try and key in on something that gave him a great deal of pleasure, was of a shadow box. A box that sat within a box until Tom unpacked it back at the couple's new Carolina home. A box displaying fresh and saltwater flies that a friend had given him as a gift, just before the couple sold their home and moved south from Oyster Bay Cove, Long Island. It was a beautifully framed case that remained unpacked and cherished, while everything else was repacked and shipped back to New York, to where, once again, the couple relocated in order to *escape*—seemingly ironic in Tom's troubled mind—a single memory. The horrific crushing crash.

Tears filled the man's eyes as he related his tragic story to Justin there in the finished basement of the couple's home in Aquebogue. "Sorry," the retiree apologized. "I still get very emotional whenever I talk about that incident. I cry very easily."

"That's okay. Really. We can stop for a moment if you like."

"No, it's all right. I like to talk about fly-tying and fly-fishing. It's the only thing I remembered after I got out of the hospital. Everything else I had to relearn. But not fly casting," he said enthusiastically. "That, I can do with my eyes closed. I know because I fish at night. And believe me when I tell you, I'm good." Tom said it in such a way that did not come across as bragging. "I'm going to be holding a seminar in August, I think I told you. Free. Down by the . . . that Marina in . . . uh . . . . Jamesport . . . ." Tom was trying desperately to remember the name of the boat basin, although he had been there many times before—as recently as a week ago, instructing those who had begged him for pointers after watching him practice for a period of time. "Sorry. I sometimes forget the littlest of things," he said with embarrassment, searching his mind while scratching the side of his head for the name of the marina before frantically searching through the many pockets of his fly-fishing vest for the boatyard's business card. "You know . . . that public boat ramp in Jamesport."

"Oh, you mean Great Peconic Bay Marina?"

"That's it!" Tom said with a sigh of relief. "You really have to forgive me."

"Tom, there's really no need—"

But Tom was excitedly trying to explain. "You see, when I hit my head in the accident—you know how the Honda has that—well, I mean most every car today has, I guess—" he laughed "—the . . . ah, molded hump in the roof that houses the safety belt and buckle. Well, it got me right here," he declared, sending a shaky finger to a spot above his right temple. "You see, the brain sits on a shelf, if you will, in the skull. And when my head struck that goddamn protruding metal piece with such force, it jostled loose my brain, actually shifting it." Tom launched back in time to past careers as an educator and a New York City school administrator, as if to compensate for his disability. "And I used to write grants and raise—"

Justin gently took the animated man's hand into his own.

"Tom."

"Yes?"

"Tell me some more about the flies you tie. Tell me about the menhaden in particular and the man who asked you all those questions," he pressed patiently.

"Sorry, I have a tendency to jump all over the place, don't I?"

"That's all right. I want to hear everything. I really do. But you already told me all about District 3," Justin said and smiled compassionately.

Tom wiped a tear or two from behind his glasses. "Sorry."

"What about this man?"

"I already told you what he looked like."

It could have been more of a question than a statement, so Justin politely nodded. "That you did, Tom."

"Well, he wanted to know everything there is to know about the materials used to tie the fly. Especially the eyes. I told him about the plastic ones already made up and packaged. Lead ones, too; like a little dumbbell that you tie around the shank of a hook. I told him about the peel-off and stick-on kind. But he was more intent on perfecting a prototype. So, I suggested acrylic paints and how to apply them. Showed him a little trick I learned a long time ago," he explained. "See, when it comes to tying flies, I never forget. Funny what's stored in the brain and what can suddenly be erased as the result of an accident."

"What was this little trick you passed along, Tom?"

Tom reached for an artist's brush across his cluttered workbench. "Here. Hold this like so."

Justin held the ends of the narrow wooden brush horizontally.

Tom took a sharp, thin serrated blade and cleanly sawed off a series of smooth inch-long sections from the tapered length, discarding the head of the brush. Next, he opened a bottle of red acrylic paint and poured a small amount onto a piece of scrap cardboard. "Now watch." He carefully dipped the tip of one end of the wood into the paint, then dabbed it onto a small pad of white paper, repeating the process with the other ends until all the sections but the narrowest were used. A series of different size circles lined the pad. "See? Each diameter is different."

Justin stared down at the group of tiny circles. "Neat. Very neat, Tom."

"We're not finished," he stated emphatically, picking up the tiniest dumbbell in the world between his thumb and forefinger, then placing and locking it within the needle-nosed jaws of a rotary fly-tying vise. Taking the remaining pointed piece of wood, which had been the end of the handle, Tom dipped it into the red acrylic paint and made a perfect pupil appear on one side of the lead eye, rotated the vise, wiped the wooden tip clean, dabbed it into the paint again, then made the other pupil. "How's that?"

Justin studied the concentric circle within a circle. "Cool."

"Of course, it doesn't have to be that perfect to fool a fish, but some tiers want perfection at any cost. Like the fellow you're asking me about."

"Tell me everything, Tom."

"Well, he wanted to make the eyes out of Mylar, using different colors and shades to 'affect the perfect eye,' he said. Talk about overkill. He even wanted them to have contour. Believe that? I asked him if he ever tied before. He said he hadn't but that a man he knew did."

"Did he want you to tie them?"

"No, but if he had, I'd have told him truthfully that what he wanted was too intricate. I'm good, but not that good. Besides, it would take forever to tie just one. Cost prohibitive," Tom made clear.

"Did he say who this other person was? Did he use a name?"

"Yes he did!" Tom searched the ceiling for the name. "Wait. Something like with a color to it. Give me a minute because when it comes to color and fly-tying, I don't forget."

Justin practically spit the name out for him, but held his tongue.

"Something like . . . syrupy or something."

Justin wanted to jump out of his skin. "Take your time, Tom." *But don't take too fucking long,* he wished to add.

"Got it on the tip of my tongue. Syrupy. No. Honey. Pretty silly," he said decidedly. "Wouldn't call him honey unless he was kind of funny," he recited in a childlike tone, shaking his head impatiently while running a series of brown and amber, then lighter, brighter, whiter shades through his damaged brain. "Got it! Milky. The man's name was Milky. Know how I know?"

Justin shook his head so hard that he could not help but smile at the possibility he might have shifted his own brain off its shelf as Tom had described.

"I know because when he told me, I immediately thought of the Milky Way. You see, I like to fish at night." Tom took his words right back. "I mean, I *love* to fish at night. It's my Magic Time!" He wept happily, the tears pouring down his face like two tiny waterfalls. "Maybe someday I'll tell you about Magic Time," he considered, momentarily removing his glasses and wiping both eyes with fingers that worked themselves like erratic miniature windshield wiper blades.

But Justin already knew all about Magic Time and Tom Cousins' poetry from a write-up and exhibit of his work at the public library in Riverhead, prudently taking the time to recite a line of the poet's verse rather than eagerly pursue the line of questioning. "'Be wary, little adventurers. For there are many hungry mouths out there to feed. It's Magic Time,'" Justin quoted.

Tom nodded excitedly and, from off the workbench, grabbed a section of a fly rod coupled to an empty reel, sharply bringing both hands shoulder-high . . . his body, mind and soul mystically being transported to a favorite nighttime, shoreline haunt. There, before an illusory body of water, the man stripped and whipped yards of fanciful fly line from the silvery reel, affecting an airy-feathery phantom out and over the ". . . flat, glistening, inviting, smooth black water," the ardent figure recited. "Be wary, little adventurers. For there are many hungry mouths out there to feed. It's Magic Time!" Tom exclaimed gleefully, slowly lowering the butt section of his four-piece, nine-foot graphite to his side.

"What did this fellow say next, Tom?"

"Huh? Oh, nothing that I can recall. But he did buy all the materials he needed to tie a dozen menhaden the way he wanted them. I told him how the segments for the eyes would have to be cut and layered. I told him, too, that for what he wanted to achieve, this man he had in mind would have to be an artist along the lines of Michelangelo: sculptor, architect, painter and poet," Tom added quite seriously.

"What did he say to that?"

"Nothing. He just smiled."

"Pay you in cash?"

"One hundred dollars. Oh, and he told me to keep the change. Materials were worth about twenty-five bucks when you figure in the stainless steel Gamakatsu long shank 3/0 hooks. I told him fifty would be fine, but he insisted. He told me the information and my time were worth their weight in gold."

"Anything else, Tom? Like where he lived or where this man he knew was staying. Anything like that?"

Tom shook his head. "That was it. He took the materials and left."

"Didn't buy or ask where he could purchase a vise or scissors or bobbin; hackle pliers or dubbing needle? Any equipment like that?"

"I don't have any of those things to sell. Just the materials and hooks, like I said."

"Tom, when you have this clinic in August . . . clinic the right word?"

Tom nodded. "Clinic. Seminar. Over three consecutive days. A talk. A little tying. And finally, fly-casting lessons on the beach in Jamesport. No charge. At Great Peconic Bay Marina!" he exclaimed proudly.

"I'm gonna be there," Justin promised. "You gonna teach me how to cast? But I wanna warn ya, I'm a little slow at catching on to certain things at first," he admitted freely.

"Not any slower than my having to relearn the things I once enjoyed," Tom assured him. "But I can promise you that you're going to learn to cast proficiently, where people will turn their heads and stare at you in awe and say, 'Can you teach me to cast like that?' And do you know what you're going to do then?"

Justin nodded in understanding. "Take the time to teach them, and then tell them to pass it on, Tom?"

"Oh, I think you catch on to things mighty fast, Detective Barnes," Tom Cousins declared, casting a broad smile that matched Justin's. "I just know you're going to do perfectly fine."

Chapter 55

Justin kept one hand on the steering wheel; the other gripped his cell phone. The Cadillac was barreling south along County Road 105.

"Theo?"

"Go ahead, J."

"I got a line on Emery and the fly-fishing material," he reported with elation. "May be our first real break."

"Tell me you got a line on his safe house," Theo prayed.

"No."

"Didn't think so."

"You gonna listen? Or you gonna denigrate?"

"Whew! Denigrate. If you spent half as much time looking for clues as you do words in the dictionary, as Ursula tells me, maybe you'd be further along the line," he ribbed. "Tell me what you got."

"First, I'll tell you what I don't got. Time for your snide remarks."

"Sensitive, we are today. Now, give."

"I just spoke to a guy who sold Emery the materials needed to tie that fly. Several of them, in fact. Eyes and all. Well, not the eyes themselves but the sheets of Mylar, along with feathers, glue, thread, hooks and acrylic paint. He even told Emery how the eyes had to be —"

"Who told Emery?"

"Fellow by the name of Tom Cousins. Aquebogue. Listed in the book. He's a member of Eastern Flyrodders. That's a club. Not the kind you hold, Theo; though it's where you sometimes golf—and rather poorly, from what I hear," he razzed. "Indian Island Golf Course is where the members meet. Only, Emery was in the man's home three days before Milky was murdered. I'm on my way back from there and—"

"Whoa! Slow down. Any possibility our boy could still be

around there?"

"Doubt it seriously. I think he's still back there in The Greens, Theo. Perfect cover for a safe house."

"What are you going to do?"

"Head back there tonight. I tell you, I got this feelin' in my bones."

"Just going to bang on everybody's door?"

"Somebody had to see something, Theo."

"Like who? I got a couple of undercover guys snooping all around that seedy neighborhood. They're even the right complexion, like you asked for. Nothing back there—"

"Pull 'em. Immediately, if not sooner."

"So, that's the lead you give me? A hunch. A feeling in your bones?"

"That and a poem and a prayer."

"What?"

Justin didn't say anything. He just drove.

"All right. You want me to have Mosely meet you there later this afternoon?"

"Absolutely not. I'm goin' in deep and dark and alone, Theo. I'm gonna turn that place inside out and upside down. I'm gonna *spook* 'im out," he jawed. "I'm telling you, we're close."

"Just don't get in over your head. And I want to hear from you every few hours. Hear?"

"Right."

"Know what I need from you before you put yourself in harm's way?"

"My bank account numbers? Power of attorney? What?"

Theo held back a laugh. "A full report on that Cousins interview. Now. Write it. Find a fax. Then send it to me before you step one foot inside The Greens. Got it?"

"Got it."

The two hung up.

Two hours later, the lieutenant stuck his head out of the office. "Get Underwood in here immediately," Theo told a detective sitting at a desk across the hallway. "No. Make that sooner," he blasted.

"Yes, sir," the woman said, getting up and marching down the hallway toward the men's room.

Detective Noel Underwood was sitting on a commode reading a boating magazine when the door to the stall flew open.

"Jesus Christ, Pam! What the fuck do you want?"

"It's not what I want. It's what Theo wants; on the double."

"I'm taking a shit, for cryin' out loud. What the fuck you want me to do?"

"Flush," she said, turning around and exiting.

Within two minutes, Underwood was standing tall before the lieutenant's desk. "Sir?"

"Didn't you go out to Indian Island and interview members of that fly-fishing club?"

"Yes, sir. I certainly did. Eastern Flyrodders." Underwood glanced down at his report in an open folder on the lieutenant's desk.

"And did you not interview a seventy-year-old male Caucasian by the name of Thomas Cousins?"

"Yes, sir. It's all right there in my report."

"What's right there in your report?"

"I . . . well . . . ."

"Nothing's right there in your report on Cousins, except his name and age and something about past employment and a head injury."

"That's because he had nothing of importance to say."

"I see."

"Sir, with all due respect to the man, his age, and what he did before retirement, the guy's a raving lunatic."

"That a fact?"

"That's a fact, sir. I asked him the name of his boat, *Reel Estate*, which he still owns and operates, and he couldn't tell me because he couldn't remember. He started crying and wouldn't stop."

"Wouldn't stop."

"Yes, sir. I mean, no sir. He wouldn't stop."

"So you stopped the interview."

"Well, yes sir. He had nothing important to say," the detective repeated.

"Did you even bother to show him a photo of the menhaden fly?"

"Sir, the man's a lunatic."

"Have a seat, Detective."

Detective Underwood sat.

"Spending some quality time with your son?" Theo asked the rookie detective calmly.

"Oh, absolutely. We go fishing twice a week," the young man said in earnest.

"Snapper fishing. Yes?"

"That's right, Lieutenant," he answered rather cheerfully.

Theo nodded. "What I'd like you to do right now, Noel, is to sit here for a moment and read this account." Theo took a copy of Justin's fax out from underneath Underwood's report and handed it to the young man. "After that, I'd like you to start thinking about going after *bigger* fish. Might help. All right?"

Underwood took and put the sheets of paper upon his lap and started reading . . . deliberately . . . setting the first page beneath the second . . . shaking his head somewhere between the poles of shame and disbelief.

Chapter 56

The lowest of low income housing. That would certainly be one way to describe The Greens, Justin ruminated, gnawing away at many heartfelt memories as he entered the predominately all black neighborhood, located just south of Route 58 in Riverhead.

The Greens, he stewed.

It was anything but green; green in name only, with an even darker countenance that sat sprawled across its acreage, largely made up of dilapidated shacks and shanties neglected by greedy landlords that the maverick revisited with a heavy heart.

Justin's eyes widened as he rounded a corner and avoided a pothole the size and shape of a crater. He steered the vehicle hard to the right and onto the shoulder before returning to solid pavement. Not much had changed, he maintained. Certainly not the conditions of the roads or poor street lighting.

In Justin's mind's eye, the bucolic ghetto was, had been, and always would be connected to an inherent factor. A component carried forth from cradle to grave with gusto. In a word—crime. Crimes involving incest; the theft of pure innocence. From that point forward evolved the metamorphosis of prepubescent tykes into demented teens and adults engaged in all sorts of sordid trysts—aberrant behavior unimaginable to most outsiders.

Next came those marginal misdemeanors that, for the most part, magically manifested and magnified themselves into more serious felony offenses. From simple pilfering, to the more ingenious and daring thefts committed just outside the community. No place was immune to the larceny. Certainly not the new and thriving Tanger Mall, nor the high-security banks and vaults of big and small businesses: beverage centers and liquor stores, gas stations and car lots, even heavy machinery warehouses. All fell victim to a crooked hand.

The added insult to an already precarious enclave came with the wheeling and dealing of drugs. From the back streets of downtown Riverhead, through woods, fields and meadows, then back across the tracks to their shabby dwellings where the dispirited hid or hung their heads till morrow. Some awakened much later on in life, only to face new charges: manslaughter and felony murder. Justin was all too familiar with the latter, being privy to piles of confidential reports.

Such was Justin's portrayal of life among his people; a realization that he carried around daily in his heart and mind. In essence, the pockets of poverty throughout the country were really not that different from one another. As a black youth, he had witnessed the indigence firsthand, having subsisted within the impoverished neighborhoods of New Haven and Harlem through most of his adolescence before moving to Mastic/Shirley. It was neither God nor country that saved him from himself and the conditions he was forced to live with. His saviors were two detectives who resided in East Moriches—one male, one female; one white, one black; interracially joined in the holy bonds of matrimony. To Justin, Detectives Brain and Kim Archer served as a beacon of bright *white* light—and a life to go along with it—discovered at the end of a long, pitch-black tunnel.

A far better path to follow than that of groping around in the dark until one's dying day, the maverick mused with mixed emotions. *Amen to that.*

Riverhead was not really rural. Nor was it suburban or urban either. What it was, essentially, was a rapidly and radically changing microcosm. What it had once been was God's little acre to a population of Poles who settled there decades ago. The Greens, however, to a sane person—black or white—was now viewed as the Devil's lair. A den of inequity. *The Greens.*

"A jungle of tar shacks and tinderboxes" was the way one Riverhead police officer described the section as he and Justin rode through the wretched area one bloody night, many a year ago: the black officer behind the wheel, Justin in the backseat wearing handcuffs. Black or white, no officer wanted to go into The Greens alone. Not on your life. Cleaning latrines back at the precinct would have been the preferred duty of the day.

But tonight, Justin Barnes was back in his element. He felt right at home. It was hardly a feeling of nostalgia. It could best be termed as a welcome dread. It was a hot, muggy midnight hour as he pulled up and parked in the front yard between two tricycles, directly behind a rusted out '86 Chevy station wagon, sitting up on cement blocks before the front stoop. He stepped from the car, locked it, then walked up to the dimly lit dwelling, rapping on the door repeatedly.

Less than a minute later, a tall black figure crossed the front room and approached the threshold . . . a man taller than Justin by a hair. Broader across the shoulders. Faces of the owner's family appeared at the corners of the open windows on either side of the crooked frame. Two children and a woman.

The man unlocked, then opened the door the length of the chain that secured it. "Yeah?"

Justin pushed a photo through the opening. "Ever see this little fella before?"

The big man glanced at the colored picture of the menhaden streamer fly, closed the door, slid the chain off its track, then reopened the thick but warped and cracked paneled sheet of plywood.

"Hey, Lanelle. Com'ere. We got a comedian for a visitor at this midnight hour."

Zeke Idler's wife stood five-foot-eleven in stocking feet and a wrinkled housedress, her coal-black hair pulled severely back in a bun. She looked beautiful to Justin and truly was . . . unchanged since the day he met her near a park in another lifetime, or so it seemed. Justin had recovered her shoulder bag from the ravages of two teenagers set on making a hasty withdrawal and a neighborhood name for themselves. He probably saved Lanelle from a fate worse than death. If the two local boys had had their way with her, it would have been a safe bet that she would have wound up severely disfigured, like other young women the thugs had sliced with box cutters after raping them for kicks and currency. Justin had kicked their proverbial asses, putting them both in the hospital for a good, long spell.

Not a word was ever spoken about the incident in public. In private, only one word was ever uttered in Justin's ear. *Thanks.* Her gratitude was sealed with a sincere kiss one week later when Lanelle and Zeke came by with a hot dish of sweet-potato pie. The two hoods were off the streets, and that was that. Justin's form of justice. Cheap. Efficient. Orderly. The hoodlums' attack and Justin's counterattack were over in less than sixty seconds. Less time than it took a professional car thief to jack a Jaguar.

Lanelle stared in wonder. "Jesus, is that really you, J?"

"Yeah, that's him." Zeke cracked a smile a little wider than the crack across the face of the door.

"So, you gonna let me in, or all the air conditioning out," Justin kidded.

"We don't got no air conditioning, mister," their littlest tyke innocently announced as she exposed her stomach by leaning so far back that Justin thought her head might touch the floor. Suddenly, like his Palooka punching bag from childhood, she sprang back up.

"Get!" Lanelle scolded, moving the child aside and taking Justin slowly into her arms.

"Does Mommy have a boyfriend?" the oldest asked, covering her oval mouth and a high-pitched giggle with a tiny ebony hand.

"Be the day," was all that Zeke could think to say.

Lanelle released Justin as warmly as she had pulled him to her breast.

"I'm gonna tell-el," the tiny one threatened to tattletale.

"Yeah, who you gonna tell, girl?" her daddy demanded to know.

"EVERYBODY!" his oldest declared at the top of her lungs.

"Me, too," the little one promised. "Gonna tell everyone at summer school."

"That's if you ever see school again," Big Zeke swore. "She's been out sick a week," he explained. "Flu."

Justin sank to the floor before the two darlings, scooping them into his arms before they knew what had grabbed them. Tears came to his eyes, and he dabbed them away on their clean white T-shirts, pretending it was more a matter of horseplay than the fact that he was using them both as a pair of handkerchiefs.

"You're beautiful," he said, looking them both squarely in the eyes. "What're your names?"

"Quanah," said the oldest.

"I'm not telling," said the other.

"It's Quanika," Lanelle answered, smiling down at the three of them.

"Mom-mieee," Quanika pouted. "You're not supposed to tell."

"Why not?" her mother questioned, a feigned look of

annoyance written across her face.

"'Cause."

"'Cause why?"

"I don't know."

"That's what I figured. Now, you know what?"

The two of them saw it coming.

"Noooo," Quanah protested.

But Lanelle was nodding an affirmative, *yes*.

"There's no school tomorrow," Quanika whined.

"That's *right*," Quanah argued, agreeing with her younger sister. "It's Sunday."

"You, you have no say," Zeke decided. "You're sick. And it's late."

"I'm not sick anymore. I swear."

"Good, 'cause you're gonna be up early for church. Now, off to bed. Both of you. And I do mean now. And say good night to your Uncle J."

Quanah brought the heel of her hand to her forehead. "Oh, God! Another uncle. How am I *ever* going to keep all of them in my head?" she questioned, delivering the line dramatically with repeated taps to her brow—stalling for all it was worth.

"Good night, Quanah. Good night, Quanika," Lanelle said with an edge to her voice that, apparently, they had come to know and understand quite well.

"Good night, Mommy, Daddy, Uncle J," the girls surrendered, doling out hugs and kisses laden with disappointment and sad yet angelic faces.

Justin got off the bare wood floor and stood before the parents. "You're blessed," he said sincerely. "You really and truly are."

"Well, I got a feeling I'm about to be cursed," Zeke said half-jokingly, then added congenially, "This ain't no social call at this hour. So state your business, and we'll see what we can do, J."

"Excuse me for a moment while I go tuck them in," Lanelle said demurely, giving Justin the space she figured he wanted.

Justin stole a glance as the pretty woman took her leave.

"Sit, sit." Zeke directed Justin to a table in a corner of the room. "What gives?"

Justin came right to the point. "I need pairs of observant eyes scoping out the neighborhood. Ain't nobody, I'm sure, knows this place and its people better than you two. Let's wait for Lanelle."

Zeke nodded. "How 'bout a nice tall glass of lemonade? Freshly squeezed."

"Love some."

"Stay put."

When Lanelle and Zeke returned, and drinks and sweet cakes were passed around, Justin explained the situation, holding back certain facts that the couple needn't know: facts relating to the case; undisclosed information concerning the most recent murders, which the police were keeping under wraps, literally as well as figuratively. For the moment, no mention was made by the media concerning the fact that Melvin Milken and Vito Vitalo were both albinos. Justin wished to keep it that way.

"I believe there's a white dude in this neighborhood, passin'," Justin put forth.

Zeke and Lanelle looked at one another then back at Justin.

The term *passing* was reserved for light-skinned black folk passing themselves off as white.

"Go on," Zeke said.

"He's a really sick dude, Zeke, Lanelle. Serial killer. Brilliant. Former professor. Gourmet chef. Actor. I could go on and on. I'm sure you've heard about him."

"Clarence Emery," Zeke said knowingly.

Justin nodded.

"Oh, my God," Lanelle said, shooting a glance toward the girls' bedroom.

"Does he know you're looking for him?" Zeke asked in earnest.

"Yeah, but believe me, he doesn't know I'm here. So relax."

"Relax, he says," Zeke muttered, sending his hands into the air, then smack down upon his knees.

"What is it that you want us to do, J?" Lanelle asked gravely.

"Keep your eyes and ears open for anyone who looks or acts suspicious. *Acts* is the operative word. You dig? He's good. I ain't talkin' Al Jolson in blackface. I'm talkin' gooood."

"You positive he's here in The Greens?" Zeke questioned,

setting down his glass.

Justin shook his head. "I *believe* he's around here," he answered, pointing a finger to his temple. "But if not, I *know* he's got to be close by," he stated solemnly, laying a hand across his heart. "This is the perfect place for him to lay low. No cops unless somebody calls them. And then there's only a fifty-fifty chance they'll show. Know which fifty I'd take?"

"Yeah, the fifty in my pocket that says a no-show; givin' out odds of ten-to-one or better," Zeke remarked.

"Got that right," Justin agreed.

"So, what's with this photo?" Zeke asked, reaching for and holding up the picture of the streamer fly.

Justin went through most of the story, leaving out information that they need not know.

"If I could get a handle on his safe house, well, you both know what I'd do. No suits or uniforms. In and out and over with."

Lanelle knew better than her husband could ever imagine. Zeke only received a secondhand account involving the incident of long ago. But she, of course, had firsthand knowledge of her savior's savagery. Vicious, yet controlled. He could have easily killed the two brothers if he had wanted to that evening. Instead, he fixed it so that they'd never walk again. She could well imagine what Justin would do to Clarence Emery if he found him. The couple had no radio or television. Nor did her husband have fifty cents in his pocket, let alone fifty dollars, like he bragged. But Lanelle read the daily paper: *Newsday*. Picked up nightly in the trash. She knew what was going on in the world around her. She knew how to read between the lines. Emery, from all written reports, was more than likely still in Suffolk County. He probably *was* hiding in their neighborhood, based on what Justin had just told them; she mulled over the situation anxiously in her mind.

Lanelle looked up from a spider crawling along the floor. She stared directly into Justin's eyes. "You know we'll do anything we can to help you, J," the woman said with conviction.

"Goddamn right we will," Zeke said with bravado, then scratched his head and chin.

Justin smiled appreciatively, moving his eyes like a cautious cat from Lanelle to Zeke. "I think I know what you're thinking, Zeke.

I repeat. He doesn't know I'm here. No one does. The car I came in? It's *bor·rowed*. So please relax."

"You stole a car to come here in?" Big Zeke brayed. And then he laughed quietly. "If I didn't know any better, which I do, I'd be concerned that we got double trouble on our hands, bro. But I'm gonna tell you somethin'. No white boy passin' through this neighborhood gonna pass hisself off as a brother; no way, nohow. Hear me? I don't care how good an actor he is. And now that my antenna's up—" Zeke waved a hand in back of his head, then turned it in all directions like a periscope "—I'd spot that honky a block away."

"Good. Just don't underestimate this guy. Either of you. You hear or see anything, you let me know immediately. Night or day. I'm gonna leave you my cell phone number. You tuck it away." He removed his wallet and handed Lanelle a card with only a number and the letter **J** printed on it. "Zeke." Justin opened wide his billfold and handed Big Zeke twelve hundred dollars in one hundred dollar bills. "Expenses. Anybody asks, you got lucky at OTB. Understand? No whiskey, Zeke," the maverick stated quite firmly. "You spread this money around wisely as needed. I'm counting on you. All right?"

"OTB? Whiskey?" Zeke questioned, scratching his head in apparent confusion.

"Ezekiel," Lanelle scolded.

Zeke bent forward and brought two palms noisily to his knees, laughing uproariously. "Just want to show 'im that I can be an actor, too," he declared, sticking the money deep into a pants pocket, then withdrawing his hand and patting the denim fabric affectionately.

"You hearin' me, Zeke?"

"Oh, I's hearin' you, boss. I's hearin' you real good. Know why? 'Cause you done shoooowed me da money," Zeke bleated, doing a little in-place dance step with his bare feet while seated in the chair.

Lanelle rolled her big brown eyes, pointing to the bedroom as a reminder that the kids were probably asleep.

"You'll snoop around. Ask questions, but be discreet. *Comprende?*"

"*Sí, señor.* What else, Santa Claus?"

"Everyone knows what a stand-up guy you are. Right?"

"Kick their black asses if they didn't," Zeke swore through a smile.

"Pay attention," Lanelle ordered.

"So, you wouldn't run out and spend some of that money on yourself without first thinking of the wife and kids. Right?"

Zeke reached back down into his pocket and pulled out the folded bills. "Fuck 'em all."

"Zeke! Stop it," Lanelle snapped. "That's not funny."

"I'm an actor. Remember? So just relax. He tells me to relax. I'm telling you both to relax."

"Stardom has gone to his head," she offered as an excuse for her husband's bad behavior.

"Actor," Zeke repeated smugly, kissing the money before shoving it back into his shabby dungarees.

"An actor who must remain in character," Justin warned him. "An actor who must play himself. That's why you're gonna go out and buy Quanika, Quanah and Lanelle new shoes and outfits first. Then you spread a little bit here. A little bit there. Got it?"

"Oh, I got it, J," he teased, tapping his pocket solidly like Quanah had tapped her pretty little head before she went to bed.

"Think you can pull this off, Zeke? Or you gonna screw it up? This doesn't call for brawn, you know. It calls for brains."

"You sayin' I ain't got brains?" Zeke asked indignantly.

"I don't know, Zeke. Long time's passed. You look a little soft around the middle there," he stabbed verbally, as well with an accusing finger. A twinkle in his eye belied the ensuing remark. "Figure you might be a little light upstairs, as well."

"Soft around the middle? Light upstairs? You think you could wup my ass?"

"Know I'd put you down to the flame," Justin said, giving Lanelle a little wink.

"Yeah, you tried but couldn't do it last time around. Remember? Two hours, twenty minutes. Then *you* gave up."

"I didn't give up. You had a studio apartment not far from here, and Lanelle had to be up for work the next morning."

"That was your excuse."

"No excuse now. Tomorrow's Sunday, Zeke."

"Oh, you're on, baby. Gonna wup your ass good."

"We'll soon see."

"Well, you know what to do, woman. Don't just stand there

givin' me that reproachful look. He opened up his big mouth first. Not me."

Lanelle shook her head, stood, then disappeared into the kitchen area before returning a moment later with two ice-cold Budweisers, two votive candles and a pack of matches.

"There you go, guys. Just like old times. But remember that we're still going to church in the morning, Zeke. Early. I'm going to bed."

She gave both men a kiss upon the cheek, then left the room.

"No mercy," Zeke promised.

"'*No más*' is what you'll be cryin' within the hour."

"We'll see. It's you, not me, who's gonna be runnin' to the cupboard for the Crisco."

"Shows how much you know. You don't put shortening on a burn."

"No? Then whattaya do?"

"You run cold water on the back of your hand, dummy. Shortening retains the heat."

But Zeke was shaking his head. "You're the dummy. You *have* to use shortening."

"Why?"

Zeke could not help but grin from ear to ear. "You really want me to tell you *how* and *where* to stick it?"

The two men laughed, lit and placed the candles three feet apart from the center of the table, opened their beers, clinked bottles, took a long pull and swallowed satisfactorily before locking their hands in a vise-like grip—black, bare elbows planted solidly on the white Formica surface.

Chapter 57

Front counterman, Frankie Sunseri, pushed the hold button and signaled a waiter, who, in turn, found the manager in the back dining area preparing a cup of cappuccino.

"Call for you on 0-three, Jackie," a waiter said and signaled, holding three fingers high above his head at the threshold of the crowded back dining room.

The caller had to wait; Jacqueline was in the middle of the process. Her cappuccino was an art form, and she prided herself in its presentation. Steamed skim milk was essential in obtaining a high, creamy head. Two waitresses out of the many employed at the Bella Sera could make a fairly decent cup; however, no one had *perfected* the drink the way Jacqueline had. There were some customers who insisted that only she prepare it for them. If Jacqueline was too busy with other responsibilities, they'd rather wait or simply pass than have someone else make the hot beverage. She was that good. Of course, the machine the employees worked with cost several thousand dollars, and only the best espresso was used. Still and all, it was the young woman's finesse that produced perfection.

Jacqueline shut off the steam, then poured and spooned the bubbly mountain of milky foam from a miniature stainless steel pitcher into a cup of fresh espresso before handing the finished product over to a Spanish waiter. "Table ninety-three, *per favore*," she directed, brushing a wisp of lustrous black hair away from her beautiful face. Tonight she looked radiant. The server gingerly took the cup and saucer and wended his way around a group of tables. Jacqueline picked up the phone. "Hello?"

"You know what really gripes me, Jackie?" a male voice on the other end of the line complained.

Jacqueline stiffened. She knew who the caller was and hit RECORD on the device that sat beside the phone. "No, what's that?"

"Restaurants that really rip you off."

She was signaling for a waitress to get Phil or Tomas. *Pronto.*
"I'm listening."

"Good, Jackie. That's very good because I wouldn't want to think I'm talking to a wall."

"You have a complaint with our restaurant, sir?"

"Oh, good heavens, no. Not *your* restaurant, dear girl. Estrada's Restaurant on Old Country Road in Riverhead. Know it?"

"Yes, I've heard of it."

Tomas came running toward her.

"It's him," she communicated silently, forming two syllables upon her lovely lips and turning her husband around with a circular gesture from several yards away.

Tomas ran to the closest exit to inform a fed.

"Well, let me tell you how they treated me, Jackie. First of all, I was in time tonight for their early bird specials. Two dinners for $24.95 as advertised on their billboard. But that's not the menu the waiter put in front of us, my dear. No, ma'am. He set down the regular dinner menu bound in burgundy—all very nice—followed by a separate pink sheet listing specials *other* than the early bird. No prices, mind you. This way, the unsuspecting customer thinks he's ordering the early bird special, when in fact he's not. Are you with me, Jackie?"

"I understand."

A field agent and a homicide detective now stood behind the bar with Jacqueline, the former attempting to run the trace.

"Good girl. Because we really don't have much time," Emery continued.

The agent was motioning for Jacqueline to stall the caller.

"Well, I really don't understand what this has to do with the Bella Sera, sir. I'm the manager here, and if—"

"I know who and what you are, my dear. And I know you know who this is. I also know what you're tryin' to do there. Therefore, please listen up. All right?"

The agent nodded excitedly, practically pulling the tiny earphone and its wire from the recording unit.

"All right."

"Now, where was I . . . ah, yes. Their wine list was on the table in front of me as well. I chose a nice Shiraz. Anyhow, I had to *ask* for the early bird menu, which the waiter finally brought after trying to seduce us with the more expensive specials. No dice. I ordered the pork chops. My companion ordered the veal and eggplant dish. Then I noticed at the bottom of the menu that an eighteen percent gratuity would be added to the check. Fine, but rather tacky. Don't you think, Jackie, dear? Usually, a restaurant would reserve that right for a party of eight or more. But okay, because I always leave thirty percent or better if the fare and service are up to speed. Then again, I'm sure there are folks on this splashy South Fork who don't look carefully at their check and wind up putting an additional twenty percent on top of the eighteen. Bear with me, Jackie. I'm getting to the good part." Clarence Emery was talking rapidly. "In the middle of the meal, the owner's brother comes over and says the charge card machine is broken and would I mind paying in cash. Can you imagine? What if I were low on cash or had none at all and relied solely on my credit card? Would I have had to wash dishes while my companion dried? Gee, I hope not."

"We got'im," the agent said in a sotto voche, jotting down the crossroads on a slip of paper and ripping the wire from his ear.

Tomas looked down at the location. "That's right near here," he snapped, pointing just to the west of the restaurant.

"You keep him talking," Detective Kilpatrick instructed Jacqueline.

The agent and the homicide detective disappeared in a flash.

Tomas nodded encouragingly to his wife as she turned away in a concentrated calm, injecting an occasional note of interest and understanding to the caller.

"I'm sure you'll be surprised to learn who my companion was for dinner this evening, Jackie. Anthony Notaro. Hates to be called Tony. Almost bit my head off. He had absolutely no idea who I really was until soon after we left the restaurant. But by then, it was too late. You see, he let his guard down. I believe he was falling in love with Officer Ruth O'Connor. I know for a fact that she was head over heels in love with him. I lured Anthony out with a promise of Clarence Emery's whereabouts. You see, I wasn't lying. I always keep my promises, Jackie. Ruth, they'll find in Anthony's bathroom along with his little boy. Anthony, they'll find behind this phone booth from which I'm speaking to you. I even put his phone card back into his wallet."

Jacqueline was crying softly.

"What?" Tomas whispered.

She jotted down a message in Sicilian.

"I won't be here when they come for me because I've been talking to you via a prerecorded tape since the point I told you about that nice Shiraz. Did you know that they use Mylar in recording tape, Jackie?"

Jacqueline could hear a commotion in the background. The sound of vehicles coming to a screeching halt. Car doors opening and slamming shut. A grating noise emanating from an old-fashioned phone booth door. And then there was the sound of loud cursing. Not Emery's. But rather a familiar voice. Jacqueline handed the phone over to her husband.

"Jackie, this is Detective Kilpatrick."

"Detective, this is Tomas."

"Tomas, is everything okay back there? Is Jackie all right?"

Tomas held Jacqueline's message in a trembling hand and stared at where his wife stood crying in the corner behind the bar. Her back was to her customers who dined in the din, oblivious to what was happening around them. *Thank God at least for that,* the husband seethed.

"Tomas!"

"No, she's not all right," Tomas answered coldly. "She thinks Ruth, Anthony and the boy are dead."

"Listen to me. We've got men stationed all over the restaurant. Not to worry."

"That's real comforting, Detective."

Kilpatrick hung up the receiver.

A patron saddled up to a bar stool.

"Sorry," Tomas said politely. "This bar is closed."

"Well, I want a cappuccino."

"Please go to the bar up front, or I can have your waitress bring it to your table."

"Yeah, well I want Jackie over there to make it. No one else. Got it?"

"Jackie's off for the evening."

"Who says?"

"I says."

The man laughed at Tomas' English and accent, looking down disparagingly at the cook's soiled apron, then back up and into the Sicilian's face. "And who are you? The dishwasher?"

Tomas didn't answer.

"Are you all right, Jackie?" the customer asked with some concern, suddenly realizing that she was quite upset and crying.

Jacqueline turned around abruptly.

"Jesus, Jackie. This guy bothering you?"

"Mr. Monterro," Jacqueline managed through her tears. "This man is my husband." She brushed aside the wisps of hair from her face. "He cooks the food that you've been eating now for several months. You're new here, and I appreciate your business and concern. But you show him and anyone else here who tries to help you some respect. *Capisci?*"

"Yeah, sure, Jackie. I meant no disrespect."

"Not from where I'm standing. I want you to apologize to Tomas. Tomas, I want you to take the man's hand. Olivia!"

A waitress hurried over.

"Olivia, you make Mr. Monterro here a cup of cappuccino, on the house."

"That's really not necessary, Jackie. I—"

"Shut up. Shake hands. Good."

"Jackie, I—"

"I'll say good night now, Mr. Monterro. We hope to see you soon." She did not give Mr. Monterro her hand or the kiss upon both cheeks that she usually reserved for her *special* customers.

Mr. Monterro returned red-faced to his table.

"I think they're dead, Tomas," she reinforced through a whisper. "I think Emery murdered Anthony, Ruth and the boy," Jacqueline blubbered beneath her breath.

Tomas took his wife well into his arms.

Chapter 58

Anthony Notaro's corpse had been punctured like a pin cushion, laying in a fetal position behind a phone booth less than two blocks from the Bella Sera Restaurant. Twenty-two deep stab wounds, quick and to the point, marked the man's entire body. Conversely, Ruth's remains, found in Notaro's bathtub, had been worked over quite skillfully, reminiscent of a surgeon dissecting a cadaver for the benefit of eager first year med students. What Clarence Emery did to Notaro's two-year son, Nicholas, was unspeakable—and few elaborated—except in purely clinical and technical terms.

Theo and Justin were in a room down the hall from the lieutenant's office, listening to the tail end of Emery's prerecorded tape—the part that Jacqueline Rubino did not get to hear after the authorities had arrived at the phone booth:

> . . . I was in a hurry, otherwise I would have carved him into steaks and sent prime or choice to the Bella Sera, Jackie. But Ruth was the one who really pissed me off, so I made time for her and Nicholas while I waited for Anthony to call. I told him I was a private detective and had a good lead on Clarence Emery, which I said I passed along to Ruth, explaining that she left a little while ago with the boy, but insisted that I wait there for his call. He demanded to know exactly where she and the boy went. Demanded, Jackie. I told him I wouldn't dare give him that information over the phone, that I'd meet him at a spot on Old Country Road, where I picked him up and drove him to dinner at Estrada's. His last supper, you could say. And the last time I'll ever go back there again . . . .

Emery concluded with a chuckle that positively manifested itself into a peal.

Theo stopped PLAY, then hit REWIND. "That's it."

Justin just shook his head and got up to leave.

"Sit. I've got something interesting to show you, J," the lieutenant said encouragingly. "It might prove to be nothing at all, but the techies seem to think otherwise. Townsend and his crew believe they've stumbled on to something."

"What?"

"Numbers."

"What fucking numbers?" Justin was in no mood.

"Numbers taken from the Mylar that formed the menhaden's eyes. At least, they could be numbers."

"What the hell are you talkin' about?"

Theo pushed two blowups across his desk for Justin to examine. "Those eyes are from the outside looking in. Look closely. First, the left eye, labeled A, like you saw magnified on the screen when Townsend was presenting. Tell me what you see in terms of numbers or letters, or anything at all."

Justin shook his head. "Just the blemish . . . the spot Townsend pointed out."

"Now the right eye; labeled B. See anything that could be a number?"

"Nope. Only those triangular growths."

Theo handed him a second set of photos. "How about from the inside looking out? Either eye."

Again, Justin shook his head.

"Focus on the veins in the right eye, J. Forget about the left."

Justin studied the squiggly lines. "Maybe a 1 in the middle of the other two marks."

"Turn the image around."

Justin turned the photo. "Could be a backward 7 followed by a 1, and perhaps a backward 4."

Theo handed Justin a magnifying glass and a small hand mirror.

"What am I supposed to do with these?"

"Read. Mirror-writing, or numbering as the case may be. Hold them up to those veins in the eye. Tell me what you see now."

"417."

Theo nodded in accord. "That's right, if you stretch those squiggly little lines a bit and not just our imaginations," he said with a wink.

Speechless, Justin's mind was working at the speed of light. He set down the items.

Theo stood and handed him a duplicate of the last enlargement, except for the fact that it was upside down on a transparent sheet.

Justin shook his head. "We're back to the backward numbers."

The lieutenant simply flipped the image over.

Justin reached for the mirror and magnifying glass.

"You don't need those now," Theo insisted. "See?" As the lieutenant spoke, he noticed a burn on the back of Justin's hand but said nothing, not daring to break the man's concentration.

Justin recognized what he had seen just seconds before but without the aid of the mirror or magnifier.

"417," Justin repeated.

"As plain as the nose on your face."

"Sweet Jesus."

"Townsend and his team surmise, and I'm inclined to agree with them at this point, that Milky was trying to communicate these numbers to you, J. Otherwise, why would he even bother with acrylic paint for the veins, and in only one eye? Furthermore, have you ever seen veins in a fish's eye? I haven't. By inverting and setting a darker film of pink Mylar over a lighter shade, Milky was able to obscure those numbers. Even a mirror couldn't pick them up once they were set in place. Milky knew that Emery or Vitalo would be watching him pretty carefully, so your friend had to come up with an elaborate way to outwit them. I think he did. The thing that puzzles Townsend's people, aside from not knowing what those numbers mean, is the fact that Milky used black and white and finally pink thread to wrap the shank of the hook, then completely covered it over with green dubbing material. We both know what all those colors symbolize: black and white—you and Milky, respectively; pink—pinkeye, or the conjunctivitis you contracted in prison; *dark* green—The Greens. Not to mention human hair—taken from Milky's own scalp. Take note." Theo showed him a blowup of the streamer minus its hackle, hair, and wrappings. "But back to those numbers, J. Any ideas? Any clue, whatsoever, as to the numbers?"

Justin hunched his shoulders and shook his head. "None, boss.

I'm going to have to reflect on that."

Theo accepted Justin's response. "You know, you didn't call me last night or the night before. I told you, I want to hear from you every few hours. I need to know where you are and what's going on."

"I wish I had a mother like you, boss. I really do."

"Call me."

"In the middle of the night?"

"Yes, in the middle of the night. On my home phone. If I'm sleeping, the machine will answer. That way, at least I'll know whether you're alive or dead or in trouble come morning," he chided.

"Believe me, if I'm dead, I'm sure you'll either get a recorded message or hear it from Emery himself." Justin reached across the desk and hit the REPLAY button, faced about, then walked smartly from the office.

Hello?
You know what really gripes me, Jackie?
No, what's that?
Restaurants that really rip you off.
I'm listening.
Good, Jackie. That's very good because I wouldn't want to think that I'm talking to a wall . . . .

With all the new developments and intrigue, Theo suddenly realized that he forgot to ask Justin what happened to the back of his hand.

Chapter 59

If Milky had been trying to communicate a message through his art, did Emery actually turn a blind eye to the artisan by allowing him to select and assemble the materials in order to perfect the streamer fly? Justin entertained. Or was it, perhaps, Emery's orders and, therefore, The Teacher's message?

The color green surely had to symbolize The Greens, in Justin's own mind's eye.

Has to.

Whether it had been Emery's instructions or Milky's magic, or both, for whatever reasons, Justin believed he had part of the puzzle figured. But the unsettling question still remained as to whether it was a trap—bait to lure him in. In any event, the information proved to be pure unadulterated detective work on the part of the police. Still, was the exterior *green* dubbing Emery's diversion, a clue meant to mislead and put the maverick on an erroneous path? Again, the numbers, 417, had to mean something.

Has to. If, indeed, they are actually numbers at all. What, if anything, can they possibly mean? How, if at all, do they figure into the scheme of things? Justin kept turning over in his mind.

If the crypto boys had not figured it out, Justin wondered how in hell he was supposed to . . . unless the message was meant solely for him, he pondered . . . masked in mystery by his friend, Milky. Rumor was that even a numerologist had taken a peek but came away with a big fat zero.

The Greens.

That was all that Justin really had to go on. But it was something more than just a hunch he held. It was an aching feeling in the center of his gut that wouldn't let go.

Two days of snooping about the neighborhood, and Big Zeke turned up nothing.

Justin thought about getting Zeke and Lanelle a cell phone because as things stood, he would have to get dressed and drive over to the couple's home at ungodly hours. But at least from Ursula's residence, he was close by. He tried to grab a catnap on her couch but only dozed.

Ten minutes had passed when a detective and Ursula let themselves in through the front door. The man immediately switched on the light, then turned off the alarm. It was after midnight. He saw Justin awake on the couch, nodded, then said his good-night to Ursula. Detective Kilpatrick, along with three other detectives, relieved a pair posted just outside the premises before taking up positions around the home.

"Why are you still up, J?" Ursula asked as she put her Coach purse down on the coffee table.

"Had a good nap," he fibbed, rubbing his eyes with his knuckles.

"You look like you haven't slept in a week."

"Try two days, but see how I look again in another five," he soured, reaching for his shirt.

"And where do you think you're going now?"

"Out."

"Out where?"

"Better you don't know."

Ursula sat down as Justin tied his shoes. "Jesus, J. What happened to your hand?"

He sloughed off her concern with a yawn and a silly grin. "Just a little burn."

"That doesn't look funny to me at all."

"Well, you should see the other guy."

Ursula shook her head and began to cry.

"Now what's the matter?" Justin jawed. "You're in here two seconds, and its pick, pick, pick. Two days I didn't see you. I hardly got any rest, but I sure as hell had peace and quiet."

"Yeah, I heard all about your peace and quiet. I heard about Ruth and—and I told you this would happen. Didn't I? I have four detectives following me around every place I go. I can't even go to the bathroom in my mother's own home without one of them standing near the doorway."

"Remember when we had *one* guy for security? And many times that guy was me. Huh? And now you're complainin' 'cause I made you a *ce·leb·ri·ty.*"

"Oh, I think you're ready for the loony bin, I truly do."

"Good. Because when I go *really* mad, maybe I'll finally figure out how to find this fuck."

"Well, let me tell you something, sweetheart. You ain't got very far to go."

"Thank you very much, sweetcakes. I love you, too."

"You know, I have half a mind to turn right around and walk the hell out of here. Only this is *my* place."

"I'd say you have half a mind, period," he threw out flippantly. "And if you do leave, set the alarm 'cause I'm goin' in to shave."

"Why would I set the alarm when you're already up and ready to run off?"

"Not the alarm clock; the security alarm."

"Then say what the hell you mean," she blubbered, suddenly clenching her fists and balling them against her chest. "Do you have any idea how old that Notaro child was? Well, do you? Two. Two years old, J. *TWO!*" she shouted then shivered before sinking slowly to the floor in a state of sheer anguish.

Chapter 60

Justin sat across from Zeke and Lanelle. It was well after midnight, and the kids were fast asleep. From a leather portfolio, he removed a blowup photograph of the artificial eye and placed it flat upon the kitchen table, displaying the three numbers.

"417. Mean anything at all to either of you?"

Both of them stared, thought for a moment, then shook their heads in unison.

"You sure?"

"How about an address?" Lanelle suggested.

"First thing I thought of," Justin said. "Here in The Greens. But where? The post office has nothing. Still, I drove all around this area and turned up zip."

"Zip code," Zeke thought aloud. "Part of a zip code."

"Three out of nine digits, Zeke? Come on," Lanelle expressed with annoyance. "And stop touching those burns. Idiots. The both of you."

"Maybe if you read it backwards, J. 714," Zeke proposed. "Huh?"

Justin shook his head. "Been there, done that. Same deal. No such number, no such zone," he put forth giddily in sing-song fashion.

"How about switching them around? Like 174. 147. 471. 741, et cetera. Or add them up. Twelve. A coded address," she submitted.

"Ran them all. Good try, though. I had a 12 Laker Lane. Had a spotting scope on that family till I lost the light yesterday. They're cool." Justin looked down at the numbers. "You can rearrange them all you want. I don't think Milky made this any more complicated than he had to. I think it's staring me right in the face, but either I'm too thick or blind to see it."

"May I see that a minute, please?" Lanelle muttered, sliding the photograph toward her. "You mind?" Lanelle carefully studied the characters, along with some of the other squiggly marks surrounding them, before turning the picture upside down. She examined the image meticulously.

"What is it, woman?" Zeke asked with a smirk. "You Dick Tracy now? You want a microscope or somethin'?" he mouthed off jocularly.

"Or somethin'," she threw back. "I'll be right back." Lanelle got up from the table and headed for their daughters' room.

"Yeah, you wake them, and you'll sit with them till they fall back to sleep," Zeke promised.

"Always do."

"Wise-ass woman," Zeke called out.

Lanelle stopped in her tracks, then turned around sharply. "Keep your voice down! *You're* the one who's going to wake them, jerk."

"Woman needs a good ass-wuppin'," Zeke said in a whisper as Lanelle stepped from the room.

Justin decided he wasn't going anywhere near that comment. "How's your hand?"

"Sore. How's yours?"

Justin studied the burn above his wrist. "Not as bad as yours," he said decidedly.

"I'll get you next time."

"In your dreams."

"Two-and-a-quarter hours, bro."

"And we ain't as young as we used to be," Justin reminded the man.

"Two bad-ass motherfuckers. Whoops, here comes the sleuth," Zeke whispered through a titter, poking fun at Lanelle holding the kids' magnifying glass.

Justin was tired and frustrated. He needed to be alone to think. He would offer his apologies for keeping them up late once again, extend his thanks, bid them both good night, then get the hell out of there and maybe get some badly needed sleep.

Lanelle sat back down at the table. She repositioned the photo under her nose and studied the squiggly little lines beneath the lens. "You know, these could be letters, J, instead of numbers," she offered, lifting her eyes from the glass. "To me, they're clearly an **L** and an **I**."

"The police considered that. They believe they're more in line with numbers than letters," Justin explained patiently.

Lanelle rocked her head from side to side rather skeptically, refocusing the lens. "But if you look carefully, see how the lighter marks above and below the middle character almost touch it to form a capital **I**?"

Justin took the magnifying glass and turned the page around to appease her.

Lanelle got up and walked behind Justin's chair, leaning over his shoulder. "And see how that upside down four is shaped? More like an **h**. A capital **H,** if you note that wavy line there that's practically touching the tip of the seat. See? Now, show me how you make your fours. Go ahead."

Justin humored her, withdrawing a pen from his shirt pocket and writing the number four by printing an **L** with a line drawn vertically through its horizontal axis.

"Right. Nobody I know makes their fours the other way," she said, taking the pen from his hand and forming a typewritten 4. "True? That is, unless you're working on a typewriter or computer," she expanded. "I'm telling you that's a letter—not a number."

"You know, you could be right, Lanelle," Justin hedged.

"Didn't I tell you she was smart?" Zeke asked excitedly. "Didn't I?"

Justin shook his head dubiously. "Told me somethin' 'bout an ass-wuppin', though," he needled mischievously, suddenly alert and settled.

"Yeah, that'll be the day," Lanelle reproached, directing their attention back to the color photograph. "So, let's see what we got here."

"L - I - H," Zeke said succinctly.

Lanelle was nodding her head in agreement. "All uppercase letters," she posited. "So, now we're back to square one. What the hell could it stand for?" Justin questioned irritably.

The three of them put their heads together in thought, staring down at the letters.

"Long Island something, I'll bet," Lanelle said and went to get the Suffolk County phone book, turning to the business listings.

"Where'd you dig that up?" Zeke barked. "We ain't got no

fuckin' phone."

"Watch your smart mouth," Lanelle warned, setting down the directory and flipping to the business listings at the back of the White Pages as Justin casually put away the enlargement.

Zeke covered his mouth in mock surrender.

"Let's see, now: **Long Island Abstract**, **Agency**, **Angels**, **Aquarium**," she began, running a finger quickly down the alphabetical listings, continuing through to the **H**'s. "Here we go. First one. **Long Island Hand Rehabilitation Center**. Maybe I should send both you guys over there," she scowled. "**Long Island Hardware**, **Health Network**, **Health Plans**, **Hearing**, **Heritage**," she scanned the columns. "Here's something that rings a bell: **Long Island Honda**. Didn't that nutcase, two blocks over from us sell stolen Hondas from his house, Zeke?"

"Those were Harleys."

"You're right. So why isn't Harley listed here with Honda?"

"Because no self-respectin' nigger gonna deal in rice bikes," Zeke affirmed.

"Where's Honda located?" Justin questioned, setting them both back on track, believing that the bike shop was somewhere way back west. "Gotta search close to The Greens."

"Gotcha. 1660 Sunrise Highway in Bay Shore. So scratch that. **Hotels**, **Humane & Dog Protective Assoc. Inc.**; now we're into the **I**'s. **Insurance**, **Interiors**, yada, yada, yada."

"Maybe we need the Yellow Pages," Zeke suggested.

"Shh," Lanelle silenced him, running through the list again. "We're doing something wrong here, fellas. Because I know there's a Long Island Harley that I don't see here," she mumbled mostly to herself, returning to the beginning of the listings for Long Island, spotting a note at the bottom of the preceding page:

LONG ISLAND (LI) LISTINGS ARE ARRANGED AS IF SPELLED IN FULL. SEE ALSO THE BEGINNING OF THE 'L'S FOR THE LISTINGS BEGINNING WITH L I

"Damn it. **LI** written together and **L I** written with a space between." Lanelle impatiently flipped back to the beginning of the **L**'s and over to the second column: "**LIAFE**, **L I Airports Limousine**

Svce Corp," then down to a listing for, "**L I Home Inspections Inc.** in Massapequa. *Nada*. I can't believe they've got just one **H** listing." She searched ahead and found the other Long Island section listed as **LI**; no space. "I don't believe this crap. Who puts these books together anyhow?"

"White Pages? White folk," Zeke declared and slapped both knees followed by a guffaw.

"Here it is! See?" she asseverated. "Told you there was a Long Island Harley. Only it's **LI Harley Owners Group** in Oakdale. What I think we need to do is start at the beginning and just run through *all* the **L I**, **LI**, and **Long Island** business listings because maybe there's something we're missing that might just fit the **H** we're looking for."

"Like what?" Zeke asked.

"Like I don't rightly know," she answered quite frankly.

"Maybe like **Long Island Cycle**—see? Same address as **Long Island Honda**, that sells Harleys," Justin noted, having jumped two columns ahead.

"Right!" Lanelle agreed.

"Sounds like we'll be here forever," Zeke said wearily.

"Why don't I put up some coffee first?" she suggested. "Then the three of us can go back and tackle this. It shouldn't take too long."

"Better yet, I'll make the coffee," Zeke offered. "You two work together 'cause I'm good for nothin' when it comes to readin' with these eyes of mine. Need new glasses. Print that size is just one big blur."

"Fine. J, why don't you work from one end of a list, and I'll start at the other. All right?"

"Sounds good. Can I make a suggestion that might save us some time?"

"Of course."

"We start with the addresses first, homing in on Riverhead Township: Wading River, Baiting Hollow, Riverhead, Calverton, Aquebogue, Jamesport and South Jamesport. Any place near enough to The Greens. See what we can come up with that we can leash to an **H**. Anything that might strike a chord; give us some clue. How does that sound?"

"Sounds like you just saved us a ton of work," Lanelle said with savvy.

Zeke laughed. "Gee, if you was lookin' for a legitimate business *in* The Greens, you'd both be through before I could fill this pot with water."

"Pessimist," Lanelle replied without lifting her brown eyes from the book.

"Pessi-who?" he retorted with a frown. "Always with them fancy five-dollar words."

"All right. Let's see how this is gonna work." Justin worked backwards from the end of the list. "**Long Island Vault & Box Co Inc**. What might we connect to an **H**, Sherlock?"

"Heirlooms," Lanelle answered crisply off the top of her head.

Justin was impressed. "**Long Island Kosher Fish**."

"Herring!"

Justin paused just long enough to pull a memo pad from a shirt pocket and jot down a note. "**Long Island Costumes & Balloons**."

"Halloween."

He shook his head in amazement. "One more. **Long Island Arena**."

"Hockey."

"Your woman belongs on a game show, Zeke. I kid you not."

"Yeah, *The Gong Show*."

"No, I'm serious."

"So am I."

"Any of the companies in Riverhead Township, J?" she asked, ignoring her husband's slight.

"Not a single one."

"So why are you wasting valuable time?"

"Hey, don't beat up on me. I'm on your side. I'm the one who'd put up good money for you to appear on *Jeopardy* in a heartbeat, girl," Justin rallied with a winning white smile.

"Get to work."

"Right."

A minute later, Justin scratched his head. "Thought I had something here," he said quite seriously. "Shit."

"You watch your mouth, too, mister."

"Yes, ma'am."

"Piss, shit and corruption. I thought I had one, too," she swore, covering her mouth to hide a lasting grin.

Chapter 61

A quarter of an hour later, Zeke returned to the table carrying a tray filled with cakes and corn bread, coffee, cups and saucers, teaspoons, cream and sugar. "Here we go, folks. Nourishment. How're the two sleuths doin'?"

"Making headway in getting through the listings, Zeke," Justin answered. "But not much luck connecting any **H**'s to the area, I'm afraid."

"Me, either," Lanelle murmured.

"Well, I happen to know a lot of **H**'s with listings in the area, bro," Zeke took liberty in explaining. "There's Tamika, Latoya, Shaniqua, and Precious. One day, I'll tell you all 'bout them ladies, J," Zeke promised with a leer. "Girls got themselves *several* listings, my man. Yep. Four, four-star hookers known from here to Orient Point. Point bein', all four pull down better than a hundred grand a year. Each. Ain't got no Uncle Sam or Stable Man to tax or touch their booty, either. Hear what I'm sayin'? All free and clear. I gotta tell ya jus' one little story 'bout Tamika, J," Zeke insisted, setting the stage by bowing and slapping his hands on opposite knees before spinning completely around—laughing quietly, yet outrageously.

"Never you mind, Zeke," Lanelle carped. "We're having coffee and cake now. Those kind of stories you can save for another time."

The threesome took a break and enjoyed the delicious homemade corn bread and sweet cakes that Lanelle swore their eldest daughter, Quanah, had made from scratch, "—with just a tiny bit of help," the mother confessed most modestly. "Even Quanika gave a helping hand," she boasted proudly of the five-year-old.

Zeke went on to reminisce about the old days.

After a spell, Justin complimented Lanelle on the treats and told her to extend his praises to the two little cooks. He thanked Zeke, too, for brewing and serving the pot of fresh, rich coffee. Then the trio went back to work.

Zeke cleared, washed, dried and put away the dishes while Justin and Lanelle, their heads but an inch apart, continued to comb the columns for a clue. Forty minutes later, the pair finished up, their fingers meeting together in mutual defeat.

"Well, that was a total waste of time," she decided.

Justin smiled. "Not really. Consider it a heads-up. Because, like Zeke said earlier, we now know for certain we'd have no competition if we started a small *legitimate* business on the block."

Lanelle stretched and yawned. "Yeah, dream on."

"Listen, I want you two to know that I really appreciate this," Justin said sincerely.

Zeke looked down at his new Nike sneakers. "Me, too."

The three of them laughed with restraint so as not to wake the kids. Lanelle stood and proudly showed off her new housedress for the second time that evening.

"Hope it's true what you said 'bout them Keystone Kops kickin' in the cash fo' all these presents, J," Zeke said. "I'd feel bad if it was you who's footin' the bill."

"Right out of petty cash, Zeke," Justin lied. "Every penny of it, bro."

"Good, 'cause them honky motherfuckers—" Zeke stopped himself in mid-sentence. Not because of his wife's warning. No. But because something apparently flew into his brain like a freight train. "Jesus!"

Neither Lanelle nor Justin said a word.

Zeke walked up to the table in a trance and slowly sounded out the initials. "**L-I-H**. We got a guy lives less than a mile away . . . yeah . . . right here in The Greens. Drives for Long Island Heating. Ain't gonna find them in no phone book 'cause I tried lookin' them up when we lost the furnace last year. Small outfit way back west. He covers this area out here from his house with the company vehicle. Panel truck. Passes right by here most mornin's fo' the sun comes up."

"You know, he's right, J! White van. Black lettering."

"'Course I'm right. Whitey's been drivin' fo' that company goin' on eight or nine years."

"What was that?"

"What was what?"

"What did you call him?"

"Whitey. Why?"

"Whitey, like in honky. Or Whitey, like in his name?" Justin questioned with the intense eyes of a killer cat.

"Whitey, like in the color of his skin." Zeke grinned. "Not a Michael Jackson. Just an old nigger with a scar. Light-skinned; white hair. We call him Whitey, 'cause that's his nickname. Why you lookin' at me like that?"

"And when's the last time you saw this Whitey fella, Zeke?"

"Oh, maybe two, three days ago. Jeez, J. You look like you've seen a ghost, my man. Hey, where yo' goin', bro?"

"We. You and I are gonna take a little ride, Zeke."

"At two-thirty in the mornin'?"

Lanelle had both hands covering her mouth, shaking her head slowly back and forth in anguish.

"It's all right, Lanelle," Justin said reassuringly. "Zeke's just gonna point out where this Whitey lives, and we're both gonna come right back. Swear. Listen, can you two put me up for a few hours? I promise to be up real early and outa here before the kids wake up."

Lanelle still had her hands over her mouth, nodding her head up and down as though it were controlled by someone working the strings of a marionette.

"It's gonna be all right. I promise."

Lanelle went over and put herself into Justin's arms.

"Jeez, woman," Zeke bellyached. "We're just gonna take a little ride. Hey! Am I gonna get a hug like that, or what?" Zeke asked a bit uneasily.

Chapter 62

Justin quietly backed the *borrowed* mid-size sedan off the front of the property and onto the deserted, dark and deeply rutted street before turning on the headlights. He headed down and around the corner as Zeke directed. The two had been sitting in virtual silence for several blocks when Justin finally blew.

"Christ, Zeke! Why didn't you tell me about this Whitey before?"

"Before what? You told me to keep my eyes and ears open for a white guy passin' for black. Not no bro workin' for a heating oil company for almost a decade."

"And you saw this guy within the last few days, you said."

"Uh-huh."

"You're sure?"

"'Course, I'm sure. Wouldn't tell you I was if I wasn't. Make a right, then another left. Last house at the end of the block. Guy works hard for a nigger," Zeke jawed. "Long hours. Hardly ever home till very late."

"Right or left side of the street?"

"Last house at the end of the block, I said. Note that I didn't say no shack."

Dead ahead, Justin saw a white van parked in front of a modest but well-maintained home and lawn. "Fuck, Zeke!" he blared and immediately killed the lights. "You couldn't tell me this was a dead-end street? I might just as well be shining a flashlight in his fucking face. And who builds a house smack at the end of a road like this?"

"Relax. The guy's probably dead to the world."

"That's exactly what I'm afraid of." He immediately turned the car around and headed back.

"I don't understand what you're getting so uptight about."

"Might not be Whitey in there. Might be our man. Clarence Emery."

"No way."

"Why do you say that?"

"Told you. How many times do I have to say it? I just saw Whitey, and he waved."

"He waved?"

"Yeah, he waved. Whitey waved good mornin'."

"Mighty neighborly. Ever wave to you before?"

Zeke looked at Justin oddly. "Gee, now that you mention it . . . I'm not sure."

"You're not sure. Guy drives by your home most mornings for years, and you're not sure?"

"Well, what I mean is, he waves to our kids. And they wave back." Zeke's mind was reeling.

"Thought you said the guy drives by your house before the sun comes up. Kids up that early getting ready for school?" he questioned suspiciously.

"I mean, he used to wave to them when they was little . . . and on weekends."

"I see."

"You know, you sound just like a fuckin' cop. Know that? You tell me you're freelancin', J. Paid informant. I don't know, man. Sure you ain't workin' undercover and just blowin' smoke up my ass?" he remarked. "I bet you're the real *thang*. Badge and all, buddy."

A sudden shiver shot up Justin's spine and spread across his shoulder blades. He glanced at Zeke strangely. "With my record, Zeke? You got to be kiddin', right? They just need a nigger in this woodpile, and they're payin' me beaucoup bucks for Emery's hide."

"You sure you ain't on any kinda permanent payroll, pal?" Zeke pressed.

"I just go door-to-door lookin' for the score, bro. Jus' like you. That's our lot in life," he lied.

"If you say so."

"Just a little luckier than most, I guess."

"I suppose."

The two drove back to the ramshackle house in silence. Justin killed the lights.

Lanelle was waiting by the open door.

Justin looked over at Zeke. "Tell her to go back inside, that we gotta talk—be in shortly."

Zeke rolled down his window and poked his head out.

Lanelle didn't have to be told anything; she seemed to know, stepping back inside—closing the rickety door behind her.

A look of sadness and disappointment spread across Justin's face.

Zeke was staring straight ahead through the cracked windshield.

"417 was your badge number. Wasn't it, Zeke?"

Zeke sat there in silence for what seemed like an eternity before he spoke. "That was in another lifetime, J. A long, long time ago," he said, fidgeting with his wedding band. "When you first came to the door the other night, I didn't know whether you had all the pieces put together or not." Zeke smiled so sorrowfully and shook his head. "Guess it was just a matter of time."

"You weren't gonna tell me on your own, were you?"

"Couldn't"

"How come?"

"Lanelle. The kids."

"He threaten to hurt them?"

Zeke gave a short laugh.

"You know, the two of you really had me going in there. That was beautiful, I'll admit."

Zeke was shaking his head. "Wrong."

"Played me like a fiddle. Or should I say a fish? A big fish. Took the bait and ran with it. You two really cranked me in. The magnifying glass. The phone directory. **L-I-H**. Wow! What kinda fish, Zeke? A sucker," Justin said decidedly. "I was at the bottom of your game."

"Not my game, J. Emery's."

Justin nodded. "How much did he pay you?"

"Fifty grand."

"Betcha he would have paid a hundred."

"I wasn't in any position to negotiate."

"How'd Emery get a line on you?"

"Vitalo."

"Were you there for the grand finale? Milky's, I mean."

Zeke shook his head. "Just Vito's."

"And 417? How did that all come into play?"

"I was in uniform. Borrowed. But I always kept the badge."

Justin nodded his understanding. "I see. An ex-state trooper and an ex-cop. Explains a lot of things. Doesn't it? So, how did Milky manage to conceal his art work with the three of you standing around?"

"You kidding me? Emery misses nothing. Milky tried, though. But he could barely keep his hands from shaking. He knew, of course, they were gonna kill 'im in the end."

"What are you saying? That Milky didn't tie that fly? That he didn't fabricate those eyes?"

Zeke sadly shook his head. "Until tonight, I didn't know the real meaning behind the message Emery was sending. I didn't know it till the moment you came through that door and presented those three numbers."

"Then who constructed those eyes, if not Milky?"

"Who?" Big Zeke Idler had to laugh. "Who do you think?"

"Mother of God!" Justin suddenly realized.

"He told me he couldn't wait to hit the flats in Florida and work his way south from there. Central and South America are his stomping grounds. His fly-tying ability would rival some of the best tiers in the world. Including your friend Milky's. All Emery wanted from Milky was information to use against you to further the game."

"So, Emery had me going nuts trying to decipher clues he himself planted. He knew that I'd pick up on that Indian Island lead and lead me down the primrose path."

Zeke rocked forward in his seat, implying an implacable yes. "Sorry it turned out like this, J."

Justin fixed his cold eyes on the doorway. "Lanelle's good, Zeke. I gotta hand it to her. I really do."

Zeke shook his head assertively. "Nothin' to do with her, I told you. Nothin' of the kind. To tell you the truth, I was even surprised Lanelle saw what she saw. She saw letters. You and your boys saw numbers. End of story."

"Not quite. What about Long Island Heating? That white van? Whitey? If she hadn't—"

"If she hadn't picked up on letters, I'd have gone into my little act way before coffee. You wanted an actor; well so did Emery. **L-I-H**. I had the whole thing rehearsed as directed. I told you. I didn't know from 417 until you dropped that bomb tonight."

"But Emery did!" Justin marveled aloud.

"If I thought he was back at that safe house, I'd go there and kill him myself."

"What about this Whitey? Is he real or part of Act Two?"

"Oh, he's real all right. Only he's probably dead like you said." Zeke hung his head mournfully. "Drivin' for that company all those years. Light-skinned nigger; not no wigger. Genuine albino. Mean as they come. Never waved to nobody in his entire life. Waved to me the last couple of mornings, though. 'Course, it probably wasn't Whitey."

"Look at me, Zeke."

Zeke looked over at Justin somewhat tentatively.

"Emery in that house or not?"

"Already told you. Wouldn't think so."

"Why not?"

"He knows you're comin' for him."

Justin nodded mindfully. "That's his game."

"He's a player, J. Best I've ever seen."

"You're a player, too, Zeke."

"That's right. And when this is over, me, Lanelle and the kids are out of that rattrap," he swore, gesturing toward the shack.

"Interesting to note who you listed first and foremost, Zeke. Not to mention those you listed last."

"Don't pull that kind of crap with me."

"You hate yourself and me that much, Zeke? Tell me."

"You know why I hate you, don't you?"

"Lay it on me nigger, because I haven't got a clue."

"You and Lanelle."

"What about me and Lanelle?"

"He told Emery what you told him in prison."

"He, who?"

"Your friend. Milky."

"What did I tell him, Zeke?"

"About your affair with Lanelle."

Justin laughed out loud. "And you believed Emery?"

Zeke was nodding and crying. "I see the way you two look at one another. The way she holds you in her arms."

"Zeke. I love Lanelle. I'm not *in* love with her. Nor is she in love with me. You know me; or you used to. If that were the deal, I'd come to you and say, 'Hey, chump—me and Lanelle's got this *thang*; now fuck off.' Would I not? She loves you, Zeke, or she wouldn't stick around here. Kids or no kids. Off with them she'd go if she didn't care. Look at this dump. You're a broken man, Ezekiel. You were once a decent cop until you got greedy and lost it all. You sold out then, and you sold out now. What ever changes? Not too many things. You think fifty grand is going to solve your problems? Your problems are just beginning. Gonna tell you one last thing. I had a good friend. Met 'im long time ago in prison. His name was Milky. As white as white can be. I had another friend. Back in another lifetime. Black as the ace of spades. Chauffeured me all around this neighborhood as I sat in the backseat of his patrol car, shortly after putting' two white punks in the hospital. And then, he let me go. His name was Ezekiel. Big Zeke, to the boys in the hood. He died right in front of me tonight. Now get the fuck outa my stolen car fo' I make your wife a widow."

Zeke Idler got out of the car and slammed the door violently.

The veins were bulging along Justin's neck and temples.

Chapter 63

It was 9:00 a.m. when the phone rang. Justin was in bed, about to finally fall asleep. He picked up the receiver and put it to his ear, staring at the ceiling and thinking maybe it was Ursula calling from her mother's.

"You know another thing that gets my goat, J?"

"What?"

"How they serve the soup."

"What soup?" He was half-listening. Not taking any notes. Not bothering to record or trace the call, although he was equipped and trained to do exactly that.

"I don't think you're really paying attention, sport."

"Tired."

"Anthony Notaro was tired, too. That's how I got to him. All good things come to those who wait. Who said that, buddy? Doesn't really matter. You're going to come to me, J. You're going to come running into my arms. You'll soon see."

"Silly question, but why did you have to kill Whitey Hawkins like that?"

"Was that his full and legal name? We were only on a casual first name basis." Clarence Emery sighed. "I guess I must be getting a little tired, too. Impatient would probably be a better word. Usually, I know every detail there is to know about a person's life before I claim it. Or why bother? God, that was some scene this morning at Whitey's. Yes? I never saw so many police around. I mean, for The Greens. Find everything you guys and gals were looking for? All that fly-tying paraphernalia? I hope you appreciate the trouble I go through to keep the game alive, J. I really and truly do." There was a pause and, even though it was morning, Justin pictured Emery sipping expensive Champagne from a crystal glass.

"I was really wondering how long it was going to take you to key in on The Greens and Whitey, sport. You're really not a very good detective, I want you to know. Much too slow on the uptake. Then again, you're not really a detective at all. Now, are you? You're a paid assassin. Off the books, but on target. Yes?" Emery giggled. "I'm using the word assassin in lieu of bounty hunter for a couple of reasons, J. Number one, I'm worthy of it. I'm not just anyone. I'm The Teacher. And I'm going to *teach* you all a lesson you'll carry to your graves. Number two, my capture and arrest—as far as both you and Suffolk County homicide are concerned—are entirely out of the question. Is that not true, J? I understand, of course, that bounty hunters can and sometimes do conduct their business according to their own discretion, meaning that they may choose to bring their prisoner in either alive or dead. But the term *assassin* so suits your silly and single-minded purpose. Still, it has such a lovely flavor to it. Which brings me back to the soup. Listening?"

"The soup."

"Yes. I was recently in that seafood restaurant in Mastic/Shirley. Right around the corner from your flat. Well, I ordered a cup of their seafood bisque. Guess what came out? Three quarters of a cup. So, I politely told the waitress to take it back and fill it, watching her every move to make sure that they didn't piss in it to bring it to the top. You see, they have an open, airy kitchen back there, and you can kind of tell what's going on. Well, she was back in a jiffy with the cup, along with a message from the cook. 'That's a measured cup,' she said rather rudely. Fine. I swallowed my pride, along with the soup, then left.

"They got me like that once before," Emery went on. "Only it was with a glass of red wine, couple of years ago. Once again, three quarters full. Now, I don't mean a sixteen fluid ounce claret glass, which they usually fill halfway so that the wine can breathe, they tell you. I'm talking three quarters of a four ounce glass. Three ounces, J. Seven bucks. Malcolm Columba could have told you similar stories before you deep-sixed him. So, what do you have in store for me, Justin Barnes? Death by chocolate, sweetheart?"

"The most unmerciful death I could conjure up. Gonna fuck you up real good," Justin promised Emery, unequivocally.

"My goodness, J. I do believe you're having an erection as you're saying that," he said and sighed rather satisfactorily.

"Got that right. 'Cause I'm gonna fuck you real good when I get my hands on you. You'll pay dearly for what you did to Milky. You'll pay for what you did to all of them."

"Holy mackerel there, Andy," Emery uttered in a disparaging black dialect. "I finally figures out what kind of fish you really be. Why, you be da Kingfish," the lunatic lashed his words through an uproarious laugh. "Oh, and one more thing, J. Jackie? I'm going to snatch her right from underneath your nose," he said before he hung up the phone.

Exhausted, Justin hung up, too, then fiercely punched his foam pillow. He kicked the top sheet off the bed with a vengeance before falling fast asleep for several hours. It had been a long night.

Chapter 64

Justin sat alone in the records room down the hall from Theo's office, ruefully reviewing the case files of all the senseless murders dating back to the first day he worked the investigation: The two Pipes Cove female victims from Greenport; Grace Littleton from San Francisco; her father, Doctor Timothy Littleton—also, the passengers and crew members en route from New York to California, including flight attendant Desirée Notaro; Howard Urban and Laura Ingrilli of Maryland; David Klein, East Quogue; his friend, Milky; ex-State Trooper Vito Vitalo of Monroe; Anthony and little Nicholas Notaro, along with policewoman Ruth O'Connor; and now, Whitey Hawkins from The Greens. When would it end? The simplistic answer was when Clarence Emery was finally dead . . . the more pragmatic question being, how soon?

As far as the police could determine, Emery started his killing spree better than a decade ago, butchering young, attractive women of Italian descent. Now, it was clearly evident that he was a nondiscriminatory serial killer who delighted in toying with and torturing his victims before allowing them to die a horrible death. Anyone was fair game.

The one constant that Justin duly noted was the fact that Emery, without question, always used a blade or needle-like instrument on his victims, confronting them up close and very personal—mutilating their bodies, if time allowed. Grace Littleton's fall to her death, the bomb set aboard the airline that claimed the lives of passengers and crew, and Milky's brutal murder—in which his skull was shattered—were, in all likelihood, as Theo had pointed out earlier, the work of accomplices . . . a gift bestowed by Emery as a show of gratitude before they, too, wound up dead.

Justin also discerned that never once did the serial killer wield, as weapons of cruelty, any cutlery or equipment other than those employed in the fields of culinary art or surgery; for example: fillet knives, cleavers, butcher knives, larding and brining needles, scalpels and such—operating or brandishing those implements with deft precision, as evidenced on the Howard Urban teenager and, especially, the Notaro child.

Accomplices, Justin pondered. *Who would be Emery's next accomplice? Did he already have one? Or was he looking for one at present?*

He was sorry he hadn't recorded or taken notes of Emery's earlier call. However, most of the maniac's monologue was logged in Justin's head, bringing to mind several key phrases that piqued his curiosity.

Chapter 65

Justin arrived at Alfredo's Restaurant in downtown Baltimore at 4:00 p.m. the following day. The place was not very busy. Two waiters and a waitress were standing around chit-chatting by the back door off the kitchen.

Justin walked up to the trio. "Excuse me."

"Have a seat anywhere you like, and I'll be right with you," the waitress said mechanically.

"I'm looking for Xavier Sanchez," Justin said as the young woman started to walk away.

"Doesn't work here anymore," she responded and kept walking.

Justin took a seat close to the kitchen, his feet sticking out in the aisle.

A moment later, the waitress came up to the table with a menu in hand. "Staying or takeout?" she snapped.

"Have any idea where I can find Mr. Sanchez?"

The woman smirked. "Mr. Sanchez collected his check and hasn't been back since."

"How long ago was that?"

"Staying or going, mister?"

"Staying."

The waitress abruptly laid the menu on the table.

Justin placed a badge on top of it in like manner.

She glanced at it quickly. "What do you want?"

"Information."

"You'll have to speak to the boss."

"Send him over."

"He's not here right now."

Well, that's a relief, he said to himself. Justin collected the badge and handed her back the menu. "Got a bag or a purse? Get it."

Brenda Harrison stood her ground. She was not easily intimidated. "I'm working."

"You're unbusy, lady. But I'll order, if you like," Justin promised. "Wait you out until your shift is over, then waste your time downtown."

Brenda cast a searing glare. "You *are* downtown."

"Huh. Well, we'll just start with a glass of water, honey-bunny. Then let's see if I can keep you hoppin' till quittin' time. I'm a very finicky eater, so I might have to send things back several times till you finally get it right. In the end, you'll see it wasn't worth the trouble and still have to answer my questions. Now. Just make sure the *agua's* mighty good and cold. And you'd better pour it in plastic 'cause I don't wanna drop a glass and break it. Oh, and no ice cubes, please, 'cause it tends to bother my very sensitive teeth," Justin pushed the envelope, smirking from ear to ear.

Brenda slowly lowered herself into the seat across from him. "He left here a little over a week ago."

"Did he say where he was going?"

She shook her head. "Only that he could do better than what he was doing here."

"He say anything else?"

The waitress laughed and nodded. "Yeah, he said, and I quote, 'Remember the Alamo.'"

"Remember the Alamo?"

"That's what he said. 'Remember the Alamo.'"

Justin took out his notepad and jotted down the phrase. "What's your name?"

"Brenda."

"Brenda, what?"

"Brenda Harrison."

Justin nodded sadly.

"What is it?"

"You're the young lady who found Laura and Howard's bodies. Aren't you?"

"Is that what this is all about?"

Justin nodded.

"Well, why didn't you say so? I thought you were like from Immigration, or something."

He shook his head.

"They come in here and check sometimes. Al, my boss, handles them. Ask you a question?"

"You can ask," he answered.

Brenda took the man into her shiny blue eyes. "Laura was my friend. A good friend. Are you any closer to catching this guy?" She sat rigid in the seat, staring into the black man's very serious face—waiting for his reply.

"We're trying, Brenda. We're trying damn hard. That's why I'm down here."

Brenda gave a hopeful nod, laboring a narrow smile.

"Tell you a little something I'm not supposed to tell," Justin whispered. "Promise to keep it to yourself?"

Brenda hastily crossed her heart.

"He murdered a friend of mine, too."

"Oh, my God! Was he a cop?"

Justin smiled sadly. "No."

"I'm so sorry." She reached across the table and tentatively touched the back of his hand. "Oh, sorry. Is that a burn?"

"It's nothing."

"Listen, how about something to eat or drink?" she coaxed. "I mean, if you promise not to spill or drop things on the floor."

"Maybe in a minute. I got another question or two to ask you about Xavier Sanchez."

"Okay."

Justin swung his legs under the table and leaned forward, taking her into his confidence. "This goes absolutely nowhere."

Brenda nodded her understanding.

"Is Mr. Xavier Sanchez gay?"

Brenda took her time in answering. Thinking. Reflecting. "You mean because he let Mike, I mean Clarence Emery, stay with him?"

"Something like that."

"I don't think so."

"How about Emery? You worked with him part-time. You had time to observe him. Yes?"

Brenda was fidgeting with her fingers and gnawing away at her bottom lip. "I don't know. He did spend a lot of time with the fellas. Took an immediate liking to Howard. How could he kill him and Laura like that?" She was starting to lose it. Tears came to her eyes.

Justin capped her hands with his. "Take your time. Was there anything you observed, obvious or otherwise, that might cause you to wonder—"

"Brenda? Is everything okay?" one of two waiters asked in concern, staring down at the pair of black hands covering Brenda's. The other waiter stood doggedly beside his coworker.

Justin didn't wait for Brenda to answer. "You two take a hike."

The pair turned on their heels and left immediately.

"I'm fine," she called after them.

"Anything that might make you suspect Emery is a homosexual?"

Brenda was shaking her head. "The only thing I recall is that one night after work, after we closed up, Xavier was really upset about something, and Mike—sorry—Emery was rubbing the back of his neck. I really didn't think much of it. Probably nothing like what you're thinking."

"What about Howard?"

"Howie?" she questioned incredulously. "Howie was in love with a customer's daughter. Cute girl. She took it pretty hard when she heard what happened."

Justin nodded and removed his hands from hers.

"What's your name, Detective?"

"Barnes. But Justin will do just fine."

"Well, Justin. There's a customer who just took a seat up front, and I'm afraid you've frightened away the help," she noted with a smile, handing him the menu. "Have a look-see. Everything's pretty good here. Not like when Mike was here, though." This time, she didn't bother to correct herself. "Hard to believe it was him." She shook her head sorrowfully. "I'll be right back. Beer in the meantime?"

"Sure. Bud?"

"Bottle or draft?"

"Bottle."

"You got it."

"Ice-cold."

"You got it," she repeated.

Justin disliked the expression. He liked, believed, and trusted Brenda Harrison, nonetheless.

Chapter 66

There was no one presently living in Xavier Sanchez's apartment, although the landlady informed Justin that she had already rented the place to a British woman from Dover, England. The young divorcée would be arriving in another week with her Persian cat.

"All the way from Dover, England to Baltimore," the owner of the rooming house elaborated. "Usually, I don't allow pets. But I figured, what the heck. Twenty percent increase in rent. Two months security. References here in the states, which I checked out thoroughly, mind you." The middle-aged woman stopped dusting just long enough to pull a Kleenex from her housedress, sneeze and blow her nose. "Allergies," she explained. "Won't be coming up *here* much, you can bet," she swore. "But at least cats are clean."

"Did Mr. Sanchez leave anything behind, ma'am?" Justin asked, following her around Xavier's empty room.

"Not a scrap of paper. You're welcome to look around. Police already went through this place with a fine-tooth comb. Vacuums, too. I asked one nice detective if he wanted to rent the place. Do you know they even wiped their feet before they came in?"

"Are you trying to make me feel guilty, ma'am?"

The landlady waved away the notion with her rag. "It was raining out that day. Anyhow, I didn't ask Xavier to leave. He just did that on his own. I guess it got a little awkward as time went on or something. Nosy neighbors were always asking me questions. Tell me, Detective. He didn't do anything wrong, did he? That's not why you're here."

"No, ma'am. I just have a couple of questions I want to ask him, is all. You have no idea where he might have gone?"

"You asked me that the second you came here. Second question, in fact," she said, turning the cloth over and passing it along the top of the table. "You don't think I'd lie to a policeman, do you?"

"No, ma'am. I surely don't."

"I should hope not."

"Well, you have a nice evening. I'll see myself out."

Chapter 67

Security at the Bella Sera Restaurant, as well as the Rubino home and surrounding property, was especially tight. No one in authority really believed for a moment that Emery would be foolish enough to risk his life by trying to kidnap Jacqueline, or any member of her immediate family for that matter. The concern was that Emery might put an accomplice up to the deed, to make good on the madman's threat.

As a precautionary measure, Jacqueline was restricted to the kitchen and rear dining room where undercover cops and FBI agents could watch her and her surroundings like hawks.

A presumed blind man sat at a back table with his Seeing-Eye dog, trained in bomb detection, in case anyone had the bright idea of carrying in explosives. The side and rear exists to the building were secured. Customers entered and exited only from the front of the restaurant. Federal agents were posted just outside the doorways. Throughout the busy workday, the parking lot was surveilled by undercover personnel wearing workmen uniforms and aprons: sweeping, cleaning, or picking up litter. Delivery and garbage trucks periodically moved about the building. The men who drove them knew exactly what was coming in and going out—and when. There would be no surprises as there had been with the Airborne Express, Omaha Steak delivery. Every shipment, along with every item, was checked and double-checked: flowers, fish, meat, poultry, vegetables, linens, and restaurant supplies.

After a week of tension, the Rubino family began to feel a bit more relaxed. Even Jacqueline seemed to unwind; but not the men and women of law enforcement who were busy watching the family day and night. Jacqueline's Uncle Phil wanted to have a party for family and friends, expecting to close the restaurant to customers the following Monday. However, authorities strongly advised against it—

for no good reason that Phil could comprehend.

Justin understood perfectly. Suffolk County and the federal government were not about to foot the bill for security for Phil to throw his own private party behind closed doors while there was an outside chance that Emery or an accomplice might show. Therefore, a compromise was finally reached whereby Phil and a limited number of close friends and family members could hold their get-together in the back of his older brother's newly opened restaurant, La Siciliana, in Noyack, by the bay. As far fewer tables graced the establishment by comparison, less security personnel would be needed to provide the necessary protection. It was agreed that Bella Sera would close its doors for an evening. La Siciliana would remain open, but with limited seating in the front section of the restaurant for its customers. Takeout, too, conducted behind its lengthy counters, would operate as usual—in the hope that law enforcement agents might take out Clarence Emery or an associate in a body bag if either culprit made their move.

The authorities figured that maybe—just maybe—Emery, or more likely a newly recruited accomplice, might see the way clear to strike at the new location. Unlike the Bella Sera, the kitchen facilities at La Siciliana were located downstairs: a catacomb of passageways and chambers where food was stored and prepared. Undercover police would be stationed at each doorway. Entry or exit would be accessed solely from the front of the eatery.

The party was scheduled for Monday evening at 8 p.m.

Chapter 68

Phil Cancilla was the first to arrive at La Siciliana, followed by his three daughters and their husbands. Minutes later, Frankie Sunseri stepped into the restaurant carrying a huge arrangement of flowers as his wife held the door open for him. Soon after, relatives and several close friends began appearing and were directed to the back room. Phil's older brother and two sons were busy preparing food. Another son carted wine up from the basement. Jacqueline and a nephew lent a helping hand by fetching freshly baked bread from the adjoining bakery, which Raymond Cancilla owned and operated, too. Everyone was working, mingling, joking, laughing, waving and throwing kisses. Immediate members of both families were orchestrating the event.

One of Jacqueline's cousins was busy directing several busboys and waiters who were carrying pitchers of water and large trays filled with mountainous plates of appetizers over to guests standing before or seated at the tables. Aunts and nieces, volunteering as last-minute waitresses, were opening and pouring and serving glasses of fine wine while, at the same time, planting loving kisses on kin and kind.

"You know what I like best about this group, Phil?" an in-law quizzed.

"What's that?" Phil Cancilla responded with a smile, putting an arm around the older man.

"No goddamn kids!" he swore at the top of his voice.

The volume in the room was rising.

Laughter and music filled the refreshingly cool air.

"You gonna smoke, you take that outside, young man," Raymond ordered a nephew. "You know better than that."

"Hey, Ray. You want me to break his legs?" one of the boy's neighbors called over.

"You? I break *your* legs you ever lay a hand on that young

man. *I'm* the only one who can break his legs," Raymond stipulated, poking his cigar in jest at the young man.

"How come he gets to smoke in here and not him?" a wise guy questioned, adjusting the Windsor knot of his white-on-white silk tie.

"Because it ain't lit, and because he owns the place, nitwit," a cousin to the boss replied. "Hey, Jackie! You look beautiful as always. Who's that funny-lookin' guy standin' next to you?" the relative called out.

"Hi, Eugene," Jacqueline acknowledged warmly as Tomas blew the guy off by giving him the bird.

Jacqueline's mother came over and gave her son-in-law a great big hug and a loud, wet smooch.

"Hey, Tomas," Eugene persisted, "my ex-mother-in-law never gave me a hug and a kiss like that until the day I divorced her daughter. Then her father came up and offered me a thousand bucks and his prize racehorse," the wannabe comedian started.

"For what reason?" an unwitting straight man seated at a nearby table asked in earnest.

"To take her back, of course—and in the bargain, ride his ol' lady out of town."

"So, what did you do?" a relative insisted, egging his grandson on.

"What did I do? he asks." Eugene straddled an empty chair and grabbed the back of it like a rein. "I took the man's money, jumped on his mare, and rode away like the wind. Solo!"

"What? Without the women?" the grandfather questioned with mock surprise.

"Hey—" Eugene replied, grinning from ear to ear, setting one hand on his crotch and the other around the slim waist of the woman nearest and dearest to him "—I'm Siciliano!" he announced most proudly, inviting his new bride to come and share his saddle-seat, then pretending they were riding off in tandem.

The men around him roared. A group of older women from across the room came quickly forward and starting beating him playfully with their fists. Eugene's twin sister, Carla, waved an arm his way in sheer disgust.

"It's cads like you who give Sicilians a bad name," an elderly aunt swore, using the bottom of her heavy handbag against his head and shoulders in a fashion falling just short of playfulness. "Hear me?"

"Hey!—all right, already—"

"Say you know. Say it!" his Aunt Ileana commanded.

"—enough, already—I know, I know," he admitted freely, releasing his riding partner and escaping to center stage. "Ladies and gentlemen, this joke you're gonna like a lot. Even you, Aunt *Il Duce*. There's these two lesbians—hey! Whattaya guys doin'?"

Eugene was moved out of the limelight and replaced by Raymond's youngest son, Victor, an up-and-coming comedian making the nightclub circuit, performing at theater clubs and improvs throughout many cities along the Eastern seaboard. Without introduction, as everyone present knew Victor Cancilla, the ironically shy young man blushed and politely waited for the applause and whistling to subside. A moment later, the room grew silent, and the heavyset entertainer launched into one of his new routines. At the end of the hilarious act, uproarious laughter filled the room and lasted for a good two minutes. For an encore, Eugene and a nephew both insisted that Victor tell their favorite, all-time joke. After more than a bit of prompting from the audience, the young comedian continued rather shyly.

"Well, there were these four Northern Italian women—not Sicilian, mind you, Aunt Ileana," Victor proffered disarmingly, carefully setting the scene, "but rather four *dumb* blondes from Verona, who died somewhere in their mid-twenties. Anyhow, they found themselves standing before the pearly gates. So, Saint Peter explains to them that in order to enter heaven, they have to pass a little test. He asks the first blonde to come forward and explain the annual Christian festival of Easter, and what it celebrates.

"Well, the first blonde scratches her head and says, 'I think that's when all the children dress up once a year in costume and go around the neighborhood trick-or-treating.'

"Saint Peter shakes his head with disappointment, explaining that's the eve of All Saints' Day: Halloween. He then asks the second blonde to come forth.

"The woman steps forward, trips, recovers rather clumsily, then begins to explain that Easter is a day set aside once a year for friends and family to gather around the dinner table, hold hands, and give thanks to God for His divine favors and blessings before everyone begins feasting and fighting over white and dark meat turkey.

"Saint Peter winces, waves her away without even bothering to explain that she's confusing Easter with Thanksgiving, then summons forth the third blonde. Well, this blondie bean is pulling anxiously on her ponytail and asks Saint Peter to repeat the question, which he does with restrained irritation: 'Blondie,' he says. 'Can you explain the annual Christian festival of Easter, and what it celebrates?' The young woman nods awkwardly, conveying she believes she can. She proceeds to tell Saint Peter that Easter commemorates the birth of Christ, celebrated as folks assemble excitedly to deck the halls with boughs of holly, hang mistletoe, trim the tree with lights and ornaments, followed by the exchanging of lovely gifts.

"The apostle is appalled, vehemently shakes his head and tells the poor soul that she is quite mistaken, explaining that she is confusing Easter with Christmas. He then calls upon the fourth blonde to approach, asking the fair-haired, pigtailed pixie if she, too, would like the question repeated. But the young woman rolls her head confidently from side to side, explaining that the question is an easy one for her. Peter smiles rather pessimistically but patiently awaits her answer.

"'Saint Peter,' she emotes. 'Easter is the annual Christian festival which commemorates the Resurrection of Our Lord and Savior, Jesus Christ, whereby Judas, in exchange for thirty pieces of silver, had betrayed Jesus with a kiss: a form of greeting commonly used among His disciples,' she elaborates, 'thereby exposing Him before the Roman soldiers. The Son of God was led away wearing a thorny crown and forced to carry a heavy wooden cross, to which He was crucified upon a hill called Calvary, thereupon dying for our sins.' The blonde bravely brushed away her tears, dramatically took a deep breath and composed herself. Peter is very impressed and deeply moved, encouraging the woman to continue. 'Well, three hours later, Jesus' body was taken down, wrapped in shrouds, and put into a cave. On the third day, following His Crucifixion, Christ emerged from the mouth of that very cave on a sunny Sunday morning, saw His own shadow, and all of Jerusalem suddenly realized that they were in store for six more weeks of winter.'"

The crowd went absolutely wild.

When the laughter and applause finally subsided, a proud Raymond Cancilla walked over and hugged his son affectionately. "I believe you truly found your calling, Vic, my boy. You follow your dream of stage and screen like you always wanted, with your mother's and my blessings. But you know you'll always have a place here with your brothers and me if things don't pan out quite the way you plan. *Capisci?*"

Victor smiled proudly. "Thanks, Dad."

"I mean it. It's the stage for you, my boy," he declared.

From their seats, two hecklers had their shot at Victor.

"Yeah, the stage," an envious older brother shouted. "The next one outa town."

"Or the Stage Deli in Manhattan," the other shouted.

The pair was merciless.

Victor was turning red with embarrassment.

"See? Stage fright," Raymond's middle son directed, pointing out his younger brother's crimson cherub cheeks.

"What are you two *spronci* talking about?" their mother jeered her two older boys in jest. "Why, he's a regular stage-door Johnny," she teased her youngest, cheering him on in the very next breath.

Victor waved them all off good-humoredly before wending his way to their table.

Chapter 69

Heading for the basement, Jacqueline informed an FBI agent that she needed sauce from one of the refrigerators downstairs. At the bottom of the steps, a plain-clothes detective was standing tall.

"What's up, Jackie?" the cop and longtime customer asked politely.

"We're running out of marinara," she explained.

"I guess that's a little like running out of beer and pretzels during the Super Bowl," the Irishman declared in a lilting thick brogue while smiling pleasantly.

Jacqueline laughed lightly. "Did you have something to eat yet, Ted?"

The detective patted his stomach satisfactorily as she walked by. "Entirely too much. Need a hand?" he called after her.

"No, I'm just going to grab a couple of quarts. But thank you."

Jacqueline disappeared around the corner in a fashionable yellow pantsuit, a folded apron encircling her trim waist and concealing the weapon she was licensed to carry.

Detective Ted Donahue was happy for the assignment. Smiling. *Beautiful girl,* he entertained. *Nice girl.* Probably one of the nicest he had ever known, he reckoned.

Jacqueline knew most of the police officers, detectives, and a few of the FBI agents by their first and last names. She felt safe and secure around them. Some of them she even considered her friends. Ruth O'Connor had been her friend. And whenever Jacqueline thought of her and Anthony's little boy, all alone with Emery before he brutally butchered them in cold blood, she almost always cried—if not outwardly, then silently from somewhere deep within her being.

Sadly, she thought a lot about Anthony, too. He was a good man. During the time they spent together, he always treated her well. She knew he felt more than a bit uncomfortable when they were out together in public, putting on their little act. He tried not to show it. But she knew. He had loved his wife dearly and missed her terribly. As time went on, he felt more relaxed around the both of them. Especially Ruth. He was growing very fond of the undercover cop.

Ruth had confided in Jackie and confessed that she believed she was falling in love with him. Ruth and Anthony had made quite a team. Neither of them was acting beyond the midway point in their relationship.

Jacqueline brushed away a tear as she reached inside the locker and withdrew two containers of marinara sauce. From out of nowhere, a busboy suddenly appeared, wheeling a large stainless steel cart across the tile floor. She stepped abruptly back from the refrigerator door, practically dropping the containers while reflexively reaching for her weapon.

"Excuse me, *Señora*," the Mexican said politely. "Everything okay?"

"God, you gave me quite a start is all," she admitted, withdrawing her gun hand from the small of her back, recovering and removing a tissue at the front of her apron.

"Sorry I startle you. I see you crying. You all right?"

Jacqueline dabbed her eyes with the tissue. "You're new here."

"Yes. Mr. Raymond . . . he tell me to call him Ray," he said rather shyly, "—which is very hard for me—started me here one week ago."

"Yes, I saw you upstairs before. What's your name?"

"Felix," the busboy said rather anxiously. "Felix Zamora."

"I'm Jackie, Felix." She offered the young man her hand, cradling the containers in her other arm.

"Pleased to meet you, *Señora*."

"Jackie," she insisted with a sincere, yet saddened, smile. "Him, Ray. Me, Jackie," she teased in a sweet, low voice, gesturing with an elbow toward the ceiling. "Neither of us bite," she swore.

"Here, let me take these for you, Jackie."

"Thanks."

"You need couple more?"

Jacqueline put away the tissue and brought a finger to her chin. "You know, we just might need another container."

"Marinara or meat?"

"Marinara. Uncle Ray's got plenty of meat sauce upstairs."

"One more marinara, coming right up," the handsome young man smiled broadly, removing the container and closing the door, setting the sauces atop the stainless steel cart.

"What's in there?" she asked curiously.

"It's a surprise for end of party tonight. Mr. Raymond, I mean Ray, told me to keep this under wrap. Shh," he sounded soberly, putting a finger to his lips.

"What is it?"

"I don't want to get in no trouble," the young man answered, glancing up and down the long hallway.

"You won't," the pretty woman promised, making the sign of the cross across her chest.

"It's a cake," he whispered.

"A cake?"

The young man nodded.

"In a bin that big?" she questioned with surprise.

"A very big, expensive cake. Special message for a special someone."

"But I saw a quarter sheet upstairs. A flat box," she explained.

The young man smiled. "Decoy," Felix clarified. "This one is the big surprise."

"But—"

"I'm the one they sent to pick up at Frank's Bakery in Mastic," Felix explained.

"My, God! You could feed a large wedding party."

"All I know is Mr. Ray say he break both my legs if I don't come back with this cake in one piece."

Jacqueline and the young man heard a pair of footsteps coming around the corner.

"Everything all right here, Jackie?" Detective Ted Donahue asked.

"Everything's fine, Ted. But you better have saved some room for dessert," she warned. "If not, I have a feeling you and everybody else is going home with a big piece of cake." Jacqueline pointed to the unit.

The busboy was deliberately shaking his head. "You're going to get me in big trouble. I just know it."

"No, I'm not. Am I, Ted? Not a word about this cake, all right?"

The detective raised the tips of ten fingers to his to his lips, his eyes, his ears. "Today, I speak no evil, see no evil, hear no evil, although I do deal with it most every day."

"See?" Jacqueline reassured the young man.

The detective turned and went back around and down to the other end of the hall.

A bakery upstairs, and Uncle Ray orders from Frank's Bakery in Mastic, Jacqueline had to smile. Then again, La Siciliana was not equipped to handle a tiered cake quite that large. *Besides, Aunt Ileana's fiftieth wedding anniversary is this week,* she remembered. "Huh," she wondered aloud. "You didn't by any chance happen to see what was written on the cake, did you, Felix?"

The busboy smiled knowingly, removing the containers of sauce from the top of the steel bin and setting them down carefully on a small aluminum table in back of him. Next, he wheeled the unit around and raised its lid so that the writing atop the vanilla icing was facing her.

Jacqueline looked down at the beautiful cake and couldn't believe her eyes.

Our Jacqueline
The Bravest Girl In The Whole Wide World.
Your Loving Family

"*Diós mío!*" the busboy exclaimed. "Jacqueline . . . Jackie. Tell me you're not—"

"It's all right. Honestly."

"No, it's not. I ruined your surprise."

"No one's going to know. I promise you, Felix," she swore so sweetly. "Please don't give it a second thought."

"I'm so sorry."

Jacqueline was deeply touched by her family's sentiments, still staring down at the beautifully decorated cake when Felix Zamora, real name, Xavier Sanchez, stepped behind her and pulled a large folded handkerchief from a Ziploc, pressing the cloth forcefully against her face. Jacqueline fought fearlessly, but in vain. Within moments, she was unconscious and still as stone. Xavier removed the 9 mm PPK Walther from its holster at the small of her back, placing the handgun in his waistband, beneath a stark-white, full-length smock.

Xavier Sanchez had to work fast. He carefully lifted the top tiered section from the refrigerated unit, setting the tray down upon the table next to the quarts of sauce. Quickly, he lifted and placed Jacqueline's trim body inside the bin, tucking her beneath the empty shelf, replacing the tray back inside and atop the cooler. He closed the cover then grabbed the containers of sauce, wheeling the unit around the corner and down the corridor toward the detective.

"Sir, *Señora* Jackie ask if you wouldn't mind helping me with the you-know-what," Xavier said with a sly smile. "She wants it put out back and out of sight till after the dinner. If you wouldn't mind holding the door for me. But first I got to run this sauce upstairs. Be right back."

"Where is she?"

"In bathroom."

Xavier ran upstairs with the sauce.

Detective Donahue opened the top of the bin, smiled and shook his head.

Xavier was down in a jiffy.

"That was pretty fast, fella."

"Mr. Ray got me hopping. Mind giving me hand with the door?"

"Sure thing, kid."

"And please don't say anything about cake, or it'll be my head. It's supposed to be a big surprise."

"Jackie take a little peek inside?" he questioned through a grin.

The young man nodded nervously.

"Can't put anything over on that girl. You're a good lad," he said sincerely. "Felix Zamora, right?"

"Yes, sir."

"Come, Felix."

Together, the pair rolled the bin across the tile floor and up the concrete ramp toward the back of the building. The detective unlocked and pushed open the door, helping the young man pull the unit through the narrow passageway, parking the cooler just outside the doorway in a shady corner. The busboy went back upstairs, and the detective secured the exit.

Chapter 70

Eugene's sister, Carla, moved through the crowd of forty guests gathered in the dining area at the rear of the restaurant.

"Anybody see Jackie?" she asked around.

Several friends and relatives shook their heads. Carla made her way along the buffet table to a small group standing at the threshold between the restaurant and the bakery.

"Did you see Jackie?" she kept asking, a look of concern written across her face.

Again, aunts and uncles, nieces and nephews, cousins and friends responded in the negative.

"She went downstairs for more marinara, last I saw," a great-aunt replied from a work station off a corner of the room.

"I know that," Carla said impatiently. "We were running low, so she went to fetch some containers."

"A busboy brought up some sauce a little while ago," Eugene mentioned casually.

"But we got plenty of marinara up here," Raymond's oldest son said with some surprise.

"Yeah, but it's all frozen," a waiter interjected. "I checked."

"Not all of it. Can't be. I just filled the case before. We got plenty."

"So, where is she?"

"Someone said she went back downstairs looking for calamari in the locker."

"Will someone please go downstairs and find her," Carla insisted. "And where the hell is Tomas?"

"He's in the bathroom, for cryin' out loud. Cool your jets, girl. I'll go look for Jackie," Eugene volunteered, getting up from the table after taking a sip of wine.

"Yeah, don't strain yourself," Carla snipped.

"Anything else you need while I'm down there?" he asked, ignoring his sister's remark.

Carla shook her head. "Just go look."

"She's probably in the downstairs bathroom fixin' her hair or something," Victor offered reassuringly.

"Yeah, or busy talkin' to one of them slick detectives," Eugene joked. "On second thought, why don't you go look for her, Vic? Cops give me the creeps."

"Why don't you say it a little louder?" Carla lowered her voice, running her eyes along the wall and fixing them on a young man in his mid-twenties, standing not ten feet away.

"Him? I thought he was family."

"He is."

"Not on our side, he ain't," he snickered.

"Very funny. You gonna go look for her or not?"

"We're both gonna look," Victor answered, rising from his chair. "Come on, Eugene. Show you where my dad hides the lobsters and *good* champagne."

"Who he gotta hide them from?"

"Me, myself, and I."

"That's what I figured."

Minutes later, Detective Ted Donahue, followed by Victor and Eugene, came bounding up the stairs.

Raymond and Phil were busy talking business in a corner of the room.

"Where is she?" Jacqueline's mother demanded.

"Gone," was all that Victor could say, standing there in a daze.

"She just disappeared," Eugene managed, his hands trembling.

"What do you mean, gone—disappeared?" Carla was crying, her fingers gathering the black voile material into fisted balls at the front of her dress.

"They can't find her anywhere," Eugene swallowed.

Raymond and Phil were suddenly flanked by two detectives. The two brothers listened carefully to what the detectives had to say before asking a dozen questions themselves.

The brothers went up to Ted Donahue.

"Ray, I'm tellin' you. I even opened the lid and *physically* saw the cake myself," Donahue whined. "I read what it said. The busboy said that Jackie said to put it out back. Ray, listen—"

"Never mind, *saw*. Did you even think to *search* the cooler, Ted?" Raymond shouted. There was no response. "That's what I thought," he said with utter disgust.

Jacqueline's mother watched in horror as several FBI agents and pairs of detectives moved across her space . . . in slow motion . . . tilting out of the perpendicular . . . seemingly falling forward as her world suddenly turned black.

Tomas broke his mother-in-law's fall a split second before she dropped to the floor. "Someone call a doctor!" he shouted.

Both Raymond and Phil were yelling and shaking their heads back and forth excitedly.

"The cake I made is still in *there*, Ted!" Raymond exploded, pointing to the adjacent room. "A quarter sheet. Flat. Not a layered mountain covered with vanilla icing in some goddamn bin, like you said."

"We ordered no other cake!" Phil blasted in support.

"She's going to be all right," a neighbor promised, raising the woman's head a fraction, then placing Tomas' jacket beneath it.

Tomas made his way to Donahue's side. "Where's my wife, Ted?" he demanded.

Phil stepped next-door into the bakery. "Here, you wanna see?" he said angrily. He tore off the top of the box. "Look. No inscription to Jackie. There's nothing to celebrate until they catch this murderer. See? It says ~COWARD~. And all of us here were going to take a bite out of crime."

"What murderer?" an elderly man wanted to know. "Who's he shouting at? Who's Howard?"

"Not Howard. Coward, Daddy."

"Danny in trouble again?" the old-timer wanted to know.

"Danny's been dead quite a while, Grandpa," a daughter-in-law explained.

"Who's he talkin' about?"

"Never mind," said the man's son. "It's not your business."

"Whattaya mean, it's not my business? If it's family, it's *our* business."

"Pop, listen—"

"Don't you 'Pop' me."

"Please, Pop."

"Agggh." The old man waved off his son.

Fifteen minutes later, a call came through and Detective Donahue answered his radio. "Yeah ... Uh-huh ... No ... Right ... Okay."

"What?" Raymond snapped.

Another call came into the restaurant. Raymond snatched up the receiver. It was Raymond's eldest son.

"Yes, Mario. Where are you now? ...Phil, pick up; it's Mario."

Phil went behind the counter and grabbed the other phone.

"Go ahead, kid."

"The police found the vehicle ten blocks from here," Mario reported excitedly.

"What vehicle, ten blocks from where?" his father blew. "Speak English, man."

"Bella Sera's van, parked ten blocks away. Uncle Phil's delivery van," the young man choked.

"Any sign of her? They know anything?" Phil questioned quietly.

"Nothing."

"You stay with them, hear?" Raymond ordered.

"All right."

"Where's my Jackie?" Tomas was crying uncontrollably. "Where is she, Ray?"

"Hang on a second, son." Raymond held the receiver against his chest. "I don't know, but I promise you we're gonna find her, Tomas." He took his nephew-in-law into his other arm. "Stay on the line, Mario." Raymond put his son on hold, then took another call. "... Phil! Take the call on 0-one. Important." Raymond hit the flashing button. "Mario, you call in every fifteen minutes. Hear me?"

"Sure, Dad."

"But first I want you to call me right back on my cell phone. Do it now, son."

Thirty seconds later, Raymond grabbed his cell phone off the counter, turning his back to everyone. Cupping a hand alongside his mouth, he spoke quietly and distinctly to his eldest boy. "Mario, I want that busboy. You call your Uncle Dominic in Trabia. You have his number stored in your cell phone. You fill him in on exactly what's happened here. Tell him to call me tonight on a secure line. We should have handled this business ourselves from the beginning," he stated gravely. "Remember, you report back to me every fifteen minutes. Got it? ...Good."

Justin came barging through the front door. Tomas immediately charged toward him, reaching angrily for the black man's throat. Several men grabbed the husband, pulling him away.

"All your fucking fault!" Tomas kicked and cursed.

Two detectives held Tomas at arm's length as Phil went running over.

"Hey, hey, hey! That's not going to get us anywhere, Tomas. *Capisci?*"

Tomas and Phil went back and forth at one another in Sicilian.

Although Justin could not understand a single word, he had no need for an interpreter. One man, Tomas, simply wanted to kill him; the other held a *let's wait and see* attitude. It was as simple as that.

Chapter 71

Raymond and Phil Cancilla told invited friends and family to go home and not discuss—with anyone—what had happened. Fortunately, most of the customers dining up front were regulars, respecting and accepting the owner's wishes and explanations for having to close the restaurant early. Tomas and Justin remained standing in neutral corners as relatives and personnel were finally leaving.

"Tomas, please. Go home and wait for us," Phil pleaded, trying to persuade his nephew-in-law from remaining there another second.

"I'm not going anywhere," Tomas said firmly. "This is family business. Jackie is my wife."

Phil looked over at Raymond.

Raymond remained silent.

"All right, stay as you wish." Phil turned to Justin. "J, with all due respect, this is not your business any longer."

"Wrong."

"Excuse me?" Phil said, his face turning red with anger, barring embarrassment.

"I said, *wrong*. They're my family," he repeated, pointing to the police. "You're my family, too." Justin held the palms of his hands face up, turning them over slowly. "I'm just looked upon as the black sheep—by some—is all," he added without change of expression. "Besides, I have important information you'll want to hear."

"Let him stay, too," Raymond said.

"Now, hold on just a second here," the case agent for the FBI ordered. "You'll speak to *us*, Barnes, before you speak to anyone, if at all," Federal Agent Dale Fulton challenged.

"Who the hell is he?" Tomas barked.

"SSRA. Supervisory Senior Resident Agent in charge of an

operation that's gone out of control," Justin clarified. "Now. I know who this busboy is, and I have an idea where to find him. We find him fast, we find Emery. We find Emery, we find Jackie. Hopefully, still alive," he said without pulling any punches. "We work as a team—meaning all of us together—we have a chance. Divided, we'll be working at cross-purposes, I can assure you. And that will spell disaster for everyone concerned."

"Barnes," the agent snapped. "Listen very carefully to what I have—"

"I'm not finished. I have Commanding Officer Detective Lieutenant Theodore Groche's full cooperation in this matter. He's supported by the commissioner, himself. I just got off the phone with them."

"You've got your nose so far up Groche's ass that—"

"That you won't even see the brown spot, sport," Justin, again, interrupted calmly.

Agent Fulton glared. "This is a kidnapping! I think you're forgetting who's running this show, Barnes."

"No, I'm not. As of this moment, and until further notice, I'm second in command of a squad of twenty-two homicide detectives and four sergeants. As we speak, our gods are talking to your gods." Justin turned to Raymond and Phil. "Can I, maybe, convert the two of you? Just till we take Emery down and get Jackie back?"

"You're so full of yourself, along with a barrel full of shit, Barnes, that it's coming out of your ears," the FBI agent glowered. "You have no idea how things work."

"Call your field office, Fulton. I guarantee you they got the call by now."

Reluctantly, Raymond Cancilla nodded his cooperation, biting down solidly on an extinguished cigar. "What exactly is it that you know, J?"

"The busboy who you hired on recommendation, Felix Zamora. He's just been found murdered. Xavier Sanchez, who kidnapped Jackie, stole his identity. Xavier is the one Emery was staying with in Baltimore. He's The Teacher's new accomplice. As I said, I think I know how to find him. Again, it's important that we all work together." Justin abruptly shook his head. "Scratch that. It's imperative."

Suddenly, phones started ringing throughout the restaurant as well as the bakery next-door. The entire building was buzzing like a busy switchboard, tantamount to a telethon.

"D-Day, Daddy-o," Justin declared, taking Fulton fully into his sights.

Chapter 72

After much talk and discussion by high-ranking officials, compacted into less than a quarter of an hour, ground rules were set in motion.

"It's still our case," SSRA Dale Fulton decreed. "You'll coordinate the efforts, but Clarence Emery and Xavier Sanchez are ours for the taking," he fumed. "Do we understand one another, Barnes?"

"Just as long as you understand the 'coordinate the efforts' part, chump. You move your people how and where and when I tell you to move them. Not a second before. And I'll have people watchin' you just in case you slip up; then maybe one of mine just might slip, too. Follow?"

Fulton's eyes narrowed with hatred. "You don't threaten the FBI."

"I'm threatening *you*, asshole."

If no one stood to bear witness within the walls of Raymond Cancilla's establishment, Justin honestly believed that Fulton would have drawn his weapon and shot him on the spot.

"Let's get out of here," the federal man said to his people. "Just remember what I said, Barnes."

"Ditto, Dale."

Dale Fulton turned to face Raymond and Phil. "Just remember that your niece's life is in the hands of this lunatic. We got a file on him as thick as a phone book."

Raymond nodded. "Probably got one on this family, too. Maybe you ought to review it," he said in all seriousness.

The two men stood eyeball to eyeball. Dale was the first to turn away. He stormed out the front door of the restaurant.

"Whew," Phil exhaled. "Got us some pretty heavy shit goin' down," he said to Raymond,"

Wisely, Justin kept his mouth shut. They had no idea just how heavy.

FBI agents checked the Alamo Car Rental Airport-Serving Reservation's counter in Newark, New Jersey and hit pay dirt. A young man fitting the description of Xavier Sanchez, but using the alias, José Estrella, had flown into Newark International Airport a week earlier. The rental car had been driven to and dropped off at an Alamo office in Patchogue, Long Island. The handwriting unquestionably matched Sanchez's in signing off on the vehicle in Newark. But Justin Barnes already knew that. It was he who tipped off Cancilla's people and the feds, for the maverick had been a busy bee.

As new precedents were being set and parameters established to the letter of the law, the Federal Bureau of Investigation had little choice than to work and fully cooperate with Suffolk County homicide. Raymond and Phil's middle brother, Dominic, along with certain underworld contacts in Palermo, proved to be an added bonus.

The triumvirate was formed: a coalition working closely as a cohesive unit, sharing vital information that would unequivocally increase the chances of ultimately finding Clarence Emery and Xavier Sanchez, while hoping to rescue Jacqueline Rubino—provided that she was still alive. The trinity was seemingly of a single Godhead.

"How in God's name did Barnes ever figure it?" a senior FBI agent from the Melville field office located on Long Island wanted to know.

"Beats me," another answered, scratching and shaking his head.

The feds drew a single line between Newark and Patchogue.

"Big area to cover, people."

"What do we have to go on?"

"Only what Barnes' people gave us."

"I hear you've each been assigned a list."

"Yep."

"Well, let's hear it."

"I got gay bars and clubs."

"Halfway houses," said another.

"Wetback cantinas—other than the heterosexual kind," a

supposed cripple reported, still practicing his walk around a conference table.

"Oh, yeah? I got stuck with so-called *better* Mexican eateries, if you can believe that one. I've already been to Salsa Salsa, Green Cactus Grill, Oaxaca, Bali's Tropical, and Pancho's Border Grill. Immigration would have themselves a fucking field day," the disenchanted agent unfolded through a frown.

"Well, consider yourself lucky, pal," an exhausted, overweight Hispanic agent complained. "You got the high-end. I got the low-end of the shitlist. Believe me. Meson Olé. I had to cover both the South and North Forks all the way out to Montauk and Greenport. Seven shithouses. Don't ever eat refried beans twice in the same day. I had to hit the can back at that cantina in Patchogue twice."

"Why's that? Thought you might have missed something on the menu the first time out, Pancho? Or were you playing Cisco on the second go-around, Pablo ?"

"Yeah, one hell of a Margarita," the man confessed. "Had two, in fact."

"Oh, was that their names?"

"You didn't drink the water there, did you?" a pretty redhead asked.

"Why?"

"I don't know. I just thought it was a neat thing to ask," she deadpanned.

"Anyone ever tell you you're weird, Nancy?"

"I get that a lot. It's one of the reasons I get results. How about you, Dale?"

Chapter 73

Realistically, homicide's objective, not unlike the feds', was to stop Emery and any accomplice dead in their tracks. Idealistically, Jacqueline Rubino's life would be spared in the bargain. Justin's concern, first and foremost, was to find, rescue and return his charge safely to her family. The Cancilla family's single-minded goal was to deliver Jacqueline from captivity, at any and all cost—period. In truth, the thinking among the parties was as different as black and white, night and day, and life and death.

Who would assume the role of the Almighty in the end? Justin wondered. *The feds? Theo's teams? The Cancilla clan? He? Or God Himself?*

Unofficially, and for the moment, the maverick was in charge of Operation Teacher; that is, until such power might otherwise be seized from his hands. Meanwhile, Justin and his troops were the leading gatherers of information, outperforming the FBI hands down. The homicide teams' assimilation and dissemination of that information would hopefully prove of paramount importance in effecting the desired result. Real progress in the case was beginning to take shape.

Down the hall and around the corner from Theo's office at police headquarters in Yaphank, brainstorming continued in the squad room. Two of the lieutenant's top homicide detectives had just returned from a second trip to Western Europe, where they were following a lead regarding Rubino's kidnapping—a lead that suddenly dead-ended in Amsterdam. Brian Archer and his partner took a seat.

"So, why would Xavier Sanchez rent a car from Newark Airport, then drive all the way out to Patchogue, when he could have flown directly into Islip?" the lieutenant asked the assembled teams. "Assuming, of course, that Alamo is of significant importance."

"Maybe because there's no Alamo car rental agency at Islip Airport, or at any airport on Long Island," one homicide detective from Team Two answered up quite accurately.

"No Alamo car rental at any airport in the five boroughs, for that matter," a detective sergeant from Team One elaborated.

"No Alamo car rental at any airport in the entire state, except for Buffalo," a member of Team Three expanded.

"So, he flies from Baltimore to Newark International Airport and rents a car from Alamo," Theo reiterated. "Not Avis. Not Hertz. Not Budget. But Alamo. Then drops the car off at one of their neighborhood locations in Patchogue. Not Huntington, Smithtown, or Babylon. But Patchogue. Which tells us what?"

"I know it's not the answer you're looking for, Lieutenant, but it tells us that he's smart. Tells us he knows that if he simply abandoned the vehicle, he would have drawn attention to himself. This way, he doesn't raise a red flag," Noel Underwood answered up.

"Good."

"Or that someone else is smart. Like Emery. Telling Sanchez exactly what to do," another member of the team amplified.

"All right. Anyone else?"

"Tells us maybe he's a stone's throw away from us," an undercover cop in coveralls said with wishful thinking, as the two towns were but several miles apart.

"Or maybe the car's left in Patchogue to misdirect us," the rookie detective suggested, taking a different tact.

"Okay. Back to the word Alamo, in general. What could it possibly mean?"

"You mean, what it might mean to a young Mexican boy of his generation," posited a middle-aged, seasoned detective sitting up front —pointing a gun-finger for emphasis at Theo standing behind the podium.

Theo smiled. "Shoot from the hip, Lacy. Elaborate."

"It could mean that the kid has a hard-on for Davy Crockett," a voice from the back of the room remarked.

Everyone laughed except Theo.

"Sorry, Lieutenant."

"No, that's fine. Really, Mark. Back to you, Lacy."

"Well, I was going to say something right along those lines.

Might evoke some strong emotions in an impressionable young man."

"Fine. J, why don't you come on up here and tell us what you picked up in Baltimore."

"Crabs," Detective Kilpatrick roared, standing off in a corner and scratching his crotch.

The members of all three teams had a good laugh at Barnes' expense.

Justin stepped up to the podium and shook a friendly fist at the veteran detective. When the group grew quiet, he began his talk.

"I paid a little visit to Xavier Sanchez's place of employment and spoke with one of the waitresses down there. The one who discovered Laura Ingrilli and Howard Urban's bodies. Brenda Harrison. Right after Sanchez collected his check, he told her rather angrily, 'Remember the Alamo.'" Justin paused for the full effect.

"Anyone care to expand on that?" Theo invited.

"Well, it could just be some kind of subliminal thing," the case detective, Brian Archer proffered. "Guy arrives at the airport and has to rent a car. Like the lieutenant said, there's Hertz, and Avis, and Budget . . . and then there's Alamo. Strikes an unconscious chord in the boy."

"Yeah, but wouldn't Alamo trigger more of a negative reaction, like Lacy and Mark suggested?" a female detective tabled. "Subliminal level or not. I mean, if I were a rebellious young male Mexican, wouldn't I avoid the name Alamo and pick another rental counter?" she presupposed.

Justin waited politely for someone else to reply. No one did, so he launched into an abridged response, having carefully researched the topic of 'subliminal seduction' to the nth degree.

"Not necessarily," Justin addressed the woman's point. "Remember that Santa Anna's men kicked some ass back then, putting down legends like Crockett, Travis and Bowie, before getting their own butts seriously fucked. Not to get too heavy, here, keep in mind the way some Madison Avenue advertising executives once upon a time promoted products for their clients." Justin went on to explain the use of symbols, such as skull and crossbones. ". . . or the negative word-equivalent, *Poison*, for example, obscured within their packaging design to stimulate a desired consumer response. All illegal practices today. But it really doesn't matter whether you're subtly depicting poison or penises, Margaret," the presenter enunciated with a wide grin. "Big breasts or boogeymen. Positive or negative. It doesn't really matter. It's the level or degree of subliminal shock value that's important in motivating someone to behave a certain way. And it works, gang."

"Even like murdering someone?" the woman asked skeptically with a smirk.

"I'm told it doesn't carry over to that extent; that a person wouldn't act upon something he or she wouldn't ordinarily do," Justin elaborated. "In any event, I don't think Xavier Sanchez, posing as the busboy, Felix Zamora, murdered the kid," he declared emphatically. "I think that was Emery's handiwork."

"But there were no fingerprints or trace evidence of any kind this time around," Brian Archer's partner, Gary York, explored. "Emery always leaves his calling card, whether its prints, hair or fiber, or his own admission."

Justin nodded in agreement. "I don't have an answer for you, Gary. All I can say is that Emery's heavy into mind games. I think what we need to do for now is focus on the word Alamo, either as a symbol or something more concrete. There's got to be a connection. I *don't* know what it is. Haven't got a clue, in fact. But it did point us in the right direction, didn't it? Also, I think homosexuality is somehow linked to this Alamo business, as well."

"Are you saying that this Sanchez guy is gay, J?"

"I think they're both gay. Emery and Sanchez. Just a gut feeling. With Emery, it's because of certain words and phrases he used in his last conversation with me. His intonation, too."

"I'd like to hear them," Kilpatrick said.

"Yeah, you don't have to tell us how you responded," Brian Archer joked.

Justin smiled uncomfortably. "His use of the word 'lovely,' for one. But more to the point, 'You're going to come running into my arms,' he told me. And, 'I do believe you have an erection as you're saying that,' when I told him that I was gonna fuck 'im up real good."

"He didn't refer to you as *Shaft*, did he?" a black detective needled.

"Cute, Mosely. Very fucking cute."

"Cute sounds like a fag word, if you ask me," Bobby Lee

snickered, scratching an itch at his elbow, just beneath the plaster cast.

"No one's asking you," Theo remarked coldly.

Chapter 74

Fortunately, the Cancilla brothers' contacts were not embroiled in any red tape involving court orders for wiretaps, searches, seizures and such. They just went about their business efficiently and effectively. Most importantly, expeditiously. There was no boss of all bosses. Only one facilitator. Dominic. Jacqueline's father. Dominic owned and operated a restaurant in Trabia, a town just east of Palermo —although it appeared as if he were residing right around the block. Dominic's finger was on the pulse of activity. Feds. Homicide. Locals. Justin's carotid artery, or so it seemed.

Dominic's people took Justin at his word. The watchword was Alamo. A symbol or a sign. One sign read, ALAMO MAIL SERVICE. Hauppauge. Every square inch of that property was scoured. Every employee was checked and double-checked.

Two residences right out of the telephone directory were surveilled and subsequently searched as well. One home belonged to a woman in Coram: a divorcée, Blanca Alamo. The other residence was rented to a couple in Hampton Bays: Wilfredo and Gloria Alamo. A variation of the surname, Ala*i*mo, was also looked into—as were forty respective dwellings.

Dominic's associates were widening the net.

Twenty-four hours later, a clandestine call was made from East Patchogue to Trabia.

Dominic picked up. "Go ahead."

"We found an Alamo Motel here, if you want to call it that; not listed in any directory." "Yes?"

"I think we found the Sanchez boy. Cut up into little pieces and left in a storage bin."

Dominic closed his eyes and prayed. "How do you know it's him and not Jackie?"

"ID. Male anatomy. Clothing. Wristwatch. It's not her, Dom.

Feds are typing the DNA to see if it's actually the kid, but I wanted to call you immediately."

"I appreciate that."

"I'll get back soon as I hear more."

Dominic opened his eyes and thanked God profusely, although he wasn't completely sure about anything at the moment . . . anything, that is, except the full and true meaning of the word *hope*.

Chapter 75

The call was initially made to Justin's apartment, although it had been automatically rerouted back to a computer terminal at police headquarters in Yaphank. Justin, Theo and Agent Dale Fulton were standing beside the computer maven who was monitoring high-end reel-to-reel ADC (analog to digital converter) equipment.

"Hey, J. How are you doing, good buddy? I thought I'd catch you in. How's tricks? I must say it's remarkable how fast you fellows found him. Poor Xavier. I bet when they lifted the lid, their first reaction was, 'Oh, God!' Were you present for the grand opening? I'm sure Xavier's mother's reaction will be more like, '*Diós mío*!' Oh, well. We all have our crosses to bear. I want the Cancilla family to feel rest assured that Jackie says her prayers every evening; though, granted, it's only been two nights. She even works them in during the day when she thinks I'm not watching."

Justin's heart was racing like a Thoroughbred's.

"Let him keep talking," Agent Fulton both mouthed and gestured, winding one index finger around the other like a miniature makeshift recording machine. The wall of electronic recording equipment standing before them stood taller than his ego.

Justin nodded.

"Are you there, J?" Emery asked.

"I'm here."

"Where is here, dear?"

"Right here in my bedroom. Is Jackie—"

"Stop it!" Emery snarled.

Justin looked at Theo. "Stop what?"

"Stop the trace and I'll put Jackie on. But just for a moment. She's only allowed three words. We rehearsed them together, both she and I."

"Let me speak to her."

"You're not listening, J. She'll speak. You'll listen, sweetheart."

"I'm not your sweetheart."

"Oh, but you will be. Don't you remember what I told you?"

Justin kept his tongue.

With face and hand motions working like a mime's, Theo and Dale were prompting him to go on.

"Yes, I remember."

"Let me hear you say it, darling."

"'I'll come running into your arms.'"

Justin waited for Emery's next sentence, word or demand. But all he heard was the caller's breathing.

Fulton was scribbling something down on paper.

"Well, J?"

"Well, J, what?"

"Are you going to stop the trace? You know, I could have called you on your cell, which would have made matters a bit more difficult to home in on, as I'm sure you know. But I figure we still have a little time left to establish trust."

Justin looked down at Detective Kim Archer.

The programmer shook her head.

The agent thrust a note under Justin's nose.

Ask him what he really *wants*, it read.

"What do you really want?"

"I want you to go over to the window and open the shade," Emery insisted, knowing full well that Justin was in a concealed space at headquarters.

"I'm in bed," was all that Justin could think to say.

"Are all of you in bed together, dear? Or just in cahoots?"

Kim indicated that she wasn't getting anywhere.

Theo nodded and told her to stop the trace.

Dale Fulton drove his fist against a metal file cabinet.

"My, but it's getting noisy over there."

"It's done," Justin said, clenching his teeth.

"Swear?"

He could picture Emery smiling. "I swear."

"You know something? I believe you, J. I truly do."

"Put her on."

The recording equipment—not the trace, however—was operating and functioning flawlessly. At least they'd have precise, undistorted copies of the conversation with which to work.

"I just want you to know, J, that this is really a very *safe house* that we're all staying in."

"Who's *all*?"

"Jackie, my new assistant, and I. Who's all over there, pussycat?"

Justin looked at Theo, and Theo nodded.

"My commander, an FBI agent, and a technician."

"And you."

"Yes, and me."

"You're sure it's you now, J, and not another fellow in your bed?" Emery laughed.

"Put-her-on."

"Jackie, would you come here, please? Ollie, would you help her? There, there now. It's all right. Three words, remember. Blubbering won't count as one of them, and contractions are quite okay."

Justin heard another's laughter and cringed as the sobbing sounds drew closer.

"Go ahead, Jackie. It's that troublemaker, Justin Barnes. Speak directly into the mike."

"I'm s-so . . . s-scared."

A lot more crying was heard as Jackie was presumably led away.

"Oh, I guess stuttering and stammering are all right, too," Emery expressed through an impatient sigh. "I'll allow it under the circumstances."

Justin's heart locked tight. His head became light. He had to sit down. "I want to speak to her."

"No."

"Now!"

"No."

"How do I know that's not a prerecording?"

"You don't. But I thought that we had established trust."

"Her family is prepared to pay you a small fortune, Emery. Would you like to hear the number?"

"It's not about money, J. I think you know that."
"Ten million dollars, sent anywhere you want."
"You're not listening."
"What do you want in exchange for her?"
"You."
"Done. When and where?"
"I'll be in touch. Toodle-oo."

Chapter 76

Dale Fulton was pacing the room while Justin sat with his head in his hands.

"How could Emery know, Kim?" Theo asked his computer wizard. "How could he possibly know?"

"I think it's pretty obvious, Lieutenant," Fulton fumed, pressing and passing both palms along the sides of a shiny scalp.

"I don't know, Theo. I really don't," Kim answered her superior. "It's like the guy has radar. It's uncanny."

"Uncanny!" Fulton laughed incredulously. "You people are unbelievable. I'll tell you what the guy's got. The guy's got a mole inside your ranks, hotshot. That's what he's got. An accomplice working right underneath your noses, and you don't know it. I'll need that deck and tape before I leave here. Not a copy of the conversation. Hear me? You guys and gals can work from whatever you want. But my people are going to analyze the original before she really screws things up." The agent looked down with disdain at Kim Archer. "I leave here with the unit."

"The only thing you'll leave here with is that chip on your shoulder, unless I decide to knock it off," Justin menaced caustically with clenched fists. "Maybe clock your head clean off in the bargain," he added for good measure.

Fulton ignored Justin as though he weren't even in the room. "And another thing," the agent barked. "I want—"

"I want you to shut up for a minute and listen to me," the lieutenant interrupted. "Kim is the best at what she does. I'll match her against anyone you got. No one here is going to screw anything up. You want to do this on your own? Fine by me. You'll leave here with a copy and like it or lump it. If you're unhappy with that, bring whoever you want over here, and we'll run it for you. But the equipment stays where it is so that *you* don't screw things up. And if you're smart, Fulton, you'll come back with a team and work with this woman who will probably teach your people a thing or two."

"You know I can have this whole goddamn area sealed in twenty minutes, and *all* this fucking equipment impounded. What do you think about that, Groche?"

Without batting an eye, Theo told him. "Exactly what I always thought, Dale. You're an idiot."

Fulton fixed his steely blue eyes on the head of homicide as if he wanted to murder the man precisely where he stood. Seconds later, the angry agent smiled down derisively at the black pair seated next to one another, surrounded by a wall of computers, hard drives, phones and microphones, loud speakers and laptops. "Like monkeys, I guess you can train them to do just about anything," he stated arrogantly and glared.

Justin launched from his seat like a rocket, propelling the agent back against the same file cabinet upon which the agent had vented his anger moments earlier. Fulton managed to throw a feeble punch, but Justin caught him in the gut, followed by a left hook that nailed the agent squarely in the jaw. Dale was down for the count. Unconscious. Justin was standing over his opponent like a disappointed prizefighter who had demanded someone more challenging from the start of the bell. "Round one already over, chump?" the champ chomped as though wearing a protective mouthpiece.

"Some folks never learn," the woman said rather sadly. Then, as if nothing of significance had happened, Detective Kim Archer swung herself back around in her seat and went to work on an earlier assignment, cross-referencing the word Alamo with books, illustrations, newspaper articles, brochures, historical documents, ad infinitum . . . starting with the obvious and working her way into the recesses of the arcane. If there was a link, Kim would find it. She had already connected several dots.

Looking wearily from Justin to the figure lying motionless on the floor, the lieutenant shook his head in a sign of surrender and disgust. "We got ourselves a real problem here, J," he remarked.

"Well, unless he's dead, I'd say *you* got the problem, bossman." Justin squeezed Kim's shoulder affectionately before he started from the room.

"And just where do you think you're going?" Theo barked.

Justin disappeared around the corner.

Theo turned to Kim. "You made backups of those recordings?"

"Uh-huh."

"How many copies?"

"One of each, for now. I'll run others later."

Agent Fulton was starting to come around.

"Justin's getting out of hand, Kim. I can't control him anymore. I'd like you to talk to him. He listens to you."

"I'm not his mother, Theo."

"Then try playing nursemaid," he pressed.

"I've got work to do," she said politely, her eyes glued to the monitor. "But speaking of nurses," she remarked, allowing her words to hang there as a palpable reminder.

The fed was sitting up, groaning and playing with his jaw.

The lieutenant stooped and tried to help the man to his feet, but Fulton flagged him away angrily. "I think it's broken," he muttered, flexing his lower jawbone and looking as though he was about to cry.

"You deserved exactly what you got," Theo told him flatly.

The man mumbled something incomprehensible about the federal government, the agency, and pressing formal charges.

Theo asked him if he wanted a copy of the conversation or not.

Dale reluctantly accepted.

Kim propelled herself over to a computer, hit an eject button, and out popped a CD. She removed the item and passed it to Theo, who placed the disk in a protective plastic case. He handed the copy to the agent. Dale took the disk and stuck it in his pocket, struggling clumsily to his feet before leaving the room in a huff.

Kim went back to work. Theo watched as a set of flamboyant fingernails flew across the keyboard. Her eyes never left the screen, even as she waited, sometimes interminably, for a classified piece of information to be retrieved.

Before he left the room, Theo, too, fondly squeezed Kim's shoulder.

Kim reached back and held his hand in place while her other continued working solo. "We're going to figure this out and nail the son of a bitch," she said determinedly.

"Of this, I have no doubt," the lieutenant replied quite confidently, praying it would be sooner rather than later—before another innocent person was murdered at the hands of Clarence Emery or one of his accomplices.

Chapter 77

Detective Kim Archer worked Big Sister much like a concert pianist would play his or her instrument. Lovingly. However, there were times when the beige behemoth simply did not produce the desired notes needed to help connect the necessary dots. Occasionally, Kim could be heard raising her voice several decibels—rather threateningly, in fact—at which point she would maniacally dance her decorative nail art back and forth across the keyboard, pausing just long enough to enjoy those dulcet tones. The timbre of the audio frequency resonated a series of signal connections linking a central database in Washington, D.C. to the Justice Department, or other key locations around the globe—first, through a central satellite bank conjoining a series of underwater cables beneath Baltimore, followed by the sweet din of a secure system booting up before sending out the most sensitive of confidential reports—sealed documents notwithstanding.

"Here we go loop-de-loop. There we go loop-de-li," she'd sing in soprano.

If ever a person truly knew where a good part of the country's tax dollars were constantly and clandestinely being funneled, Kim Archer certainly knew, but she would never tell a single soul. More often than not, after seemingly solid information had been painstakingly compiled by both man and machine, and a viable theory fed into the works, sheer frustration rather than harmony was frequently the hallmark of orchestration. It was during such moments that Big Sister was monikered The Big Bitch by Detective Kim Archer, as well as every member of the team.

"The Big Bitch is really giving me an Excedrin headache today," Kim would complain aloud.

But for the most part, the players knew that failure was often the result of a series of dead-end leads, oversights, nonexistent records, even flawed or purposely misleading information set in motion. Kim had seen and heard it all, never leaving any note unsung. Re-reviewing research and/or starting completely anew took time and patience. Casting new light upon the shadowy gray areas of an investigation usually required innovation and creativity, along with the reinvention of the wheel.

Detective Kim Archer, the former Miss Kim Booker, together with her husband Brian, had been the two detectives responsible for bringing Justin into the fold. The recently married interracial couple was an essential part of Team Three's surreptitious network. Both Brian and his partner, Gary York, a no-nonsense veteran detective, helped seal serial killer Howard Mills' fate several years back. Mills' arrest and conviction brought an end to a spree of murders involving prostitutes in three boroughs. It was the first death penalty case on Long Island in a quarter of a century.

York had secured Mills' confession, it was rumored, by misrepresenting himself as Mills' attorney in the 8 x 8 foot interrogation room, right down the hall. In actuality, it was fact, not fancy. In private circles, York was known as The Closer. A damn good cop but, nonetheless, quite the ladies' man. Yet, in the workplace, he never carried his charm or used his good looks beyond the second plateau, defined as, and limited to, harmless flirting in and around the offices. A single step beyond the threshold of headquarters, and Detective Gary York would rival Don Juan.

"Gary," Kim called out, her eyes fixed on the monitor as though she were in a trance. "I think I got something here." There was a long pause as she reran and double-checked the information. "Yes, indeed, I do!"

Gary stepped over and stood directly behind her.

"Look," she said. "**ANONYMOUS' LATIN AMERICANS' MEXICAN ORDER.** ANONYMOUS is the umbrella organization. ALAMO is an acronym. Alamo is but one specific fraternal order of four."

Kim set up and boldfaced each initial letter in a column for Gary's benefit.

Anonymous'
Latin

Americans'
Mexican
Order

"They're a gay organization made up of mostly Latinos; that is, Columbians, Cubans, Mexicans, and Spanish," Kim explained. "Now, watch." She hit a series of keys, and the abbreviated form for each fraternity appeared.

ALACoO. ALACuO. ALAMO. ALASO

"See?" Kim clarified excitedly. "Anonymous' Latin Americans' **C**olumbian **O**rder: abbreviated **ALACoO**. Anonymous' Latin Americans' **C**uban **O**rder: **ALACuO**. Anonymous' Latin Americans' **M**exican **O**rder: **ALAMO**. And finally, Anonymous' Latin American **S**panish **O**rder of operation: **ALASO**," she said with a flourish, prominently displaying the information across the screen.

Gary saw and understood perfectly. "Where's ALAMO located?" he asked excitedly.

"Guess."

"Patchogue?"

Kim smiled and shook her head. "Guess again."

"Newark, New Jersey," he suddenly knew.

Kim nodded. "In an office building next to Holiday Inn North; right by the airport." She brought up and highlighted the address. "Unpublished number; so, of course, they're not listed in the directory."

Alamo 160-A Frontage Road, Newark, New Jersey 07114

"How'd you find them, Kim?"

"They take out advertising space semi-annually in *The Star Ledger*. That's what made it so damn difficult to trace."

"Where's Anonymous headquartered?"

"Don't know, but I'm working on it."

"You're a frappin' genius, Archer."

"To tell you the truth, I think you and Brian are going to learn the answers to some of your questions well before I do," she said

335

confidently, tilting her head back and off to one side while raising her keen dark eyes to meet his.

"You're probably right about that," he agreed.

"You guys be careful. All right?"

"We will," Gary assured her.

Kim leaned forward and sat up straight. "Now, massage my shoulders. I've been at this for fourteen hours straight, not including analyzing Emery's conversation with J."

"Ask Brian if I can take you home and maybe massage—"

"Never mind, Detective York. Just rub my shoulders or your partner will be going to Newark alone, followed by your funeral," she assured him with an affectionate smile.

Within twenty minutes, Justin Barnes, along with Detectives Brian Archer and Gary York, were off in a helicopter on their way to Newark Airport.

Chapter 78

Theo and Kim held a briefing in a windowless room right around the corner from the computer maven's restricted area. Twelve federal agents from the Melville field office stood before a long rectangular conference table set up with electronics equipment and a large monitoring screen. Agent Dale Fulton was not among the group. Kim continued with a discussion of her findings and feelings with regard to Justin's recorded conversation with Clarence Emery.

"Next, I'd like to go over parts of the conversation where I believe Emery is being truthful with us. After that, we'll juxtapose those against his other statements. To begin, voiceprint analysis indicates veracity and consistency in these phrases right there," she stated unequivocally, pointing to a printout similar to that of a polygraph recording, "where he says, '*I must say it's remarkable how fast you fellows found him,*' and, '*...feel rest assured that Jackie says her prayers every evening, although it's only been two nights.*' And again, here. '*She even works them in during the day....*'"

After studying the graph beneath the wording, one of the agents interjected. "Fine, but is the Rubino woman still alive after we hear her speaking *those* three words to Mr. Barnes? '*I'm so scared.*' Emery could have easily prerecorded it. That's one of the rubs; isn't it, Detective Archer? This could all be moot," he added impatiently.

Kim agreed with the man to a degree. "True. There's no way for us to know that for certain. Yet, we find no signs of tampering. No digital or analogic editing of any sort: no splicing, no acoustic irregularities such as dropouts, spikes, cross fading, et cetera. My gut, together with these measurements when Emery says, '*But I thought that we had established trust,*' tells me he's being truthful here," she continued, getting the agent back on track. "Look at the bar indicator. It's consistent with, '*I believe you, J. I truly do.*' And once again over here. '*Jackie, my new assistant, and I.*'"

Several heads were nodding in agreement.

A female agent who knew Archer's work and reputation still wasn't sure. "I don't know, Kim."

"All right. Let's compare an obvious falsehood with a fact, then note how they contrast. Then we'll match the measurements with other lines in question. First, '*I thought I'd catch you in.*' The intonation *seems* clear that he thinks he's calling Justin at his home and not elsewhere. Everyone agree?" Indeed, everyone did. "Good. Because we know that Emery knew damn well that Justin was here at headquarters. Note the wave pattern on the graph. Now, look at this. '*Stop the trace and I'll put Jackie on.*' And he does. See the reading you have now? Truth-telling time."

Everyone was nodding in the affirmative.

Kim hit arrow keys and scrolled up and across the display screen. "Getting back to, '*I must say it's remarkable how fast you fellows found him,*' note the wave-form and compare it to, '*Stop the trace and I'll put Jackie on.*' The fact that it's remarkable to Emery as to how fast Xavier Sanchez was found, tells us what?" Detective Archer asked the feds as though she were conducting a class, which in a very real sense was exactly what she was doing.

"It tells us that Emery doesn't know shit from shinola about the Alamo connection," an agent answered up smartly.

"Exactly," Kim said emphatically. "And that's our edge."

"The problem is that we don't have a firm handle on that ourselves," another fed put forth.

Kim looked over at Theo for a cue.

The lieutenant shook his head. "Not just yet," he put forth prudently. Although the remark was meant for Kim, it was construed by every agent present to be an acknowledgment of the commander's ignorance as well, which was precisely what Theo intended it to mean at that particular moment.

"Why would Emery call Justin Barnes at home knowing that he was here at headquarters and that the call was patched through?" the female agent wanted to know.

"Good question, Nancy, and one that cost me a night's sleep," Kim confessed. "Besides it being part of his game, to let us know how smart he is, he's probably doing exactly what we're doing here."

"Analyzing *us*," the agent posited.

"You got it," Kim agreed. "Of course, we don't know the answer to the big question. Is Jacqueline Rubino alive as we speak? But my gut, together with what I see and hear, here, tells me she is."

"So, why didn't Emery allow Barnes to speak to her rather than just listen?" the redhead pressed.

"Control," Kim said flatly. "Total control. To keep us guessing. To maintain the competitive edge."

All twelve heads were nodding in absolute agreement.

"Now, I guess we wait to hear from Emery regarding an exchange," a senior federal agent said, his face framed in a frown.

Theo smiled. "Not exactly, Lou. Can I see you in my office for a minute?"

"Sure thing, Theo."

Chapter 79

Theo relaxed in a chair behind his desk across from the veteran federal agent, Louis Tempone.

"Cup of coffee, Lou?"

"Never touch the stuff."

Theo smiled. "Should I take a peek at what I might have stashed away in a bottom drawer?"

The agent waved him off appreciatively. "Too early in the day, Theo. But thanks."

"So, I guess we'll get right down to it."

"Fire away."

"I want you to drop whatever might be pending regarding Justin Barnes."

"No can do," Louis said in no uncertain terms. "He fractured Fulton's jaw, Theo."

"Personally, I think he had it coming."

"That may be, but—"

"But we located Alamo."

Louis looked confused. "Yeah, the motel in East Patchogue."

Theo uncharacteristically radiated excitement, yet reticently shook his head. "There's more to it than that."

Louis looked at his friend in disappointment. "Theo, we all agreed that we'd work together. Share and share alike. You can't hold back vital information, then that loose cannon of yours over my head. It's simply not going to fly. First you refuse to give up the recording equipment, and now this? I'm supposed to receive any information immediately."

"Kim only pieced things together a little while ago, and I called you directly. But your Signal Analysis Branch people were hot to trot regarding that recording. 'Top Priority,' they said. You were already headed here for our meeting. I tried to inform one of your subordinates about this new development. He didn't want to hear of it. Said to speak to you when you got here." Theo pointed to the phone. "Want to hear the conversation, Lou? Date and time digitally recorded," he offered along with a smile. "Furthermore, you can take that tape and deck back to the office with you, now that we're finished with it. Your people can analyze Emery's conversation into the next century, but you're not going to find anything that's not already in Detective Archer's report. That's what I told Fulton, and that's what I'm telling you."

"Oh, I'm sure of that, Theo. I'm quite impressed with the findings, along with some of the state-of-the-art equipment I saw back there. Probably rivals Quantico's. I'm also very impressed with Detective Archer. She's topnotch."

Theo turned cold stone serious. "Lou. I know all about Quantico's equipment and technology. A tad more sophisticated than what we have here. The only problem is with those dinosaurs they've got operating things down there. Present company excluded, of course," he said without cracking a smile. "Time, Lou. Time. I'm not fighting the agency so much as I am the clock. That's why Fulton wasn't walking away from here with that ADC unit. Not until *we* were satisfied."

Louis nodded his understanding. "Still, our people are going to want to satisfy, if not sanctify, themselves."

"Fine. Now that we've gotten that settled, what about Justin Barnes?"

"What about Alamo?" Louis asked straightaway.

"A gay order; part of a larger network. Newark, near the airport."

"Go on."

"I want a guarantee, Lou."

"I'll talk to Dale."

"And I'll talk to the commissioner."

"Meaning?"

"Meaning that there's more to Barnes than meets the eye. It goes way beyond this operation, Lou. He's got a sixth sense. He's indispensable. Only I'd never tell him that."

Louis fixed his eyes on Theo's. The agent drew his lips in tightly before speaking. "I've heard certain rumors. I think I'm hearing them confirmed."

"Just rumors," Theo replied wisely.

"All right then."

"Thanks."

"But you owe me one."

"You'll have to collect before I file my papers in January," Theo announced.

"Yeah, I've been hearing those kinds of rumors, too."

Theo looked down at the framed picture of his wife and three daughters. "Well, Lou. You can make book and bank on it. How does that sound?"

"A little like insider trading, I guess."

"Thirteen years behind this desk."

"Amen to that."

"And you?"

"Maybe another two. Three at most. The only chair I want to sit behind after that is a fighting chair aboard a forty-footer off the Carolina coast."

"Amen to that, Lou."

"Know something?"

"What?"

"I think I will have that drink you offered—if you'll join me."

Theo pulled open the bottom right-hand drawer and removed a bottle of Sambovca, along with two shot glasses wrapped in clear packaging. "Got this as a gift, maybe ten years ago," he said quite truthfully. "Never touched it."

"Good stuff, I hear. Never had the urge?"

"Well, I certainly had the urge and the need, but never the opportunity, if you can believe that. Beer or some wine with the troops at the local watering holes. Then home to bed early . . . if that's even a word that can be defined."

"Half a shot. Whoa!"

"Half a shot at half past nine in the morning. Guess I *am* ready for retirement."

"To crime," Louis toasted. "Where would we be without it?"

"Probably in Utopia," Theo answered without batting an eye.

"Great. I'm drinking with an idealist."

"Nope, just a realist with a wish list, I guess."

"Well, you got one of them answered here today." Louis raised his glass and hailed a great man. "*Salute*. Now, let's hear *all* about Alamo."

Chapter 80

Detective Gary York waited a good fifteen minutes before the Alamo receptionist finally got off the phone. The short, bespectacled, well-dressed suited gentleman stood, walked over to the waiting area, then took and shook Gary's hand vigorously, cupping it completely while sympathetically extending his condolences.

"Any friend of Xavier's is a friend of mine," the man said sincerely. "We're so sorry to hear what happened. Horrible. Absolutely horrible. And I do apologize for having you wait so long, but we had to check out your story first. We get an awful lot of stories here," he explained. "An awful lot."

Gary nodded, wiping away an artificial tear or two.

"Please, sit back down and we'll talk some," the receptionist insisted.

Gary took back his hand and sat. "Thank you, Mr. Ramirez."

"Hector. Please call me Hector."

"I'm amazed the police haven't contacted you yet, Hector."

Hector Ramirez grinned. "I'm not. You have to understand that we're an extremely discreet club. We keep a very low profile. As a matter of fact, people think we're an agency for actors," he said, then giggled outlandishly.

Gary gave up a little smile. "I did a little acting once upon a time."

"Oh, I'll bet you were positively magnificent. Broadway?"

Gary shook his head. "Little bit of summer stock. *Streetcar.*"

"Oh my, Mr. York. I'll bet you had the lead. 'Stellaaa!'" Hector called out in a husky, manly, southern accent that took Gary by surprise.

"That's really good. No, I mean it," Gary swore.

"*Streetcar* is one of my all-time favorites," Hector went on, hunching his shoulders as high as a hilltop before relaxing them along with a sibilant sigh of satisfaction. "I still get goose bumps. So, tell me. You were Stanley, yes? Yes, yes, yes? Do tell me yes."

"Well, to tell the truth, I auditioned for Blanche DuBois, but they said they already had a leading lady and would I mind giving Mitch a shot," Gary put on in the best affected drag queen demeanor he could muster.

The two shared an uproarious laugh together.

"I really wasn't bad," Gary said immodestly.

"Oh, I'll bet not!" Hector swore, swooning and fawning and falling instantly in love with the handsome man. "I just know you were divine. Tell me. What else did you do, Mr. York?"

"Please call me Gary."

"What else did you do, Gary? A little Shakespeare in the Park, I'll bet."

Gary lowered his head into his hands and rocked sadly back and forth as if unable to continue the conversation. "That's where I met Xavier."

"Oh, dear boy. Please. Please don't say another word until I make you a cup of tea or coffee or anything you like. I know! We can order in. They have the most marvelous deli right up the block. I want you to use the office inside. There's a private bathroom where you can freshen up. And I won't take no for an answer. Oh, Gary. They have the most heavenly soups and sandwiches. In fact, they're having lobster bisque today, I believe. And their quiches—" Hector smacked his lips together "—to die for. Let me first find a menu, and then you just tell me what you'd like to order. Compliments of the club."

While Hector and Gary ate a light lunch together, discussing theater, gardening and the little the detective knew about Xavier Sanchez from a recent Baltimore city police report, Detective Brian Archer surreptitiously entered a back room to one of Alamo's offices where records were kept, jotting down pertinent information from Xavier Sanchez's confidential file.

Chapter 81

Detective Gary York drove the assigned sedan back to the helipad while Brian Archer read aloud from his notes. Justin and Gary were all ears.

"And check this out," Brian beamed, furtively shielding the zinger from them like a child. "Sanchez's got a name, address and phone number listed to call in case of an emergency."

"Tell me it's somebody we already interviewed who lied to us about Alamo," Gary challenged. "Tell me, so I can ring his or her neck while you tighten up some ass with promises of perjury charges."

Brian shook his head. "No, but you're going to love it just the same."

Gary glanced over from the wheel. "Well?"

"Where it reads, <u>Relationship to Club Member</u>, Xavier wrote down, '*close friend.*'"

"So, am I gonna have to play twenty questions?"

"You wouldn't get it if I gave you a hundred and twenty."

"We know this guy or not?"

Brian nodded in the affirmative.

"And we didn't interview him?"

Brian shook his head.

"Oh, so *we*, meaning you and me, are A-OK; but somebody else is gonna catch some heat. Is that it? Or did Justin, here, drop the ball?" Gary needled, catching a glimpse of their silent partner in the rearview mirror.

Again, Brian shook his head.

"Christ, not someone from our own team?" Gary squawked. "Gotta be the rookie, right? Underwood. Like he screwed up with Tom Cousins. Yes?"

"Nope."

Justin leaned forward and put his head between the two

detectives, attempting to sneak a peek at Brian's notes. But the man promptly closed the little book.

"Sit back there and behave yourself," Brian toyed and tarried.

"Dat's exactly what da po·lice officer tol' me las' time I takes a backseat to da law. Only problem wif dat today, Detective, is that *I's* callin' the motherfuckin' shots."

Gary laughed. "Yeah, you're callin' the motherfuckin' shots when you're ridin' roughshod over Dale and some of those other G-men jerks. But when you're ridin' with us, sport, you don't even have the privilege of being a backseat driver."

"I wouldn't be so sure about that, Gary," Brian said in all seriousness. "This black cat may be going in—and soon."

Gary looked over at his partner. "Say what?"

Brian opened his notes for Justin and pointed to the name in question.

"Jesus motherfuckin' Christ," Justin said slowly and as solemnly as if he were reciting the Lord's Prayer.

"Oh, you guys are really something," Gary snapped, snatching the memo book out of Brian's hand, glancing at the name of Xavier Sanchez's close friend. "Holy hen shit!"

"Eyes on the road or we'll all be hamburger meat," Brian cautioned, grabbing back the book.

"Address and phone number, too, you said?"

"Yep."

"That I can't believe. Probably bogus," Gary stated pessimistically. "It's just got to be. Some phony address Emery gave the kid before he iced 'im."

"Or could it be that the gods are finally smiling down upon us, and we have that fucker's safe house where he's hidin' and holdin' Jackie?" Justin prayed, pulling a Suffolk County Hagstrom from his briefcase.

"Sounds too good to be true," Brian's partner offered openly, praying inwardly that they had finally caught a break.

"Well, we'll find out soon enough," Brian stated optimistically, although he, too, had his doubts.

Gary ran a series of facts through their heads like a computer. "The kid flies into Newark International Airport and rents a car from Alamo, then heads to a club called Anonymous, with its Mexican chapter but a block away, back there. A chapter he's affiliated with as a dues paying member through a branch office down in Baltimore, paying a little visit up here a week ago, according to the receptionist."

"As confirmed in my notes," Brian said in agreement, scrutinizing the entry.

"So, how did Xavier Sanchez come to wind up as mincemeat in East Patchogue?" Gary continued. "Because he secured the name of some other fag in the area he could party with before going off and doing Emery's dirty work, conveniently dropping the car at a neighborhood rental office in Patchogue beforehand, where there just happens to be an Alamo fleabag in nearby East Patchogue."

"And where *this* address just happens to be located not too far from the flophouse," Justin said, consulting the map.

Brian leaned over the seat and studied the area where Justin had his finger. Foxcroft Lane.

Suddenly, Justin smacked the heel of his hand firmly against his forehead, poking an index finger at the bold red letter **H** located near the bottom of the page, half an inch away from Brian's thumb. Finally, the pieces of the puzzle were beginning to fit.

"What?" Brian questioned.

But Justin kept tapping the letter **H** for Hospital with his fingertip. "I think Emery's victims were murdered in or near the towns or cities where they were born," he blabbered. "Like Whitey Hawkins from Riverhead. Born and raised in The Greens. My main man, Milky. Delivered by a midwife not far from Ursula's home, near The Greens, too," Justin added. "Spent most of his life out west in Wyoming. But like Hawkins, he was born in Riverhead."

Gary began nodding in agreement. "Doctor Littleton's daughter, Grace, was born in San Francisco."

"What about Doctor Littleton and the flight attendant, Desirée Notaro?" Brian queried, trying to make some sense out of what the pair was positing. "Those two died in a mid-air explosion. They weren't targeted at or near their birthplace . . . were they?"

Justin was staring at Brian oddly. "I know this sounds crazy, but air-traffic control said the aircraft never it made it out of Kansas' air space before it blew," he stated gravely. "I'm not sure about Timothy Littleton, but I remember hearing that Notaro's wife's family was from the great Kansas prairies. She might have been born there.

The plane was flying according to schedule. So, if Emery timed it properly . . . ."

Gary was nodding to himself, recalling something Ruth O'Connor had told him about Anthony's wife living in the Midwest before moving to Italy, then returning to the states in her teens. He was beginning to formulate the picture, coming out of a heavy cloud of contemplation. "And I think the Urban boy was born in Baltimore."

"I'm positive the Ingrilli woman grew up there," Justin stated. "And not far from the hospital where she was born. I remember the Harrison woman telling me that."

Brian held the wheel for his partner as Gary grabbed his cell phone to call Kim at headquarters.

"Brookhaven Memorial Hospital," Justin said excitedly, back to tapping the bold letter **H**.

"What about it?" Brian barked.

"I'll bet that's where Jackie was born," he answered straightaway. "Emery will kill her near where she was born."

"I thought she was born in Sicily," Brian stated assumingly.

"She grew up in Sicily. But she was born in Patchogue. I remember her telling me that. *East* Patchogue, I'd wager. And I'll lay odds it was *that* very hospital. Right around the corner from Foxcroft Lane, leading into Hospital Road."

"Christ, J. You could very well be on to something here. I'll call Theo and tell him to set up a command post near the hospital," the lead detective decided on the spot.

It seemed more than ironic to the trio that the net was narrowing so close to home: one in which the Suffolk County homicide squad sat housed within the Police Department, located at 30 Yaphank Avenue in Yaphank; the other, perhaps Emery's safe house, situated one town over in East Patchogue. The distance between the county facilities and Foxcroft Lane was approximately four miles as the crow flies. A readied copter could chopper there in a matter of minutes.

Could Clarence Emery and the Rubino woman be right under our noses? the two detectives wondered. As for Justin, he knew the psychopath was close at hand. He could feel it in the very marrow of his bones.

Chapter 82

Theo elected to set up a command post south of Brookhaven Memorial Hospital and Foxcroft Lane, on the other side of Patchogue-Yaphank Road, in fact. Justin did not like it. But who was he to argue? *Second in command, my foot,* he knew at a late point in the game. Still, he understood the commander's reasoning. There was no time to be wasted waiting until dark, then surreptitiously move men and equipment into position. Bringing in troops and vehicles at either end of Robinson Avenue during daylight hours would prove risky in light of its proximity to the clapboard frame house located at the end of the lane. The same would hold true of Andreano, Neptune, and Fairfax Roads. Therefore, a spot was selected along Dahlia Drive South, just south of Orchid Road.

FBI agents and Suffolk County homicide detectives were strategically put into position along Sunrise Highway, Hospital Road, Patchogue-Yaphank Road, and Hewlett Avenue. The modest single-story home on Foxcroft Lane was surrounded. No escape route was possible.

A helicopter was standing by less than a mile away.

God only knew where Dominic's people were, Justin entertained.

Law enforcement personnel dressed as repairmen, joggers, delivery boys, surveyors and window and siding salesmen went about their routines along the outskirts of the area.

As tomorrow would be Recycling Pick-Up day, Justin moved with purpose along Exeter, the block behind Foxcroft Lane, busy searching for deposit returns through twenty-gallon plastic pails before the row of homes. Occasionally, he stooped to pick up a can or bottle off the side of the road, depositing the empties into a rusty, wobbly supermarket cart. He never once set his eyes on the house or lot located over his right shoulder, for that was being surveilled with high-powered binoculars and spotting scopes. Justin was talking a blue streak to himself.

" . . . which brings me back to you, Ma . . . wherever the fuck you are. Oh, you'd be so proud of me, now. So, if you jus' happen to be lookin' down, it ain't what it seems. Seldom is. You see, I'm a kick-ass motherfucker for the Suffolk County *hom·o·cide* squad, bitch. 'Course, you'd already know dat if you was up there in heaven 'n all. Which I tend to doubt, 'cause you was nothin' but a whore-ass motherfuckin' slut. But nevertheless, I made somethin' of myself, you see. Oh, how I wish that you could see, Ma. Oh, how I wish that you could see your little boy. All growed up now. Even learned to read and write."

"Barnes."

Justin pressed the transmission button from underneath his ragged raincoat. A light drizzle soaked the soiled material and at the same time hid his tears.

"Yeah, chump."

"There's no activity inside," Dale Fulton jawed painfully. "Copy that?"

"Yeah, I copy."

"I want you to keep this line open. Two-way. Understand? I want to hear everything that's going on. Hear me?"

"Yep."

"Told you before, this channel is secure. God couldn't come in on it if He wanted to. And talking about God, you got those Bibles handy?"

Justin tapped loudly upon one of the hardbound cloth covers from somewhere inside his coat.

"You don't listen; do you, Barnes? I don't want sound signals. I want to hear your goddamn mouth flappin'. I hate it, but I want to hear it. Clear on that?"

"You sound awful, Dale. Does it hurt? I hope it fuckin' hurts when you open wide. Can you say Wide World of Wales, chump? Instead of just fracturing it, I wish I would have broken your fuckin' jaw in hopes they'd have wired it shut."

Both Theo and Louis were in the command post doing a slow burn. The pair wanted to reprimand their two hotshots but thought better of it, knowing they were at the point of no return.

On Fulton's orders, Justin moved up the block with his cart, shed the filthy wet raincoat in the shadows of a building, then moved through a backyard—just as confident as any *elderly preacher man* in a wrinkled three-piece suit had ever ambulated. He held up a pair of Holy Bibles in each hand. Miraculously, the rain let up.

Justin rounded the corner and walked right on up the block toward the targeted clapboard-framed house.

"What the hell are you doing, Barnes?" Fulton raved. "You're supposed to go door-to-door. Slowly. You're an old man. What's wrong with you?"

"That'll take forever. That's what's wrong. Ring the phone *now*, Fulton. I'll ring the bell. Pairs of eyes on every window, chump. Just remember, Jackie could be in there. In which case, *I* negotiate this show."

"I hope Emery or someone shoots your ass, Barnes. Swear to God I do."

Justin cut the communication short.

The telephone sounded inside the house. Justin rang the front bell simultaneously.

Someone inside the home ignored the phone and came to the front door.

Justin stood propped before the entranceway as the barrier between them opened inwardly on its hinges. In one arm, the *preacher man* held two black and gold Bibles. In the other hand, he gripped a deadly matte black and brushed stainless steel Kimber Eclipse .45 semi-automatic, held to one side of the doorjamb.

"Come on in," the figure standing to the left of the doorway invited. "For a minute, there, I thought you were Methuselah."

Justin stood there in shock.

"I don't want one of your sharpshooters putting a bullet in my brain," the man said. "Now, step inside. Quickly."

"No sharpshooters until the word is given. Besides, they'd probably miss and put a hole in that cigar."

Raymond Cancilla cracked a grin and, for a final time, told Justin to come inside.

"Just don't answer the phone," Raymond said.

"Why?"

Raymond shrugged. "Like a good soldier, I just listen and

follow orders."

"Any sign of her?" Justin asked, crossing the threshold and stepping into the tidy room.

The man sadly shook his head.

"Anyone else here with you?"

Raymond gestured. "Somewhere out there. They've already gone through this place. I'm here alone. Waiting."

Justin nodded, putting away his gun and setting down the books. "Give me a second." Justin turned on the transceiver and adjusted the volume as well as the wire in his ear, speaking over the angry voice of the case agent. "Just shut up and listen to me, scamp. Ray Cancilla and a crew have already used this place as a pit stop. The race is on, and time is running out. The house is secure with just him and me standing in it. No sign of Jackie. And tell them to hang up the goddamn phone. It's giving me a headache."

The phone stopped ringing immediately.

"Exactly what the *hell* is going on in there, Barnes?" Fulton demanded. "Tell me right now, damn it. You tell me, and you tell me the truth. Every goddamn detail."

"Well, Dale. Ray is lighting up as we speak. Cuban, if I had to guess. I could ask. And to tell you the truth, I don't see a THANK YOU FOR NOT SMOKING sign anywhere in the room. You want me to find him an ashtray?" Justin sounded off through a smirk.

"You don't touch a fucking thing until I get there."

"Didn't think so."

"And you tell him to put that cigar out. Now!"

"I'll be sure to do that." Again, Justin terminated the conversation.

"That's that Fulton fellow?" Raymond asked heatedly.

"Yes. So, please put the cigar out before he has a kitten."

Raymond snuffed the head of the cigar into a marble ashtray. "He was supposed to let us know."

"Looks like you did all right on your own."

"We were all supposed to work together. Recall?"

"Oh, I recall. How long you been here?"

"Long enough for a team to sweep this place and the area out there clean."

"And?"

"And nothing. Think I'd be waiting here if we had something solid to go on?"

"Then why *are* you still here?"

"Finished up and heard you were coming."

"How'd you hear?"

"Ways and means committee."

"Yeah, well, your ways and means committee could get people hurt, Raymond."

"No, that idiot out there you have running things is going to get people hurt. Best not be Jackie."

Simultaneously, several men and a woman from the SWAT team stormed through the front and rear doors. A second later, a dozen men in similar outfits and weaponry materialized, seemingly from out of nowhere.

"WE'RE COOL!" Justin shouted. "Just relax."

Chapter 83

Federal Agents Dale Fulton and Louis Tempone soon followed the SWAT team through the front door of the summer residence on Foxcroft Lane in East Patchogue. A rental. Detective Lieutenant Theodore Groche and several of his homicide detectives entered through the rear.

"Where is he?" Fulton demanded.

"You mean Barnes?" a SWAT team operative asked the SIAC.

"Yes, for Christ's sake. Justin Barnes."

"He left."

"Left?"

"Yes. He said he was changing sides and left. He wanted to take this fellow with him, but I figured you wanted to talk to him first."

"Well, I guess that makes you a half-wit. Doesn't it?" Fulton flared.

"Sir, Barnes is second in command and in charge of—"

"Barnes is not in charge of his own faculties, let alone this operation," the agent blew, turning around angrily to face the civilian.

Raymond Cancilla shrugged nonchalantly and sat down in one of two chairs, inviting the federal agent to do likewise. "Sit. We'll talk," the Sicilian man said calmly, gesturing toward the seat.

Dale looked down incredulously at Raymond, assuming a pompous tone. "Mr. Cancilla. We're not in your restaurant now. We're on my turf. Clear on that? I give the instructions, and I set the stage."

"Sit," Raymond repeated. "Please."

Pairs of eyes, which focused fully on the two men, suddenly moved to other areas of interest around the room. Theo spoke with Louis and another agent. Detectives Brian Archer and Gary York made their way around and through the two bedroom cottage.

Dale began his rebuke. "You cannot—"

"You lied to me, Fulton."

"No one lied—"

"We found Xavier Sanchez, and we called you immediately."

"I—"

"Immediately," Raymond repeated. "But no more."

"You cannot interfere with—"

"My niece's welfare?"

"This is warfare, Mr. Cancilla. Do you understand that?"

"More than you could ever imagine."

Dale Fulton was shaking his head. "Where did Barnes go?"

"Probably off with our people."

"Your people? Or Dominic's soldiers?"

"Family," Raymond stated evenly.

"I see," Dale replied disdainfully. "And I suppose you think these people are going to find your niece. Alive. You think Emery is just going to let your people walk in and take her back? Is that what you think? You think your *family* has better resources than the FBI? Do you?"

"If you're implying that we're mobsters—"

"Is that what you're inferring, Cancilla? You're a restaurateur. Just like your brothers Phil and Dominic. We know that. But it's the company one of them is keeping, Raymond. Bad news. If your niece is alive—and I stress the word *if*—those people are going to kill the only chance you have."

Raymond Cancilla drew a deep breath. "I believe my family and I stand a better chance working with people we can *trust* rather than cooperating with you, and for a very basic reason. Your agenda is to apprehend Emery, at all cost. Ours is to find and free Jackie, at any price. Selfish on both our parts, yes? You operate under a banner of the common good. We operate under a banner of what is *good* for family. So, on the surface your endeavor seems the more noble cause. But let me tell you something, Agent Fulton. *You* do what you do to advance your own career. *You* do it to add another feather to your cap. It's true that three parties working together as a team stand a better chance of finding Jackie than if we worked apart. But you ruined that chance. In the final hour, God will ultimately decide how things get sorted out. I honestly believe that. I think Justin Barnes believes that, too. I also believe that we can alter the course of events right up to that final moment by being honest with ourselves and others, just as I am being brutally honest with you right now. You lost our family's trust when you broke your promise to Phil and me. Nothing can or will change that. I also want you to know that your dishonesty is not something that surprises us. We're not naive."

"You finished?" Dale railed.

"With you I am."

"Fine. But I'm telling you not to interfere with this operation any further, or I'll have each and every one of you out there—" Dale pointed toward a yellow curtained window "—put behind bars. I'm not playing around, Raymond Cancilla. You have no idea what's in store for you and your family if you persist. Clear?"

Raymond leaned forward and picked up the extinguished cigar from the ashtray on the end table between them, sticking the Havana into his mouth before leaning back in contemplation. He weighed his words carefully before he spoke. "You're right, Dale. I'm only a restaurateur. But you'd be absolutely amazed at what I could cook up for you."

Dale Fulton and Raymond Cancilla looked deeply into one another's eyes before Theo and Louis went over to the pair.

"Everything ironed out fellows?" Theo asked pessimistically, noting the tension between the two.

"Everything's fine, Lieutenant," Raymond replied, refusing to take his eyes off Fulton. "We were just working out a recipe for success."

Chapter 84

Detective Kim Archer worked away indefatigably with Big Sister. Justin had definitely put the computer wizard on the inside track, for she was categorically connecting several dots. To save time, the maven had decided to jump ahead in her search by eliminating those victims Clarence Emery was *suspected* of butchering, dating back well over a decade, to those who authorities positively *knew* the serial killer murdered, or was responsible for annihilating through accomplices. She began with the double homicide at Pipes Cove in Greenport.

Carmela Fontana and her roommate, Theresa Pelicano, had been residents of the North Fork. Both were born in Eastern Long Island Hospital in Greenport, information which Kim had easily secured from County Records. *We'll see where all this business leads us,* she said inside her head.

Grace Littleton. Just as Justin had recalled. Born as well as murdered in San Francisco. *Interesting.*

Her father. Doctor Timothy Littleton. Born in Hutchinson, Kansas. Blown to bits in an aircraft explosion thirty thousand some odd feet above the state. *Strange.*

Desirée Notaro; maiden name, Milo. Born in central Kansas, too. McPherson—just north of Hutchinson. *Very strange.* "There are no coincidences," the wizard whispered to no one in the room but herself.

Clarence Emery's known accomplice: William Baxter. No legitimate birth record. Phony birth certificate, social security number, drivers' licenses, et cetera, et cetera. *Figures.* Billy Baxter died on that plane, along with passengers and crew. MasterCard records revealed that he had spent a good deal of time in and around Salina, Hutchinson, McPherson and Wichita: three cities and a town running north and south, virtually through the center of the state. *Totally bizarre.*

Laura Ingrilli. Born in Good Samaritan Hospital; Baltimore, Maryland. Her body cruelly butchered and beheaded in a bathtub just several blocks away. *Sickening.*

Howard Urban. Born in Sinai Hospital; Baltimore, too. Found sadistically tortured next to Laura. "Getting weirder by the moment, girl," Kim said directly to Big Sister itself.

David Klein. Born in a water taxi along Quogue Beach, she learned after surfing the net. Murdered in his waterfront home in East Quogue.

Melvyn A. Milken: sobriquet, Milky. Justin's friend. A relationship formed in a Wyoming prison. Murdered several blocks from where the albino was born with the aid of a midwife in The Greens in Riverhead. Killed in Ursula's own home along the outskirts. Actually, on the line of demarcation, Kim discovered. "Bizarredosville," she positively swore.

Kim noted that the home on Shelter Island where Vito Vitalo was born in the early seventies had been demolished decades ago. The ex-state trooper from upstate New York was murdered on the site where the house once stood. The fact that the man was in law enforcement, before becoming Emery's accomplice, made Detective Kim Archer want to vomit. The way in which he was found butchered gave her some relief. "Bastard."

Rufus (Whitey) Hawkins. Born and raised and executed in The Greens in Riverhead, never having ventured past the county seat, insofar as Kim could determine. The child was delivered into the world by a volunteer fireman, both an old article and Hawkins' most recent obituary had reported—his remains delivered to the county morgue. Kim simply, yet sadly, shook her head.

Anthony Notaro. Born in an ambulance en route to Southampton Hospital, traveling from Hampton Bays. The vehicle never made it to Montauk Highway before the mother gave birth to an eight pound, four ounce boy . . . the man's body recovered behind a phone booth a block away from the scene, thirty-one years later.

Ruth O'Connor. Kim paused long enough to wipe away her tears. She did not have the luxury of a grieving period. None of them did. To date, four wakes and/or funerals regarding their serial killer case that she and Brian had attended. Kim did not want to see or hear or even think about number five. Her tears kept coming as she backed away from the monitor for fear she might flood and seize the keyboard. Kim dried her eyes then continued to feed and retrieve information. Elizabeth Scala had been born secretly within a safe haven for abused and battered women at an undisclosed location in Wading River—legally adopted and raised in Manorville as Ruth O'Connor. Today, the Wading River refuge, Connie's Shelter for Victims of Domestic Violence, was but a mile from where Ruth was found brutally murdered in the Notaro home.

The Notaros' two-year-old son, Nicholas, unquestionably failed to fit the pattern, having been born in northern Italy where Anthony and Desirée were vacationing with her parents at the time. Yet the placement of the boy's body, found folded in a fetal position and tucked within the gutted cavity of Ruth's abdomen, told a telling, sickening tale of sheer madness. For the boy was still alive at the time Emery removed him from one world and metaphorically returned him to another . . . *as if the child were in the mother's womb,* Kim mulled over in her mind.

Felix Zamora. Born and murdered in Southampton, Long Island.

Xavier Sanchez. Born in Patchogue, Long Island, long before the town fathers set up new boundaries: Patchogue, North Patchogue and East Patchogue.

Detective Kim Archer satisfactorily confirmed Justin's theory that each murder occurred within proximity to where the deceased was born—the single exception being the Notaro boy. Of course, there were the victims of the downed aircraft, of which three known targets aboard were blown to smithereens somewhere over the middle of Kansas, and therefore fit the profile as far as she was concerned.

Kim did not waste another second.

"One more name, girl," Kim spoke to the machine. "Among the living, I can only pray. Then we'll give us both a rest. Promise." Kim accessed the information from Albany's Records Bureau through the young woman's social security number and maiden name. Ten seconds later, the data appeared on the screen.

Cancilla, Jacqueline Maria. Birth date: June 6th, 1970. Brookhaven Memorial Hospital Medical Center, 101 Hospital Road, East Patchogue, New York. 11772 (631) 654-7100

The proximity of the vacant rental on Foxcroft Lane, in relationship to the hospital—less than a mile away—was as disturbing to Kim as it was to Justin, but for an added reason. Out of sheer habit, she hit several keys to confirm that the facility had not closed its doors or relocated to a different address, as other hospitals certainly had, noting that the Center was established in 1956, forty-six years ago.

Kim suddenly had a nagging suspicion in the center of her gut. "I should just get off my butt and walk straight into records and pull his file. But that isn't going to help me *specifically* with what I need to know. Hate to break a promise, girl, but that's the way it has to be," she addressed Big Sister as if she were a living entity.

Kim typed in the man's social security number and name, recalling that he was born and reared in New York before moving out to the California coast in his early twenties.

"Here we go."

Emery, Clarence. Birth date: December 30th, 1956. Brookhaven Memorial Hospital Medical Center, 101 Hospital Road, East Patchogue, New York. 11772 (631) 654-7100

Kim sat stunned for half a minute, berating herself for not having begun with Jacqueline's and Emery's names and place of birth in the first place, instead of wasting valuable time.

"Think, by God. Think! Help me clear away the cobwebs. Come on, you Big Bitch. Give me something to go on."

Kim was staring blindly at the monitor before she focused on the number that was staring her smack in the face. She picked up the phone and dialed.

An elderly woman answered on the third ring. "Brookhaven Memorial Hospital. May I help you?"

"Patient Information, please."

"One moment."

Kim was connected immediately.

"Yes, do you have a Rubino listed? That's R-u-b-i-n-o?"

"Um . . . I have a Rubano. R-u-b-**a**-n-o."

"Jacqueline?"

"No, a Geoffrey with a G. But let me check something . . . hold on a second, please."

"Thank you."

"No, nothing like that. I'm checking the discharge sheet for this morning, as well as yester—"

"Could you try Cancilla? She might be listed under her maiden name. That's C-a-n—"

"Got her right here. Jacqueline Cancilla. C-a-n-c-i-l-l-a. Room 251. Would you like me to—"

"NO!"

"Well, that was quite emphatic, my dear."

"I'm sorry. I just want her to rest. Please excuse me. I've been a wreck. I've got to go. I'll call back later. And thanks." Kim hung up and caught her breath. "Oh, my God!" She immediately called Justin on his cell phone, using her own cell.

"Yeah, Kim."

"Oh, thank God I got you."

"What's up?"

"I think I found Jackie. Can you talk?"

"I'll listen."

"I hear you. Brookhaven Memorial Hospital. Room 251. Under her maiden name, Cancilla. Jacqueline Cancilla. That's all I got. No it's n-not," she corrected herself, trembling as she spoke. "Emery was born there, J. Do you want me to call the command post?"

"NO!"

Kim couldn't help but smile. "Glad I asked."

"Gotta go."

"Listen to me."

"What?"

"This whole business is insane. You be careful. I can't remember when I've been so afraid."

"Oh, how right you are, love. How right you are."

Chapter 85

Instinct told Justin to start with the Care Center across the street from Brookhaven Memorial Hospital. The tall, striking black administrative nurse stood at the threshold to her office and raised a single but serious finger to signal that she was on an important call. "Be right with you," she said, smiling at the handsome figure and noticing immediately that the man wore no wedding band. Not that it was necessarily the sign of eligibility. But at least it was a sign of hope.

Justin waited impatiently and was about to interrupt. A moment later, it became evident that the woman was waiting to leave a message on someone's answering machine.

"Hi. This is Doctor Ames' office," she began, absently twisting the extension cord around the bare ring finger of her left hand. "This message is for Sarah Fernbach. We just received your pathology report, and it's good news." She smiled up at the man as though it might have been his own report. "Everything's all right. It's all good pathology. No signs of malignancy. Doctor Ames has reviewed it and said to pass that on to you. If you have any questions, he's handling Doctor Booth's cases while he's on vacation. You can give him a call at 654-9021. But everything is fine. Okay? Bye."

The nurse hung up the phone and went over to Justin. "That woman is going to sleep very well tonight," she said with satisfaction.

"Linda?"

"That's me. Linda Carter. Now, what can I do for you?"

"Mary, at the reception desk, said that you might be able to help me." Justin opened his wallet and flashed a badge and credentials.

"And I had you pegged for a soap star. Silly me."

"I think Mary took me for a porn star," he kidded. "Can we go someplace private to talk? It's very important. Kinda like your business; sometimes a matter of life and death. Only mine's more immediate. Real urgent, Linda."

"You bet. Follow me."

If Justin's mind was not one hundred percent on Jacqueline and Clarence Emery, a fraction of it homed in on the woman's derriere. "Later."

"Excuse me?" Linda said, swinging her head and shoulders around while walking dead ahead.

"Talkin' to myself."

"I do it all the time. How's this?" She led him into a very private office, then closed the door.

"I need the names of all those doctors who are filling in for other doctors. Notably, new arrivals. I need their photo IDs and a general history. I especially need the name of the doctor who is treating Jacqueline Cancilla across the street; room 251—her records and anything else you have. And here's the kicker, Linda. I need and want it *now*." Justin removed a recent photo of Jacqueline from his jacket pocket. "You see her?"

Linda shook her head solemnly, then looked back up at Justin. "May I see your identification once again?"

"Anything you want, dollface." Justin withdrew his wallet, placing it down upon the desk in front of her.

Linda gave the credentials a more careful look, studying both Justin and the woman's photo intently before going to work for him at a hundred miles an hour.

Chapter 86

Brookhaven Memorial Hospital was big and busy. Visitors and personnel were moving about between the lobby and the information desk. Administrative Nurse Linda Carter and Justin Barnes stepped into an elevator. The two rode the car in silence to the second floor, exiting and walking briskly along passageways—past a nurses' station. The pair paused after rounding the corner.

"Room 251 is in the middle of the hallway on your right," Linda said, pointing down the corridor. "Doctor Yreme is handling Doctor Jordon's cases while he's on vacation till the end of this month; Yreme's making his rounds at the moment. How do you want to handle this? I could page him if you like."

Justin shook his head and toyed with the borrowed stethoscope hanging around his neck. Against the side of his leg, he held Jacqueline's file. "I'm going to take a walk down there and have a peek. It's a private room, you said."

Linda nodded.

"I'd like you to wait right here," he cautioned uneasily.

"Yes, Doctor," Linda said with an alluring smile, adjusting the collar of his lab coat, then the stethoscope, both on loan from the building across the street where the two had met, not thirty minutes earlier. "There. You look fine. You even look like a doctor."

"Maybe from one of them soaps?"

"Even better," she assured him.

At the end of the hall, two doctors exited one of the rooms and were headed their way. One wore a white cotton coat like Justin's. The other was covered from head to foot in green scrubs, a matching mask hanging from his neck. They were walking straight toward Linda, waving and craving attention.

"Shit. What do I say; R-x or something?" Justin choked.

Linda laughed and covered her mouth. "Say nothing and stick

your nose in that file. Just ignore them. They're both jerks."

"Hey, Linda," the shorter of the two said with genuine surprise.

"What are you doin' over here, woman?" the other wanted to know.

"Slumming," Linda answered succinctly, poking a finger in the patient's chart and jabbering away in medical lingo that Justin wholeheartedly agreed with as positively prudent advice, demonstrated by dynamic nods of his curly crop.

"Can't you see she has no time for you, Lincoln?" the white coat told his black colleague.

"What I see is that Linda's done found herself a Mandingo medicine man."

Justin looked up from the file.

"Whew! Check out those angry eyes. Guy looks like he could handle you and the whole damn tribe," Doctor Aaron Goldstein declared. "Better we just keep walking, my man," he suddenly decided.

"Nah, I don't think he could whip Marcus Welby's white ass, Aaron," the one in scrubs remarked.

Justin handed the file over to Linda, staring down the pair.

Aaron giggled. "Maybe you're right, but the guy might be carrying; or worse yet, be a carrier."

"See you later, Linda," Lincoln lamented and leered.

Arm in arm, the two men marched quickly by, heading toward the other end of the corridor.

"Those guys are doctors?" Justin asked in disbelief.

"Both surgeons," Linda answered. "Damn good ones, but jerks as I said. The likes of Hawkeye Pierce and Trapper John, or so they think."

"More like Aaron 'n Andy," Justin excoriated, alluding to the fifties Amos 'n Andy comedy show. He watched the two buffoons disappear around the passageway, took back the file and immediately headed for room 251. "Wait."

Nurse Carter waited as instructed.

A moment later, Justin signaled Linda toward him.

Carter walked briskly down the hallway.

"It's not her," Justin stated evenly.

Linda went into the room, smiled pleasantly at the patient, then checked the woman's chart at the foot of the bed. "How are you doing today, Mrs. Antly?"

"Like I just told the doctor, here. I'm ready to go home."

"Well, Doctor Barnes is not your doctor, dear. Can you tell us the last time Doctor Yreme looked in on you?"

"I haven't seen him since yesterday, when they put me in this room. He said I could go home today. He promised me."

"Well, I'm just going to have to have a little talk with Doctor Yreme, and then we'll get you out of here. All right?"

"Thank you, dear," the middle-aged woman said cheerfully. "Just don't beat up on him too badly because he's been really very nice. He had me transferred to this private room and told me it was being handled similar to an upgrade in a fancy hotel. 'No extra charge,' he said," she made perfectly clear.

"That's my man," *Doctor* Barnes smiled keenly. "Good ol' Doctor Yreme." Emery spelled backwards, Justin had gotten it from the get-go. Not very original—although Justin did appreciate the impostor's true given name. Clare. Abridged from Clarence. Simple. Male or female. Take your pick. From the Latin word meaning *clear one*. Things were becoming a bit clearer for Justin. "May I ask you something, Mrs. Antly?"

"Ask me anything you like, Doctor."

"What nationality would you say Doctor Yreme is? Not necessarily by his name—but judging from his appearance and speech. Where might he be from?"

"Oh, India, without a doubt. No, wait! Pakistan. As a matter of fact, East Pakistan. I know because it came up in conversation when Doctor Yreme was arguing with a doctor from New Delhi. Something about nuclear weapons testing—then over some territory that each felt belonged to them. I can tell you that they did not like one another very much. Why do you ask?"

"Quota," Justin replied with a wink. "We're letting too many of them in here," he whispered next to her ear.

"Oh, but Doctor Yreme is very nice," she repeated. "Him, you should keep around."

"Thank you, Mrs. Antly. We'll certainly take that under consideration."

"Don't mention it."

"Don't *you*," Justin rejoined shrewdly, putting a finger to his lips.

The woman laughed and coughed and wheezed. "You won't forget about me, will you?"

Linda assured the woman that she wouldn't be forgotten.

Justin withdrew his cell phone, stepped from the room, and placed a call.

The pair headed back around the corner, then stepped into another borrowed, private office. Linda closed the door.

Justin was the first to speak. "Work with me," he said to Linda, sounding more like her boss than a cop.

Linda was upset and confused. "Doctor Yreme doesn't look or sound like he's from *either* India or Pakistan," she stated determinedly.

"So, what would you say he looks and sounds like?" he asked. "That *was* a pretty piss poor picture you showed me of him back there."

"Like I told you before. Australian. Definitely Australian . . . at least in speech. In looks? Well, I'm really not sure, Detective."

"Listen to me, Linda. The guy could be a scorpion on that wall and you'd swear it was a harmless insect. Follow what I'm saying?"

Linda looked at him queerly. "Oh, my God!" the administrative nurse said with alarm, the exclamation hanging there before her open mouth.

"What?"

Linda put both hands to her face. "He's that guy. Isn't he? The guy the papers call the chameleon; The Teacher."

Justin nodded.

"You're a *homicide* detective."

"You liked me better when you thought—"

"I thought you were a detective-detective. Not *homicide*," she whispered, although the door to the office was shut.

"Did I, or did I not tell you my business was kinda like your business? Sometimes a matter of life and death. True?" he offered lamely.

Linda was shaking her head. "I think you should talk to the director. I really do." She turned her face away from Justin's, staring at the door like she wanted to run.

Justin gently reached out and took her by the shoulders.

"Look at me, Linda. I need *you*. No director. A director or anyone else in charge is going to blow this for me. And that young woman, Jackie, is going to die. You're cool, baby. I sense it. Don't fall apart on me now. I have a plan." Justin was not commanding the nurse, nor was he asking her any longer. He was pleading with her. "Please."

"What do you want me to do?" Linda could not believe she even asked the question.

"You have candy in this place?"

"Gift shop."

"You know a decent perfume when you smell it?"

"Well, I sold several good name-brands in Cosmetics & Perfume at Macy's, to put myself through school. Why?"

"You know Lancôme?"

"Uh-huh. Joy. Lancôme. Beautiful. Chanel. You name it. But you're not going to find those here in the gift shop."

Justin's smile was broad. "Could you still recognize Lancôme on someone who maybe hasn't bathed or showered in say a couple of days?"

"Maybe."

"Could you detect it from those other perfumes you mentioned?"

"Absolutely."

"Where do women generally spray perfume on their person?"

Linda smiled a beautiful smile. "That depends mainly on the person and who they're with. And they usually don't *spray* perfume, unless they've got cash to burn. You're not talking cologne, now are you, Detective?"

"Doctor."

"Are you, Doctor?"

Justin shook his head. "Perfume. Lancôme. Thirty-two dollars an ounce. Believe me, I know." *No wonder Tomas hates me*, Justin realized, adding insult to injury to a growing list of gifts he had given Jacqueline over the course of time.

Linda delicately touched the tips of two fingers to the inside of both wrists, lightly rubbing them together; next, her temples—then down along the sides of a lovely swan-like neck. "For a little more intimacy . . . ." Linda ran a forefinger partway down the inside of her blouse.

Justin nodded. "I think I got the picture, Linda. Do you? Jackie probably doesn't look anything like herself right now."

"You're telling me Lancôme is Jackie's perfume. You want me to buy some candy. Hand out pieces to patients who are allowed to have them, like mints or Hershey Kisses. If they're not permitted sweets, I give them all a little kiss upon the hand and cheek and determine if one of them might be Jackie."

"It might be an old woman—or even a male midget," Justin exaggerated, making clear the lengths Emery would go to achieve an end.

Linda took a moment to think, then thought better about thinking at all—putting out the palm of her hand.

"What?"

"Money."

"You can't shell this out yourself, or as part of a public relations program?" he joked to disguise his own apprehension.

Linda passed her hand like a collection plate beneath his nose. "Before I change my mind."

Justin opened his wallet wide and took out a fifty dollar bill.

"Another," she demanded.

"You're kiddin'?"

"I'm going to the *gift shop*, downstairs. Not the corner bargain basement store. You don't want to know how many patients I have to see, or how much things cost."

"What if you find her on the very first floor?" he balked in jest. "Any refund?"

"I'll return the candy and take you out to dinner with what's left over, sport. Assuming we both get through this thing together—in one piece."

Justin gave her another fifty. "You all right with this?" he asked awkwardly. He was *not* talking currency.

"I've got to be crazy."

"That's how I know we're going to get him, Nurse Carter. Crazy is the watchword."

"What if I see him, or he comes by while I'm in one of the

rooms?"

"Just walk the hell away. You're being shadowed by people as we speak."

"You serious?"

"Deadly. Just do your *thang*, girl. If you find her, or there's the slightest possibility you feel it could be her, you immediately come back to this office. Understand? You don't call or speak to anyone. You just keep moving. All right?"

"I understand. But I have to let them know across the street that I'll be busy over here."

"Okay." His mind was racing like his heart. "Is there any way to narrow down the number of patients you'll be visiting, maybe by screening those who might be heavily sedated?"

"Yes, but it will take some time."

"But less time than if you went through *every* room. Yes?"

Linda smiled uneasily. "You're very good at what you do, aren't you?"

"Want to know the truth?"

"I'm not sure."

"I'm winging it."

"Want to hear *my* confession?"

"I'm not sure, either."

"I wing it every day."

Justin nodded. "Ready?"

"Ready as I'll ever be. I guess."

Chapter 87

Justin had apprised Dominic Cancilla's people as to exactly what transpired. Throughout the wards, in and out of elevators, and along trafficked corridors, dauntless soldiers dressed as doctors, orderlies, nurses, technicians and maintenance people, vigilantly, yet furtively, observed Nurse Linda Carter navigate the hallways.

Zeroing in on the wards for the terminally ill, Linda Carter moved forward with a heavy heart. Bed after bed, ranging from infants to the infirm, patients were stationed along a netherworld. It was the single reason why she had chosen administrative duties across the street the day she had her druthers.

The conscious or semiconscious who shared semiprivate space with the comatose were not immune to Carter's kindness. From room to room, Linda made the rounds with her sobering basket of cheer. Little candies for those patients who were allowed the luxury of sweets. Miniature bars of perfumed soaps and sachet for the others. Hugs and kisses were doled out like so many petals or pennies—perhaps appearing trivial or cursory to those more fortunate patients recuperating nicely just steps beyond those somber walls, yet proven positively precious to the peaked and impoverished within. Blanket tucks or the freshening of pillows were bestowed upon everyone she came in contact with, whether they were wide awake or not.

Linda was at it for a good fifty minutes when she thought her efforts might be in vain after having observed several orderlies and a practical nurse who had the task of shaving, sponge bathing, and assisting several patients to the shower. Any one of them could have cleaned and freshened Jacqueline Rubino as one would a soiled bed sheet; that is, quite thoroughly in fact. If the woman were indeed incapacitated, and therefore predisposed to using a bedpan—not having had the opportunity to wash up or shower properly—there could be a chance that Linda might still detect a balm. Hence, she built up her hope anew and persevered.

One female patient revealed a hint of lilac. Another, the overpowering fragrance of Clinique. One man bore the odor of urine. Still another reeked from the overly sweet smell of Canoe. Linda was surprised at the reliability of her olfactory sense when put to the test, cynically figuring that if she had any sense at all she wouldn't be there in the hospital but back across the street in the Care Center, where she belonged.

At the end of the hall was a very private room with a DO NOT DISTURB sign on the door. Linda removed it, then stuck it into her pocket. She gently knocked and quietly entered the space. There she spied a single soul, curled up at the foot of the bed in a ball. The figure's face was ashen. Vapid. An intravenous solution contained within a clear plastic bag hung suspended from a fingered metal pole pointing ominously toward the ceiling. Its length of tubing barely stayed the needle in the patient's arm, as if the person had tried to free herself before crawling into a neutral corner.

Nurse Carter went over and adjusted the stand and tube. She took the woman's pulse and read the name printed on the hospital ID bracelet, secured around the thin wrist. She raised both lids of Eve Parisi's unfocused eyes; first one, and then the other. Linda lowered her face and placed it gently alongside the young woman's neck, then against the woman's ear, perceiving the subtle fragrance of Lancôme. She tenderly took a damp, limp hand into her own.

"Can you hear me?" Linda whispered.

There was no response.

"If you can hear me, I want you to try and squeeze my hand. It's important that you do, dear."

After what seemed like an eternity, Linda felt the slightest, faintest pressure around her fingers. So slight, in fact, that she thought she might have only imagined it.

"Please. Try and move your fingers for me," she persisted. This time, Linda knew she felt a movement as light as a feather within her hand. "Good girl." Softly, she caressed and kissed the woman's cheek as if they had been friends for a hundred years. Linda held the woman's hands in a relaxed grip, speaking slowly and distinctly. "I want you to know that I know how difficult this is for you to do. But I want you to try even harder. I want you to tell me if your name is

Jackie by folding your fingers for me and making a fist. Do nothing if you're not. Please. For me. For your family. For Detective Barnes, who sent me to find you. Is your name Jacqueline Rubino?" she repeated. "Tell me if it is."

It was as if a sleepy infant's hand had taken hold of Linda's. The nurse nodded in understanding and watched a single tear roll down Jacqueline's cheek. And then another.

Linda stroked the woman's hair. "Jackie. I have to go now. I have to go downstairs and get the detective. But I want you to know you're perfectly safe." Linda looked into Jacqueline Rubino's half-dead gray-green eyes again and gently squeezed her hand. "I'm getting help. I promise," she said so sweetly.

Linda wanted to rip the needle from the woman's arm but thought better of it should Doctor Yreme, or whomever, return before Justin arrived.

"Excuse me."

Linda turned around abruptly.

"What do you think you're doing?" the doctor asked.

Linda smiled brightly. "I'm giving Miss Parisi, here, a little cheer." And with that pronouncement, the nurse took a tiny bar of soap along with a miniature bag of sachet from the basket, then placed the items on top of the patient's bureau.

"Fine. Now would you please leave? Miss Parisi needs to rest."

"Certainly, Doctor. Is Doctor Yreme around?"

"No, he is not. I'm his associate, and I have instructions that this patient is not to be disturbed. There was a sign on the door. You didn't happen to remove it, did you?"

"No, sir. But I think I know who did."

"And who might that be?"

"The candy striper who couldn't finish this floor because she was feeling queasy," the administrator invented on the spot.

"Why would she remove the sign?"

Linda smiled mischievously. "Because she's lying down at the other end of the hall in a private room and doesn't want to be disturbed."

The doctor stepped over to Linda's basket and poked through the soap, sachet, and little candies. "You didn't give her anything, did you?"

"Miss Parisi?"

The doctor nodded his head with annoyance. "Are you a little slow? Yes, of course, Miss Parisi. Who do you think? Did you give her anything, or not?"

"Of course not. Just the soap and sachet. You were standing right there," Linda said defensively.

"What's your name?"

Linda stepped right up to the doctor and pulled her laminated ID badge several inches forward of her blouse—a foot away from his —helping him along. "Nurse Linda Carter. I'm from the Care Center across the street."

"I see. Please leave now, Nurse Carter, and let Miss Parisi rest in peace." The doctor handed her the basket.

"Would you like me to go downstairs and get another sign for the door?"

"I'll take care of it."

Linda took her leave, heading across the hall to the next room to avoid suspicion.

Chapter 88

Justin waited anxiously as Nurse Linda Carter came briskly down the hallway toward him.

"Jackie's in room 417," Linda said breathlessly, briefly explaining exactly what transpired. "The doctor's name is Sydney. Oliver Sydney. He says he's Doctor Yreme's associate."

Justin reflected on the room number. *Should have figured*, he sighed, shaking his head in sheer frustration then refocused on the moment at hand. "How does she look to you?" he questioned anxiously.

"Extremely weak. He has her heavily sedated—just like you said. Propofol, would be my guess. She can barely move a muscle but understands what's going on around her."

Justin was on his cell phone, ordering and moving people into key positions. First Dominic's soldiers. Then homicide. Finally, the feds were notified.

"You did real good, Linda Carter," the maverick managed to mention.

"I know. I've never been so scared, but I wouldn't let that bastard know it."

"You stay right here."

"You'll get no argument there."

Justin took the elevator to the fourth floor and followed the arrows to Room 417. Daytime phantoms trailed after him. He made his way along a hallway, then went right up to the door.

Another DO NOT DISTURB sign hung in place.

Patients and personnel in the immediate vicinity had already been evacuated.

Justin withdrew his weapon and turned the doorknob.

The door was locked.

He knocked.

There was no answer—nor a single, solitary sound.

Justin hurried back down the corridor and rounded a corner near the nurses' work station. "Key to open room 417," he told a hospital official on high alert.

The administrator and a security guard searched through drawers and cabinets. "The master keys are missing," the former finally said.

Justin ran back to the room.

SWAT stood on either side of the door, their automatic weapons at the ready.

One of Dominic's soldiers boldly stepped forward and easily picked the lock, gesturing that the room was ready for entry.

Justin signaled for the man to step aside.

The stocky Sicilian put the tool back in his vest-pocket, then moved to the sidelines.

Justin held his handgun shoulder-high; he turned the doorknob —pushing the door open wide.

SWAT instantly had the deadly duo dotted with lasers and aligned within cross hairs—but held their fire.

The two impostors stood equally tall, their prisoner supported securely between them. The pair were outfitted from head to foot in mint-green cotton surgical garb and latex gloves, each holding a pistol firmly against their captive's temple. Jacqueline had journeyed from prisoner to patient to hostage in seemingly a heartbeat. Her chin drooped upon her chest like that of a broken doll. A curtain of dark hair draped the helpless form and hung as still as a furled flag—frozen before the figure's fleur-de-lis hospital gown.

"Well, well, well. I really must congratulate you, J," the man just steps ahead and to Justin's right said in a thick Australian accent. "I'm Doctor Sydney, and this is my colleague, Doctor Yreme."

"No, no, no. *I'm* Doctor Oliver Sydney, and *he's* Doctor Clare Yreme," the Pakistani contradicted in a nerve-grating, high-pitched tone.

Justin had the sights of his Kimber Eclipse fixed on the bridge of the Australian's nose, then swept it past their prisoner to the Pakistani standing alongside her.

The pair angled the muzzles of their pistols ever so slightly, so that if either man suddenly pulled the trigger they wouldn't annihilate the other.

"Tell them to put down their weapons, or she dies right here and now," the one supposedly from Pakistan said, switching to an Australian accent.

"He said now, nigger," the Australian spoke with a Pakistani inflection, then smiled.

Justin ordered the members of SWAT, Team Three, as well as Dominic's people to put their weapons down and back off.

"DO IT NOW!" the Australian warned.

Every man but Justin did as they were told.

"Now, you, J," the other kidnapper ordered.

Justin held his sight fixedly on the duskier-complexioned man. "I'll take one of you with me if the other harms a hair on the girl," Justin swore.

"The *girl*, mate? Oh, that *is* rich," the Pakistani said insanely, mixing affected accentuations for effect.

"Did he say, 'the *girl*,'?" the other questioned, gawked and giggled.

"That he did."

"Oh, she's so much more than just a girl to you, J," the Australian said with an American intonation.

Or is he actually the genuine article? Justin wondered and weighed.

"Why, I think she's a bright penny in the center of your heart, J. I truly do."

"Want to play our lit'l game, J," the swarthy figure baited, switching back to a Down Under modality, "'fore we kill you, I mean?"

Justin fixed his sights on the center of the man's forehead. "No, but you're gonna play *my* lit'l game and like it," the maverick mocked.

"And what game might that be, mate?"

"Yeah, tell us 'fore we split a gut."

"It's a game of survival, and it goes like this. You see, one of you is Clarence Emery. And the other is his sick assistant. Of course, I don't know who is who, just yet. But I do know one thing. One of you is a killer who always uses a knife, or the like. The other does his dirty work."

"Yeah, but like you said, you don't know which of us is which. And if you look to your right, J, you'll see that you have rudely interrupted an important surgical procedure that we were about to undertake with much ado," the one closer to the foot of the bed said sadistically.

All eyes but Justin's flashed to the row of shiny scalpels and other blades laid out neatly along a narrow blanket of black leather.

"All one of us has to do is take the gun from Jackie's ear, then point and paint your face," he continued. "Blood red."

"While the other pulls the trigger and expedites this operation. Either way, it's going to be a success," the Pakistani promised with a pleasant smile.

Justin smiled, too. "And in that very instant, I pull this trigger and obliterate one of you, like I said. Wanna play?"

"But you don't know which one of us is going to pull the trigger on poor Jackie, here. Or which one is going to shoot you. Is it me?"

"Or me?" the other tormented, the two of them speaking perfect English, both sounding exactly like the voice Justin had come to know so intimately over the phone.

"*I* might be the one to launch and lodge a bullet in your brain, J. And, as you pull that trigger, you can bid your Jackie dearest goodbye. So, what makes you think one of us won't pull the trigger, just because the other always uses a knife—or the like, like you say? Huh? Tell us."

"Yeah, our backs are to the wall, you see. If he or I have to shoot her, we will, indeed. I promise you this is *not* going to remain a Mexican stand-off much longer. *Sí?*" the other needled.

Justin shook his head emphatically. "One of you would and one of you won't for the simple reason that one of you is not a killer; just like Xavier Sanchez wasn't a killer."

"Ah, but Billy Baxter was."

"And so was State Trooper Vito Vitalo."

"Therefore, how can you be so sure one or the other of us isn't?"

"Don't you think I have the stomach for it, J?"

"Don't you think *I* have the stomach for it, J?" the other mimicked.

The pair giggled in unison like two silly schoolgirls.

"Yeah, you never met either of us face to face, until now."

"That's right, J. You only spoke to one of us on the phone."

"And that was me," the other swore quite madly.

"Was not. It was me."

"No, it was me. I'm the madman."

"Are not."

"Am, too."

"Now stop it, Doctor Yreme. You're going to confuse Doctor Barnes. Then he'll wind up shooting himself in the foot."

The two of them absolutely roared, pressing the muzzles of their weapons solidly against Jackie's skull.

Justin studied the pair from head to toe. "Tell you what. You're both damn good actors. I gotta give you guys that. But only one of you is ever going to see and set foot on the stage again. It might not be for many, many years, but at least there'll be light at the end of the tunnel. Pull the trigger on the girl, and you'll both burn in hell. That's a given."

"But you'll burn in the bargain, J. Want to gamble with your life? You go right ahead."

"Gambling might not be a bad choice if the odds are in one's favor," Justin set forth brashly.

"Well, let me tell you something, J," the darker-skinned figure spoke. "You lost those odds when the troops put down their weapons. Up to that point, you really had me a wee bit worried, I must admit. Still, you *know* Jackie would have gotten it right between the ears. And she will if we don't walk the hell out of here. And I do mean, *now.*"

"You're not walking anywhere," Justin said most assuredly, moving his instrument of death from one man, then back to the other, deciding their fate. "Last chance to save yourself. Whoever the fuck you are. What's it going to be?"

"J. Look at me. Do you really want to see—"

In that very instant, Justin squeezed the trigger and shot the speechless one—the nitro bullet exploding and shattering the top of the man's skull like a bowl of tomato soup being hurled against the stark white wall.

The talker immediately threw down his gun; nonetheless,

Justin thwacked him squarely in the throat with another powerful round fired from the .45. The figure flew and fell rearward as if struck with a wrecking ball, the assistant's neck barely connected to his shoulders at the back.

I take no prisoners, Justin said inside his head. *That first bullet clearly had Victoria Littleton's initials on it, Clare Yreme. Literally. You see, I, too, keep my promises.*

Jacqueline had dropped between the bodies as Dominic Cancilla's soldiers went rushing to her aid.

SWAT swiftly swept inside the private quarters, throwing open a closet and bathroom door. One officer quickly retrieved the two scattered weapons then announced that the room was secure. Team Three holstered their guns as several FBI agents came barreling around the corner.

Two of Dominic's men helped carry Jacqueline from the room, whisking her away to doctors and nurses waiting in the wings.

"Show's over, fellas," Detective Gary York announced to the feds.

Brian Archer went over to Justin and put an arm comfortingly around the man's shoulders before making a call on his cell to Theo.

The Sicilian who had picked the lock for Justin suddenly stepped forward with a dark and angry face. "I have never in my life witnessed anything so reckless and irresponsible," he practically shouted. "You could have gotten her killed. The fact that you didn't does not excuse your actions. You gambled with Jackie's life. You are a heartless fool."

Justin simply shook his head. "I have to admit that I didn't know who was who at first, but I finally figured it out. I took Emery out for openers. He *would* have pulled the trigger and killed Jackie if I hadn't put him down," Justin stated unequivocally. "That one over there really didn't want to die. Believe me."

"How could you possibly know which one was Emery? How could you conceivably know the other man didn't want to die?"

"Come." Justin crossed the threshold toward one of the fallen gunman.

The Sicilian followed.

The maverick pointed down to one of the dead man's street shoes. "See anything unusual about the footwear?"

The man looked, but shook his head.

"Look at how they're laced. Crisscrossed. Just like yours and mine."

Although the light in the room was dim, both shoes and laces black, the man could plainly see that it was so. "So?"

"Look carefully at the left lace."

Dominic's man shrugged. "Broken shoelace; tied in a knot."

"Not just a broken shoelace. Note how the lace on the left shoe is different than the one on the right. What happened is that the one on the right shoe broke, too, but was replaced. See how one lace is flat and the other rounded—in addition to that sloppy knot? Quickly and carelessly tied. Clarence Emery was neither quick nor careless. Emery was methodical. Obsessive. Now, let's look over here," he continued, stepping over to the other body. "See how this guy's laces are tied like a little ladder? No crisscrosses. Takes time and patience to lace up shoes like that—to make the laces even."

The man noted that the laces were, indeed, tied like tiny railroad tracks.

"This is Clarence Emery," Justin said with conviction. "And that freak over there is—was—his new accomplice." Cancilla's man unfolded his arms from across his barrel chest and nodded his understanding. "But how could you possibly know that the one over there wouldn't shoot Jackie, after you shot Emery?" he repeated.

"May I?" Justin asked, removing the picklock tool from the man's vest-pocket. The two stepped back around to the Pakistani pretender. Justin stooped beside the body. Using the tool as a probe, he pushed up the dead man's sleeve.

Agent Dale Fulton suddenly stormed around the corner, pitching a fit as he came upon the scene. He went absolutely wild. "What the hell do you think you're doing, Barnes? This is a crime scene. This is *my* crime scene!" he exploded inarticulately.

Justin Barnes looked up. "It's going to be a crime if I *break* your jaw this time out. Won't it?"

Fulton marched maniacally from the room, mumbling and grumbling incoherently. Justin turned the Sicilian's attention back to the clear, thin plastic hospital bracelet on the decedent's wrist. "Nurse Carter showed me the files of the doctors who are on vacation. This guy, Oliver Sydney, was Doctor Jordon's patient and psychiatric referral. An out of work—out of his mind—actor. The last patient Jordon saw that day before he left on vacation. See?" The bracelet clearly bore Oliver Sydney's name.

The two stood up, and Justin returned the tool to the man's pocket.

"I saw that bracelet, too. You're not going to stand there and tell me you could read the name Oliver Sydney from where you were standing."

"No, of course not. All I saw was the bracelet, like you."

"Then how could you know?" he persisted. "You heard the way they switched dialects. You saw the way they switched roles. Why not the bracelet? Emery could have had that bracelet on."

But Justin was shaking his head in the negative. "Those bracelets are not something you snap on and off at will. They have to be cut off. So there was no switching bracelets back and forth like dialogue. Besides, Emery wasn't wearing one. There was only one bracelet. Oliver Sydney's. Sydney, here, was clearly the patient. Emery, there, was surely his mentor. They didn't know we were here to end their sick game. That was to our advantage, and I made the most of it."

"It still doesn't explain how you knew this Sydney didn't want to die."

Justin nodded, then took his time explaining. "Doctor Jordon is a heart specialist who successfully, I'm sorry to say, performed quadruple coronary bypass surgery less than a month ago on Oliver Sydney, right before Jordon left for vacation. Why would anybody, after going through an extensive operation like that, be so anxious to die?" Justin questioned.

"Because, as you yourself said, he's crazy!" he flared. "Ever stop to consider that?"

"Stop?" Justin asked evenly. "I don't think you would have wanted me to stop, sir."

The man studied Justin carefully before speaking. "I don't know," he said and shook his head. "You're either very smart or very crazy yourself, Justin Barnes."

"Maybe a little bit of both," Justin responded without expression. "You see, I had the added advantage of *two* mentors," he affirmed, staring over at Detectives Brian Archer and Gary York.

As if to corroborate Justin's accusation, Detective York went over to the foot of the bed and picked up one of the scalpels from the black leather strip. Squatting before the body of Oliver Sydney, Gary quickly cut through and removed the plastic ID strap from the man's wrist. Scrunching back a bit upon his haunches, the detective ran an end of the decedent's shoelace through one of several holes in the wristband, tying and securing it firmly with a double knot. "There. Toe tag," Gary concluded. "Really doesn't matter much now who or what he was or wasn't. What matters is that Jackie's alive and that I won't have to go to court to testify," he announced, then smiled up at everyone.

"Detective York always has to have the last word," Justin said, fixing his eyes on the Sicilian.

The man held Justin's stare before extending his hand. "No, you just worked that in quite cleverly," he declared. "Go with God, young man. I think maybe you lead a charmed life."

Justin took the man's hand and wisely remained silent.

Chapter 89

Jacqueline Rubino was recuperating satisfactorily under Doctor Jordon's associate's care: a board certified, middle-aged neurophysiologist affiliated with another nearby hospital. After Justin was certain that Jacqueline's family and friends had left for the evening, and the coast was clear, he went into her room.

"Hi there, kid. I see you got your very own ID bracelet," he quipped, gently taking hold of her hand. "Didn't want to mix you up with someone else."

The patient did not open her eyes but surrendered a little smile, withdrawing her hand from his. "You know I hate you," she said rather sluggishly.

Justin gave an awkward little laugh. "Believe me, I know."

"If Tomas were here now, he'd try and kill you . . . ." her words trailed off.

"Yeah, I know that, too. You Sicilians are so ungrateful," he jawed playfully.

Jacqueline slowly opened her eyes. "I suppose you want us to thank you?"

Justin shook his head. "Got you into this mess."

"Got that right."

Justin shrugged. "What can I say?"

"Nothing. How's Ursula?"

"Ursula left me."

"Smart girl."

"I guess."

"What are you going to do now?" she asked sleepily, allowing her eyes to close by themselves.

"About what?"

"About everything."

Justin pulled over a chair.

"Please don't."

"Don't what?"

"Don't sit down."

"Your orders? Or marching orders from your family?"

"Both."

"I see."

"I'm very tired, J."

"You asked me what I'm going to do."

"Just tell me, and then let me sleep."

Justin folded his hands across his chest and took in the ceiling. "Really want to know?"

Jacqueline opened her eyes again and stared. "Yes," she said weakly.

"Well, my relationship with Ursula is over and done with, as is probably my stint with the Suffolk boys when Theo retires in January. So, I really don't know what I'm going to do."

"How about looking for honest work?"

"Oh, right. Put my résumé together in a heartbeat, girl. Experience. Contract killer for Suffolk County homicide. Or I *could* go it alone. Freelance."

"Doing what exactly?"

"Vigilante," he answered crisply. "Certainly not as exciting as assassin or bounty hunter, but with a rather nice ring to it. Maybe even as colorful. How about I order a new set of business cards? **Have Gun–Will Travel.** Think that might be misconstrued as a form of plagiarism? Whattaya think, Jackie?"

"I'm too tired to think nonsense, J."

"I guess. I guess, too, nothing good lasts forever."

"If you want to call what we did good."

"Oh, indeed, I do. We were *very* good together, kid."

The weary woman gently rocked her head from side to side. "We were positively crazy."

Justin disagreed. "We wiped the slate clean of several killers, Jackie. You and me. In another lifetime, or so it seems. Don Ciccio, for one; along with a high-ranking, crooked, city cop. Not to mention Malcolm Columba and associates. And today, Clarence Emery and his last accomplice. Columba and Emery, Jackie," Justin emphasized. "Two of the most prolific serial killers perhaps the world has ever known."

"We put ourselves way above the law."

"Maybe closer to God," he offered up for consideration.

"I think not."

"You think on that some more," he suggested and was about to leave.

"J."

Justin turned to face her.

"Uncle Phil and the family feel it best that you don't come by the restaurant anymore. I'm sorry."

Justin smiled sadly. "To tell you the truth, I think I've exhausted the menu," he said sillily, attempting to save face.

"Good night, J."

"Well, looking on the bright side, that wasn't a goodbye."

Nurse Carter suddenly appeared and stepped inside the doorway. "I'm sorry, but visiting hours are long over. You have to go, Justin. Jackie needs her rest."

"We were just saying good night, Linda." Justin turned and walked away.

A tear rolled down Jacqueline's wan cheek. And then another.

She had the queerest feeling that she had seen and heard the pretty nurse somewhere earlier in time.

Robert Banfelder is an award-winning novelist and outdoors writer. He has written five psychological thrillers: *No Stranger Than I, The Author, The Teacher, Knots* and *Trace Evidence. The Author and The Teacher*, the first and second books in the Justin Barnes series, both received "Best Suspense Book" accolades from NewBookReviews. *Knots* is the third thriller in the Justin Barnes series. *The Good Samaritans*, the final in the series, is scheduled for publication in 2014. Robert weaves his knowledge and love of the outdoors through his novels.

In addition to his novels, Robert Banfelder writes outdoors articles which have appeared in numerous publications; e.g., *Nor'east Saltwater, The Fisherman, On The Water, Big Game Fishing Journal, Hana Hou! The Magazine for Hawaiian Airlines*, *New York Game & Fish*. Banfelder presently maintains a monthly online report for *Nor'east Saltwater*. He is a member of the Long Island Outdoor Communicators Network and the New York State Outdoor Writer's Association.

Robert also co-hosts (with Donna Derasmo) Cablevision TV's *Special Interests with Bob & Donna*. They have interviewed a number of outdoors enthusiasts, artists and writers such as Bob Bourguignon, Eileen Gerle, Pat Mundus, Christopher Paparo, Tony Salerno and Mary Van Deusen.

www.RobertBanfelder.com
Facebook @Robert Banfelder
Twitter @RBanfelder.

www.ingramcontent.com/pod-product-compliance
Lightning Source LLC
Chambersburg PA
CBHW051441260626

47162CB00001B/195